FORGOTTEN REALMS®

R.A. Salvatore's

WAR OF THE SPIDER QUEEN BOOK V

Annihilation

PHILIP ATHANS

R. A. SALVATORE'S
War of the Spider Queen Book V: Annihilation

Distributed in the United States by Holtzbrinck Publishing. Distributed in Canada by Fenn Ltd.

Distributed to the hobby, toy, and comic trade in the United States and Canada by regional distributors.

Distributed worldwide by Wizards of the Coast, Inc. and regional distributors.

Printed in the U.S.A.

Cover art by Brom
First Printing: July 2004
Library of Congress Catalog Card Number: 2004101047

9 8 7 6 5 4 3 2 1

US ISBN: 0-7869-3237-6
UK ISBN: 0-7869-3238-4
620- 96553-001-EN

U.S., CANADA,
ASIA, PACIFIC, & LATIN AMERICA
Wizards of the Coast, Inc.
P.O. Box 707
Renton, WA 98057-0707
+1-800-324-6496

EUROPEAN HEADQUARTERS
Wizards of the Coast, Belgium
T Hofveld 6d
1702 Groot-Bijgaarden
Belgium
+322 467 3360

Visit our web site at **www.wizards.com**

FORGOTTEN REALMS®

R.A. Salvatore's
WAR OF THE SPIDER QUEEN

For Deanne

Acknowledgements

The people who made this book and the others in this series possible are: Peter Archer, Mary Kirchoff, Matt Adelsperger, Liz Schuh, Mary-Elizabeth Allen, Rachel Kirkman, Angie Lokotz and her outstanding team, and the workflow masters Marty Durham and Josh Fischer.

Needless to say there would be no Book V without Books I, II, III, IV, and VI so I owe a huge debt of gratitude to the other Spider Queen authors: Richard Lee Byers, Thomas M. Reid, Richard Baker, Lisa Smedman, and Paul S. Kemp. Thanks to Elaine Cunningham for helping us with a particular continuity problem and Ed Greenwood for Creating the World in the first place. Brom, thank you for the cover paintings; masterpieces all. Thanks also to game designers Eric L. Boyd, Bruce R. Cordell, Gwendolyn F.M. Kestrel, and Jeff Quick for lots of fun new Underdark toys.

But most of all I have to thank R.A. Salvatore, who gave so much more than just his name to this series. He gave his limitless creativity, energy, and generosity of spirit in portions larger than any of us had a right to expect. If any of these six books are good at all, it's because of him.

She was the strongest. She had feasted on more than any still alive. She had killed more than any still alive. She had killed all those around her and hadn't even bothered to devour their carcasses before moving on to those outside the zone of the dead.

She was the strongest. She knew she was the strongest as yet another fell before her snapping mandibles. She was the one who would rise through the carnage and rule.

She was the strongest.

The others soon knew this as well.

So she was dead.

Within the chaos, there was intelligence and purpose. Within the hunger and the slaughter, there was common cause. She was the strongest and would kill them all or rule them all, so they bonded together and tore her eight legs from her, devouring her fully before turning again upon each other.

Another rose to prominence through deed and fearsome assault.

That one, too, fell to the common cause.

The mortal test continued. The strongest died, but the smartest remained. The manipulative remained—those who hid their strengths beyond what was necessary to kill the present opponent.

Those who stepped forward, who rose above the tumult, died.

Through all the millennia, she had recognized those who were stronger than she, and she had persuaded them to do her bidding or be killed. Strength came not from the size of her muscles but from the power of her cunning.

In the frenzy of the birthing, in the contest of the slaughter, these traits paved the road to victory.

To find the moment when individual strength was beyond the collective power to defeat it.

To intrigue amidst battle to destroy any who were stronger.

And for some, to admit defeat before oblivion's descent, to escape and survive, new demons of chaos to run wild about the planes and in the end to serve the winner.

The numbers dwindled. Those left grew in power and size.

Each waited and watched, deciding who must die before she could reign supreme, sorting through the tumult to facilitate that desired end.

Those driven by uncontrollable hunger were dead now.

Those driven by simple self-defense were dead now.

Those driven by foolish pride were dead now.

Those driven by instinctual survival were dead or were fleeing.

Those driven by cunning remained, knowing only one could emerge in the end.

For all the others, it would be servitude or oblivion. There were no other choices.

As she had manipulated the mortals who served her and the mortals who feared her, as she had maneuvered even other gods through the centuries, so she controlled her offspring. This was the test of her decree.

There were no other choices.

One

Gromph found himself growing accustomed to seeing the world through his familiar's eyes. It was that feeling that prompted him to do something about it. Gromph Baenre, brother of the Matron Mother of the First House of the City of Spiders, Archmage of Menzoberranzan, would not look through the eyes of a rat any longer than he had to.

Kyorli's head bobbed from side to side and up and down as she sniffed the air. The rat was bound to look where Gromph willed her to, but she was easily distracted. She didn't see as well in the dark, either, which in the Underdark meant she didn't ever see well, and there were no colors. Gromph perceived the casting chamber, like the rest of the world, in dull hues of gray and black.

Gromph knew the chamber well enough, though, that he didn't need the rat's vision to reveal its limits. The fuzzy blurs at the edge of Kyorli's vision were the great columns that rose to a series of flying buttresses, eighty feet into the gloom overhead. The carvings on the columns were sparse, and what they lacked in beauty they made up for in magical utility. The chamber, deep in the maze of Sorcere, was there for a purpose and not to impress. Spells were cast there in the course of training the students, testing the masters, in researching new spells, straining the limits of their powers, and for the odd summoning or scrying.

Gromph stepped into the center of the room, and from the corner of Kyorli's eyes he saw the two drow waiting for him. They bowed. The rat was sniffing the air, her nose angled up in the direction of the circle of giant mushroom stems that had been secured to the floor in the center of the cavernous chamber. There were ten of them, and to each was bound a single drow male.

"Archmage," one of the two wizards in attendance whispered reverently, his voice hissing off the distant walls in a thousand echoes that Gromph doubted he would have heard if he still had his eyesight.

The archmage willed Kyorli to turn her head to face the wizards, and he was satisfied to see that they were dressed and equipped as he had commanded.

During his time away from Menzoberranzan, thanks to the traitorous lichdrow Dyrr, certain elements within the Academy had revealed themselves. It had taken Gromph less time that he feared but more time than he'd wished to reassert himself at Sorcere. Triel had, to Gromph's surprise, actually done well in maintaining the House's hold over the school of wizards, but still there were traitors to kill and conspirators to bring back into the fold. All that had delayed his efforts to regain his eyesight. No more.

"All is prepared," the whispering mage—his own distant nephew, Prath Baenre—said.

Prath was young, still barely an apprentice, and though Gromph couldn't see the two dark elves' faces since Kyorli insisted on occasionally scratching her own hindquarters with her sharp front teeth, he was sure that the other—a Master of Sorcere named Jaemas Xorlarrin—was looking at the younger drow with impatience. Baenre or no, Sorcere had its hierarchies.

"Master Xorlarrin," Gromph said, making his own feelings on the necessity of that hierarchy clear, "as is obvious, I have some trouble seeing. I will require simple answers to some simple questions. You will stand at my left. The boy will step aside until called."

"As you wish," the Xorlarrin mage replied.

The rat left off her scratching when Gromph snapped his fingers. He watched through the rat's eyes as Kyorli scampered up his leg, to his hand, up his arm, and sat, twitching and sniffing, on the archmage's shoulder. Seeing himself through the rat's eyes unsettled Gromph, and feeling the rat's feet on him—both senses detached from each other—was something the archmage was determined not to experience again.

Gromph stepped toward the bound dark elves, sharply aware of the Xorlarrin mage following close behind him. As they came closer, a shadowy form revealed itself—another drow standing inside the circle of captives. It was Zillak, one of the archmage's most trusted assassins.

"Is the boy prepared with the sigils?" Gromph asked.

He was answered by a faint clang of metal and the sound of scurrying steps that finally slid to a halt.

"Yes, Archmage," Jaemas Xorlarrin replied.

Gromph stepped close to one of the bound dark elves. All ten of them were cousins—the wicked sons of House Agrach Dyrr and traitors to Menzoberranzan every last one. Gromph had asked for the youngest, the strongest, the ablest of them to be spared.

"Dyrr," the archmage said, doing his best to fix his sightless eyes on the captive's face.

The prisoner squirmed a little at the sound of his family's name. Gromph wondered if the boy felt the shame his traitorous House had inflicted on every last one of his kin.

"I . . ." the prisoner muttered. "I know why I'm here, Baenre. You can do your worst to me, and I will not betray my House."

Gromph laughed. It felt good. He hadn't had a good laugh in a long time, and with the siege of Menzoberranzan only digging in, with no word of Lolth or break in her Silence, he didn't think he'd be laughing much in the days, tendays, months, or even years ahead.

3

"Thank you," the archmage said to the boy. He caught the edge of the captive's confused, surprised expression as Kyorli began again to worry at her itchy hip. "I don't care what you might have to say about your doomed House. You will answer only one question . . . what is that sigil?"

There was a silence Gromph took as confusion.

"The sign," the archmage said, letting impatience sound in his voice. "The sigil my young nephew is holding up in front of you."

As ordered, Prath had taken up a position some yards away, against the wall of the giant chamber, and was holding up a small placard maybe six inches on each side. Painted onto its surface was a simple, easily recognizable rune—one any drow would recognize as marking a way to shelter, a place of safety in the wilds of the Underdark.

"I could compel you to read it, fool," the archmage drawled into the prisoner's hesitation. "Tell me what it is, and let us move on."

"It's . . ." the captive said, squinting. "Is it the symbol of Lolth?"

Gromph sighed and said, "Almost."

The archmage mentally nudged the rat on his shoulder and turned her head to see Zillak wrap a thin wire garrote around the prisoner's neck. When blood began to ooze from under the wire and spittle sprinkled from his mouth, Kyorli paid closer attention. Gromph waited for the prisoner to stop struggling, then die, before he stepped to the next traitor.

"I won't read it!" that one barked, the fear coming off him in waves. "What is this?"

Gromph, aggravated at the waste of time a spell of compulsion would take, tipped his head to the Xorlarrin mage who still stood right behind him and asked, "What color?"

"A garish magenta, Archmage," Jaemas answered.

"Well," Gromph replied, "that won't do at all, will it?"

That was enough for Zillak, who slipped the garrote, still dripping with the first Dyrr cousin's blood, around the second's neck. Gromph didn't bother waiting for the prisoner to die before stepping to the third in the circle.

There was a sharp stench of urine that almost made Gromph step back, and a spattering of droplets echoed on the hard stone floor. The archmage blew air out his nostrils to clear the smell.

"Read it," he said to the terrified captive.

"It's a way shelter rune," the terrified Dyrr cousin almost barked. "A way shelter."

Gromph could tell by the feminine timbre in his voice that he was a younger cousin. That was positive in itself. Kyorli, perhaps sensing the boy's fear or drawn to the stench of piss, looked the prisoner in the face and Gromph did his best to keep the rat's gaze fixed on the boy's eyes.

Jaemas Xorlarrin leaned in from behind and said quietly, "A pleasing blood red, Archmage."

Gromph smiled, and the bound prisoner did his best to look away.

"The smaller," Gromph said then listened to the sounds of Prath's robes rustling behind him. "Read it," he said to the prisoner.

The boy looked up, tears streaming down his cheeks, and blinked at the young Baenre, who Gromph knew was holding up the other side of the placard upon which was drawn, half again smaller than the way shelter rune, the number . . .

"Five," the prisoner said, his voice squeaking in a most unseemly way.

Gromph smiled and stepped back, Jaemas moving smoothly to get out of his way.

"Yes," the archmage said, "this one."

Jaemas snapped his fingers and Prath came quickly back to attend his superiors. The sound of a dark elf being strangled again echoed through the chamber, then again, and seven more times as Zillak executed the rest of the captives, save the one with the sensitive, blood-crimson eyes.

As Zillak went methodically about his bloody work, Gromph, Jaemas, and Prath stripped off their robes to stand barefoot, naked from the waist up, covered only by simple breeches. Gromph concentrated on the sounds of the executions, keeping his mind as clear as he could.

In his rise through a demanding House, then through the ranks of Sorcere, Gromph had seen and done much. He was no stranger to pain and sacrifice and was able to withstand much that would break even other noble drow. He told himself that he would bear the proceedings that day as well, for his own good and for the sake of Menzoberranzan.

He kept mental note of the number of strangulations he heard, and when Zillak was squeezing the last of the life out of the last of the Dyrr captives, he said, "Bring in the table when you're through there, Zillak. Then leave us."

"Yes . . . " the assassin grunted as he strained through the last execution, "Archmage."

When that last life was spent, Gromph caught a glimpse through Kyorli's eyes of Zillak walking quickly out of the circle of dead, wiping his hands dry on a rag. The surviving Dyrr was crying, and by the sound of it Gromph thought the boy was more ashamed than afraid. He had broken, after all. He had behaved like some . . . goblin—certainly not a drow. Dark elves didn't wet themselves at the prospect of death or torture. Dark elves didn't cry in the face of their enemies—didn't cry at all. If the boy hadn't proved his keen darkvision, Gromph might have thought him half human.

An example, he thought, for us all.

Zillak wheeled in a table upon which were secured four sturdy rothé leather straps. At one end was a drain that emptied into a big glass bottle hanging from the bottom of the table. Zillak left the table where Jaemas Xorlarrin indicated and quickly left the room.

Gromph took hold of Kyorli and cradled the rat in his arms as he sat on the table. Holding the rat, he found he could turn the beast physically to keep her eyes focused where he wished. Gromph chuckled at the odd timing of that revelation and turned the rat's face to Jaemas. The Xorlarrin mage was making a point of not acknowledging Gromph's sign of humor. Young Prath just looked nervous.

"This is something," Gromph said to his nephew, "that few masters have seen in a centuries-long lifetime, young nephew. You will be able to tell your grandchildren that you were here to witness it."

The apprentice mage nodded, obviously unsure how to respond, and Gromph laughed at him even as he lay down on the table. The steel was cold against his back, and Gromph broke out in gooseflesh. He let out a long sigh to keep from shivering and held Kyorli to his bare chest. The rat's claws pricked him, but Gromph didn't mind. There would be greater pain soon, and not only for the archmage.

Reeling at first from the dizzying perspective, Gromph held the rat aloft and turned it to face the Master of Sorcere. From the bowl that Prath was holding Jaemas had taken a polished silver spoon. No ordinary eating utensil, the edges of the spoon were sharpened to a razor's keenness. Jaemas gestured for Prath to step closer to the prisoner, and Jaemas began to chant a spell.

The words of power were like music, and the sound of them sent a shiver through Gromph's already freezing spine. It was a good spell, a hard spell, a rare spell, and one that only a handful of drow knew. Jaemas had been chosen carefully, after all.

As the cadence rose and fell, the words repeating then turning upon themselves, the Xorlarrin mage stepped closer still to the shaking, terrified captive. He held the spoon in a delicate grip, like an artist holds his brush. With his other hand, Jaemas held the prisoner's left eye open wide. It wasn't until the shining silver spoon was an inch from the boy's eye that the captive seemed to understand what was about to happen.

He screamed.

When the sharp edge of the spoon slipped up under his eyelid, he screamed louder.

When Jaemas, in one deft, fluid motion, scooped the eye from its socket, he screamed louder still.

When the eye fell with a soft, wet sound into the bowl that Prath held under the prisoner's chin, he shrieked.

Seen through the rat's eyes, the blood that poured from the empty socket looked black. Jaemas held open the prisoner's right eye and the young drow started to beg. All the while, the Master of Sorcere continued his incantation, not missing a beat, not missing a syllable. When he slid the spoon under the right eyelid, the boy began to pray.

When the eye came out, all the traitor could do was shake, mouth open wide, cords showing in his neck, blood flooding over his face.

Gromph had a fleeting thought of telling the prisoner, paralyzed with agony and horror, that at least the last thing he saw was a drow face and the simple line of a silver spoon. The next thing Gromph would see might drive even the archmage mad.

Gromph, of course, said nothing.

Through Kyorli's eyes, Gromph saw Jaemas slip the silver spoon into the bowl, careful not to cut either of the fragile orbs. The Xorlarrin mage, still incanting, took the rat from his master's hands, and Gromph's vision reeled. He heard Prath set the bowl gently on the floor, and Jaemas turned the rat so that Gromph could see himself lying on his back on the cold steel table. He could see Prath's hands shaking as he gently, almost reluctantly, folded the leather straps around Gromph's right wrist. He fastened the strap, but not nearly tight enough.

"Tighter, boy," the archmage growled. "Don't be squeamish, and don't be afraid you're going to hurt me."

Gromph allowed himself a laugh as his nephew tightened the strap then moved on to his right ankle. Jaemas continued to chant the words of the spell as Prath finished strapping his uncle to the table at both wrists and both ankles. When Gromph was satisfied that he was properly secured, he nodded to the Xorlarrin mage.

Odd, the Archmage of Menzoberranzan thought as Jaemas set Kyorli down on his bare chest. If Lolth wished it, none of this would have been necessary, but whether she answers her priestesses' prayers or not, all of it would still be possible.

That thought brought a tentative peace to Gromph. The knowledge—no, the certainty—of his power had always reassured him, and it did still. It was that certainty that helped him breathe normally and remain still as he watched, from the rat's own eyes, Kyorli's meandering, reluctant march up his chest and onto his chin. The rat paused and Gromph saw black fingertips—Jaemas's—descend over his left eye with a twisted bit of wire. The Xorlarrin's touch was cool and dry on Gromph's eyelids. The archmage held still while the

Xorlarrin mage set the wires gently, carefully, to hold his eyelid open. That was repeated on his right eye while Jaemas continued to chant, and Kyorli looked on with uncharacteristic patience. The rat was slowly coming under the influence of the spell, and it was that magic that was focusing the rodent's attention on Gromph's eyes.

Though he could feel the wires holding his eyes open, Gromph, when he let his concentration fall away from his familiar, could see nothing. There was not a hint of light or shadow, not a sliver of reflection.

Gromph took a deep, steadying breath and said, "Proceed."

His concentration off the rat and onto himself, Gromph couldn't see Kyorli crawl over his face, but he could feel every needle prick of her claws, could smell her musk, and could hear her sniffing. A whisker slipped across one of Gromph's open eyes, and he flinched. It stung. His eyes might have been useless, but they could still register pain.

Well, thought Gromph, too bad for me.

The first bite sent a wave of burning agony blasting through the archmage's head. Gromph's entire body tensed, and his teeth ground together. He could feel the rat back off and could feel the blood slowly drip down the side of his face. Jaemas continued to chant. The pain didn't stop either.

"Kyorli," the archmage grunted.

The rat was hesitating. Even under the influence of the spell, even offered the tasty morsel of a living—if sightless—eye, the rat knew that she was mutilating her own master, a master who had proven in the past to be anything but forgiving.

Gromph slipped his consciousness into his familiar's, and despite the one already ruined eye sending blood dripping down the side of his head, Gromph could see. It was the same colorless, dull rat's vision, though. He could see the bite the rat had already taken out of his right eye, could see the blood, could see himself shaking, could see the grim set of his jaw, and the open, helpless orb of his other blind eye awaiting the rodent's reluctant ministrations.

Gromph compelled the rat to finish her work.

Kyorli might have hesitated at the orders of Jaemas, but she responded to her master's invitation to feed without a second's pause. For at least three bites, Gromph watched his own eye being chewed out of his head, then Kyorli's vision blurred as she plunged her head into the ruined orb to tear at the tender, blood-soaked bits inside.

The pain was unlike anything Gromph had ever imagined, and in his long, uneasy life, the Archmage of Menzoberranzan had imagined a lot.

"Scream if you have to, Archmage," his nephew whispered into his ear, barely audible over the sound of the feeding rat. "There is no shame in it."

Gromph grunted, trying to speak, but kept his jaw clamped shut. The young apprentice had no idea what shame was, but even in his maddening agony, Gromph promised himself that his nephew would learn and that would be the last time Prath Baenre offered his uncle advice.

Gromph didn't scream, even when the rat moved on to the other eye.

The demon steered them to the darkest part of the lake, and not one of the drow thought anything of it. Bobbing at anchor in the deep gloom of the Lake of Shadows, the ship of chaos—*Raashub's* ship of chaos—stood out stark white against the inky darkness. The water itself was a black matched only by the deep ebony of his drow master's skin. The wizard, the one they called Pharaun, had found him, bound him, chained him to his own deck, and had done so with no humility, no respect, and no fear. The thought of it made the wiry black hairs that dotted the demon's wrinkled gray flesh stand on end. For a few moments, the demon stood reveling in the hatred he felt for that drow and his haughty kin.

The drow had been gating in one servile, simpering, weak-willed mane after another. The damned souls of petty sinners were food in the Abyss, and they were food for the ship of chaos. The uridezu took note of the number of manes the drow wizard brought in at any given time in hopes of gauging the dark elf's power. If it was an exact science, the gating in of lesser demons, Raashub didn't know its finer points, but so many of them were coming through there could be no doubt that the drow was skilled. Raashub wasn't helping the drow and was happy to let them not only feed his ship but exhaust their spells, efforts, and attention in the process. The presence of all those wailing, miserable demons must have clouded the drow priestess's senses enough that at times Raashub could push the boundaries of his captivity.

A rat's primitive consciousness intruded on his own, and Raashub sent only the tiniest hint of a glance its way. He'd been calling them, subtly, for two days—ever since the drow had first come aboard. The rodents swam the surface of the Lake of Shadows, and they inhabited the spaces between decks and under steps on the ship of chaos the same way rats everywhere swam, hid, and survived. Raashub, an uridezu, was as much rat as anything else a mundane prime could understand, and he knew the rats of the Underdark as he knew rats in every corner of the endless planes.

The rodent responded to Raashub's glance with a silent twitch of its whiskers, a gesture the uridezu felt more than saw. It scurried behind the thick base of the main mast and crept cautiously toward the draegloth.

They called the half-breed Jeggred. As draegloths went he was an average specimen. If Raashub were stupid enough to engage him, the draegloth would win a one-on-one fight, but the uridezu would never be that stupid. He would never be as stupid as the draegloth.

The rat didn't want to bite the half-demon, and Raashub had to silently insist. It was a gamble, but the uridezu didn't mind the odd risk for the odder reward. His psychic urging drew the attention of one of the female drow again, though, and the uridezu backed off, looking away before they made eye contact. All of the drow deferred, if grudgingly, to the female named Quenthel, who was apparently some high priestess of the drow spider-bitch Lolth. That one was as conceited and as unworthy of that conceit as the rest of them, but she was sensitive. Raashub worried that she could actually hear him when he didn't want her to.

Darting in fast, the rat nipped at the draegloth's ankle. The half-demon swatted it away with a grunt, and the tiny rodent flew through the air, out into the darkness. The splash was almost too far away to hear. The draegloth, whose skin was unmarred by the puny creature's teeth, locked his eyes on Raashub's and glared at him.

The draegloth had been doing little the past two days but glare at him.

Annoying little vermin, Raashub sent into the draegloth's mind, *aren't they, Jeggred?*

The draegloth blew a short, vile-smelling breath out of his nostrils and his lips peeled slowly back to reveal fangs—rows of dagger blades as sharp as razors and as piercing as needles. The half-demon hissed his anger, and boiling spittle sizzled on his lips.

Pretty, Raashub taunted.

The draegloth's eyes narrowed in confusion. Raashub allowed himself to laugh.

The high priestess turned and looked at them both. Again, Raashub avoided eye contact. He moved his foot enough to let the chain that bound him rattle against the single dragon bone that comprised most of the deck of his ship. Above him, the tattered sails of human skin hung limp in the still air. The demon heard Jeggred turn. Raashub liked the game—they were both caught by a sternly disapproving mother in their boyish mischief.

Quenthel looked away, and Jeggred locked his eyes on Raashub again. The uridezu didn't bother taunting him anymore that day. It was becoming boring. Instead, the demon contented himself with standing quietly, occasionally nudging the ship a little closer to the deeper gloom along the cavern wall.

Patience was not normally a quality enjoyed by his kind, but Raashub had been trapped in the Lake of Shadows for a long time. The appearance of the drow had been something of a godsend—though by the tone of their conversations and the snippets of facts regarding their mission the drow had let slip, Raashub knew it was hardly a god or goddess who'd sent them. They had managed to release his ship and release him. If he was anything but an uridezu, a demon born in the whirling chaos of Mother Abyss, he might have been . . . ah, what was the word? Grateful? Instead, he was patient, a little patient for a little longer.

Soon the drow would slip into their Reverie, their meditative trance so like sleep, and the high priestess would look inward. When that time came and she couldn't sense what he was doing, Raashub would bring another of his kind across the limitless infinity between planes. He had already called one of them the day before. The drow, over-confident in their measure of control over him, hadn't sensed him calling, failed to notice his cousin Jaershed cross from the Abyss, and still didn't realize that the other uridezu was even then clinging to the keel, wrapped in conjured darkness, waiting.

Jaershed hadn't learned patience the way Raashub had, and the lust for blood and chaos sometimes came out of him in waves. When it did the damnable high priestess would look around as if she'd heard something, as if she thought she were being watched. Raashub would silently wail, then, adding his mental voice to the anguished moans of the parade of manes they brought in and led into the hold one by one. Quenthel would be curious, disturbed even, but she would ultimately believe.

The dark elves had bested Raashub after all. Their powerful mage had trapped him on that miserable plane, chained him to his own deck, cowed him, enslaved him . . . and none of them could imagine that as true as that was, nothing—not in the Abyss, the Underdark, the Lake of Shadows, or aboard a ship of bone and chaos—lasted forever.

Raashub closed his eyes, suppressed his anticipation, and smiled.

Ryld Argith peered into the darkness of the Velarswood night and sighed. In the places where the trees were tall enough and close enough together to block out the star-spattered sky, it almost felt comfortable for him, but those times were few and far between in what the weapons master had come to learn was a relatively small forest. The sounds didn't help—whistles and rustling all the time from every direction, often not echoing at all. His hearing, sensitized by decades of training at Melee-Magthere, was tuned to the peculiarities of the Underdark, but in the World Above, it was making him a nervous wreck. The forest seemed always alive with enemies.

He turned to scan the darkness for the source of some random twittering—something he'd been told was a "night bird"—and instead he caught Halisstra's eye. She knew what he was doing—startling at every sound—and she smiled at him in a way that only days before Ryld would have taken as a sign that she'd identified a weakness in him, one that she'd surely exploit later. The twinkle in her crimson eyes seemed to imply the opposite.

Halisstra Melarn had confused Ryld from the beginning of their acquaintance. The First Daughter of a noble House from Ched Nasad, at first she had been every inch the haughty, self-possessed priestess she'd been raised to be, but as her goddess turned her back on her, her House fell, then her city crumbled around it, Halisstra had changed. Ryld abandoned his long-time ally Pharaun and the rest of the Menzo-berranyr to go with her, and he didn't regret that, but he wasn't sure he could turn his back forever on the Underdark the way she so obviously had. Ryld still had a home in Menzoberranzan—at least he assumed he did, absent any news from the city that was already feeling the effects of Lolth's Silence when they'd left. When he thought about it, he felt certain that someday he would return there. When he looked at Halisstra he saw a dark elf like him but also unlike him. He knew that she would never be able to go back, even if she had a House to go back to. She was different, and Ryld knew that eventually he would have to change too or go home without her.

"Are you all right?" she asked him, her voice a welcome respite from the cacophony of the forest.

He met her eyes but wasn't sure how to answer. Thanks to the Eilistraeen priestesses Uluyara and Feliane, he was not only alive but unwounded. The poison that had nearly claimed him had been pulled from his blood by their magic, and his wounds and Halisstra's had been healed, leaving not even scars to mark their passage. The alien goddess of the surface drow had granted him his life, and Ryld was still waiting for her or her followers to present a bill.

"Ryld?" Halisstra prompted.

"I'm—"

He stopped, turned his head, and when he heard Halisstra inhale to speak again, he held up a warning hand to silence her.

Something was moving, and it was close. It was on the ground, and it was moving toward them. He knew that Feliane had gone ahead of them—the Eilistraeeans were always sensitive about giving the two newcomers time alone—but she was farther away and in a different direction.

Behind you, he signaled to Halisstra, *and to the left.*

Halisstra nodded, and her right hand moved to the enchanted blade at her hip. Ryld watched her turn, slowly, and as he drew his own mighty greatsword from his back, he took the briefest moment to admire the curve of Halisstra's hip, her mail glittering in the starlight against the dark background of the forest. Her feet whispered in the snow, and Ryld tracked the sounds. Whatever it was wasn't moving in a very deliberate way, and it sounded as if there was more than one, though the lack of echoes still made it hard for him to be sure. He didn't detect any change in the way it was moving when either of them drew their swords, so Ryld thought it unlikely the trespasser had heard them.

A spindly plant devoid of green—the Eilistraeeans had called one like it a "bush"—quivered, but not from the wind. Halisstra stepped back and held the Crescent Blade in the guard position in front of her. She had her back to him, so Ryld couldn't communicate with her in sign language. He wanted to tell her to step back farther, to let him take care of whatever it was, but he didn't want to speak.

When the thing rolled out from behind the bush, Halisstra hopped back three fast steps, keeping her sword at the ready. Ryld rushed at the bundle of bristly brown fur assuming Halisstra would clear the rest of the space for him. When she didn't he was forced to stop, and it looked up at him. The closest thing to the creature Ryld had ever seen was a rothé, but it was no rothé. The creature was small, the size and weight of Ryld's torso, and its wide eyes were wet and innocent, weak and—

"Young," Halisstra whispered, as if she was finishing his thought.

Ryld didn't let down his guard, though the beast sat calmly on the ground, looking at him.

"It's a baby," Halisstra said, and slipped the Crescent Blade back into her scabbard.

"What is it?" Ryld asked, still not ready to let down his guard, much less sheathe his sword.

"I have no idea," Halisstra answered, but still she crouched in front of it.

"Halisstra," Ryld hissed, "for Lolth's—"

He stopped himself before he finished that thought. It was another habit he would have to change or take home with him.

"It's not going to eat us, Ryld," she whispered, looking the little creature in the eyes.

Its nose twitched at her, and its eyes held hers. It seemed curious, with a face vaguely elflike, but its gaze betrayed an animal's intelligence and no more.

"What are you going to do with it?" he asked.

Halisstra shrugged.

Before Ryld could say anything else, two more of the little animals wandered out of the bushes to regard their comrade and the two dark elves with a meek curiosity.

"Feliane will know what to do with them," Halisstra said, "or at least be able to tell us what they are."

It was Ryld's turn to shrug. One of the creatures was licking itself, and even Ryld wasn't wrapped so tight that he could still see them as a threat. Halisstra sent out a call the Eilistraeeans had taught them—the sound of some bird—and Ryld slipped his greatsword back into its scabbard.

Feliane would hear the call and come to them. Ryld cringed when he realized that when she got there and saw the two of them dumbfounded by what looked like harmless prey animals . . . they would both look foolish again. At least, Ryld would.

Feliane came stomping through the underbrush. Ryld was surprised by not only how fast the Eilistraeen was moving but by how loud she was. He'd come to respect their ability to slip through the forest un—

He realized at that moment that what he heard crashing at them through the pitch-black forest wasn't Feliane. It wasn't a drow, or a surface elf, or even a human. It was something else—something big.

The thing burst out of the thick tangle of underbrush like an advancing wall of matted brown fur. Ryld managed to get his hand on Splitter's pommel but couldn't draw it before the beast rolled over him. The weapons master tried to tuck his body to protect his belly from the monster's trampling claws, but he didn't have the time.

The creature stomped on him, tripped on him, rolled on him, then stepped on him. All Ryld could do was keep his eyes pressed closed and grunt. It was heavy, and when it first punched him into the ground Ryld heard then felt at least one of his ribs snap under its weight. It finally came off him, and Ryld rolled off to one side—any side—ending up curled under a spindly "bush" with thorns that harried at his armor and *piwafwi*. Snow packed into the spaces between his armor's plates and chilled his neck and hands.

The creature stopped, rolling all the way over in the end and coming back onto its feet still facing away from Ryld. The weapons master looked up and blinked at it. It looked like a bigger—much bigger—version of the little animals that had wandered up to twitch their noses at the drow. It was a clever ruse and surely a successful hunting strategy: Disarm and distract your prey with your curious young, then trample it into the ground when it isn't looking.

Still, the Master of Melee-Magthere grimaced at his having fallen for it, however clever it was.

I'm getting slow, he thought. All this open air, all this talk of goddesses and redemption . . .

Shaking the distracting thoughts from his mind, Ryld spun to his feet at the same time he drew Splitter and whirled it in front of him. The lumbering animal turned to face him, and Ryld was ready for it.

The beast looked him in the eye and Ryld winked at it over the razor edge of his greatsword.

Steam puffed from its nostrils as it coughed out a series of loud grunts. It scratched at the snow with one of its front paws, and Ryld saw its black claws, the size of hunting knives, at the end of surprisingly well articulated hands. The look in the creature's eyes was a mix of slow-wittedness and feral anger—a look Ryld had seen before and had learned to respect. Stupid foes were easy to defeat and angry foes even easier. Mix the two together, though, and you're in for a fight.

The beast charged, and Ryld obliged it by meeting it in the middle. When it reared up at the end of its charge, the animal was nearly three times the drow's height. That display would likely frighten lesser opponents, but for Ryld all it did was open the thing's belly. The weapons master brought his greatsword in fast at shoulder height in a hard slash meant to open the animal's gut and end it quickly. The beast was faster than it looked, though, and it fell backward, rolling onto its back as the edge of Ryld's sword flashed past it, missing by a foot or more. Ryld had no choice but to follow through with the swing, but he managed to make use of the inertia to send him dodging off to the left when the creature slashed at him with its hind claws.

Ryld spun to a halt, blade up high, while the animal continued its roll and flipped back onto its feet. Both of them blew steam into the frigid air, but only Ryld smiled.

They went at each other again, and Ryld was ready for it to try to either trample him or rear up again. The animal did neither. It reached out for the drow warrior with both hands, obviously trying to grab him by the shoulders—or by the head. Ryld slid toward it at the end of his run, stabbing up with his greatsword as he passed under the animal's chin. He intended to impale it, maybe even behead it, but his opponent proved still more surprisingly agile. It ducked its head to one side, and all Ryld managed to do was nick one of its ears.

The weapons master continued his slide, bringing his arms in so he could stab again and at least get the creature in the gut, but the animal jumped to one side and rolled off, again managing to elude the drow's attack.

Ryld hopped to his feet, and the two opponents faced each other again. Ryld heard a voice to his left and glanced over to see Halisstra, bent in an attitude of prayer, mumbling her way through some kind of chant. The animal took advantage of Ryld's momentary attention gap and leaped at him, clearing easily eight feet before crashing to the ground in front of the drow. The creature had to dodge back, unbalancing itself, to avoid another slash from Splitter. It opened its jaws wide, revealing nasty fangs, and let loose another series of angry, frustrated grunts.

It swiped at Ryld with one set of claws. Ryld was ready to meet it, fully engaged to sever the animal's front leg at the elbow—when both of them jerked backward to avoid something that whizzed through the air between them in a flurry of feathers, talons, and turbulent air.

Ryld followed the animal's eyes as it followed the new player's mad course through the air. It was some kind of bird, but with four wings. Its multicolored feathers blended well into the dark background of the forest, and Ryld actually lost sight of it for a second. The huge furry beast stepped back, trying to look at Ryld and look out for the bird-thing at the same time.

Even Ryld wasn't able to do that, and since the furry animal was in front of him and at least a little off its guard, the weapons master stepped in to attack again—and again the bird-thing flashed between them, raking the air with its needle-like talons.

Ryld barely twitched away, but the big animal all but fell onto its back to avoid the newcomer. Ryld, already in mid-slash, quickly changed the direction of his attack and was half an inch from cutting the fast-flying bird-thing in half when Halisstra called out from behind him.

"Wait!" she shouted, and Ryld tipped the point of his blade down barely enough to let the bird fly past. "It's mine. I summoned it."

Ryld didn't have time to ask her how she'd managed to do that. Instead he stepped back three long strides, keeping his eyes on the beast, which was already back on its feet. The bird-thing slashed in from the darkness behind the animal and dragged its talons across the beast's head. The creature howled in pain and surprise and snapped its jaws at the passing bird-thing, missing it by a yard or more.

"What is that?" Ryld asked, not looking at Halisstra but keeping his eyes on the furious forest animal.

"It's an arrowhawk," Halisstra answered.

Ryld could hear the pride and surprise in her voice, and something about that sent a chill down his spine.

The animal looked at him, grunted, and came on. Either it had forgotten about the arrowhawk or had given up trying to see it coming. Ryld crouched, Splitter out in front of him, awaiting the beast's charge. He kept his shoulders loose and told himself that the fight had gone on long enough. He was not going to be made a fool of by—

—and the arrowhawk swished over his head, missing the top of his close-cropped white hair by a finger's width.

Ryld tucked his head down as it shot over him. The bird flew as fast as an arrow shot from a longbow, and it was easy for Ryld to understand how the creature had received its name. It looked as if the hawk was flying straight for the furry creature's eyes. Half of Ryld wanted the arrowhawk to kill it, the other half didn't want to be shown up by some conjured bird. At least not in front of—

That thought too went unfinished when Ryld heard himself gasp at the sight of the huge ground animal grabbing the arrowhawk right out of the air with one huge, clawed hand.

The bird let out an ear-rattling squawk, and the creature looked it in the eyes as it started to squeeze. Ryld didn't doubt for a moment that the big animal could break the long, slender arrowhawk in two with one hand. It was half a second away from doing just that when the arrowhawk flipped its long, feathered tail up and pointed it at the animal's face. An eye-searing flash of blinding light arced from the arrowhawk's tail to the tip of the animal's nose. Ryld snapped his eyes shut and gritted his teeth against the pain. There was a loud rustle of feathers, another angry squawk, and a high-pitched wail that could only have come from the big ground animal.

Ryld opened his eyes and had to blink away an afterimage of the graceful purple spark that had shot from the arrowhawk's tail. The animal had let go of the bird, which was nowhere to be seen. A tendril of smoke rose from its burned nose, and the stench of singed hair quickly filled the still night air.

Halisstra stepped up to Ryld, and they shared a glance and a smile as the big animal writhed in pain.

"Not bad," the weapons master joked, and Halisstra responded with a pleased smile.

"Praise Eilistraee," she said.

As if it understood her and had no love for her goddess, the big animal looked up, coughed out two more feral grunts, and started at them. Ryld put out one hand to push Halisstra behind him, but she had already skipped back into the darkness. He set his feet, ready for the charge, and saw the arrowhawk shoot out of the darkness again. The arrowhawk whipped its tail forward, and Ryld, knowing what was coming, closed his eyes and lifted one arm—both hands on Splitter's pommel—to shield his sensitive eyes.

There was a sizzle of electricity, the faint smell of ozone, and the none-too-faint stench of burned hair again. The furred creature growled in agony, and Ryld opened his eyes. Again, the arrowhawk was nowhere to be seen, likely whirling through the forest dodging tree trunks, circling back for another pass.

"Wait!" a woman's voice called. Ryld thought at first that it was Halisstra.

"No, Feliane," Halisstra called back. "It's all right. Between Ryld and the—"

"No!" the surface drow cut in.

Ryld would have turned to watch Feliane approach, but the animal had decided to charge him again. Not sure what Feliane was trying to stop, exactly, Ryld stepped in toward the big animal. He saw the arrowhawk coming, though and slid to a stop in the snow. The animal must have realized why the drow came to such a sudden halt, and when the arrowhawk came in low for another slash with its talons, the creature saw it as well.

Jaws snapped over the arrowhawk. There was a loud confusion of fluttering wings, screaming, growling, snapping, and popping—and the arrowhawk fell to the snow in two twitching, bleeding pieces.

"What's going on here?" Feliane called, her voice much closer. "What in the goddess's name are you doing?"

Its long, fang-lined jaws dripping with the arrowhawk's blood, the animal looked fiercer, more dangerous, and angrier than ever. Ryld smiled, spun his massive enchanted greatsword in front of him, and ran at the thing head on.

Behind him and off in the underbrush, Halisstra and Feliane were talking in urgent tones, but Ryld's trained senses put that aside. They were allies, and the only opponent of note was the furious beast. Whatever they were discussing, they could tell him about it later, after he had dispatched the vicious, cunning predator.

The creature reared up again as Ryld came in, and the drow slipped Splitter in low in front of him, slicing a deep furrow in the beast's exposed underbelly. Blood oozed from the wound, and quickly soaked the matted, dirty brown fur around it. Ryld spun his greatsword back around and pointed it forward, held in both hands above his head, for a final impaling stab.

The forest predator again proved it wouldn't go down easily. Before Ryld could plunge Splitter home, the thing's huge, handlike claw wrapped around his right arm, digging into the space between his pauldron and vambrace to puncture the skin of his underarm.

Ryld tucked his right arm down, pressing the claw against his armored side to keep the beast from tearing away his pauldron—and a good portion of skin and muscle with it. That had the unfortunate effect of tipping the point of his greatsword up. The animal pushed down, and its weight was enough to send Ryld sinking, slipping, then falling onto his back. Splitter's tip passed harmlessly past the animal's shoulder. When he felt the other claw clamp onto his left pauldron, Ryld knew he was pinned.

The beast snapped at his face, but Ryld still had enough room to jerk his head out of the way. With all his considerable strength, the weapons master pushed up, but with his arms trapped over his head and his sword all but immobile next to the animal's ear, he had to use his back and shoulders to try to lift himself off the ground—carrying the fifteen-foot animal that must have weighed a ton at least with him. He didn't move it far, but when the animal felt him trying to push up, it pushed down, extending its arms the fraction of an inch Ryld needed to muscle his sword down and under. Twisting his wrists painfully, Ryld managed to get the greatsword's tip up under the beast's chin.

The animal rolled its dark, dull eyes down and stretched its neck up and away from the sword. The two of them were stuck that way, and Ryld feared that that was how they were going to remain for a very long time: it pushing him away, he trying to stab it through the throat.

"Halisstra!" Feliane screamed. "No!"

The sound was shrill, panicked, and close enough that it finally registered on Ryld that the two females were still there. He wasn't alone. As females were wont to do, they were letting him take the brunt of the punishment, but they wouldn't leave him like that—or would they? From the sound of Feliane's voice, it was exactly what she intended to do.

Ryld redoubled his efforts, but so did the beast and they got no closer to a resolution—until Ryld heard a woman growl in an odd way, realizing it was Halisstra. The thing dipped that fraction of an inch forward that Ryld was hoping for.

The tip of the greatsword bit into the animal's throat, and blood poured down the blade. The animal grunted, opening its mouth a quarter of an inch—and allowing the blade to slip that much farther in. Hot red blood exploded from the wound, then pumped out of the monstrosity's neck in rhythm to its speeding heart—Ryld had found the artery he'd been hoping for.

He saw Halisstra's boot to his right and heard a sword come out of its sheath. She had jumped onto the animal's back and was straddling it, drawing the Crescent Blade to deliver the killing blow.

Ryld celebrated that realization by twisting Splitter's tip into the creature's throat, bringing more blood and sending a shiver rippling through the creature's fur.

Feliane ran up next to them and must have hit the side of the animal hard. Halisstra grunted, and the hulk started to topple sideways. Ryld sawed into its neck for good measure, not sure it was actually dead.

Feliane's boot scuffled in the snow next to him, and she said, "Stop it. For Eilistraee's sake, that's not what the Crescent Blade was meant for."

Ryld let the quivering carcass roll off him and fall into a dead sprawl in the underbrush. Wincing from the pain in his shoulder and underarm, he slid his blade out of the dead animal's neck and got to his feet, stepping back a few steps before he had his legs under him.

Halisstra and Feliane were standing next to the fallen animal, and Feliane's hand was wrapped tightly around Halisstra's sword arm.

"I couldn't . . ." Halisstra said, her voice quavering, each word punctuated by a puff of steam that rolled into the frigid air. "I couldn't let it kill him."

Both of the women turned to look at Ryld, who could only shrug.

"She was only protecting her young," Feliane said.

She was looking at Ryld, but the weapons master got the distinct impression she was talking to Halisstra. Ryld didn't understand. Who was protecting . . . ?

"The animal?" he asked.

"She's a giant land sloth," the Eilistraeen said, releasing Halisstra's arm and stepping away from her. "She *was* a giant land sloth. They're rare, especially this far north."

"Good," Ryld said. "It was tougher than it looks."

"Damn it!" Feliane cursed. "She was only protecting her young. You didn't have to kill her."

Halisstra was looking at her sword, the blade glowing in the darkness.

"Why," Ryld asked, "would it attack an armed drow to protect its young? It could have lived to birth more."

Feliane opened her mouth to answer but said nothing. A strange look came over her, one that Ryld couldn't remember ever seeing on the face of a drow.

Halisstra looked down at the dead sloth and whispered, "She. . . ."

Ryld shook his head. He didn't understand and was beginning to think he never would.

THREE

It had been two days since Pharaun had contacted his master, and the news that sending had brought still sat heavily on the wizard's shoulders. The spell allowed only a short message to travel through the Weave from the Lake of Shadows into Menzoberranzan and an equally short message back.

Ship of chaos is ours, Pharaun had sent, careful to use no unnecessary words though that was against his natural tendencies. *Advise on proper diet. Don't trust captain. Any word of Ryld Argith or Halisstra Melarn? Sent home to report details.*

He'd waited the interminable seconds for a reply, all the time wondering if the time he had been waiting for had come—the moment when Gromph Baenre, Archmage of Menzoberranzan, would fail to answer. That would be the moment Pharaun would know that they had failed, that they had no city to return to, no civilization to protect.

That time had not yet come.

Feed it manes, the archmage had replied. *As many as you can. Captain will serve power. Master Argith and Mistress Melarn not here. Stop your squabbling and get moving.*

Pharaun didn't stop to wonder how Gromph had known that the tenuous alliances within the expedition were fraying. Gromph was a drow himself, after all, and probably assumed it. If he thought he'd had the time, Pharaun might have studied that point much more closely, tried to determine the degree to which Gromph was aware of their actions, but there was work to do.

A manes demon was hardly the most daunting creature to either summon or control, but it was a demon nonetheless. He would have to use powerful spells to summon and bind them, all the while maintaining some measure of control over the uridezu captain who gave his name as Raashub. It had been two long, difficult, and tiring days for Pharaun. He had taken only enough Reverie to replenish his spells and was doing everything his considerable training allowed to push his casting to its limit. The parade of hideous, groveling, snapping subdemons he brought to the ship's deck began to amaze even himself, and Pharaun hoped that Quenthel and the others were taking note. Those among them capable of gauging such abilities would have to be impressed, and if they were impressed they would be scared. So long as they were scared, he would be safe.

As he led a string of the vile-smelling fiends into the gnashing jaws of the demonic ship's hold, Pharaun let his mind wander back to the rest of that sending. Ryld hadn't made it to Menzoberranzan, but that could mean anything. He could be dead anywhere between that cave on the World Above and the City of Spiders, or he could still be on his way. There was no straight line between any two points in the Underdark, and he could be only a few miles as the worm bored from Menzoberranzan and still have a tenday's travel ahead of him.

Ryld might still hold a grudge for Pharaun's having abandoned him all those days before, back in the city, but Pharaun knew he still had a powerful ally in the Master of Melee-Magthere. The warrior might have fallen under the spell of the First Daughter of House Melarn, but if Halisstra herself still lived, surely she would be on her way to Menzoberranzan herself. Pharaun couldn't imagine the homeless priestess had anywhere else to go.

Without Ryld at his side, Pharaun had given Quenthel and her draegloth nephew Jeggred as much room as the cramped deck allowed. They hadn't appreciated Pharaun leaving them to spin while he'd gone to pick up Valas and Danifae first. Even Valas and Danifae had been surprised by that one, but Pharaun had long ago learned that whenever possible a cautious drow lets his enemies twist for a while, if only to remind them that he can.

Still, the Mistress of Arach-Tinilith had been more than a little displeased, and Jeggred had made another serious attempt at a physical assault. Quenthel had held him back, if reluctantly, and charged the draegloth with guarding the uridezu. They were two of the same: demons on the wrong plane, pressed into the service of drow who were ready to take them back to the Abyss that spawned them. Pharaun let himself sigh at that thought. He knew it was a bad idea on its surface, going to the Abyss, but they had passed up the acceptable a long time before. They were in new territory. They were headed for the Spider Queen herself, and right when Lolth seemed least inclined to greet them.

Pharaun was sure he wasn't the only one who had second thoughts about the expedition, even as strenuously as he'd argued for their going forward. For a Master of Sorcere, it was a mission that could make him Archmage of Menzoberranzan. For her part, Quenthel had already achieved the highest post she could hope for. As Mistress of Arach-Tinilith, Quenthel was the spiritual leader of all Menzoberranzan and the second most powerful female in the city. Some would argue that she was indeed more powerful than her sister Triel.

Of all drow under Faerûn, she would surely be welcomed into Lolth's domain—assuming there was either a Lolth or a Demonweb Pits at all anymore—but still the high priestess was on edge. Her normally stern countenance had gone nearly rigid, and her movements were jerky and twitching. Any talk of the journey ahead made her pace around the deck, all but oblivious to the lesser demons that often snapped at her or reached out to grab her.

Even Pharaun, cynical as he was, didn't want to believe that the Mistress of Arach-Tinilith might be losing her faith.

The fact that Jeggred also noticed Quenthel's unease didn't make the wizard feel any better. The draegloth's expressions weren't always easy to read, though the half-demon was the least intellectually capable of the party, but since coming to the Lake of Shadows—perhaps even before—Jeggred had looked at his aunt quite differently. He could see her agitation, though he might have thought it fear, and he didn't like it. He didn't like it at all.

Pharaun closed his eyes and took a deep breath as the last of the day's manes went down the ship's gullet. He felt tired enough to sleep like a human. Without even bothering to cross the deck to the place where he'd set his pack, Pharaun sank to the fleshy planks and sat.

"Before you slip into Reverie," Valas Hune said from behind him, "we should discuss practical concerns."

Pharaun turned to look at the Bregan D'aerthe scout and offered him a twisted smile.

"Practical concerns?" the wizard asked. "At this point I'm too tired for any kind of concerns . . . other than . . . the . . . ones that are . . ."

Pharaun closed his eyes and shook his head.

"Are you all right?" the scout asked, his tone comfortably devoid of real concern.

"My wit has failed me," Pharaun replied. "I must be tired indeed."

The scout nodded.

"We'll need supplies," he said, addressing all four of them.

Quenthel didn't look up, and Jeggred only glanced away from the chained demon for a second.

The draegloth shrugged and said, "I can eat the captain."

Pharaun didn't bother to look at the uridezu for a response, and the demon, sensibly, didn't offer one.

"Well, I can't," Valas replied. "Neither can the rest of us."

"There will be no opportunity to stop along the way?" Danifae asked.

Pharaun regarded the beautiful, enigmatic battle-captive with a smile and said, "We'll travel from this lake across the Fringe and into the Shadow Deep. From there to the endless Astral. From there to the Abyss. Any roadhouses along the way will be . . . unreliable to say the least."

"Which is to say," Valas cut in, "that there won't be any."

"What did you have in mind, Valas?" Pharaun asked. "How much are we talking about?"

The scout made a show of shrugging and turned to Quenthel to ask, "How long will we be away?"

Quenthel almost recoiled from the question, and Jeggred turned to stare daggers at her back for a heartbeat or two before returning his attention to the captured uridezu.

"One month," Pharaun answered for her, "sixteen days, three hours, and forty-four minutes . . . give or take sixteen days, three hours, and forty-four minutes."

Quenthel stared hard at Pharaun, her face blank.

"I thought your wit had abandoned you, Master of Sorcere," Danifae said. She turned to Quenthel. "An impossible question to answer precisely, I understand, Mistress, but I assume an educated guess will do?"

She looked at Valas, her white eyebrows arched high on her smooth black forehead. Valas nodded, still looking at Quenthel.

"The simple fact is that I have no idea," the Mistress of Arach-Tinilith said finally.

The rest of the drow raised eyebrows. Jeggred's eyes narrowed. It wasn't what any of them expected her to say.

"None of us do," she went on, ignoring the reaction, "which is precisely why we're going in the first place. Lolth will do with us as she pleases once we are in the Demonweb Pits. If we must be supplied, then we will need supplies for the length of our journey there and perhaps our journey back. If Lolth chooses to provide for us while we're there, so be it. If not, we will need no sustenance, at least none that can be had in this world."

The high priestess wrapped her hands around her arms and hugged herself close. All of them saw her shiver with undisguised dread.

Pharaun was too taken aback to see the further reactions of the others. A low, rumbling growl from Jeggred finally drew his attention, and he looked over to see the draegloth's eyes locked on Quenthel, who was successfully ignoring her Abyssal nephew.

"You talk like humans," the draegloth growled. "You speak of the Abyss as if it was some feral dog you think might nip at your rumps, so you never rise from your chairs. You forget that for you, the Abyss has been a hunting ground, though you do most of your hunting from across the planes. Are you drow? Masters of this world and the next? Or are you . . ."

Jeggred stopped, his jaw and throat tight, and returned his steely gaze to the uridezu. The demon captain looked away.

"You assume much, honored draegloth," Danifae said, her clear voice echoing across the still water. "It is not fear that prepares us for our journey, I'm sure, but necessity."

Jeggred turned slowly but didn't look at Danifae. Instead, his eyes once more found the Mistress of Arach-Tinilith. Quenthel appeared, to Pharaun's eyes at least, to have succumbed to the Reverie. Jeggred blew a short, sharp breath through his wide nostrils and turned a fang-lined smile on Danifae.

"Fear," the draegloth said, "has a smell."

Danifae returned the half-demon's smile and said, "Fear of the Spider Queen surely smells the sweetest."

"Yes," Valas broke in, though Danifae and the draegloth continued to stare at each other with expressions impossible to read. "Well, that's all well and good, but surely someone knows how long it will take us to get there and how long to get back."

"A tenday," Pharaun said, guessing for no other reason than to get on with it so he could rest and replenish his magic. "Each way."

The scout nodded, and no one else offered any argument. Jeggred went back to staring at the captain, and Danifae drew out a whetstone to sharpen a dagger. The vipers of Quenthel's scourge wrapped themselves lovingly around her and began, one by one, to sink into slumber.

"I'll be off then," Valas said.

"Off?" Pharaun asked. "To where?"

"Sshamath, I think," the scout replied. "It's reasonably close, and I have contacts there. If I go alone, I can be there and back quickly, and no one who doesn't fear Bregan D'aerthe will even know I was there."

"No," Danifae said, startling both Valas and Pharaun.

"The young mistress has a better suggestion?" Pharaun asked.

"Sschindylryn," she said.

"What of it?" asked Pharaun.

"It's closer," Danifae replied, "and it's not ruled by Vhaeraunites."

She sent a pointed look Valas's way, and Pharaun allowed himself a smirk.

"I'm tired," the Master of Sorcere said, "so I will weaken enough to speak on Valas's behalf. He is Bregan D'aerthe, young mistress, and his loyalty goes to she who is paying. I don't believe we'll have trouble with our guide jumping deities on us. If he can get to, through, and out of Sshamath faster, then let him do what he's been hired to do."

"He will go to Sschindylryn," Quenthel said, her voice so flat and quiet that Pharaun wasn't certain he'd heard correctly.

"Mistress?" he prompted.

"You heard me," she said, finally looking up at him. She let her cold gaze linger for a moment, and Pharaun held it. She turned to Valas. "Sschindylryn."

If the scout had any thought of arguing, he suppressed it quickly.

"As you wish, Mistress," Valas replied.

"I will accompany you," Danifae said, speaking to Valas but looking at Quenthel.

"I can move faster on my own," the scout argued.

"We have time," said the battle-captive, still looking at Quenthel.

The high priestess turned to Danifae slowly. Her frigid red eyes warmed as they played across the girl's curves. Danifae leaned in ever so slightly, eliciting a smile from Pharaun that was as impressed as it was amused.

"Sschindylryn. . . ." the wizard said. "I've passed through it a time or two. Portals, yes? A city crowded with portals that could slip you in an instant from one end of the Underdark to another . . . or elsewhere."

Danifae turned to Pharaun and returned his smile—impressed and amused.

"How much time do we have?" Valas asked, still ignoring the more subtle, silent conversation-within-a-conversation.

Pharaun shrugged and said, "Five days . . . perhaps as many as seven. I should have provided the ship with adequate sustenance by then."

"I can do it," Valas replied. "Barely."

The scout looked to Quenthel for an answer, and Pharaun sighed, pushing back his frustration. He too looked at Quenthel, who was gently stroking the head of one of her whip vipers. The snake swayed in the air next to her smooth ebon cheek while the other vipers slept. Pharaun got the distinct impression that the snake was speaking to her.

A sound caught Pharaun's attention, and he saw Jeggred shifting uncomfortably. The draegloth's eyes twitched back and forth between his aunt and the viper. Pharaun wondered if the draegloth could hear some silent, mental exchange between the high priestess and her whip. If he could, what he heard was making him angry.

"You will take Danifae with you," Quenthel said, her eyes never leaving the viper.

If Valas was disappointed, he didn't let it show. Instead, he simply nodded.

"Leave when you're ready," the high priestess said.

"I'm ready now," the scout replied, perhaps a second too quickly.

The viper turned to look at the scout, who met its black eyes with a furrowed brow. Pharaun was fascinated by the exchange, but exhaustion was claiming him all the more quickly as the discussion wore on.

Quenthel slid back to rest against the bone rail of the undead ship. The last viper rested its head on her thigh.

"We will take Reverie, then, Pharaun and I," the Mistress of the Academy said. "Jeggred will stand watch, and the two of you will be on your way."

Danifae stood and said quietly, "Thank you, M—"

Quenthel stopped her with an abrupt wave of her hand, then the high priestess closed her eyes and sat very still. Jeggred growled again, low and rumbling. Pharaun prepared himself for Reverie as well but couldn't help feeling uneasy at the way the draegloth was looking at his mistress.

Danifae slipped on her pack as Valas gathered his own gear. The battle-captive walked to Jeggred and put a hand lightly on the draegloth's bristling white mane.

"All is well, Jeggred," she whispered. "We are all tired."

Jeggred leaned in to her touch ever so slightly, and Pharaun looked away. The draegloth stopped his growling, but Pharaun could feel the half-demon watch Danifae's every move until she finally followed Valas through a dimensional portal of the scout's making and was gone.

Why Sschindylryn? Pharaun asked himself.

It was the battle-captive's calming touch with the draegloth that accounted for the wizard's uneasy Reverie.

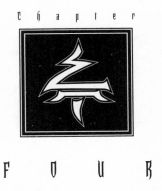

FOUR

A little more than half a mile under the ruins of the surface city of Tilverton, two dark elves ran.

Danifae breathed hard trying to keep up with Valas, but she stayed only a few strides behind him. The scout moved in something between a walk and run, his feet sometimes appearing not even to touch the slick flowstone of the tunnel floor. As they'd emerged from the last in a rapid, head-spinning series of gates, Valas had told her they were more than halfway to Sschindylryn, and it had been only a single day. Danifae admired the mercenary's skill in navigating the Underdark, even as she dismissed his obvious lack of ambition and drive. He seemed content in his position as a hired hand—scout and errand boy for Quenthel Baenre—and the idea of that sort of contentment was utterly alien to Danifae.

After all, she thought *in time, Valas is only a male.*

The scout came to an abrupt halt, so abrupt in fact that Danifae had to stumble to an undignified stop to avoid running into him. Happy for the chance to pause and rest, though, she didn't bother to complain.

"Where—?" she started, but Valas held up a hand to silence her.

Even after all her years as a battle-captive, a servant to the foolish and slow-witted Halisstra Melarn, Danifae hadn't grown accustomed to shutting up when told to. She bristled at the scout's dismissive gesture but calmed herself quickly. Valas was in his element, and if he wanted silence, both their lives might well depend on it.

He turned to her, and Danifae was surprised to see no hint of annoyance or irritation on his face, even as her one word still echoed faintly in the cool, still air of the cavern.

Another portal up ahead, he told her with his fingers. *It will take us far, almost to Sschindylryn's eastern gate, but it's not one I've used in a very long time.*

But you've used it before, she replied silently.

Portals, especially portals like this one, Valas explained, *are like waterholes. They attract attention.*

You sense something? she asked.

Danifae's own sensitive hearing detected no noise, her equally sensitive nose no smell but her own and the scout's. That didn't mean they were alone.

As if he'd read her mind, Valas replied, *You're never alone in the Underdark.*

So what is it? she asked. *Can we avoid it? Kill it?*

Maybe nothing, he answered in turn, *probably not, and I hope so.*

Danifae smiled at him. Valas tipped his head to one side, surprised and confused by the smile.

Stay here, he signed, *and keep still. I'll go on ahead.*

Danifae looked back along the way they'd come then forward in the direction they were going. The tunnel—twenty-five or thirty feet wide and about as tall—stretched into darkness in both directions.

If you leave me behind. . . . Danifae threatened with her fingers and with her cold, hard eyes.

Valas didn't react at all. He seemed to be waiting for her to finish.

Danifae again glanced to the seemingly endless tunnel ahead, only for half a heartbeat. When she turned back, Valas was gone.

Ryld drew the whetstone slowly along Splitter's razor edge. The enchanted sword hardly needed sharpening, but Ryld found he was always better able to think when he was performing the simple tasks of a soldier. The sword had no outward signs of an intelligence of its own, but Ryld had convinced himself some years before that Splitter enjoyed the attention he gave it.

He was alone in the crumbling, weed-choked hovel he shared with Halisstra. The sounds and smells of the forest all around him managed to invade even that personal time with his sword and his thoughts. He knew he was as relaxed as he would ever be on the surface in the daylight under the endless sky—at least, when Halisstra wasn't with him.

The Master of Melee-Magthere was alone because he hadn't been invited to the circle that Halisstra had gone to join. The curious, heretical surface drow were planning something, and Halisstra and her newfound toy—the Crescent Blade—were obviously a big part of it. He had killed the raging animal that attacked him, and as many times as Feliane had tried to explain it to him, he couldn't imagine why that made him an outcast. Still, Ryld knew he had been left out for more than that one reason.

He sat alone also because, unlike Halisstra, he had not openly rejected the Spider Queen nor openly embraced her sun-ravaged rival, the Lady of the Dance. Ryld didn't understand that frivolous goddess of theirs. The Lady of the *Dance?* Were they to set their lives along a path defined by *dancing?* What sort of a bizarre goddess could draw, much less mete out, power from something so pointless as dancing? Lolth was a cruel and capricious mistress, and her priestesses held her power close, but she was the Queen of Spiders. Spiders were strong, resourceful predators—survivors. Ryld could see himself as a spider. Spiders knew no mercy and never asked for forgiveness. They spun their webs, caught their prey, and lived. Spiders made sense, spiders had power, and power was all any drow needed.

Apparently not every drow.

Still, Ryld knew that there was a third reason why he sat sharpening his sword while the females plotted and planned, and that was precisely because he wasn't a female. In Menzoberranzan, Ryld Argith was a highly regarded and well-respected warrior, a soldier with powerful friends and much to recommend him to his superiors. He led a comfortable life, wielded some items imbued with powerful magic—the greatsword not the least of them—and was even trusted to be a principal member of the vital expedition in search of their silent goddess. Despite all that, Ryld Argith was a male. As such he would never be anything but second, and he well knew likely not even that. He would lead other males, other warriors, but would never command a female. He would be asked his opinion, and that opinion would occasionally even be considered, but he would never make decisions. He would be a soldier—a tool, a weapon—but never a leader. Not in Menzoberranzan among the daughters of Lolth and not in the sun-baked forest among the dancing priestesses.

Three reasons for being left out, Ryld thought, while at home there is only the third. Three reasons to go home to Menzoberranzan.

One reason to stay.

In the past lingering hours of solitude Ryld had thought often of returning to the Underdark. Pharaun and the others would have moved on, continued their quest. Likely they'd all forgotten about the Master of Melee-Magthere who had left the City of Spiders with them. Ryld held no illusions about his worth to the likes of Quenthel Baenre, and Pharaun had at least once proved that Ryld's life was less important than the wizard's convenience, let alone the Master of Sorcere's own well-being.

Pharaun, however, was predictable. Ryld knew the mage and knew what to expect—even if that meant expecting betrayal. Pharaun was a dark elf, not only well tuned to, but prone to revel in, his drow nature. Quenthel Baenre was the same, which was why they so irritated one another. Those two and the others—even the laconic Valas

Hune—were like spiders too: predictable, efficient survivors. Ryld saw himself in the same terms, and being in like company had a compelling draw.

Until he thought of Halisstra.

In his years in Menzoberranzan, Ryld had enjoyed the company of more than a handful of females, but like any male in the City of Spiders he knew well enough not to allow attachments to run too deep. He had known from time to time that he was a plaything, a tool, a dalliance, a performer—but never one of those surface elf words, those oddities such as lover, companion, friend, husband. Those words had no meaning until Halisstra.

Ryld tried and tried, but he couldn't understand the hold the First Daughter of House Melarn had on him. He had even drawn upon the unique power of Splitter to dispel whatever magic she had cast on him to draw him along with her—but there was no magic. She had cast no spell, sang no *bae'qeshel* ballad, slipped him no potion to wrap herself around him so tightly. She hadn't, Ryld mused, even done or said anything too different than things he'd heard before, though in the past such things were said in tones of mockery or even cold, bitter irony by those dozen or more drow females who had had him.

Halisstra had simply smiled at him, held his gaze with hers, touched him, kissed him, looked at him with fear, longing, regret, pain, anger, desperation . . . looked at him with honesty. Ryld had never seen any of it before, not on the black face of a dark elf, not in the cool gloom of the Underdark. He could feel her when she was close, as if she gave off some ripple that tuned his senses to her. She was simply Halisstra, and the Master of Melee-Magthere was dumbfounded to find that was enough. Her mere presence was sufficient to drag him away from a life that was, and would continue to be, as rewarding as a drow male could expect.

There he was, putting up with the same things, still the male whose strong sword arm would be called into service on a second's notice but who would not dine at the same table.

The fourth reason that he was alone that day and had been alone for much of the day before roared into Ryld's mind then, and he let it come, but only for a moment.

They mean to kill her, he thought as a chill raced down his spine and the whetstone that had so slowly and so carefully and so rhythmically been drawn along his blade came to a sudden stop. They mean to kill Lolth.

Ryld closed his eyes and drew in a long breath, calming his suddenly racing heart.

It was, after all, why Halisstra had been sent to retrieve the Crescent Blade. It was why the Eilistraeen priestesses put up with the obviously unpleasant presence of the Master of Melee-Magthere—at Halisstra's demand. It was why Halisstra stayed and why she carried herself with a confidence and composure he hadn't seen . . . well, never in the outcast from the ruins of Ched Nasad. It was why Halisstra no longer trembled in fear. It was why she woke in the morning and why she drew breath during the day.

In Eilistraee's name, Halisstra Melarn meant to murder the Queen of the Demonweb Pits in her sleep.

Ryld set the whetstone in motion again and smiled.

Maybe, he thought, she's more like a spider than she wants to admit.

Valas held the crystal to his left eye and scanned the chamber. He stood in the deep shadows at the edge of where the tunnel—a very old lava tube—emptied into the pyramidal cavern. The ancient monastery was obvious to even his unaided darkvision. Set against the northern wall of the cathedral-like space off to Valas's right was a half circle of stone, perhaps seventy-five feet in radius. The curved wall rose as tall as two hundred feet before rounding to a domed roof, with the apex about thirty or forty feet above that. Two huge slit windows, not much wider than Valas was tall but eighty feet in length, were set high on the walls. A thief might have to climb the brick wall for a dangerous hundred feet before being able to slip inside. Between the two tall windows and a few feet below their bottom edges loomed a pair of small, dark holes tall enough that Valas might be able to step through them without dipping his head. Below those round holes a drooping oblong opening led into the pitch-black interior of the ruin.

The windows, the two round holes, and the oblong opening gave the ruined monastery the look—obviously intentional—of a frowning face.

Stalactites had formed along the upper edge of the mouth and hung down to form ragged fangs, and dripping water had carried centuries of sediment onto the dome so that a wide patch of smooth white flowstone capped the far end of the great head like some gaily off-kilter hat. What grim ceremonies might have been held before that giant face Valas didn't bother to imagine. The centuries that had passed since his ancient ancestors had abandoned it had been unkind to the building, but Valas knew that the ravages of dripping water, mold, and earthquakes hadn't touched the gate that rested inside it. Twice before, though many years gone by, Valas had climbed into that drooping, melancholy mouth and passed between two rune-carved pillars to step two hundred miles to the northwest shore of Lake Thalmiir, an easy walk to Sschindylryn.

Valas knew he wasn't the only one who'd used it.

A crystal normally hung on his vest—an enchanted garment that gave Valas much of his nimble footing and lightning reaction—with many other magical trinkets he'd picked up over a lifetime in the wilds of the Underdark. Through that crystal the scout could see that which others couldn't—most things rendered invisible by magic either sorcerous or innate.

Valas slowly and carefully scanned the base of the great face, then to the left along the still pool of black water that bisected the round floor of the cavern. There was a cave low in the sloping wall across from him and a smaller one—another lava tube of similar dimensions to the one Valas had come through—higher up and to the right. The scout began to scan the roof of the ruined monastery when he heard Danifae all but stomping through the tunnel behind him.

Valas didn't stop his slow, methodical examination of the structure.

He knew that Danifae would walk past him, their shoulders close to touching, and she would never see him. He had told her to wait, and if she disregarded his warning it was her choice.

Let her stomp on in, he thought. Let her—

Valas froze when the crystal revealed the tip of what could only be a talon resting on the top of the monastery. Holding his breath, the Bregan D'aerthe scout drew his head back half an inch and played the crystal, still held close to his left eye, along the domed roof of the ancient face.

The creature that rested atop the ruin wasn't too big, at least not as far as dragons go. No taller than Valas himself, with a wingspan maybe twice that, the beast was coiled comfortably but alert atop the dome. Though the crystal tended to bleed any color from the scene, Valas knew the monster was as gray in color as it appeared to him through the magic item. Even through the crystal it seemed undefined, blurred as if it had been painted onto the giant face in watercolors.

That's how you hide, Valas thought. You blend into the darkness.

Danifae passed him and strode uncaring to the mouth of the lava tube. She stood for a moment, one hand resting casually on the rock wall, gazing out into the cavern. Valas could tell she hadn't seen the dragon on the top of the face, but a last quick glimpse through the crystal showed him that the dragon had seen her. It slowly uncoiled itself, drawing up its wings.

Valas slipped into the cavern, relying in no small part on his own training and experience but not too proud to call on the power of an enchanted ring to speed his way. Mithral chain mail hushed any sound he might make as he moved, and it helped his toes find safe, quiet footing. Keeping always in shadow, always without the slightest scrape of sole on stone, without the faintest reflection of stray light on metal, Valas came down the incline from the mouth of the lava tube and along the bowl-shaped edge of the huge space to the yawning black cave across.

He risked the occasional glance up at the creature, whose outline he could only barely discern in the gloom high up in the cavern—and only then because he knew it was there. Valas also risked a glance or two back at Danifae, who was slowly, and with surprising grace, making her way down into the bowl of the cavern. She looked all around but not up. Her eyes never rested on either Valas or the stone-gray dragon.

Danifae walked slowly toward the edge of the pool as Valas drew the shortbow from his back. He nocked an arrow and drew back the string.

The female was all but offering herself on a silver platter to the beast, and though Valas ached to allow her to see her folly through, he worried about Quenthel. The high priestess seemed to have taken a liking to the Melarn battle-captive, stealing her away without a thought from the female from Ched Nasad. Valas didn't want to find out the hard way that he'd let the battle-captive die when Quenthel had plans for Danifae beyond their occasional loveplay.

"Valas?" the female called into the dark, still cavern.

Her voice echoed, Valas cringed, and the dragon took wing.

Nimor Imphraezl watched from above as the duergar engaged the spiders. Drow warriors—all male—rode the enormous arachnids into battle. The spiders skittered and whirled around them while the riders sat stiff and straight in their saddles. The mounted drow carried long pikes—weapons the duergar were unaccustomed to, as rare as the long weapons were in the confines of the Underdark—and they skewered one after another before the gray dwarves drew any dark elf blood.

The spider riders were hopelessly outnumbered by the horde of duergar who continued to lay siege to the slowly crumbling city of Menzoberranzan, and Nimor was content to lose a few gray dwarves for the chance to watch the drow fight. They were good, he would grant them that. The spiders killed as many duergar as the pikes did, but the beasts were never out of their riders' control. All in all it was a beautiful, bloody dance.

In the center of the spider riders a mounted drow male wearing

armor of the finest mithral positively glowed with magic. He carried a
pike like the others but hadn't brought his to bear. He held it up, and
from it a long, thin banner wafted in the cool Underdark air. It took
Nimor a minute or so to recognize the sigil emblazoned on the banner.
The riders represented House Shobalar—a lesser House, but one loyal
to the Baenres and known throughout the drow-settled Underdark for
their effective and impeccably trained cavalry. The dark elf with the
banner must be their leader.

One of the riders took two duergar at once, pinning them together
then using their weight at the end of his pike to topple three more of
their companions onto the flowstone floor. Nimor smiled.

He had come to that particular tunnel after hearing three separate times of unusual activity there. The duergar had managed to kill
a Menzoberranyr scout only a day before, and even the gruff gray
dwarves had admitted that other drow had been there and gotten away.
It wasn't the most well defended approach, and Nimor had been keeping an eye on it, certain the Menzoberranyr would be testing it.

When the scout was killed, Nimor had Crown Prince Horgar send
reinforcements, but only a few. Enough, Nimor hoped, to satisfy the
drow but not enough to close the approach. Nimor wanted to draw
them out, and like the arrogant aristocrats they were, they'd taken
the bait.

Nimor hung upside down, hidden by a spell of invisibility, his
piwafwi, another spell that prevented anyone using similar magic
from finding him, and another that would draw enemies' attention
away even if they thought to look up at him. Those things and the
immediate threat of the duergar soldiers were enough that he could
wait and watch in peace—wait and watch for the spider rider captain
to send his arachnid mount scurrying into the fray, scurrying right
under Nimor.

With a touch to a brooch that bore the sign of the Jaezred Chaulssin, Nimor dropped slowly, still hidden from sight by magic. As he
descended, Nimor drew his dagger—a very special dagger—and
when he came to rest on the spider, inches behind the cavalry leader,
he flicked the blade across the back of the drow warrior's neck. There

was a perfect space there between his helm and his pauldron.

The spider rider flinched and turned in his saddle. Nimor, still invisible, grabbed the drow around his neck and held the poisoned blade to his throat.

The spider rider couldn't see him, but he could hear Nimor whisper in his ear, "What is your name, Shobalar?"

"Who are you?" the warrior asked, and Nimor cut him again—not too deeply—in response.

The drow grunted, and Nimor could feel his body stiffen, jerk, and quiver.

"Yes," Nimor hissed into the slowly dying officer's ear, "it is poison. Very, very elegant poison. It will paralyze you, twist your throat closed, squeeze the last gasp of air from your lungs, and keep you from screaming while you suffocate."

The drow growled and said, his voice already quiet and tight, "My House will avenge me."

"Your House will burn, Captain . . . ?"

"Vilto'sat Shobalar," the drow answered even as his throat squeezed shut, "of the Spider Riders of House Sh—"

Smiling all the while, Nimor held the dying drow upright in his saddle as he suffocated. The Anointed Blade of the Jaezred Chaulssin waited until Captain Vilto'sat Shobalar quivered through his last attempt at a breath and his magenta eyes glazed over. Then Nimor levitated up and away from the suddenly uncontrolled, feral warspider.

The arachnid went berserk, chewing through duergar after duergar then turning on another of its kind. The rider of that spider turned his attention to protecting his mount from the wild arachnid—just long enough for a particularly enthusiastic duergar footman to take his head with a poleaxe.

Nimor killed eight more drow himself over the next ten minutes or so, while the duergar claimed three. The rest finally turned and ran back through the tunnel, past the outer siege line and back into Menzoberranzan. They had taken back nothing, and Nimor had four of their spiders and the dead drow.

Nimor ordered up more duergar to resecure the position, had the spiders bound and made ready for travel, and went back to his command post with the corpse of Captain Vilto'sat Shobalar.

Spoils of war.

Chapter

FIVE

Valas could tell that Danifae didn't know the drake was behind her until the second his arrow sliced through the fine membrane of its wing, surprising it. It made a noise deep in its throat, the arrow made a wet ripping sound as it entered, and the drake's smooth motion ended in a jerk. All that was enough for anyone to sense some disturbance behind her and turn—and it was that simple reflex that saved Danifae's life.

Though the drake forgot its intended target, it landed hard in a skidding roll and would have bowled her over if she hadn't jumped clear—and she barely managed that.

The portal drake whirled in the direction from which Valas's arrow had come. Saliva dripped from its open mouth, curling around jagged teeth and collecting on the cave floor in steaming pools. Valas saw the intelligence in the thing's eyes, the great age—centuries spent stalking the alluring magical portals of the Underdark—and the cold, hard anger.

The drake searched the darkness for him, but Valas knew it wouldn't see him. Valas didn't want to be seen; it was that simple.

Behind the creature, Danifae scrambled to her feet, drawing her morningstar at the same time. Valas already had another arrow in his hand, and as he slipped sideways along the edge of a deep shadow he set it to his bow and drew back the string. The drake mirrored that expansive movement by drawing air into its lungs. It couldn't see Valas, but it had apparently concluded that all it had to do was get close. It was a conclusion with which Valas could—unfortunately—find no fault.

After taking a heartbeat to aim, Valas let the arrow fly. The drake exhaled, releasing a billowing cloud of greasy green vapor into the air. It rolled and expanded as it left the dragon's mouth. The drake began to strain to get it all out.

Danifae struck with her morningstar—a weapon enchanted with the power of lightning—from behind, and the portal drake jerked forward. Valas's arrow bit deeply into its chest, finding the half inch it needed between two hard scales. The thing's armored skin quivered, and muscles rippled and jerked. The breath caught in its throat, and its cloud was cut short. Still the gas rolled in Valas's direction.

The scout could see it coming. It was aimed toward rather than at him, so he flipped backward away from it. He had no way to protect himself from poison gas. It was a weakness in that situation that Valas found frustrating. All he could do was avoid the gas, and avoidance, at least, was something he was well versed in.

"Hide in the dark there if you wish, drow," the portal drake hissed in Undercommon. Its voice was cold and sharp, almost mechanical, and it echoed in the high-ceilinged chamber with a sound like glass breaking. "I can't see you."

The creature turned to face Danifae, who was whirling her morningstar, looking him in the eye. She was backing up.

"But I can see her," the drake said.

Danifae smiled, and the expression sent a chill down Valas's spine. He stopped, noting the sensation but utterly confused by it.

When the battle-captive lashed out with the enchanted morningstar again, the drake dodged it easily.

"What are you expecting, lizard?" Danifae asked the drake. "Do you think he'll reveal himself to save me? Have you never met a dark elf before?"

Valas, about to draw another arrow, let it drop silently back into his quiver. He slipped the bow over his shoulder and made his way around the back of the drake, skirting the edge of the cavern wall toward the giant face. He quickly estimated the number of steps, the number of seconds, and gauged the background noise for sound cover.

"Dark elves?" the drake said. "I've eaten one or two in my years."

Danifae tried to hit him again, and the drake tried to bite her. They dodged at the same time, which ruined both their attacks.

"Let us pass," Danifae said, and her voice had an air of command to it that got Valas's attention as well as the drake's.

"No," the drake answered, and Danifae stepped in faster than Valas would have thought her capable of.

The morningstar came down on the portal drake's left side, and Valas blinked at the painfully bright flash of blue-white light. The burning illumination traced patterns in the air like glowing spider-webs. The creature flinched and growled again, its anger and pain showing in the way its lips pulled back from its teeth.

Danifae stepped back, setting her morningstar spinning again. The drake crouched, and Valas stopped and stiffened. The drake didn't lunge at her—it burst into the air with the deafening beat of wings. In less than a second it was high enough to disappear into the gloom up in the cathedral-like space.

Valas stepped forward and let his toes scrape loose gravel on the floor. Danifae looked up at him.

Run back to the tunnel, Valas traced in sign language. *Go!*

Danifae saw him, didn't bother to nod, and turned to run. Valas slipped back into the darkness, drew his *piwafwi* up over his head, and rolled on the floor until he knew he was back in a place where no one would be able to see him.

Valas watched the battle-captive run, knowing she wouldn't be able to see the portal drake. He drew another arrow slowly so that it wouldn't make a sound as it came free of the quiver. He turned and twisted a fraction of an inch here, a hair's breadth there, so the steel tip would reflect no light. Breathing slowly through his mouth, the Bregan D'aerthe scout waited—but didn't have to wait for long.

The sound of the portal drake's wings echoed from above, doubled, then doubled again, and more—not just echoes.

Five, Valas counted.

Still cloaked in auras of invisibility and the gloom of the long-abandoned cavern, Valas started forward.

Five portal drakes swooped out of the shadows in formation. The two at the far ends swept inward, and two others shifted out. They changed positions as they flew, but their target was the same.

Danifae hesitated. Valas could see it in her step. She heard them and knew they could fly faster—many times faster—than she'd ever be able to run. To her credit, though, she didn't look back.

The five portal drakes were identical in every detail, and no one who had traveled as extensively as Valas had could have been fooled for long. Only three wing-beats into it, Valas knew what they were.

Not all of the trinkets the scout wore were enchanted, but the little brass ovoid was, and Valas touched it as he ran. The warmth of his fingers brought the magic to life, and only a thought was needed to wake it fully. It happened without a sound, and Valas never missed a beat or revealed himself at all.

Danifae stopped running anyway, leaving Valas to wonder why.

Similarly confused, the portal drakes drew up short, fluttering to a halt, crossing each others' paths and coming within fractions of an inch from collision.

Danifae smiled at the dragons—all five of them rearing up to shred her with claws like filet knives—and she said, "Careful now. Look behind you."

The toothy sneer that was the drake's reply played out simultaneously on all five sets of jaws.

Valas let his arrow fly, and all four of his own conjured images did the same. The little brass ovoid—a container for a spell that had been very specially crafted by an ancient mage whose secrets had long ago been lost—had done its work, and for each of the five portal drakes, there was a Valas.

For each of the five portal drakes there was an arrow.

The dragon might have heard them or sensed them in some other way, or maybe its curiosity had gotten the better of it. The creature whirled around and met the arrows with its right eye. Four of the arrows blinked out of existence the instant they met with the false drakes, and those illusionary dragons disappeared as well. The barrage left only one real arrow, one real portal drake, and one real eye.

The force of the impact made the creature twitch then stagger back a step.

Valas could tell that the dragon could see him—all five of him—with its one good eye.

"I'll eat you alive . . ." the portal drake rasped, "for that."

Valas drew his kukris, and his images did the same. The dragon, blood pouring from its ruined eye, didn't bother to pull out the arrow that still protruded from its eye socket. Instead it charged, wings up, claws out, jaws open.

Valas stepped to the side, into the drake's blind spot. The creature had obviously never fought with only one eye before, and it fell for the feint. Valas got two quick cuts in—cuts each answered with a deep, rumbling growl.

The drake lashed out, and Valas stepped in and to the side, letting one of his images cross in front of the attack. The portal drake's claw touched the image's shoulder, and by the time the talon passed through the false scout's abdomen the illusion was gone.

The dragon grumbled its frustration, and Valas attacked again. The creature twisted out of reach and snapped its jaws at Valas— coming dangerously close to the real dark elf. When the dragon's single eye narrowed and smoldered, the scout knew the dragon had pegged him.

Valas danced into the drake's blind spot, stepping backward and spinning to keep the dragon off balance and to keep his own mirror images moving frenetically around him. The drake clawed another one into thin air then bit the third out of existence.

Valas watched the image disappear and followed the portal drake's neck with his eyes as it passed half an arm's length in front of him. He looked for cracks, creases, for any sign of weakness in the monster's thick, scaly hide.

He found one and sank a kukri between scales, through skin, into flesh, artery, and bone beneath it. Blood pumped from the creature in torrents. The dragon flailed at Valas, though it couldn't quite see the scout. As the creature died, it managed to brush a claw against the last false drow. The drake started to fall, and Valas skipped out of the way. The narrow head whipped around on its long, supple neck, and the jaws came down on Valas's shoulder, crinkling his armor and bruising the black skin underneath.

The scout pulled away, rolled, and came to his feet with his kukris in front of him.

No attack came. The portal drake splayed across the floor of the cavern. Blood came less frequently and with less urgency with every fading heartbeat.

"Always knew . . ." the dying dragon sighed, "it would be . . . a drow."

The portal drake died with that word on its tongue, and Valas lifted an eyebrow at the thought.

He stepped away from the poisonous corpse and sheathed his kukris. There was no sign of Danifae. Valas didn't know if she'd kept running back the way they'd come or if she was hiding somewhere in the shadows.

With a shrug and a last glance at the portal drake, Valas turned and went to the abandoned monastery. Assuming that the Melarn battle-captive would eventually return to the cavern and the portal that was their goal there, Valas climbed into the great downturned mouth.

Inside the semicircular structure were two tall, freestanding pillars. Between them was nothing but dead air and the side of the tall cavern wall. The interior was shrouded in darkness, and from it came the sharp smell of the portal drake's filth.

Danifae stood between the pillars, her weight on one foot, her hand on her hip.

"Is it dead?" she asked.

Valas stopped several strides from her and nodded.

Danifae looked up and around at the dead stone pillars and the featureless interior of the huge face.

"Good," the battle-captive said. "Is this the portal?"

When she looked back at Valas, he nodded again.

"You know how to open it," she said, with no hint that it might be a question.

Valas nodded a third time, and Danifae smiled.

"Before we go," she said as she pulled a dagger from her shapely hip, "I want to harvest some poison."

Valas blinked and said, "From the portal drake?"

Danifae walked past him, smiling, spinning her dagger between her fingers.

"I'll wait here," he told her.

She kept going without bothering to answer.

If she survives that, Valas thought, she might just be worth traveling with.

Pharaun traced a fingertip along the line of something that hadn't been there the day before: a vein. The blood vessel followed a meandering path along the length of the bone rail of the ship of chaos. At random intervals it branched into thinner capillaries. The whole thing slowly, almost imperceptibly, pulsed with life—warm with the flow of blood. When they'd first come aboard the demonic ship, the railing was solid, dead bone. Half a tenday spent gating in minor demons and feeding it to the ship was changing it. It was coming to life.

"Will it eventually grow skin?" Quenthel asked from behind him.

Pharaun turned and saw the high priestess crouching, examining the deck the same way he was examining the rail.

"Skin?" the wizard asked.

"These veins it's growing seem so fragile," she said. Her voice sounded bored, distant. "If we step on them won't we cut them?"

"I don't know," Pharaun said. What he meant was that he didn't care. "What difference could it possibly make?"

"It could bleed," she said, still looking down at the deck. "If it can bleed, it can die. If it dies when we're . . ."

Pharaun could tell she didn't finish that thought because she was afraid to. He hated it when a high priestess was afraid. Things rarely went well if they started with that.

"Not everything that bleeds dies," he said with a forced smile.

She looked up at him, and their eyes met. He expected her to be angry at least, maybe offended, but she was neither. Pharaun couldn't tell what she was thinking.

"It troubles me," she said after a pause, "that we know so little. A ship like this . . . you should have studied it in the lore, shouldn't you? At Sorcere?"

"I did," Pharaun said. "I've been feeding it a steady diet, I've cowed its captain, and we're nearly ready for our little interplanar jaunt. I know what it is and how it works, which means I know enough. For a priestess you can be overly analytical. Will it grow skin? If it wants to. Will it bleed to death if your spike heels slice a vein? I doubt it. Will it behave exactly the same way every time for everyone? Well, if it did, it wouldn't be very chaotic, now would it?"

"Some day," Quenthel said without a pause, "I will sew your mouth shut so you'll stop talking long enough for me to kill you in peace."

Pharaun chuckled and rubbed cool sweat from his forehead.

"Why, Mistress," the mage replied with a smile, "whatever for?"

"Because I hate you," she replied.

Pharaun said nothing. They gazed at each other for a few moments more then Quenthel stood and looked around.

"I'm getting bored," she said to no one in particular.

You're getting scared, Pharaun thought.

"I'm getting angry," Jeggred cut in.

Both Pharaun and Quenthel looked over to where the draegloth sat. The half-demon was slowly, methodically, skinning a rat. The rodent was still alive.

"No one asked, nephew," Quenthel said with a sneer.

"My apologies, honored aunt," the draegloth said, his voice dripping with icy sarcasm.

"Valas and Danifae will be back soon," Pharaun said, "and we will have the ship ready when they get back. We will be on our way presently, but in the meantime we mustn't let the tedium of this cursed lake get the better of us. It wouldn't do to have a party of dark elves fighting among themselves."

"It's not the lake I find tedious, mage," Jeggred shot back.

Pharaun rejected his first half-dozen retorts before speaking, but his face must have revealed something. He could see it reflected back at him in the draegloth's amused sneer.

"Yes," the wizard said finally, "well, I will accept that gracious threat in the spirit in which it was offered, Jeggred Baenre. Nonetheless, I—"

"Will shut up," the draegloth interrupted. "You will shut your damned mouth."

Jeggred licked the dying, squealing, flayed rat, leaving blood dribbling from his cracked gray lips.

"I don't like this," the half-demon said. "This one—" he tipped his chin to indicate the captive uridezu—"is planning something. It will betray us."

"It's a demon," Quenthel replied quietly.

"Meaning?" the draegloth asked, almost shouting.

"Meaning," Pharaun answered for her, "that of course it will betray us—or try to. The only thing you can trust about a demon is that it will be untrustworthy. It might cheer you to know we feel the same way about you, my draegloth friend."

Pharaun had expected some reaction to that comment but not the one he got. Jeggred and Quenthel locked stares, their eyes boring into each other's. There was a long silence. It was Quenthel who looked away first.

Jeggred actually seemed disappointed.

Aliisza nuzzled close to Kaanyr Vhok, her long ebony tresses mingling with the cambion's silver hair.

"Have you been entertaining ladies while I was away?" the alu-fiend cooed into her lover's neck.

The cambion let out a slow breath through his nose and slid a hand onto Aliisza's back. He drew her closer to him, so their sides were pressed together. Aliisza could feel his blazing body heat, so much hotter than a dark elf's. So comfortable and reassuring. So powerful.

"Jealous?" Kaanyr Vhok whispered.

Aliisza thrilled that he was playing along. It was a rare reaction from the half-demon, who normally kept his feelings so carefully guarded.

"Never," she whispered back, pausing to let her hot, moist lips brush along his skin. "I just wish I could have joined you."

She hoped for further playfulness but instead got a dismissive chuckle. Kaanyr Vhok withdrew from her, and she plastered a coy pout on her face, narrowing her deep green eyes in a scowl.

Vhok flashed her a rare grin and put a finger gently to her lips.

"Don't cry, my dear," he said. "When this mad war is over, we'll have time for dalliances to thrill the likes of even you."

"Until then?"

He took his hand away and stepped to a small table on which was set a tray, a crystal decanter of fine brandy stolen for sport from a shop in Skullport, and a single glass.

"Until then," Vhok said, pouring a splash of the rust-colored liquid into the glass, "we'll have to occasionally break for business."

"How goes that business?"

"Menzoberranzan is under siege," the cambion answered, making a sweeping gesture to indicate their surroundings, "and will be for a very long time, unless someone manages to inject some intelligence—or dare we hope, imagination—into our gray dwarf allies."

"You don't sound hopeful," she said.

"They're as dull witted as they are ill tempered," Vhok replied, "but we make do."

He turned to look at her, and Aliisza smiled, shrugged, and sat. More accurately, she let her body pour onto a richly upholstered sofa, her lithe body draping seductively across it and her eyes playing over his body. Her leather bodice looked stiff and restraining, but it flowed over her the same way she flowed over the sofa, shifting to her will like her own skin. The sheathed long sword at her hip tucked under one leg.

Vhok's own costume was typically opulent, a tunic embroidered in a military style. A long sword of his own hung at his hip, and Aliisza knew he wore any number of magical bits and pieces, even in the privacy of his own temporary quarters.

The tent they inhabited at the rear of the siege lines was cloaked in enchantments that would prevent anyone from overhearing, peeking in, or spying on them in any conceivable way, but still Aliisza felt exposed.

"That lake," she said, her eyes drifting around the silk-draped confines of the tent, "is the dullest place I've ever been, and I've spent time in duergar cities."

Vhok took a small sip of the brandy and closed his eyes, savoring it. Aliisza had long ago gotten over not being offered any.

"It's a dreary, gray cave," she added. "I mean, the air is actually gray. It's awful."

Vhok opened his eyes and shrugged, waiting for more.

"They captured the captain," she continued.

"An uridezu?" the cambion asked.

Aliisza nodded, lifting an eyebrow at the oddly accurate guess.

"Sometimes," Vhok said, "I think you forget what I am."

"I remember," she said hastily.

Kaanyr Vhok was a cambion, the son of a human father and a demon mother. He shared the most dangerous qualities of both those chaotic animals.

Aliisza reached out a hand and shifted on the sofa.

"Come," she said. "Sit with me, and I'll tell you everything I saw. Every last detail. For the war effort."

Vhok downed the rest of the brandy in one gulp, set the glass down, and took Aliisza's hand. His olive skin looked dark and rich against her own pale flesh. Not as dark as Pharaun's of course, but . . .

"Sounds to me," the cambion said as he slid onto the sofa next to his demon lover, "as if these drow are planning a trip."

"They are past planning," she said.

"They are past foolishness," replied Vhok. "Typical drow, serving a chaotic mistress with such strident lawfulness. Always marching in lockstep, with their Houses and their laws and their infantile traditions. No wonder the spider bitch turned her back on them. I'm surprised she suffered their nonsense this long."

Aliisza smiled, showing perfect teeth—human teeth she chose for intimate occasions. She'd found over the decades that even Vhok could be put off by her jagged fangs. Aliisza smiled often and nearly as often changed the size and shape of her teeth to fit her mood.

"You think too little of them," she cautioned. "One or two drow have proven interesting. One or two of the interesting ones, together, can prove dangerous."

Vhok answered with a noncommittal grunt then said, "I suppose I should apologize for calling you back from the Lake of Shadows before you could make contact with this wizard of yours. It was unforgivably officious of me."

The alu-demon leaned in closer and let the tip of her tongue play along the edge of Vhok's pointed ear. He sat still, responding in ways more than simply physical. Aliisza could feel herself flush.

"You will get us both in trouble," the cambion whispered to her, "with the wrong dalliances."

"Or make us both triumphant," she replied, "with the right ones."

Vhok didn't bother answering, and Aliisza moved to whisper very close, very quietly into his ear, "They could do it. The ship of chaos could get them there."

Vhok nodded, and Aliisza tried to read that response. She thought he was happy with her at least for being as discreet as she was with that opinion, even in the spell-warded tent.

She began to unbutton his tunic, teasing him with each slow twist of her fingers, each incremental loosening of his clothing. Aliisza knew what to expect of Kaanyr Vhok without his clothes. Though from all appearances the marquis cambion was an aging half-elf from the World Above, his chest, arms, and legs were covered in green scales. That demon's flesh was a sight few had ever lived to see twice.

"They go in search of the spider bitch," Vhok said, twisting to help her more easily slide his tunic off.

"They mean to wake her?" Aliisza asked, turning her attention to the glistening scales on Vhok's broad chest.

"They mean to take their quest for her favor to her sticky little throne," the cambion replied, "or her sticky little bed . . . or her sticky little tomb, and wake her from her sleep. You say they've been feeding the ship?"

"A constant diet of manes," she whispered into his ear.

Vhok nodded as he began to undress her.

"The wizard?" he asked.

"Pharaun," she answered.

"He can do it, then," Vhok decided. "A Master of Sorcere no less, with the captain enthralled."

"They can get to the Demonweb Pits," she said, "but do you think they can wake her?"

"No," came a startling third voice in what Aliisza was sure was a tent occupied by only two.

Both of them stood and in a thought had their swords in their hands. The blades, identical to the finest detail, practically hummed with magical energy. They stood back-to-back, a defensive stance born of instinct more than practice.

Aliisza could see no one but could feel Vhok tense behind her. She had come to know his moods well, and what she sensed from him was anger, not fear. Aliisza continued to scan the room until a figure presented itself.

"Nimor," Aliisza breathed.

"A dangerous decision," Vhok said to the shadowy figure of the drow assassin, "walking in here unannounced."

"Believe me," Nimor replied, stepping into the warm torchlight nearer the center of the tent, "voyeurism was the last thing on my mind. As you said, Lord Vhok, there is business to be handled. Besides, I didn't 'walk' in."

Vhok slipped his sword, a blade he called "Burnblood," back into its sheath and stepped away from Aliisza. With slow, deliberate motions, he picked up his tunic and slipped it back on, covering the scaly flesh he so seldom exposed.

The edge of Nimor's thin lips slipped up in wry amusement. Something about that reaction made Aliisza uneasy—more so than normal when in the assassin's presence.

"What business brings you here now, Anointed Blade?" asked Vhok.

"That drow expedition, of course," the assassin replied. "They have found a ship of chaos, and they mean to pay their sleeping goddess a visit?"

The assassin was looking at Aliisza, expecting an answer. She sheathed her own sword and slipped back down to the sofa, never taking her eyes off the dark elf. The alu-fiend didn't bother refastening the clasps Vhok had undone on her bodice.

"There's very little reason to suspect they'll succeed," said Vhok.

"Would you agree, Aliisza?" Nimor asked.

Aliisza shrugged and said, "They have a wizard with them who could likely handle the ship. I became acquainted with him in Ched Nasad just before the end, and I found him quite capable."

"Ah, yes," Nimor said, "Pharaun Mizzrym. He could be the next archmage, or so I hear. If his name were Baenre, that is."

"They could do it," Vhok said.

Nimor took a deep breath and said, "There are a thousand things that could go wrong between the Lake of Shadows and the Abyss, and a thousand thousand things could go wrong between the edge of the Abyss and the sixty-sixth layer."

"What will they find there, Nimor?" Aliisza asked, genuinely curious.

Nimor smiled, and Aliisza momentarily thrilled at his feral expression.

"I haven't the vaguest notion," he answered.

"If they find Lolth?" asked Vhok.

"If they find Lolth," said Nimor, "and she's dead, then we can settle in for as long a siege as necessary. Menzoberranzan is doomed. If she sleeps and they can't wake her or if she has simply decided to abandon her faithful on this world, the same is true. If she sleeps and they do wake her or she is ignoring them and they regain her favor, well, that would pose a difficulty for us."

"How do we know what they'll find?" asked the cambion.

"We don't," Nimor answered.

The dark elf folded his arms across his chest and tipped his head down. His features grew tighter, darker as he wrapped himself in thought.

"Let them go, but . . ." Aliisza suggested, the words tripping over her tongue before she'd thought them through.

"Send someone with them," Nimor finished for her.

The alu-fiend smiled, showing a row of yellow-white fangs.

※　　※　　※

"Agrach Dyrr is alone," Triel Baenre said. "Alone and under siege."

Gromph nodded but didn't look at his sister. He was captivated by the sight of Menzoberranzan. The City of Spiders stretched out before him, ablaze in faerie fire, magnificent in its chaos, in its perversion of nature—a cave made into a home.

"Good," Gromph replied, "but don't assume they'll give up easily. They have loyal servants of their own and allies who make up for what they lack in intelligence with superiority of numbers."

From where they stood on a high belvedere on the outside edge of one of the westernmost spires of the House Baenre complex, Gromph had a largely unobstructed view of the subterranean city. The Baenre palace stood against the southern wall of the huge cavern, atop the second tier of a wide rock shelf. It was the First House, and its position above the rest of the city was more than symbolic.

"They may have thrown in with the gray dwarves," Andzrel Baenre said, "but no dark elf in Menzoberranzan fights on their behalf."

Gromph turned to his left and looked west across the high ground of Qu'ellarz'orl. Before him was the high stalagmite tower of House Xorlarrin and beyond that the cluster of stalactites and stalagmites that housed the treasonous Agrach Dyrr. Flashes of fire and lightning—the work of Xorlarrin's formidable and plentiful mages—flickered across the ground and in the air around Dyrr's manor. The lichdrow who was the rebel House's master was holed up inside there somewhere, and his own mages answered back with fire and thunder of their own. Gromph could feel his sister Triel and the weapons master Andzrel behind him, waiting for him to speak.

"It seems as if I've been gone a very, very long time," Gromph said, his voice subdued but carefully modulated to covey to his sister his grave disappointment at the state of the war.

He could sense Triel stiffen behind him then shake his words off.

"You have been," she said, letting no small amount of acid into her own voice, "but let us not dwell on failures in the face of such grave danger to all we hold dear."

Gromph allowed himself a smile and glanced back over his shoulder at his sister. She was staring at him, her arms folded in front of her, cradling them as if she were cold. He turned back to the ongoing stalemate around the foot of Agrach Dyrr and noted with some satisfaction how well his new eyes were seeing. The blurring and the pain were mostly gone, leaving Gromph to enjoy the irony of watching House Agrach Dyrr fall with a set of Agrach Dyrr eyes.

"Not all the Houses are at our beck and call, though, are they?" he asked.

Triel sighed and said, "It is still Menzoberranzan, and we are still dark elves. Houses Xorlarrin and Faen Tlabbar are firmly with us. Faen Tlabbar brings with it House Srune'lett, who's strongly allied with House Duskryn. Of the lesser Houses we can rely on Symryvvin, Hunzrin, Vandree, and Mizzrym to serve us."

"That's all?" Gromph asked after a pause.

"Barrison Del'Armgo perhaps still stings over Oblodra," Triel replied. "They remain loyal to Menzoberranzan, and they fight, but they keep their own council."

"And carry their own allies," Gromph added.

"Thankfully, no," Triel corrected, obviously pleased with proving her brother wrong at the same time she was pleased that that powerful House was on its own. "The other lesser Houses remain neutral but offer their assets in defense of the city. Better a dark elf neighbor you hate than a duergar in any capacity."

"Or a tanarukk," Gromph added.

"Or a tanarukk," his sister agreed.

Gromph turned his attention back to the city at large. There were very few drow in the streets and the archmage could see columns of troops moving, some at double time, through the winding thoroughfares.

"The city is quiet," he commented.

"The city," Andzrel cut in, "is hard under siege."

Gromph bristled at that but knew better than to kill the messenger, at least in that case.

"We are surrounded on all sides, but we're fighting," the weapons master continued, "and will continue to fight. Our own forces hold Qu'ellarz'orl and are moving to support House Hunzrin in Donigarten north."

"The siege of Agrach Dyrr," Triel offered, "is largely House Xorlarrin's, and they seem to have it well in hand."

"Is the lichdrow dead?" asked Gromph.

There was a pause, during which neither the matron mother nor the weapons master bothered to answer.

"Then they could have a firmer hand," the archmage concluded.

Andzrel cleared his throat and continued, "Faen Tlabbar, aside from blocking Agrach Dyrr's retreat west, guards the southwest approaches to the Dark Dominion from the Web to the western tip of Qu'ellarz'orl. They face the largest concentration of gray dwarves, assisted by House Srune'lett. Faen Tlabbar also supports House Duskryn's efforts to hold the caves north of the Westrift."

"Well," said Gromph with a wry edge to his voice, "isn't Faen Tlabbar impressive."

"They are," Triel agreed, "and Srune'lett and Duskryn require no more proof. If Faen Tlabbar were to betray us, they would take those two Houses with them at least."

"Why in all the Underdark might they do that?" Gromph joked.

Triel laughed, and the weapons master cleared his throat.

"What of the lesser Houses?" Gromph asked.

"Symryvvin assists Duskryn above the Westrift," Andzrel said.

"Another probably in Ghenni's pocket, should it come to that," Triel commented.

Gromph shrugged and said, "If they defend Menzoberranzan now, let them make plans for afterward. If we survive, we survive as First House."

"I agree, Archmage," said Andzrel.

Gromph turned to look at the warrior, letting a cold gaze linger over the drow's rough features and battle-scarred armor.

"Of course you do," the archmage said, his voice barely above a whisper.

Andzrel looked down then looked at Triel, who only smiled at him.

"House . . ." the weapons master began, obviously thinking it safer to continue his debriefing than further patronize the powerful archmage with his support. He cleared his throat and continued, "House Hunzrin is hard pressed against forces of the Scoured Legion in Donigarten north. Vandree holds well against duergar south of the Westrift. Mizzrym lends what it can to Xorlarrin's efforts against Agrach Dyrr, and they also send patrols into the mushroom forest where they've encountered the odd spy."

"The tanarukks are mostly in the east, then?" Gromph asked.

"As one would expect, Archmage," the weapons master risked. "They marched from below Hellgate Keep, which lies to our east. The duergar are from Gracklstugh."

Gromph let a breath out slowly through his nose.

"I never thought I'd live to see the day," Triel murmured. "Gracklstugh . . ."

"The tanarukks are more formidable foes," Gromph went on, ignoring his sister. "Tell me that more than House Hunzrin are holding against them."

"Barrison Del'Armgo fights well in the south of Donigarten," Andzrel replied, "against the largest concentration of the Scoured Legion."

"Mez'Barris will have her heroes," Triel sighed.

"North?" Gromph asked.

"Barrison Del'Armgo again, with help from the Academy, holds the Clawrift," replied the weapons master, "mostly east into East-myr. The duergar are thin there. There have been reports of illithid incursions—mostly one or two at a time—in the east, from beyond the Wanderways."

"The flayers sense weakness," Gromph said. "They're scavengers. They'll harry us when they can and disappear entirely when they can't. Some of them can prove . . . irritating, but they'll wait till we're weaker—if we let ourselves get weaker—before they appear in force."

Neither Triel nor Andzrel risked comment on that.

"And the other Houses?" asked Gromph.

"They protect themselves," Triel answered. "They patrol the immediate surrounds of their manors, assist in keeping the peace in the streets, and I'd prefer to believe, they await command."

"Well," said Gromph, "I'm sure we'll find out soon enough. Still, I'd have liked more allies within our own damned city."

"Tier Breche is with us," Triel said, "though I doubt I have to tell you that. In Quenthel's absence, Arach-Tinilith answers only to me. I know you have done well in your return to power at Sorcere, and Melee-Magthere will always fight should one raise a blade against the City of Spiders."

"Your gold has paid for the mercenaries, I assume," Gromph said.

Triel shrugged and replied, "Bregan D'aerthe is on extended contract, though the Abyss knows where Jarlaxle's been. It'll take every dead duergar's gold teeth to replenish our coffers in the end, but in the meantime, Bregan D'aerthe act as infiltrators and scouts and are moving forces throughout the city to monitor and support the lesser Houses."

"Much of what we've told you today, Archmage," Andzrel offered, "came from Bregan D'aerthe reports."

"Good for them," Gromph lied.

"Menzoberranzan will stand," Andzrel declared.

"But not forever," Triel added.

"Not for long," said Gromph.

There was a long silence. Gromph spent the time watching the flickering of valuable battle magic being spent against House Agrach Dyrr.

"What will be left?" asked Triel after a time.

"Matron Mother," Andzrel said, "Archmage, in my opinion the greatest threat from within the city is no longer Agrach Dyrr but Barrison Del'Armgo."

Gromph lifted an eyebrow and turned to look at the weapons master.

"Even without any of the lesser Houses at their side," the warrior went on, "they are the greatest threat to the First House's power. Matron Mother Armgo is already making overtures to many of the lesser Houses, especially Hunzrin and Kenafin."

"And?" Triel prompted.

"And," Gromph broke in, finishing on Andzrel's behalf, "they could bite off Donigarten."

"Our food supply," Andzrel added.

Gromph smiled when Triel's face turned almost gray.

"Yes, well," the archmage said, "all things in their turn. Barrison Del'Armgo will answer for their ambitions only after I've cleaned up a more open insurrection."

"Dyrr?" Triel didn't have to ask.

"It's time for our old friend the lichdrow to die again," Gromph replied. "This time, permanently."

Danifae counted the warriors in front of her—eight armed with spears, and a row of a dozen crossbowmen behind them—and waited.

"Welcome to the City of Portals," one of the spearmen said, his blood-red eyes darting quickly, alertly, between Danifae and Valas. "If you reach for a weapon or begin to cast a spell, we'll kill you before you get a single breath out."

Danifae flashed the male a smile and was gratified to see his gaze linger on her. If Valas were going to attack, he would have at that moment. He didn't, so Danifae found herself in the position of having to trust him again.

"Who are you, where are you from," the guard asked, "and what is your business in Sschindylryn?"

"I am Valas Hune," the scout answered. He paused and reached up slowly to the neck of his *piwafwi*. When he drew his cloak aside, the guard's eyes fixed on something. Danifae was sure it had to be the insignia of the mercenary company to which Valas was attached. "My business here is to resupply. Give us a day or so to gather what we need, and we'll be on our way."

The guard nodded and looked at Danifae.

"And you?" he asked. "You don't look Bregan D'aerthe."

Danifae chuckled playfully and replied, "I am Danifae Yauntyrr. And you?"

The guard was puzzled by the question.

"She is a battle-captive in the service of the First Daughter of House Melarn," Valas answered for her.

Danifae felt her skin tingle with suppressed rage. What kind of scout volunteered such information? Or did he mean to put her in her place by reminding her that while he was free, she was not?

The guard smiled—leered almost—and looked Danifae briefly up and down.

"Melarn?" he said. "Never heard of it."

"A lesser House," Valas answered again before Danifae could speak up. "It was destroyed with the others in the fall of Ched Nasad."

The guard looked at her again and said, "That means you're free, eh?"

Danifae shrugged, saying nothing. She, unlike Valas, wasn't about to give away information. The last thing she needed was for anyone to know that she'd come to Sschindylryn to address that very question once and for all.

"We want no trouble with Bregan D'aerthe," the guard said to Valas. "Get your supplies, then get out. Menzoberranyr are less than popular here."

"Why would that be?" asked Valas.

The guards visibly relaxed, and half the crossbowmen slipped the bolts off their weapons and stepped back from the firing line. The spearmen put their weapons up but still stood ready.

"It's your fault," the guard replied, "or so they say."

"What is our fault?" Danifae asked, not certain why she identified herself as Menzoberranyr, having never even been there.

"They say," the guard said, "that it was a Menzoberranyr who killed Lolth."

Valas laughed, letting a generous portion of contempt coat the sound.

"Yes, well . . ." the guard finished. "That's what they say."

"This way," Valas said over his shoulder to Danifae.

The battle-captive nodded, took stock of her belongings, and followed the scout past the guards and toward the wide, open gate into the city proper. As she passed him, Danifae gave the guard captain a playful wink. The male's jaw opened, but he managed to catch it before it dropped.

When she was certain they were out of earshot of the guards, Danifae drew closer to the Bregan D'aerthe scout. Valas flinched away from her touch then seemed to force himself to relax. Danifae, making careful note of his reaction to her, leaned in very close. With a greater than necessary exhalation of hot air from her husky, hushed voice, Danifae whispered into his ear.

"I'm not going with you," she told Valas.

"Why not?" he answered, matching her discreet volume but not her flirtatiousness.

"I never enjoyed shopping," Danifae replied, "and I have errands of my own."

For a moment it looked to Danifae as if Valas were actually going to argue or at least press her for more information.

"Very well," he said after a few seconds. "I have a way of calling you when it's time to go."

"I have a way of ignoring you if I'm not ready," she replied.

Valas didn't respond, though that time Danifae was sure she'd broken through his impenetrable armor. She turned away and stepped into the crowd that was flowing past the columned, temple-like structure that surrounded the gate. Within seconds she had effectively lost herself in the strange city, leaving the scout behind.

The city of Sschindylryn was contained in a single pyramid-shaped void in the solid rock some unfathomable distance below the surface of Faerûn. The pyramid had three sides, each more than two miles long, and the apex was two miles above. Bioluminescent fungus grew in patches all around the smooth outer walls, giving the whole city an eerie, dim yellow ambient light. The drow who called the city home lived in houses constructed of stone and brick—unusual in a dark elf city—that were built on stepped tiers. The outer edges of the city were actually trenches carved into the stone floor of the pyramid. In the center, a sort of huge ziggurat rose up into the cool, still air. There was no physical way in or out of the city. No tunnel connected the cavern to the rest of the Underdark. Sschindylryn was sealed. Locked away.

Except for the gates, and there were thousands of those.

They were everywhere. In only the first few blocks Danifae saw a dozen of them. They led to every corner of the Underdark, onto the World Above, perhaps beyond to the planes and elsewhere. Some were open to the public, left there by no one remembered whom. Others were commercial ventures, offering transport to some other drow city or trade site of the lesser races for a fee. Still others were kept secret, used only by a chosen few. Gangs controlled some, merchant costers controlled more, while the clergy maintained hundreds.

On the narrow streets Danifae passed mostly other dark elves, and all of them seemed, like her, concerned entirely with their own business. They ignored her, and she did likewise. As she walked, she became increasingly aware that she was in a strange city, alone, looking for a single drow who was very likely still making every effort to hide.

House Agrach Dyrr had been part of the political landscape of Menzoberranzan for more than five thousand years. Only House Baenre was older.

For most of that time, Houses Baenre and Agrach Dyrr had maintained a close relationship. Of course there was never trust, that wasn't something that existed in any but the must tenuous and rudimentary form in the City of Spiders, but they had had certain arrangements. They shared common interests and common goals. Agrach Dyrr had fulfilled its role in the city's hierarchy. It went to war with the city, defended itself against rival Houses, destroyed a few from time to time as necessity dictated, and in all things followed the teachings and the whims of the Queen of the Demonweb Pits.

Matron Mother Yasraena Dyrr enjoyed pain. She enjoyed chaos, and she enjoyed the blessings of Lolth. When that last bit went away, things changed.

From their palace on the wide shelf of Qu'ellarz'orl, the Lichdrow Dyrr had stood with his much younger granddaughter and watched the city turn against them. Well, that wasn't entirely accurate, the lichdrow knew. He had turned against the city, and he had done it with precise and careful timing. He had made the final decision, as he always had in times of greatest peril and greatest opportunity. Yasraena did what she was told, occasionally being made to feel as if it was her idea in the first place, sometimes merely given an order.

Most days, the youthful matron mother was as much in command of the House as any of the city's matrons. When it truly counted, though, the lichdrow stepped in.

The palace of House Agrach Dyrr was a ring of nine giant stalagmites that rose from the rocky floor of Qu'ellarz'orl, surrounded by a dry moat crossed at only one point by a wide, defensible bridge. In the center of the ring of stalagmites, behind a square wall of spell-crafted stone, was the House temple. That massive cathedral was more than a symbol to the drow of House Agrach Dyrr—it was a sincere and passionate proclamation of their faith in the Spider Queen.

In the past months, though, the temple had grown as quiet as the goddess it was built to honor.

"Lolth has abandoned us," the lichdrow said.

He stood at the entrance to the temple. A hundred yards in front of him, his granddaughter kneeled before the black altar and stared silently up at an enormous, stylized representation of the goddess. The idol weighed several tons and had been shaped by divine magic out of a thousand of the most precious materials the Underdark had to offer.

"We have abandoned her," Yasraena replied.

Their voices carried through the huge chamber.

The lichdrow floated toward her, his toes almost touching the marble floor. She didn't turn around.

"Well," he said, "what could she expect?"

The matron mother let the joke hang there without comment.

"The bridge holds," Dyrr reported, sounding almost bored. "Word from agents within Sorcere is that Vorion was captured but was later killed. I'm still finding out if he broke."

"Vorion . . ." the matron mother breathed.

She had taken Vorion as her consort only a few years before.

"My condolences," the lichdrow said.

"He had a few admirable qualities," the matron mother replied. "Ah well, at least he died in defense of the House."

Dyrr tired of the subject, so he changed it.

"Gromph has regained his sight."

Yasraena nodded and said, "He'll be coming for us."

"He'll be coming for *me*," the lichdrow corrected.

The matron mother sighed. She must have known he was right. The priestess, bereft of her connection to Lolth, was still a force to be reckoned with. She was experienced, cruel, strong, and she had access to the House's stores of magical items, artifacts, and scrolls, but against the Archmage of Menzoberranzan, she would be little more than a nuisance. If Gromph was coming, he was coming for the lichdrow, and if Agrach Dyrr was to survive, it would be the lichdrow who would have to save it.

"I don't suppose you can count on your new friends," the matron mother said.

"My 'new friends' have problems of their own," Dyrr replied. "They lay siege to the city, but Baenre and the others Houses have done a surprisingly good job of holding the entrances to the Dark Dominion."

"They have us bottled in our palace like rats in a trap," said the matron mother.

Dyrr laughed, the sound muffled and strained from under his mask. The lichdrow almost never allowed anyone to see his face. Yasraena was one of the few to whom he would reveal himself, but even then, not often. Though she wasn't looking at him, he maintained the affectation of leaning on his staff. The outward illusion of advanced age and physical weakness had become second nature to him, and he'd begun to maintain that attitude even when no one was looking. His body, free of the demands of life for a millennia, was as responsive as it had been the day he died and was resurrected.

"Don't begin to believe our own ruse, granddaughter," Dyrr said. "Not everything has gone strictly to plan, but all is far from lost, and we are far from trapped. We were meant to be in the city, and here we are. The two of us are in our own temple, unmolested. We have lost troops and the odd consort and cousin, but we live, and our assets are largely intact. Our 'new friends' as you call them, have the city hard under siege, and many of the Houses refuse to join the fight—join it in any real way, at least. All we have to do is keep pressing, keep pressing, keep pressing, and we will win the day. I grant you that it is an inconvenience that Gromph escaped my little snare. I do wonder how he managed it. But I assure you it will be the last time I under-estimate the Archmage of Menzoberranzan."

"Did you underestimate him," she asked, "or did he beat you?"

There was a moment of silence between them as Yasraena stared up at the idol of Lolth, and Dyrr waited in mute protest.

"This assassin. . . ." she said at last.

"Nimor," Dyrr provided.

"I know you don't trust him," she said.

"Of course not," the lichdrow replied with a dry chuckle. "He is committed to his cause, though."

"And that cause?" asked the matron mother. "The downfall of Menzoberranzan? The destruction of the matriarchy? The wholesale abandonment of the worship of Lolth?"

"Lolth is gone, Yasraena," Dyrr said. "The matriarchy has func-tioned, but as with all things past it too may not survive the Spider Queen's demise. The city, of course, will endure. It will endure under my steady, immortal hand."

"Yours," she asked, "or Nimor's?"

"Mine," the lichdrow replied with perfect finality.

"He should be in the city," Yasraena added before there could be too significant a pause. "Nimor and his duergar friends should be here. Every day that goes by, Baenre and Xorlarrin wear us down. Little by little, granted, but little by little for long enough and . . ."

She let the thought hang there, and Dyrr only shrugged in response.

"If you expected to do this without Gromph on their side," Yasraena asked, "what now that he's back?"

"As I said," the lichdrow replied, "I will kill him. He will come for me, and I will be ready. When the time comes, I will meet him."

"Alone?" she asked, concern plain in her voice.

The lichdrow didn't answer. Neither of them moved, and the temple was silent for a long time.

He had come for a little food and a few minor incidentals. They could drink the water from the Lake of Shadows but could use a few more skins to carry it in. Under normal circumstances nothing could be easier for someone as well traveled as Valas Hune.

Normal circumstances.

The words had lost all meaning.

"Hey," the gnoll grumbled, hefting its heavy war-axe so Valas could see it. "You wait line, drow."

Valas looked the gnoll in the eyes, but it didn't back down.

"Everybody wait line," the guard growled.

Valas took a deep breath, left his hands at his side, and said, "Is Firritz here?"

The gnoll blinked at him, surprised.

Valas could feel other eyes on him. Drow, duergar, and representatives of a few more lesser races looked his way. Though they would be angry, impatient at having to wait in line while Valas presumed to bypass it, none of them spoke.

"Firritz," Valas repeated. "Is he here?"

"How you . . . ?" the gnoll muttered, eyes like slits. "How you know Firritz?"

Valas waited for the gnoll to understand that he wasn't going to say any more. It took seven heartbeats.

With a glance at the increasingly restless line, the gnoll said, "Follow."

Valas didn't smile, speak, or look at the others. He followed the gnoll in silence the full length of the line then through a mildewed curtain into a very large room with an uncomfortably low ceiling. The space was so crowded with sacks and crates and barrels that in the first few seconds after entering, Valas saw at least one of everything he'd come for.

A single, stooped old drow sat at a table in the center of the storehouse. A dozen different types of coins were arranged in neat stacks on the table in front of him. The gnoll nodded toward him, and Valas stepped closer to the merchant.

"Firritz," the scout said, his voice echoing.

The old drow didn't turn to look at him. Instead, he slowly counted a stack of gold coins then wrote the total on a piece of parchment on the table in front of him. Valas waited.

Perhaps ten minutes went by, and in that time the gnoll left the room and came back three times. Each time he came back, he seemed a bit more perplexed. Valas hadn't moved a muscle.

Finally, when the gnoll had left the room again, Firritz looked up from his counting and glanced at Valas.

"That's about how long you would have waited in line," the old drow said, his voice reedy and forced. "Now, what can I do for you?"

"Remember that you kept Bregan D'aerthe waiting," Valas said.

"Don't threaten me, Valas Hune," Firritz said. "Menzo's reputation has become a bit less impressive of late. Gray dwarves, I heard. Why aren't you there to defend the motherland?"

"I go where the coin leads me," said the scout. "Just like you."

"The coin doesn't lead to Menzoberranzan anymore, does it?"

"Bregan D'aerthe's credit is still good here," Valas said. "I need supplies."

"Credit?" said Firritz. "That word implies that your master at some point intends to pay his debt. I run up a tab, more and more, year after year, and see nothing for it. Maybe things have changed enough that that isn't necessary anymore, eh?"

"Take a deep breath," Valas said.

The old drow looked up at him. They stayed like that for a bit, but finally Firritz drew in a deep breath then exhaled slowly.

"That's what you see for it," Valas finished, "and it's necessary I get a few supplies."

Firritz frowned and said, "Nothing magical. Everyone's been buying up the magic bits—and for twice, even thrice the market value."

"I need food," the scout replied, "waterskins, a few odds and ends."

"You have a pack lizard?"

"No," Valas said with a smile and a tip of his head, "so I'll need something to carry it in. Something magical."

Firritz swept his arm across the table, scattering the coins onto the floor with a thousand echoing clatters.

"Food, Firritz," Valas said. "Time has become an issue for me."

Danifae could feel the Binding, and she could feel Halisstra. No matter how many thousands of feet of rock separated them, they were connected.

Danifae's skin crawled.

The farther from the center of the city she walked, the higher the mix of non-drow she passed on the streets. It was with no little relief, and after enduring lewd remarks from a trio of hobgoblins that she came to her destination.

She had never been to Sschindylryn before and had never seen that one particular structure, but she had gone straight to it. She'd made no wrong turns and asked for no directions.

Danifae stood in front of a complex jumble of mud bricks and flagstones arranged into what looked like some kind of hive or termite hill. Over the wide door—wide enough to accommodate a pack lizard and a decent-sized wagon—hung a slab of black stone into which was carved an elaborate sigil. The symbol contained unmistakable traces of the Yauntyrr crest but somehow turned in on itself, imploded, perverted.

Danifae reminded herself that no matter what happened, House Yauntyrr was gone. The integrity of its heraldry was of no concern to her, nor, she was sure, to anyone else.

She stepped inside.

Zinnirit's gatehouse, not unlike the larger gatehouse they'd entered the city through, was mostly open space on the street level. There looked to be room for another floor or even two above—likely Zinnirit's private residence—but the heart of the establishment was in that single cavernous chamber.

There were three gates, each a circle of elaborately interconnected stones easily thirty feet in diameter. No seething magical light pulsed through them. All three were inactive, dark.

"Zinnirit!" Danifae called.

Her voice echoed in the empty space. There was no immediate reply. Danifae had lost track of time quite a while before, and as she called the former House Mage's name again, she realized she might have dropped in on the wizard in the middle of his Reverie.

She didn't care.

"Zinnirit!"

A quiet, slow shuffling of feet answered Danifae's third entreaty. The sound was unmistakable but difficult to trace in the huge, echoing space. Despite the echoes, Danifae got the distinct impression that there was more than one set of feet. She couldn't count exactly how many—maybe half a dozen—and they were getting closer.

Danifae drew her morningstar and set it swinging at her right side.

"Zinnirit," she called. "Show yourself, you old fool."

Again, the only answer was that same echoing set of shuffling footsteps.

A shadow bobbed back and forth at the edge of her peripheral vision from deeper into the gatehouse. Danifae reacted with a thought, calling without question or hesitation on an ability bred into all highborn drow.

Five figures blazed to life with shimmering purple light. The faerie fire ringed their bodies and outlined them against the dull gloom behind them. The figures slowly shambled toward her and took no notice of the faerie fire.

The realization of what they were hit her half a second after the foul smell did.

They were zombies: walking dead of what looked to be mostly humans, though Danifae wasn't interested in conducting a thorough physical examination.

"Zinnirit . . ." she breathed, irritated.

One of the zombies reached out for her, and a quiet, painful-sounding groan escaped its rotting, tattered lips.

In answer, Danifae stood straight, arched one delicate eyebrow, held out one slim-fingered hand, and said, "Stop."

The zombies stopped.

"That will be all," she said, her voice a perfect, level calm.

The zombies, all still aglow in purple, turned clumsily, bumping into each other, and shambled away from the battle-captive. They were moving a bit faster away from her than they had come at her.

"Well," a firm male voice said, the single word echoing a thousand-fold in the gatehouse chamber.

Danifae put her hand down, let it rest on her hip.

"You shouldn't have been able to do that," the voice said, quieter but closer.

Danifae followed that echo back to its source and saw another drow-shaped shadow at the edge of the gloom.

"No need for faerie fire," he said and stepped close enough for Danifae to see him.

"Zinnirit," she said, pasting a broad grin on her face. "How lovely it is to see you, my old friend."

The aged drow moved a few steps closer to her but still kept a respectful—no, suspicious—distance from Danifae.

"You were taken to Ched Nasad," the wizard said. "I heard that Ched Nasad fell apart."

"It did," Danifae answered.

"I honor Lolth as much as any drow," the wizard said, "but you can keep buildings made of web, thank you very much."

"That wasn't the problem," Danifae replied. "Of course, you don't give the south end of a northbound rothé what happened to Ched Nasad."

"You know me too well still," he said.

"As you know me."

"It isn't easy, you know," the old wizard said, taking a few steps closer. "What you want done. It's not something you simply . . . dispel."

Zinnirit looked different. Danifae was amazed at how stooped he was, how thin, how wizened. He looked like a human, or a goblin. He looked bad.

"You've adopted the fashions of your new home, I see," Danifae remarked, nodding at the wizard's outlandish dress.

"Yes, I have," he replied. "Good for business, you know. Doesn't frighten the neighbors as much as the old spiky armor."

"You know why I'm here," said Danifae, "and I know you knew I was coming. Were the zombies meant to scare me?"

"Another bit of showmanship, actually," the mage explained. "Drow and lesser races alike are attracted to the odd bit of necromancy. Makes me seem more serious, I suppose."

"You knew I was in Sschindylryn the second I stepped through the gate," she said.

"I did, yes."

"Then let's get on with it."

"Things have changed, my dear Danifae," Zinnirit said. "I am no longer your mother's House mage, subject to the whims of her spoiled daughters."

"You expect me to pay?" she asked.

"You expect something for nothing?"

Danifae let one of her eyebrows twitch in response. That barely perceptible gesture made the old wizard look away. She took a deep breath and concentrated on that corner of her mind in which the Binding hid.

"I know why you've come," Zinnirit pressed. "It's always there, isn't it?"

Seeing no reason to lie, Danifae said, "It is. It's been there every second since I fell into the hands of House Melarn."

"It's an insidious enchantment that binds you . . ." said the old drow, "binds you in a way that only a drow could imagine. While the Binding is in effect, you will never be free. If your mistress . . . ?"

"Halisstra Melarn."

"If Halisstra Melarn dies, so goes Danifae," he continued. "If she calls for you, you'll go to her. No question, no hesitation, no choice. You can never—much as you might like to, even as a method of suicide—raise your hand to her. The Binding won't let your body move in a way that would result in your mistress's death."

"You understand well," she whispered, "but not completely. In many ways, it's the Binding that fuels me. That spell keeps me alive, keeps me vital, keeps me listening, watching, and learning. That spell, and my desire to break its hold, is what I live for."

Danifae saw fear flash across the old wizard's eyes.

"You weren't the only member of our House to be brought to Ched Nasad," he said. "After that last raid—the one that destroyed the redoubt, that destroyed the family—others were taken by Ched Nasad's Houses, and the rest were scattered over a wide swath of the Underdark. Those who lived, anyway, and that was precious few."

"Zinnirit Yauntyrr made it to Sschindylryn," she continued for him, "and did quite well here. That never surprised me. You were a talented spellcaster. No one could teleport like you. You were the master. And teleporting isn't all you're good at.

"You're ready," she said. "I know you."

"What will you do when you're free?" he asked.

Danifae smiled at him and stepped closer. They could touch each other if either lifted an arm.

"All right," the old mage breathed. "I don't need to know, do I?"

Danifae offered no response. She stood waiting.

"I will have to touch you," the wizard said.

Danifae nodded and stepped closer still—close enough that she could smell the old man's breath: cinnamon and pipeweed.

"It will hurt," he said even as his hand was reaching up to her.He placed the tips of his first and second fingers on her forehead. His touch was dry and cool. Strange words poured from his mouth. It might have been Draconic he was speaking but a dialect she couldn't quite pin down. After a full minute he stopped and lowered his hand. His red-orange eyes locked on hers. Danifae did not pull away, much as she wanted to.

"Tell me," he whispered, "that you want to be through with it.""I want it gone," she said. Her voice seemed too loud, too sharp to her own ears. "I want to be free of the Binding."

No sooner had that last syllable left her lips than her chest tightened, then her legs, her arms, her feet, her hands, her neck, her jaw, her fingers and toes—each one. Every muscle in her body cramped and seemed to rip into shreds under her skin. She might have screamed, but her throat was clamped shut. Her lungs tried to force what air was left in them up and out through her closed throat, past her clenched jaws, between her grinding teeth. She went blind with pain.

It was over.

Her body loosened so quickly and so completely that she collapsed. Vomit poured from her, and her vision was a swirling blur. Her eyes watered, her nose ran, and she came within half a second of wetting herself.

That was over too.

Danifae was shaking as she stood. She mastered the barrage of emotions that assaulted her—everything from humiliation to homicidal rage—with a single thought:

I'm free.

She wiped her mouth on her sleeve and stepped away from her own sick. Zinnirit followed, reaching out to steady her in case she fell again, but she avoided his touch, and he seemed as reluctant to touch her.

"I can't feel her," Danifae said even as she realized that the connection was truly gone.

"She won't feel you either," said the mage. "She'll probably think you died . . . wherever she is."

Danifae nodded and collected herself. Part of her wanted to shriek with delight, to dance and sing like some sun-cursed surface elf, but she did not. There was still one more thing she needed. The battle-captive turned free drow blinked the tears from her eyes and looked at the old mage's hands.

Zinnirit wore many rings, but Danifae was looking for one in particular, and she recognized it immediately. On the second finger of Zinnirit's left hand was a band of intertwined platinum and copper traced with delicate Draconic script.

"You kept it," she said.

He looked at her with narrowed eyes and shook his head.

"That ring," she explained. "My mother's ring."

Zinnirit nodded, unsure.

"You enchanted that for her yourself, didn't you?" she asked.

Zinnirit nodded again.

"Wherever she might go," Danifae mused, "that ring would return her home to her private chamber in House Yauntyrr in far Eryndlyn. I remember she used it once when we were in Llacerellyn. The ring took us both home when an idle threat turned into an assassination attempt and someone sent an elemental after her.

"You've never used it? You've never tried to go back?"

"There's nothing there," the mage answered too quickly. "Nothing to return to. I retuned the ring years ago to bring me back here."

"Still, have you ever had necessity to use it?" she asked. "Has it ever brought you back here from some distant cave?"

Zinnirit shook his head.

"Never stepped through your own gates?"

The old drow shook his head again and said, "I have nowhere to go."

Danifae tipped her head to one side and let the tiniest smile of appreciation slide across her lips.

"You poor thing," she whispered. "All these years . . . so lonely. Waiting for one last chance to serve a daughter of House Yauntyrr."

Danifae reached out and took Zinnirit's hand. The mage flinched at her touch but didn't pull away.

She lifted his hand to her lips and kissed it. Considering she'd just thrown up all over his floor, Zinnirit winced at the gesture, but still allowed it. Danifae pressed the old drow's hand to her cheek. It felt warmer, less dry.

"Dear Zinnirit," she whispered, looking the old mage in the eye, "what has become of you?"

"I'm a thousand years old," the mage replied. "At least, I think I am. I have no House, just these three gates and whatever meager tolls I can charge. I'm a stranger in a strange city, with no House to protect me, no matron mother to serve. What has become of me? I can barely remember 'me'."

Danifae kissed his hand again and whispered, "You remember me, don't you, House Mage?"

He didn't reply but didn't take his hand away.

"You remember our lessons," she said, punctuating her words with the gentle brush of her lips against his hand. "Our special lessons?"

She took his finger into her mouth and let her tongue play over it. The old drow's skin was dry and tasteless then there was the tang of metal against her lips.

"I didn't . . ." the mage mumbled. "I don't . . ."

Danifae slipped the ring off his finger, slowly teasing his flesh with her lips all the way. She tucked the ring under her tongue before kissing the back of his hand again.

"I do," she said.

Danifae twisted the old drow's arm down and around hard and fast enough that more than one bone snapped in more than one place. Zinnirit gasped in pain and surprise and didn't even try to stop Danifae from turning him around. She brought her other hand up and cupped his chin. She was standing behind him, his broken arm twisted painfully behind his back.

"I remember," she whispered into his ear. Then she broke his neck.

For any mage, the preparation of a day's spells was part experience, part intuition, and part inspiration. Pharaun Mizzrym was no different.

From time to time he looked up from his spellbook to refresh his eyes and let a particularly complex incantation sink into his memory. What he saw when he looked up was the still, quiet deck of the ship of chaos. Larger patches of sinew and cartilage and ever more complex traceries of veins and arteries embellished the bone ship. It lived—a simple, pain-ravaged, tortured, insensible life—and when it was quiet and the others were still in Reverie, Pharaun imagined he felt the thing breathing.

The uridezu captain lay in his place, visited only by the occasional rat. He was curled into a tight ball, his body wrapped into itself in a way that made Pharaun's back ache to look at it. His breathing was deep and regular, punctuated by the odd snore.

Jeggred sat opposite the captured demon, his knees drawn up to his chest and his head down. Unlike Pharaun and his fellow dark elves, the draegloth slept. Obviously that was a trait carried over from his father, Belshazu.

Well, the Master of Sorcere thought, you can't chose your parents.

Quenthel sat as far away from the rest of them as she could, at the very tip of the demon ship's pointed bow. Her back was turned to Pharaun, and she sat straight and stiff, meditating.

Can you talk? a voice echoed at the edge of his consciousness—a voice he recognized.

Aliisza? he thought back.

You remember me, the alu-demon's voice echoed more loudly in his head—or was it more clearly? *I will consider that a supreme honor.*

As well you should, Pharaun sent back, instinctively attaching light, playful emotions to the thought. *Where are you?*

On the ceiling, she replied, *right above you.*

Pharaun couldn't help but look up, but even with his fine dark-vision, the gloom of the Lake of Shadows hid the ceiling from his sight.

How did you find me? he asked.

I'm a resourceful, intelligent, and talented woman.

That you are, he replied.

If you levitate straight up, she sent, *you'll come right to me.*

Well, Pharaun returned, *in that case . . .*

The wizard closed the book he was working on, the spell still not fully prepared, and tucked the volume back into his pack. He stood and touched the brooch that held his *piwafwi* on his shoulders.

Straight up? he sent.

I'll catch you, came the alu-demon's playful reply.

Pharaun's feet left the deck, and he accelerated, the ship falling rapidly away beneath him. When it was lost—or more properly when *he* was lost—in the pitch-dark shadows of the ominous cavern, he slowed.

"A little more," Aliisza whispered to him, her voice barely audible.

Pharaun came to a stop slowly, a defensive spell hanging on his lips in case the alu-demon turned on him—she was a demon after all, so there was always some possibility of that.

There was a surprisingly loud rustle, and Pharaun looked up. Aliisza, her batlike wings spread out behind her, was slowly sinking toward him. He turned so they were facing each other.

They were almost together when Aliisza asked, "Can your levitation hold me up?"

Pharaun almost had a chance to answer before her arms folded around his neck and her full—though not substantial—weight fell on him all at once. He concentrated hard on the brooch, almost losing his defensive spell in the process, and managed to hold them both aloft. They bobbed a bit at first, but ultimately managed a tight embrace in the gloomy air near the ceiling of the Lake of Shadows.

They were face-to-face, less than an inch apart. Pharaun could smell the beautiful alu-demon's breath. The touch of her skin against him, the curves of her body in his arms again, and the soft caress of her fleshy wings folding around him, enclosing him, made his body react of its own accord.

A playful smile crossed Aliisza's full lips, and she showed a set of perfect white teeth with the exaggerated canines of a vampire. Pharaun remembered her habit of playing with her teeth. He didn't bother wondering why he liked that about her so much.

"Yes," she whispered, "I remember you."

Pharaun returned her smile and asked, "So, what brings a bad girl like you to an evil place like this?"

That made her laugh.

"The Lake of Shadows?" she replied playfully. "Oh, I try to get here a couple times a year, if I can. To take the waters."

Pharaun nodded, smiled, but didn't bother extending the banter. Kaanyr Vhok's consort had come there for a reason, and he wasn't quite smitten, or egomaniacal enough to think it was only to see him.

"You're spying on us again," he accused.

"No," Aliisza replied with a pout, "I'm spying on you *still*. Doesn't that make you feel important, having someone like me spying on you all the time?"

"Yes," he said, "and that's precisely the problem."

"What do you hope to find in the Abyss?" she asked abruptly. Pharaun had to blink a few times to get his head wrapped around the question. "That is where you're going in that wonderful old ship of chaos you've salvaged, isn't it?"

"What would Kaanyr Vhok care what we do," he asked, "or where we go?"

"Can't a girl be curious?"

"No," he replied with some finality. "In this case, no, she can't."

"You can be quite the rodent when you want to be, Pharaun," she said, and she smiled again.

"Shall I take that as a compliment?"

Aliisza looked him in the eyes. Drow and demon were both smart and pragmatic enough to know they weren't some pair of star-crossed human lovers. They might even be combatants on opposite sides of a war that could ruin both their civilizations—if Kaanyr Vhok's ragged Scoured Legion could be called a civilization.

"Can I come too?" she asked, tipping her head, and looking almost as if she were trying to read an answer written across his brow.

"With us?" he asked. "On the ship?"

She nodded.

"I'll have to check with the purser to see if there's a cabin available, but at first glance I'd have to say no way in all Nine Hells and the Barrens of Doom and Despair besides."

"Pity," she said. "I've been there before, you know."

"Where else have you been?" Pharaun asked, intentionally jarring the subject away from her joining their expedition. "Have you visited the City of Spiders lately?"

"Menzoberranzan?" she replied. "Why do you ask?"

"News of home and all that," said the wizard.

Her wings tightened around him, and Pharaun liked the sensation. It was similar to the warmed blankets his favorite masseuse used to drape on him in Menzoberranzan. He'd been traveling too long.

"You're missing some of your comrades," the alu-demon noted. "The big fighter with the greatsword and the other one. The scout."

"You *have* been spying on us," Pharaun replied.

He couldn't imagine why she'd want to know that unless she was testing their strength, or . . .

"Reporting back to Kaanyr Vhok?" he asked.

She pretended to blush and batted her eyelashes at him.

"Menzoberranzan is under siege," he said. "I suppose you know that."

She nodded and asked, "You've sent your warriors back to aid in the defense of the city?"

Pharaun laughed, and Aliisza looked put out. He didn't care.

"Tell me they didn't run afoul of some less civilized denizen of the Underdark between Ched Nasad and here," she said. "It would break my heart."

"Your heart will remain intact then," he replied. "I don't suppose it would hurt you to tell me who lays siege to my home."

"It might just," she replied with a wink. "Let's not risk it. Of course, if I knew what you know about the fate of your Spider Queen, that might cushion the blow."

"Ah," he said, "I tell you the big secret, and you tell me the little one."

"There are no little secrets," the alu-demon replied, "if you're the one in the dark."

"You know, Aliisza," Pharaun said. "We should get together and tell each other nothing more often. It beats preparing spells or getting on with my life."

"You're a sarcastic little devil, Pharaun. You know, that's just what I love about you."

"Please assume I feel the same," was the mage's reply. "So if we're done not speaking to each other, can I go?"

"We've spoken to each other, Pharaun," said Aliisza, "I'm sure of it. For instance, until now I hadn't imagined you didn't know who was laying siege to your City of Spiders. Oh, and you told me you were going to the Abyss."

"Yes, well," Pharaun said, unconcerned that she'd drawn those obvious conclusions. "Good for you. Do run along and change the course of life in the Underdark."

"You're playing games with me," the alu-demon said, ice in her voice and in her eyes like Pharaun had never seen. "I like that but not forever."

"You're withholding information from me," he retorted. "I never like that."

They floated in midair, wrapped in a tight, familiar embrace, staring into each other's cold, uninviting eyes for a long time.

"I could be your friend still, Pharaun," Aliisza said quietly, her voice barely above a whisper.

The Master of Sorcere found himself struggling for something to say. He knew they were finished, feared they were finished forever, and found himself wishing that weren't true.

Longing, Pharaun silently mused.

Yes, Aliisza replied directly into his mind, *longing.*

Pharaun pushed her away. Aliisza hung in the air for half a second before she started to fall. She stared daggers at him even as her wings opened to slow her descent. Pharaun thought she looked more hurt than angry.

"We'll talk again," she said, then she was gone with a flash of dull purple light, and Pharaun was alone in the impenetrable shadows.

I hope so, he found himself thinking. I really do.

Chapter

NINE

Something was missing.

Halisstra could feel it—or rather, she *couldn't* feel it. She couldn't feel the Binding. She couldn't feel Danifae.

Having a captive bound to her by that obscure drow magic was a strange and subtle experience. It wasn't something she was conscious of really, not on a moment-by-moment basis. Rather it was always there, in the background, like the sound of her own breathing, the feeling of her own pulse.

She was dancing when it stopped. The priestesses who had welcomed her into their circle danced often. They danced in different combinations of certain females and danced in different places both sacred and mundane. They danced naked most of the time, clothed some of the time. They danced wearing armor and weapons and danced with offerings of fruit or works of art. They danced around fires or in the cold. They danced at night—in the dark that Halisstra still found

95

comforting—or in the day. She was still learning the significance of each of those different venues, every subtle shift in components and approach, rhythm and movement.

When the feeling came upon her, Halisstra stopped dancing. The other priestesses took no notice of her. They didn't even pause, let alone stop their joyous ritual.

Halisstra stumbled out of the circle and made her way quickly and with a sense of impending doom back to where she had left Ryld. The weapons master wasn't included in the circles of priestesses, and she could tell that was wearing on him. Halisstra was gone hours at a time, and returned to questions she couldn't always answer. She had no way to be sure Ryld loved her—she wasn't entirely certain yet what "love" was, though she thought she was learning, but the warrior stayed. He stayed there in the cold, light-ravaged forest with her, surrounded by worshipers of what to him must have still felt like a traitor goddess.

She staggered into the cool, dark chamber they shared, interrupting him in a meditative exercise she'd seen him do before. He was standing on his hands, eyes closed, toes pointed, legs bent back at the knee. The weapons master held that position for hours sometimes. Halisstra couldn't do it for more than a second or two.

He opened his eyes when she came in and must have seen something in her expression. He rolled forward in a single, smooth motion and was on his feet. There was no sign he was dizzy or disoriented.

"Halisstra," he said, "what happened?"

She opened her mouth to reply, but no words would come.

"Something happened," he said, and he looked around the room.

"Ryld, I . . ." she started to say, then watched as he began to arm himself.

He grabbed Splitter—his enormous greatsword—first then quickly buckled his sheathed short sword to his belt. He had his armor in his hands when she touched his arm to stop him. His skin felt warm, almost hot, but there was no sweat. Deep black skin was stretched over muscles so hard he felt as if he were chiseled from stone.

"No," she said, shaking the cobwebs from her head finally, "stop it."

He stopped, and looked at her, waiting. She could see the impatience in his eyes, impatience mixed with frustration.

"What is it?" he asked, and she could see him comprehending even as he spoke.

She smiled and he sighed.

"It's Danifae," she said finally. "I can't feel her anymore. The Binding has been broken."

His eyes widened, and she could tell he was surprised. Not surprised, necessarily, that the Binding had been broken, but it was as if he were expecting to hear something else.

"What does that mean, exactly?" he asked, leaning his breastplate against the wall next to the bed they shared.

Halisstra shook her head.

"She died?" he asked with no trace of emotion.

"Yes," Halisstra replied. "Maybe."

"Why does that frighten you?"

Halisstra stepped back—was literally taken aback by that question, though it was a logical one.

"Why does that frighten me?" she repeated. "It frightens me . . . concerns me, that she's free of me. One way or the other, I'm no longer her mistress, and she's no longer my battle-captive."

Ryld frowned, shrugged, and asked, "Why does that matter to you?"

She opened her mouth to respond and again could form no words.

"I mean," the weapons master went on, "I'm not sure your new friends would approve anyway, would they? Do these trait—I mean, other . . . these priestesses even take battle-captives?"

She smiled, and he turned away, pretending to be deeply involved in returning Splitter to its ready position under their bed.

"They aren't *traitor* priestesses, Ryld," she said.

He hung his head briefly in response then sat down on the bed and looked at her.

"Yes they are," he said, his voice as flat and as beaten as his eyes. "They're traitors to their race, as surely as we are. The question I keep asking myself now is, is it so bad to be a traitor?"

Halisstra stepped to him and knelt. Draping her hands on his knees. He put out a hand and brushed her long white hair from her black cheek—the gesture seemed almost instinctive.

"It's not," she said, her voice barely audible even in the quiet of their little room. "It's not so bad. We can really only be traitors to ourselves anyway, and I think we're both finally being true to ourselves . . . and each other."

Halisstra's heart sank when she saw the look on his face, his only response to those words. He didn't believe her, but she couldn't help thinking he wanted to.

"How does it feel?" he asked her.

She didn't understand and told him so with a twitch of her head.

"Not being able to feel the Binding?" he said.

She shifted her weight onto her hip, sitting on the floor, and leaned her head against his strong leg.

"I can feel everything about my old life being replaced piece by piece with something new."

He touched her again, one finger gently tracing the line of her shoulder. Her flesh thrilled at his touch.

"Lolth has been replaced by Eilistraee," she said. "Dark has been replaced by light. Suspicion has been replaced by acceptance. Hate has been replaced by love."

An unfamiliar warmth and wetness filled her eyes. She was crying.

"Are you all right?" he asked, his voice a concerned whisper.

Halisstra wiped the tears from her eyes and nodded.

"Hate," she repeated, "has been replaced by love, and apparently slavery has been replaced by freedom."

"Or was it that life was replaced by death?" Ryld asked.

Halisstra sighed.

"Maybe it was," she answered, "but either way, she's free. She's gone to whatever afterlife awaits her. For her sake, I hope it's not that empty, ruined shell of the Demonweb Pits. Maybe she still wanders the Underdark, alive and strong. Alive and free, or dead and free, she's free just the same."

"Free. . . ." Ryld repeated, as if he'd never spoken the word before and needed practice at it.

They sat like that for a long time until Halisstra's legs started to grow stiff and Ryld sensed her discomfort. He lifted her into the bed and drew her close to him as if she weighed nothing at all. His embrace was like a shell around her, a life-sustaining cocoon.

"We have to go back," she whispered.

His embrace tightened.

"It's not what you're thinking," she whispered because she knew he wanted to go back underground and never come back. "The time has finally come to find Quenthel and her expedition."

"And stop them?" he asked, the words touching her neck with each exhalation of his hot breath.

"No," she whispered.

"Follow them?" he said into her hair, his hand pressed into the small of her back.

Halisstra moved into the warrior until she felt as if she were flattening herself against him, disappearing into his night-black skin.

"Yes," she said. "They'll take us with them, whether they want to or not. They'll take us to Lolth, and we can end it."

Halisstra knew that he began to make love to her then because he didn't want to think about it, and she let him because she didn't want to think about it either.

Pharaun stood at the rail of the ship of chaos, staring into the empty darkness of the Lake of Shadows, because he couldn't think of anything else to do. Valas and Danifae hadn't returned from their supply mission, he had fed the ship enough petty demons to satisfy it, the uridezu captain was cowed and quiet, and there was no sign of Aliisza.

The Master of Sorcere went over their conversation again in his mind and was still convinced that the alu-fiend had managed to tell him nothing but had gone away having learned nothing from him. Still, she'd found him and had seen the ship. She knew where they were going and what they hoped to accomplish there—but anyone who'd been at the fall of Ched Nasad could figure that out easily enough.

He put the alu-fiend out of his mind and peered deeper into the darkness, though there was still nothing to see. Pharaun didn't have to turn around to know that Quenthel was sitting against the rail, absently chatting in some kind of silent telepathy with the bound imps that gave her venomous whip its evil intelligence. He couldn't imagine the substance of a conversation someone might have with a demon trapped in the body of a snake that was stuck to the end of a whip.

Whatever they talked about, it didn't seem to be helping Quenthel. The high priestess, as far as Pharaun could tell, was going quietly mad. She had always been sullen and temperamental, but recently she had become . . . twitchy.

Her half-demon nephew grew angrier and angrier the more bored he became. Jeggred sent a large portion of his hatred out through his eyes and into the uridezu. Raashub did an admirable job of ignoring him.

Something caught Pharaun's attention, movement out of the corner of his eye, and he stepped back from the rail as an emaciated, soaking-wet rat scurried along the bone-and-cartilage rail in front of him.

Pharaun watched the rat run, absently wondering where it thought it was going.

Anywhere dry, he thought.

Noises echoed from behind him—Jeggred fidgeting.

Pharaun stepped back to the rail and was about to let his eyes wander through the impenetrable darkness again when another rat crawled quickly past.

"Damn it," the Master of Sorcere whispered to himself.

He turned to voice some impotent complaint to Jeggred, but the words stuck in his throat.

There were more than the two rats that ran past him. There were dozens of them, hundreds perhaps, and they swarmed over Jeggred.

Something's wrong, thought Pharaun, marveling even as the words formed in his head at how slowly his mind was working after days of tedium aboard the anchored ship.

The draegloth looked more annoyed than anything else. The rats were crawling over him, tangling themselves in his hair, nibbling at any loose fold of skin, but they could not pierce the half-demon's hide. More of them were climbing onto the deck. Pharaun could hear splashing in the water on the other side of the demonic vessel. It sounded as if dozens, even hundreds more rats were swimming up to the ship.

Pharaun started casting defensive spells on himself, watching as Quenthel finally looked up and over at her nephew.

The Mistress of the Academy's eyes widened, then narrowed as she watched Jeggred smash one rat after another in his bigger set of hands, while his smaller hands brushed others off his face. Quenthel slowly rose to her feet, the vipers tangling loosely, affectionately around her legs.

"Jeggred?" she asked.

"Rats," was the draegloth's grunted reply.

Pharaun layered more magical protections over himself as Quenthel started toward the draegloth.

"Raashub," Pharaun said, keeping his voice steely and cold.

The demon flinched at the sound of his name but didn't look up.

"What are you doing, Raashub?" Pharaun asked between two more spells of protection. "Stop it. Stop it now."

The demon looked up at him with smoldering eyes and hissed, "It's not me. They're not my rats."

Pharaun couldn't shake the feeling that the uridezu was telling the truth—at least, a version of the truth.

"Pharaun?" Quenthel said, and the mage detected a trace—more than a trace—of panic creeping into her voice. "What are all these rats . . . ?"

"Pay close attention, both of you," Pharaun said, at the same time readying a more offensive spell. "There's ano—"

A globe of darkness enveloped Quenthel.

Any drow could have done it but not only a drow.

The unmistakable sounds of a physical struggle resounded from inside the slowly undulating cloud of blackness. Something hit the deck, and something cracked.

Pharaun changed direction before he'd actually begun casting the spell he'd had in mind. Instead, he formed the words and gestures to a spell he hoped would eliminate the darkness.

From inside the gloom, Pharaun could hear the shriek of metal being dragged across metal—or was it bone against bone?

His spell went off, and the darkness blew into nothingness.

Suddenly visible, Quenthel lay on her stomach on the deck. She was patting the carved bone surface in front of her, reaching for her scourge, which lay just out of her reach. Her nose was bleeding, and she winced every time she bent her back.

Standing over her was another uridezu.

The demon was, like Raashub, a humanoid rat. Smaller than Raashub, thinner, it wore tattered rags that left little of its mottled gray body to the imagination. Its long, pink tail was spattered with pustules. Cold black eyes stared down at the high priestess with murderous intent. Foam gathered at the corners of its fang-lined mouth, and angry yellow claws curved at the ends of its spindly, arthritic fingers.

"Jeggred . . ." Pharaun said, glancing over at the draegloth.

The half-demon was covered head to foot with rats of every size and description. It was as if all the vermin in the Lake of Shadows had staged some sort of family reunion—one that took place on, under, and all around the draegloth. They swarmed onto him faster than he could kill them, though he was dispatching the rodents four at a time.

Pharaun ran quickly through possible spells, stepping forward a few paces toward Quenthel.

The uridezu smashed her on the back with its tail. The high priestess's face was forced into the bone-hard deck. Blood sprayed, but not much, and she took the strong hit with a grunt.

Pharaun was impressed. Something made him set aside his first choice of spell.

Too much, he thought, for only one . . .

The Master of Sorcere looked over at Raashub. The demon captain's eyes were darting rapidly between Quenthel and the newcomer.

He's testing us, Pharaun thought. The wily bastard gated in one of his kind and is setting it against us so we can show off, reveal our strengths and weaknesses.

Raashub might have been bound, but he was a demon still, and there was always fight left in a demon—it always had a way out.

The other uridezu clawed at Quenthel's legs, opening deep gashes, and she kicked back at it. The demon danced out of reach of her boots. The high priestess extended a hand back over her head, but she still couldn't reach her whip. The vipers seemed panicked and weren't able to coordinate their movements well enough to crawl to her.

Pharaun pronounced a quick set of rhyming syllables and made a fast motion with his right hand. Pushed by his magic, the viper whip slid along the deck a few inches, well within Quenthel's reach.

As the high priestess's fingers closed around the handle of the scourge, Pharaun laughed inwardly. The spell he'd used was no more than a cantrip, a transmutation so simple any first year student at Sorcere could master it. It would tell Raashub nothing about the limits of his power.

The uridezu hissed at Quenthel, backing farther away from her, his tail twitching behind him, and his claws flickering in anticipation. The demon obviously thought he was well out of reach of the whip. He was wrong.

The five vipers that comprised Quenthel's scourge were five feet long, giving the weapon considerable reach. The high priestess was still on the deck and didn't bother to stand. She lashed the whip behind her, her jaw set tightly and her eyes wild with rage. When she brought the weapon forward, the snakes whipped outward to their full length. The uridezu flinched, though he seemed confident enough that he was still out of the weapon's range. The vipers extended farther, though, drawing themselves out, stretching thinner and thinner, farther and farther, adding another few feet to their length.

The uridezu didn't register what was happening nearly fast enough to avoid the vipers. All but one of them sank needle-sharp fangs into the rat-demon's flesh. As the whip lashed back, they dug long, bleeding furrows in the uridezu's leathery hide.

The demon screamed, high-pitched and loud enough to rattle Pharaun's eardrums.

Anything else would have been dead. Each viper possessed a deadly venom, wickedly potent. Quenthel, wild with a battle-frenzy Pharaun had never imagined, much less seen from her, wouldn't have let the snakes hold a drop of venom back. It would have been enough to drop a rothé.

The victim of that venomous lash wasn't a dumb food beast; it was an uridezu, and Pharaun had studied demons long enough to know the traits that all of them shared. Poison would never affect one. The whip had wounded the captain but hadn't killed him. Pharaun knew he could take more than that. Even a demon as relatively weak as an uridezu—and the rat-creatures were hardly the sturdiest of their kind—could withstand extremes of cold and heat and muster innate magical abilities such as the darkness he had used to ambush Quenthel. Uridezu could call on their rodent cousins, as the one Pharaun faced had set them against Jeggred. There was something about the bite of the uridezu that Pharaun knew he should remember, but that wasn't coming to him. Of course, like all tanar'ri, lightning only passed through them.

Even as that thought crossed his mind Pharaun had a hand on a wand that would have unleashed lightning bolts. Knowing that was useless, the Master of Sorcere shifted his hand an inch over and drew a different wand.

Pharaun hesitated and watched Quenthel hop nimbly to her feet and face the uridezu. The demon hissed at her, but Quenthel made no sound or sign she'd heard it. The high priestess cracked her whip at the demon again, and three of the five snakes bit deeply into the rat-demon's chest. The creature lashed out at the snakes with one set of razor-sharp claws, but the vipers withdrew in time, and the talons slashed through empty air.

Ignoring that failure, the uridezu whirled, whipping at the drow priestess with its heavy, fast-moving tail. Quenthel brought the buckler in her left hand up to meet the tail. The appendage hit her with enough force that Pharaun was sure her arm would snap, but instead she managed to bat the tail away.

The uridezu recovered more quickly than Quenthel, though, and the tail reversed and dropped lower, clipping the priestess in the ribs.

Pharaun could hear the breath driven from her lungs. She stepped to the side, almost staggering. The demon, a feral smile spread across its face, stepped in. It meant to bite her and rake her with its claws at the same time.

Pharaun drew a breath to pronounce the command word for his wand even as the demon attacked—and took Quenthel's buckler full in the face. There was a loud, wet *crack!* and blood splashed out from between the buckler and the uridezu's nose. The demon's hands flailed harmlessly in front of Quenthel and each of the five vipers took their pick of the demon's most sensitive spots in which to sink their fangs. The uridezu howled in agony.

Well, Pharaun thought, not bothering to activate the magic in his wand, looks like she's got this well in—

His eyes settled on Raashub, and Pharaun stopped. The bound uridezu was looking at him, his eyes running down the length of the wand. Anticipation was plain on the demon captain's face.

Pharaun looked at his wand then back at Raashub. Their eyes locked, and Raashub smiled at him.

With a smile of his own, Pharaun slid the wand back into his pack where it belonged. Raashub hid his disappointment well, turning his attention back to Quenthel and his fellow uridezu.

Pharaun made the decision to help Jeggred. Raashub would know what the draegloth was capable of, and if Pharaun could deal with the swarming rats and allow Jeggred to help Quenthel, the unbound uridezu could be dispatched quickly and without Pharaun having to take a more active—and more revealing—role in the fight.

As Pharaun came to that decision, a loud series of cracking and popping noises drew his attention back to Quenthel. The Mistress of Arach-Tinilith pulled up a whole section of railing. Bone and cartilage separated from the deck, snapping off like dried mushroom stems. Her whip was in her belt, the uridezu was staggering in front of her with blood pouring from its ruined snout, and she lifted the ten-foot length of railing over her head.

Pharaun quickly prepared a spell to aid Jeggred, and Quenthel attacked. The high priestess brought the section of railing down on the uridezu fast and hard. The demon, not quite blinded by its bleeding nose, skittered away from the attack and managed to leap out of range at the last second. The railing crashed onto the deck and shattered, sending bone fragments whirling through the air. Several of them bounced off Pharaun's spell-wards and shields, and he watched a couple of them slice into two of the rats that covered Jeggred.

Quenthel growled in nearly incoherent rage, and Pharaun found the noise unsettling—unbecoming to the Mistress of the Academy.

Pools of blood were collecting where the railing had smashed into the deck. The ship of chaos itself was bleeding. The wizard wasn't sure if he'd be able to repair it, and any further damage might delay or even prevent their voyage. However, Pharaun didn't want to say anything out loud, and Quenthel wasn't looking at him so he couldn't sign to her to stop damaging the ship.

Pharaun cast a spell at the rats on Jeggred. It was a simple spell, one that conjured a cone of flickering, multicolored Weave energy. Pharaun was careful in his placement of the spell so that the effect brushed along the side of the rat-encrusted draegloth. The magic didn't affect Jeggred in the least, but a goodly portion of the swarming rodents fell off him and onto the deck, where they lay twitching and writhing in a pile of wet, furry bodies.

Jeggred roared as he shook himself, sending his wild mane of snow-white hair whipping rats, blood, and water across the deck. The draegloth smashed four more of the filthy creatures—one in each hand—and stepped on three others.

Pharaun sneaked a glance at Raashub and was rewarded by a look of disappointed frustration on the uridezu captain's face. It was another easy spell the Master of Sorcere cast, one he'd learned while still a child, and Raashub knew it.

Pharaun turned his attention back to Jeggred and called, "Leave the rats, Jeggred. Your mistress is having demon troubles."

With another roar, Jeggred threw more dead or unconscious rats off him and leaped at Raashub, bringing all four of his hands up, ready to shred the uridezu captain. Raashub shrank away from the draegloth, holding up his hands and straining against his bonds.

"No!" Quenthel shouted, her voice hoarse and feral. "Not that one, damn it! Kill *this* one!"

Jeggred whirled, his eyes flashing across the scene of the ongoing struggle between Quenthel and the second uridezu.

The rat-demon, taking full advantage of Quenthel's momentary lapse in attention, slipped in and raked claws across her midsection, digging deep furrows across her armor and drawing blood. Quenthel grimaced and gritted her teeth against the pain but answered in kind with her scourge. Both of them staggered a bit, their footing treacherous amidst a pile of bone fragments from the shattered railing and pools of blood from the wounded ship.

Jeggred's lips curled back to reveal a monstrous row of vicious fangs, and the draegloth entered the fray.

TEN

Danifae sat on the floor of the gatehouse for what felt like a very long time. She hadn't allowed herself to think too much about her life before her captivity. There were only a few ways to survive as a battle-captive, including convincing yourself that you've always been one.

Before the raid that put her in the hands of House Melarn, Danifae had been taking lessons from the Yauntyrr House Mage. Zinnirit was a capable and detail-oriented teacher, and Danifae had learned much from him, especially in the fields of teleportation, translocation, and dimensional travel. They hadn't actually begun her study of the arcane Art before her House was overwhelmed, but Zinnirit had familiarized the young daughter of House Yauntyrr with a variety of enchanted items.

Danifae touched her mother's ring, feeling the cold metal warming against her skin. The ring could bounce her across the Underdark—but just her and one other. Danifae had plans that required more than that.

Her eyes settled on the still hand of the dead wizard.

"More rings," Danifae whispered, a smile playing at the corners of her mouth.

All she had to do was remember how to work them.

Even as the uridezu was bringing his tail around for another hard slap at Quenthel, Jeggred pounced on him. The draegloth caught the heavy appendage in his larger set of hands. The tail's momentum, stopped so abruptly by the draegloth's grip, staggered the uridezu and it toppled in a heap onto the ruined rail. Jagged bits of bone cut deeply into the demon's already bleeding body. At the same time, all five of the vipers from Quenthel's scourge bit into sensitive areas, released, then bit again. Waves of agony pulsed through the demon's body, and it coughed out phlegm and blood.

"We . . ." the demon gasped. "We will see you in the Abyss . . . drow bitch!"

We? Pharaun thought, stealing a glance at Raashub, who was watching with keen interest.

"Kill it now, Jeggred," Quenthel commanded, her voice still husky and mingled with deep, panting breaths. "Kill it before it goes home."

Feral light flashed in the draegloth's eyes and he brought a single claw across the uridezu's midsection. The daggerlike talon disappeared into the demon's flesh, burying itself six inches deep. Jeggred cut the thing's belly open wide enough to spill a pile of ropy yellow intestines, steaming with the demon's hot blood, onto the deck of the ship of chaos.

The demon screamed, the sound echoing unnaturally then fading even as the uridezu itself began to evaporate into nothingness. It was returning to the Abyss while it still lived.

Pharaun had to admit that he wasn't sure how long a demon might live after it had been disemboweled, but more than one breed of them could regenerate completely from even so grievous a wound.

As the demon began to fade, though, Jeggred quickly withdrew his claw and grabbed the uridezu's head in both his larger, stronger hands. The draegloth twisted and pulled, hard enough that Pharaun could see veins protrude against his straining muscles.

There was a sickly wet cracking sound and a sicker wet *pop!* and the uridezu's head came off in Jeggred's hands.

The rest of the demon's body disappeared, but the head and entrails remained. The black eyes stared, dead, at nothing. The demon's guts slowly sizzled away, being absorbed, Pharaun noted, by the ship itself. The wizard realized that most of the fragments of bone from the shattered rail had gone as well. The ship was feeding on itself, repairing the damage bone by bone.

Jeggred, obviously taking no notice of the ship of chaos's convenient regenerative capacities, tossed the uridezu's head overboard as he turned to face the captain.

Raashub, already backed away as far as his bonds would allow, put his hands up in supplication and looked away.

Jeggred, a low growl rumbling in his throat, started forward, stalking the bound uridezu with unveiled intent.

"I don't know, nephew," Quenthel said, her voice and breathing slowly returning to normal. She was bleeding but paid her injuries no heed. "I have yet to make up my mind."

The vipers seethed at the end of her whip, and Quenthel glanced at one of them as if she'd heard it speak—and certainly she had, though Pharaun was still not privy to that communication.

"Wait," the wizard said, stepping closer but not foolish enough to move between Jeggred and the uridezu. "I'm afraid we still need him."

Jeggred growled, not looking at Pharaun, but he did hesitate.

"It was to be expected," Pharaun said. "You've both worked with demons before, haven't you? So he tried to kill us and failed."

Quenthel's head snapped to look at him. The abrupt motion caused the vipers in her whip to shudder and turn on the wizard as well.

"You can't control him," she said to Pharaun. "How can you stop him from doing that again?"

"It wasn't me, Mistress," Raashub pleaded, his voice reedy and dripping with false humility. "The Lake of Shadows is home to many of my kind."

Pharaun lifted an eyebrow at that obvious lie then began to cast a spell.

"Let me eat his kidneys," Jeggred growled, his eyes still locked on the uridezu. "Maybe just one kidney."

Pharaun, ignoring the draegloth, finished his spell.

Raashub screamed.

The sound was so sudden and so loud that even Jeggred stepped back from it. Wild horror passed through the captive uridezu in visible waves. Raashub threw up his hands and clawed at the air in front of him, whimpering, sobbing, and shrieking in different combinations as Pharaun, Quenthel, and Jeggred looked on.

"What are you doing to him?" Jeggred asked, confused.

"Showing him things," Pharaun replied.

He looked at Quenthel, who obviously wanted a more detailed explanation.

"Even demons have nightmares, Mistress," the Master of Sorcere explained. "My spell is letting a few of those play out for him. I assure you both, it is an experience our dear friend Raashub will not soon forget, and he knows I can do it again."

Jeggred sighed so heavily Pharaun could smell his rancid breath. The draegloth moved toward Raashub.

"Hold, Jeggred," Quenthel ordered.

The draegloth hesitated before doing so, but he did stop.

"Raashub still serves a purpose," the high priestess said as she began to assess her injuries.

Jeggred turned to look at her, but she ignored him.

"Who told you that?" the draegloth asked in a low growl. "The dandy?"—he nodded at Pharaun—"or the snakes?"

Quenthel ignored the question, but Pharaun thought long and hard about it.

It took Danifae somewhat longer than she'd intended to remember Zinnirit's favorite command words and determine which of them powered which of the rings. Then she turned her attention to studying the finer points of the portals she had "inherited" from the late Yauntyrr House mage. Not only had she lost all track of time as she studied Zinnirit's collection of scrolls and tomes on the subject, made a few exploratory scans through open portals, and ignored a summons from Valas, but she had exhausted the limits of her own familiarity with the arcane Art. Danifae was no wizard, but fortunately she didn't have to be to use many of the features of Zinnirit's gatehouse.

The gates were used primarily for transportation—whisking someone or something hundreds, even thousands of miles in the blink of an eye—but they could also be used to *find* someone. Though the strong psychic link that the Binding had provided was gone, Danifae still had some connection to her former mistress. She knew Halisstra better than anyone ever had, even ranking members of House Melarn. Halisstra's sister had tried to kill her, and her mother had always been the model of the aloof, controlling matron mother. Danifae, though always seething with hate, had served Halisstra loyally and well every minute of every day.

Ultimately all Danifae really had to do was remember her. All she had to do was imagine what Halisstra looked like, visualize her, and activate one of the portals in precisely the right way. At least, she thought that was all she needed to do.

After several false starts and failed attempts, Danifae stepped away from the gate and began pacing. As she did she fiddled with a ring on her finger, then another ring on her other hand, and—

She stopped and looked at her hands. Danifae had taken three rings from the dead wizard. Two of them were tucked safely in a pocket. She wore the ring that Zinnirit had created for her mother, the one that would bring her back to the gatehouse from anywhere, but she wore another ring as well—one she'd almost forgotten about. It belonged to Ryld Argith, the Menzoberranyr weapons master who, like Danifae's former mistress, had abandoned the expedition.

They had been spending some time with each other, Ryld and Halisstra. Even in the cave where Pharaun had summoned the demon Belshazu, Danifae had suspected that Ryld was sneaking off to join Halisstra. If he had, she could use his ring as a focus.

It was only after several more false starts that Danifae finally found her mistress. The former battle-captive had been, like the Menzoberranyr, under the impression that Halisstra had gone to the City of Spiders to report on their progress (or lack thereof), and much of Danifae's time had been spent searching for her there. Hours later, Danifae realized that Halisstra wasn't even in the Underdark but in the bizarre landscape of the World Above.

Danifae had suspected that Halisstra was in the process of turning entirely from the worship of Lolth. They had all seen her reaction to the chaotic, empty Demonweb Pits.

Even having seen that ruined plane herself, though, Danifae had been a priestess of Lolth when she was free and living in Eryndlyn, and she had served the goddess more faithfully and more sincerely than she served House Melarn ever since, so her faith remained strong. Guarded, perhaps, more curious, but strong. Danifae wouldn't presume to question the goddess's will, and Halisstra's commitment to the Spider Queen was none of Danifae's concern. Danifae could easily enough set aside her religion if necessary, but she would never set aside her vengeance. Halisstra Melarn had to die, and not on Lolth's behalf. For Danifae it was a simple imperative.

As certain as she could be that the portal was properly tuned to the place on the World Above where Halisstra and Ryld were, Danifae stepped through. She felt as if she were being turned upside down and inside out at the same time, though there was no pain—only a dull, throbbing vertigo—then she was there.

It was night, and Danifae thanked Lolth for that. Her eyes still had to adjust to the bright glare of the starlight against the white snow, but she wasn't totally blinded. She had appeared, apparently silently and without the sort of fanfare—flashing lights and thunderclaps—that often accompanied arcane magic, in front of a ruined building. The structure was overgrown with vegetation. No light or fire glowed from inside.

Danifae drew her *piwafwi* close around her shoulders against the biting cold in the air. She stepped as quietly as she could to the entrance. Her eyes adjusted little by little, and by the time Danifae reached the ruin, she could see fairly well. Inside, Halisstra sat back to back with Ryld. The two of them were deep in Reverie and in a position that told Danifae everything she needed to know about their relationship.

The former battle-captive felt a growing respect for Halisstra, as well as a growing contempt. Halisstra had managed to outwit Quenthel and the others, seduce the steadfast weapons master—admirable, even for someone schooled her entire life in manipulation and deceit—and had set up a sweet little household for them in the freezing, animal-infested forest—a bizarre and unseemly act of betrayal against her essential nature as a dark elf.

Danifae took a deep breath and let it out in a thin, reedy whistle. Halisstra came out of Reverie without a blink and looked at her. The First Daughter of House Melarn had established that sound as their signal years before, and they had both had occasion to use it more than once.

Halisstra let one side of her mouth draw up into half a smile. She indicated Ryld with a slow movement of her eyes, and Danifae shook her head.

Halisstra stood slowly and carefully, making sure not to disturb Ryld.

"Are you all right?" the weapons master whispered, his eyes still closed.

Halisstra replied, also in a whisper, "I'm fine. I'll be right back."

Ryld nodded and returned to his meditation as Halisstra slipped out of the ruined structure. Certain that Ryld hadn't seen her, Danifae led her former mistress a good distance from the ruin, waiting for Halisstra to indicate they'd gone far enough. They stopped and faced each other for the first time as two free drow.

The Binding? Halisstra signed.

Danifae replied, *Removed by Quenthel . . . Pharaun, really, but on Quenthel's orders. We have found a ship of chaos to take us back to the Abyss.*

Halisstra visibly withdrew and signed, *I can see why you escaped.*

I didn't, really, replied Danifae. *I was sent with Master Hune to gather supplies for our doomed little voyage.*

How long before they leave? Halisstra asked.

Days still, answered Danifae.

Why are you telling me this? Halisstra asked. *You're free now. Go back to Eryndlyn if you dare, or go on with the Menzoberranyr until you all inevitably die. Do as you wish, but you no longer need seek my permission.*

I served you, Danifae replied, *and now I serve Quenthel. I'm not as free as you might think, Binding or no Binding.*

There was a short silence as the two of them studied each other in the darkness. Danifae could somehow feel how far Halisstra had strayed from the path of Lolth, but it was confirmed seconds later by Halisstra herself.

I serve Eilistraee now, Danifae. There will be no more slaves for me.

Danifae pretended to consider that last statement for a while. Internally she tried to get her head to stop spinning. The depth of her former mistress's betrayal was worse than she'd imagined. Danifae couldn't believe she'd ever allowed herself to be taken captive by so weak a mistress—one who would turn her back on her entire culture at the slightest provocation, at the first sign of weakness. It was that thought that snapped Danifae out of her confusion. Halisstra must have seen Lolth's Silence as a sign of weakness and used that opportunity to escape, just as Danifae had seen Halisstra's doubt as a sign of weakness and used that opportunity to escape herself. But would any priestess seek to *escape* the service of Lolth?

I like the sound of that, Danifae signed, *but we are all slaves sooner or later.*

We don't have to be, Halisstra was quick to reply.

Danifae blinked at how strident, how obvious, and how careless her former mistress had become.

Lolth isn't coming back, is she? Danifae asked.

I don't know, replied Halisstra, *but it doesn't look good.*

If I die still serving her, Danifae asked, *where will my soul go? There were no drow souls in the Demonweb Pits, and no entrance past the sealed doors. Where are all those souls?*

Halisstra looked at her former servant with a wounded, open look that made Danifae's skin crawl.

What, Danifae asked, *are your intentions here?*

You found me, her former mistress replied. *Tell me, what are your intentions? Spying on me for that Baenre bureaucrat?*

No, Danifae replied sharply. *I sneaked away from Valas in Sschindylryn. It was the only place to find a portal and to find you. I don't trust the Menzoberranyr.*

Why would you? Halisstra replied, eyeing her former servant carefully.

What is the weapons master doing here? asked Danifae.

She could see by Halisstra's reaction that things between she and the weapons master had gone a considerable distance toward the bizarre. The light and air of the World Above must have affected Halisstra in unpredictable ways. Danifae marveled at how such a thing might be possible.

You sit in Reverie against his back? Danifae asked,

Halisstra drew herself to her full height and tried to recapture the manner of a slaveholder. Danifae was unwilling to play the part of the battle-captive.

Instead of flying into a rage, Halisstra simply relaxed.

Do you sit the same way with Quenthel? Halisstra signed.

Danifae made a convincing show of being uncomfortable with that question. She was intimate with Quenthel not out of some alien emotion like love or compassion but because Quenthel could help her. Quenthel, in turn, used Danifae for physical pleasure and to gain a toady. It was all perfectly natural. Halisstra, however, seemed to have turned a corner with Ryld Argith, and that was something Danifae knew she could exploit.

You said that Quenthel is taking the expedition back to the Abyss,

Halisstra signed, changing the subject. *Why? Why that way? Why all that?*

Danifae could have given her some of the reasons, but some were still not clear to her.

I can explain all, Danifae lied, *but I must return to Sschindylryn. Valas will grow suspicious, then he'll leave without me. I have to go back to the Underdark then back to the Lake of Shadows. I will contact you again.*

Halisstra looked her up and down, appraising her.

"I'll be waiting," Halisstra whispered in Danifae's ear.

Danifae nodded, gave Halisstra a slight bow, and did her best to look at the First Daughter of House Melarn with a face full of sisterhood and friendliness.

When Halisstra disappeared into the dark forest, Danifae signed after her, *We'll meet again very soon, Halisstra Melarn. Sooner than you think.*

Danifae touched the ring she'd taken from the dying Zinnirit, and a second or two of bizarre sensation later and she was back at the gatehouse.

Perfect, thought Danifae. It worked perfectly.

Chapter

ELEVEN

Valas purchased more supplies than he probably should have—three large bags that carried more than would seem possible from their size or weight—but he couldn't help thinking they'd be gone longer than Pharaun had estimated. Already their journey had lasted longer than any of them had assumed when they'd left Menzoberranzan.

He sat at a small table in an open café high up and in the center of the ziggurat-city, waiting for Danifae. The battle-captive hadn't been joking, obviously, when she'd told him that she would ignore his summons. Valas wasn't necessarily anxious to return to the Lake of Shadows, but he did want to leave the city. Dark elves throughout Sschindylryn were looking over their shoulders. Tempers were short, and the lesser races had a dangerous gleam in their eyes. The city wasn't quite as bad off as Ched Nasad, but the scout could see it was headed in that direction and sooner rather than later.

"Waiting for me?" Danifae asked.

Valas turned, surprised, to see her standing behind him. He hadn't noticed her.

"Cities. . . ." the scout sighed.

He stood, quickly gathering up his bags.

"Are we really in such a hurry?" Danifae asked as she slid into the chair across the table from him.

She looked up at him with one arm raised and a wide, bright grin on her face. She looked different. Valas couldn't help but stare.

"In the Surface Realms," Danifae said, "it's customary for a gentleman to buy a lady a drink. Well, so I hear."

Valas shook his head but found it difficult to take his eyes off the female.

The chair he had been sitting in slowly slid toward him. She pushed it with her foot from under the table.

"Order us a bottle of algae wine," she purred.

Valas turned to order the wine but stopped himself.

"We should get back," he said. "The others will be waiting for us."

"Let them wait."

Valas took a deep breath and shifted the bags onto his shoulders.

"Mistress Quenthel will be displeased," he said, not caring but wanting to be on his way.

"Let her be displeased," Danifae shot back, still smiling, but her eyes grew colder. "I feel a bit like taking a holiday."

"Her House is paying," the mercenary said, still not sitting down.

Danifae looked at him, and Valas felt his skin crawl. It was as if she was peeling off his flesh with her eyes and looking inside him.

She stood slowly, unfolding herself from the chair piece by piece, and Valas watched every subtle movement that made up the whole. She held out a hand.

"I'll carry one," she said.

Valas didn't move to hand her a bag.

Whatever it was about Danifae that had changed, Valas was trying desperately not to like it.

For the drow, as with other sentient races above and below the surface of Faerûn, each individual had his own set of skills and talents, his own individual use that served the whole in some way, even if only as an irritant. In Menzoberranzan talent was something that was identified early, and skills were a commodity traded on the open market and imparted on the young only with great care and economy. Individuality was accepted only within certain limits and rarely if at all for males of the species.

"He is a lich," the Master of Sorcere said, "so his touch will paralyze."

There were a few places where male drow had some advantage, and one of those places was the halls of Sorcere. It was the females who held the power, and when things were as they should be, the ear of Lolth, but it was the males who were attuned to the Weave. Of course, not all wizards were male . . . only the best were, and Gromph Baenre, the Archmage of Menzoberranzan, had more than a little to do with that. It was his responsibility, after all, to identify talent for the Art in young drow from every House in the city, and it was his right to choose those who would go to Sorcere to study. It was his whim that decided whether or not they would ever finish their course of study. The fact that the majority of wizards in Menzoberranzan were male was no coincidence, no accident of birth or statistics, but a carefully and often less than subtly played turn in the great *sava* game of the City of Spiders. That most females preferred serving Lolth anyway only made that bit of manipulation easier.

"He will radiate an aura of fear," the Master of Sorcere continued, "but you probably won't be affected by that."

While there was no question that the priestesses had and would always have dominion over the city, his dominion over the Art was simply a small consolation—something that would warm Gromph's heart in his private moments. With Lolth silent, withdrawn, and the priestesses scrambling for answers, thrown into the sort of chaos only a demon goddess could conjure . . . well, things had changed.

"Once in each twenty-four hour cycle," said the Master of Sorcere, "he can kill with a touch."

The strangest thing, for Gromph, about the shift in power was how little he liked it. He had, after all, spent a lifetime manipulating the system to best serve his House and himself. When the system faltered, he might have been in a position to unseat his sister and the rest of the matron mothers and take control of Menzoberranzan himself—but why? What would he hope to gain? How could his position be any better? He enjoyed all the benefits of House Baenre's position and Sorcere's, but there was always someone else onto whom he could deflect responsibility, always someone who could be manipulated.

"There are a number of spell effects that will be of no concern to the lich," said the master. "These include cold, lightning, poison, paralysis, disease, necromancy, polymorph, and spells that affect or influence the mind. Best not even to bother preparing such enchantments."

Gromph was the third most powerful dark elf in Menzoberranzan, and Lolth be damned, he liked it that way.

"He will likely be wearing a robe of black silk," the Master of Sorcere continued, "that will allow him to conjure a barrier of whirling blades."

Well, he might like to be second, but still . . .

"The crown," the Master of Sorcere finished, "is more than simply a crass affectation. It can store and reflect back offensive spells."

So it was that Gromph Baenre sat on the floor of a very small, very dark, and very secret room in the deepest heart of Sorcere, surrounded by a circle of mages who were the most powerful in the city—among the most powerful spellcasters in all the Underdark. The other mages, Masters of Sorcere all, whispered or chanted and waved or gesticulated, and tossed into the air or pinched between fingers all manner of tokens, totems, focuses, and components. They showered the archmage with protective magic, doing it at so fast a pace they'd stopped even bothering to tell him what they were casting on him. Gromph had few doubts that by the time they were done, he'd be immune to everything. Surely no one would be able to harm him—no one but a spellcaster of greater power than the Masters.

And it was precisely such an opponent that Gromph meant to face.

"I should go with you, Archmage," Nauzhror Baenre said, his voice conveying a lack of real desire in that regard.

"If any of you say anything like that," Gromph replied, "even once more, I will . . ."

He let the threat go unfinished. He wouldn't do anything, and they all knew it, but out of respect for the archmage, none of them suggested going with him again. They were all smart enough to know that Gromph meant to face an enemy who, all things being equal, was the most dangerous being in Menzoberranzan. The lichdrow was a spellcaster of extraordinary, sometimes almost godlike, power. Of course they didn't really want to face him in the way that Gromph meant to: toe to toe in a spell duel that would surely find its place in drow history.

That duel was something only the archmage could fight. In Menzoberranzan, it had come down to that: male against male, wizard against wizard, First House against Second, establishment against revolutionary, stability against change, civilization against . . . chaos?

Exactly, Gromph thought—though he would never say it out loud. Order against chaos, and it was Gromph who fought for order, for law, in the name of one of the purest embodiments of chaos in the multiverse: Lolth, a goddess with the heart of a demon.

"Strange," the archmage murmured aloud, "how things work out."

"Indeed, Archmage," Nauzhror answered as if he was reading Gromph's mind—and perhaps he was. "It is strange indeed."

The two Baenre wizards shared a smile, then Gromph closed his eyes and let the others continue their casting. The protective and contingency spells were draped over him one after the other. Sometimes Gromph could feel an itching, warmth, a cool breeze, or a vibration, and sometimes he would feel nothing at all.

"Have you decided where to face him?" Grendan asked, pausing briefly between defensive spells,

Gromph shook his head.

"Somewhere out of the city?" Nauzhror suggested. "Behind the duergar lines?"

Gromph shook his head again.

"At the very least," said Nauzhror, "let us send guards to secure the arena . . . wherever it might be . . . before you arrive. They could remain hidden and come into play against the lichdrow only if necessary."

"No," said Gromph. "I said I will go alone, and I will go alone."

"But Archmage—" Nauzhror started to protest.

"What, precisely, do you think a House guard could do for me against the lichdrow Dyrr?" Gromph asked. "He would dry them up and smoke them in his pipe—precisely as I will do to any soldier Dyrr decides to bring with him. Dyrr will face me on my terms because he has to. He has to beat me, and he has to do it in front of all Menzoberranzan. If not, he will always be second, even if he manages to defeat House Baenre."

The masters continued with their spells, leaving only Nauzhror and Grendan still considering more than the magical practicalities of the duel at hand.

"Donigarten, then," suggested Grendan.

"No," Gromph said, then paused while another spell made him shudder briefly. "No."

He looked up at Nauzhror, who raised an eyebrow, waiting.

"The Clawrift, I think," Gromph said—deciding the second before he actually said it.

"An excellent choice, Archmage," Nauzhror said. "Away from any property of value and away from most of the finer drow of Menzoberranzan, of whom we have so few to spare on the best day."

A younger student entered and quickly set a small crystal ball on a short golden stand on the floor in front of the archmage. Gromph made no effort to acknowledge the student who was even then racing from the room.

He looked deeply into the crystal ball, holding up a hand to still the barrage of protective castings. The crystal grew cloudy, then flashes of light flickered in the roiling clouds inside the once perfectly clear globe.

Gromph brought a memory-image of the lichdrow into his mind's eye and held it there then did his best to convey that image into the globe. It would find the lichdrow, unless Dyrr expended some energy in avoiding it.

Gromph put his hand down, and several of the more ambitious masters started casting again—muttering incantations and tracing invisible patterns in the air—as if they'd been sitting there holding the thought.

There, Gromph thought as an image coalesced in the crystal ball of the lichdrow striding confidently across a reception hall in House Agrach Dyrr. There you are.

Gromph recognized the hall. He had been there himself on several occasions, back before things started to dissolve and Houses Agrach Dyrr and Baenre were close allies and business associates. He kept his attention on Dyrr. As he watched the lichdrow barking orders to his House guards and other armed drow, Gromph cast a spell of his own.

"Good afternoon, Dyrr," Gromph told the image in the crystal ball. "It will be the Clawrift. I know I don't have to tell you to come alone. I know you're always ready."

Gromph didn't wait for a response. He nodded to his masters and closed his eyes.

"We will be watching, Archmage," said Grendan, "and we'll be in constant contact."

"It would be irresponsible of me," Nauzhror said, "not to ask one more time if I might take your place in—"

"It would be irresponsible of me to hide behind my students," Gromph said. "Besides, Cousin, you were archmage for a little while, and by all accounts you liked it."

"I did, Archmage," Nauzhror admitted, "very much so."

"Well, if you hope to live long enough to be archmage again, you will await me here."

The lichdrow Dyrr dismissed his guards and proceeded via dimension door to the sitting room. There he found Yasraena and Nimor, who were occupied with trying not to speak to each other. Both seemed relieved when the lich stepped from the transdimensional doorway and into the room.

"It is time then?" Nimor asked.

Yasraena drew in a deep breath and held it, her eyes fixed on the lich.

"He awaits me at the Clawrift," Dyrr replied.

The matron mother exhaled slowly, and Nimor nodded.

"As good a place as any," the assassin said. "A hole in the ground . . . no sense damaging the merchandise we're paying so dearly to acquire."

"If by 'merchandise,' " Yasraena hissed, "you mean Menzoberranzan the Mighty, you—"

"Yasraena," Dyrr interrupted, his voice like ice.

The matron mother pressed her teeth together and turned away from Nimor, who stifled a laugh.

"I am prepared, as always," Dyrr said to them both, "and I will leave at once."

Yasraena turned to Nimor and said, "Go with him."

The assassin raised an eyebrow, and Dyrr—if he had any blood he would have felt it boil.

"Surely," the lichdrow said to Yasraena, "you don't mean to imply that I might not achieve the necessary victory on my own. Surely you don't . . . worry over my safety."

He locked his gaze on the young matron mother's eyes and held her there until she went gray, blinked, and turned away.

"You know that all of House Agrach Dyrr has the utmost confidence in you," she said, her voice low, stretched thin. She turned to look Nimor up and down. "But this is no time for personal vendettas. We have aligned ourselves with this . . . whatever he is. Why not use him?"

Nimor smiled, and Dyrr was reminded of the carnivorous lizards that inhabited the wilds of the Underdark.

"You wouldn't know where to begin to use me," the assassin said.

Dyrr simply shrugged off the meaningless exchange. He began to cast a series of protective spells on himself, ignoring a few more tiresome minutes of Yasraena and Nimor's verbal scuffling. Dyrr blinked after having cast on himself a spell that would make unseen things visible to him. Nimor looked different but in ways that seemed incongruous, even impossible. The drow assassin was no drow, as Dyrr had know for some time, but for the first time Dyrr could see something that might have been wings.

The lichdrow let that matter fall to the side in favor of a series of carefully crafted contingencies. After all, Dyrr himself wasn't exactly a drow anymore either. If Nimor was something else than a drow, so be it—as long as the dark assassin remained useful.

Something that Yasraena said made Dyrr stop in the middle of an incantation.

"Will House Agrach Dyrr be evacuated from Menzoberranzan," she asked Nimor, "should things not go the lichdrow's way?"

Dyrr struck her. The slap echoed in the Spartan sitting room, and Yasraena fell in an undignified heap onto the worg-carpeted floor. The lich took some of her life-force with the slap—only a taste, but enough to turn her gray and leave her gasping for breath. She looked up at him from the floor with wide, terrified eyes.

Matron mother indeed, Dyrr thought.

Nimor made no move and barely even seemed to take notice. Finally, he looked down at Yasraena as she began to struggle to her feet.

"If the lichdrow gives his leave," said the assassin, "I would like to answer that question."

The cold gleam in Nimor's eyes was enough to convince Dyrr that the assassin would give the right answer. The lichdrow nodded.

"House Agrach Dyrr," Nimor said to Yasraena, who had managed to get to her feet though her knees shook, "lives or dies in Menzoberranzan."

Yasraena nodded, rubbing her face with trembling hands, and Dyrr caught Nimor's attention.

"Precisely, my friend," the lichdrow said, "as do you."

Nimor stepped toward him, squaring his shoulders. It could never have crossed the lichdrow's mind for a second to back down, and he didn't.

"If I believe you are soon to fall," Nimor said to Dyrr, "I will rescue you."

Dyrr wanted in that moment to kill Nimor Imphraezl, but he didn't. Instead, he laughed. He was still laughing as he teleported away.

The Clawrift, a natural rent in the bedrock, cut into the northern sections of Menzoberranzan east of Tier Breche. Gromph stood at the very edge of it, looking down into the blackness. Even his newly acquired, much younger eyes were incapable of seeing the bottom. Sorcere was behind him. In front of him, across the wide chasm, was the City of Spiders. The stalagmites and stalactites that had been carved into homes and places of business for the drow were aglow with faerie fire. He could see House Baenre all the way on the other side of the cavern and the odd flash of light that marked the continuing siege of House Agrach Dyrr.

The lichdrow appeared in midair over the mile-deep chasm and hung there, a dozen yards away or more. He appeared facing Gromph as if he knew exactly where the archmage would be.

"Ah, my young friend," the lichdrow called, his voice floating over the space between them and echoing into the Clawrift itself, "there you are."

"As promised," Gromph replied, bringing a string of spells to mind.

"So it has come to this, then?" Dyrr asked.

"The two of us," replied Gromph, "fighting to the death?"

The lich laughed, and Gromph knew the sound would have sent lesser drow running.

"Why, Dyrr?" the archmage asked, not really expecting an answer.

The lichdrow turned his palms up and lifted his arms to his sides, looking around, gesturing toward the city.

"What better reason," asked Dyrr, "than the City of Spiders herself? From here, the Underdark, and from there, the World Above."

It was Gromph's turn to laugh.

"That's it then?" the archmage asked. "Mastery of all the world? Isn't that a bit of a cliché, lich? Even for you?"

The lichdrow shrugged and replied, "My existence knows no bounds, Gromph, so why should my ambition?"

"A simple enough answer, I suppose," Gromph said, "to a simple question."

"Shall we get on with it, then?"

"Yes," Gromph replied, "I suppose we had better."

They began slowly, both feeling each other out with minor divinations. Gromph could feel himself being explored even as he explored the lich. Nauzhror's voice, and Grendan and Prath's, whispered in his mind. Defenses were noted, items and clothing assessed for enchantment, notes compared. Gromph had brought a staff with him and was surprised to see that Dyrr had one too. He hadn't expected Dyrr to bring a staff.

Fire, Nauzhror told him after a tense few minutes of study. *The most effective weapon against the undead wizard from the traitor House will be fire.*

That's it, Gromph thought. Dyrr had made his one mistake.

"You're going to surprise me today," the lich called to Gromph, "aren't you, my dear archmage?"

"The only two things I'm completely sure of, Dyrr," Gromph replied, "is that we will surprise each other today and I will destroy you."

They started casting at the same time. Gromph was an experienced enough diviner to know that like himself, the lichdrow had cast his last defensive incantation.

The spells burst into being from the Weave at the same instant. A freezing wind blew from the lichdrow, carrying with it thousands of razor-sharp splinters of ice. That shredding storm met Gromph's fireball over the black depths of the Clawrift. The fire blew out even as it melted the ice. The two effects ate each other before either came close to touching their intended targets.

Well, Gromph told himself with a sigh, this is going to take a while.

T W E L V E

Things were quiet but tense on the ship of chaos. Pharaun tried not to look at Quenthel. He couldn't help but notice that she seemed unable to take Reverie. Her shoulders were stiff, and her viper-headed scourge never left her hand. The snakes writhed constantly, sliding the sides of their arrowlike heads against the priestess's warm black skin. The uridezu was surreptitiously eyeing her.

Pharaun found that curious. He was the one who had bound the demon, yet Raashub was more concerned with Quenthel. True, the Baenre priestess was still nominally "in charge" of the expedition, but her leadership had always been more ceremonial—at least in Pharaun's mind.

The Master of Sorcere couldn't quite organize his thoughts on the matter—not just then anyway—but the demon was looking at her oddly.

He sighed and stared out across the black water of the Lake of

Shadows again. He placed his hand on the rail then removed it when he felt the warm pulse of blood running through it. The ship barely moved in the dead calm of the black lake, but still Pharaun felt as if he needed to hold onto something. His hand found the twisted gray-yellow rigging—looking for all the world like a length of intestine—but he couldn't hold that much longer either.

The demonic ship didn't quite figure into Pharaun's esthetic. The wizard brushed the hair from his eyes and tried not to think about what he must look like. He hadn't bathed in far too long—hygiene had become secondary for them all, and they were rapidly beginning to stink. Jeggred was the worst of them all on a good day, but the wizard found himself avoiding Quenthel as well. Still, the thought of bathing in the cold, dark waters of the Lake of Shadows held no appeal. Pharaun could well imagine what might be living in that lake's depths, and he didn't want to offer himself up like a worm on a hook.

The ship creaked and groaned but not too much. Only rarely did there come the echo of a splash or drip or other small disturbance from the water. Pharaun was beginning to think it was the silence itself that he found so unnerving.

Something hit him in the back of the head hard enough to drive him facefirst into the bonework deck.

Surprised as much by the fact that he'd been taken by surprise, Pharaun lay blinking for a few seconds—enough time for whatever had hit him to grab him by the ankle. His foot instantly went numb, then whatever it was lifted him bodily off the deck. Still not quite having regained his wits—Pharaun hadn't realized at first that he'd been hit that hard—the Master of Sorcere found himself being spun in the air by the ankle. As he was whirled through the air, he caught glimpses of what was happening.

A party of uridezu were boarding the ship, crawling over the rail dripping with lake water and maggots. Their gray skin glistening and their pink tails twitching, the rat demons attacked in force, though Pharaun couldn't get an accurate count of them while being spun around by the ankle by another uridezu.

The wizard knew that he'd been right, that the first uridezu Raashub had gated in was meant to test them.

The demon let go, and Pharaun was sent pinwheeling through the air. He watched the rail pass beneath him, and when he was over open water he cast a spell while still in midair. By the time he hit the surface in a sprawling, stinging splash, Pharaun could breathe water.

The wizard didn't waste any time. Swimming and using the levitating powers of his brooch to help pull him downward, Pharaun dived deeper and deeper into the pitch-black water. The lake was cold enough to make him tense and stiff, but he still swam as fast as he could. All around him were the shadows of living things. There were fish, he hoped, and snakes, he feared, and other things—things crawling on the bottom.

The lakebed was covered in a fine silt that felt oddly alluring to the touch. Pharaun let himself sink into it up to his neck and closed his eyes to mere slits so that all anyone might be able to see would be his black face against the uniformly black silt.

Something brushed past his leg, but Pharaun didn't move.

The deep water and the stirred-up silt taxed Pharaun's darkvision to its limits, but he saw two uridezu dive into the water above him. Secure in his hiding place, ignoring another . . . something . . . slipping past his side, Pharaun watched the rat-demons swim with surprising agility, their heads waving back and forth as they searched the lake bed for the drow wizard. Pharaun waited for them to draw closer . . . closer . . . close enough. He threw an aura of faerie fire around them both.

The demons reacted to the magic with twitching confusion. The purple light not only outlined their silhouettes in the dark water, making them painfully obvious, it also picked out details of the folds of their skin, their whiskers, and the knitting of their worried brows.

Pharaun kicked once and rose slowly from the silt, already casting a spell. The uridezu looked over at him and swished their tails in the water. They swam quickly away from each other, smart enough not to both be caught in the same spell. Pharaun picked one at random and froze the water around it.

The Master of Sorcere knew that the ice would have no wounding effect on the demon, but it was thick enough to stop it. Pharaun smiled briefly at his handiwork. The uridezu, frozen solid in a thick block of ice, slowly sank to the lakebed, leaving a trail of bubbles in its path.

The second uridezu swam in fast, a stream of glowing purple maggots fanning out behind it. The tiny worms came from its ruined left eye, an old wound that had evidently festered for a very long time.

Pharaun tried to swim away from it, but the rat-demon was faster. It whirled in the water and brought its leathery pink tail to bear on the wizard. Pharaun took the hit with a grimace. It hurt.

As the uridezu twisted around, obviously meaning to shred Pharaun with its ragged claws, the Master of Sorcere touched his steel ring. The rapier appeared before him, and Pharaun set it against the demon with a thought. The dancing sword scored a deep slash, and the uridezu's attention—as Pharaun had planned—was drawn entirely to defending itself against the magically animated blade.

Content to let the rapier keep the demon busy, Pharaun kicked away from the duel, pulling his hand crossbow and a quarrel from his belt at the same time. When the bolt was set and cocked, Pharaun called on the power of his brooch to levitate quickly up and out of the lake. The second his face broke the surface he coughed out lungfuls of fluid. He shot into the air a dozen feet above the water and hung there, black droplets pattering off him to rain back down onto the rippling surface of the Lake of Shadows.

The wizard turned his attention to the ship of chaos. Never had the vessel seemed so aptly named. Quenthel and the draegloth fought for their lives against the rat-demon boarding party. Before Pharaun could get the whole situation sorted, Jeggred ripped a gash in the belly of one uridezu that was deep enough to spill its bowels onto the deck. It crumpled in a heap of steaming entrails at the blood-soaked draegloth's feet.

Pharaun counted four more of the demons, in addition to Raashub. The captain had gathered seven of his kind.

The wizard looked down, checking on the progress of the dancing rapier. The animated blade slit the swimming uridezu's throat. The demon shivered then went limp in the water, slowly floating to the surface. Its scalding blood sent coppery-smelling steam rising into the air below the hovering mage.

Pharaun recalled his rapier. Leveling his hand crossbow, he looked back at the ship of chaos. Quenthel held one uridezu at bay with her whip while another rushed her from behind. Pharaun couldn't get a clear shot, so he paused, and that was all the time it took for the uridezu behind her to bite Quenthel in the neck.

Blood welled up around the deep wound, and the high priestess gnashed her teeth in pain. With a hard, sharp jerk of her shoulder, Quenthel knocked the demon away. From a distance it was difficult for Pharaun to see, but he was sure the uridezu left a few teeth in the mistress's neck.

Movement from Jeggred caught Pharaun's eye. The draegloth advanced on Raashub. A wave of panic coursed through the Master of Sorcere. Attack or no attack, they needed Raashub to pilot the ship. Jeggred had been itching to kill the captain since they'd first claimed the vessel, and the boarding action was excuse enough for him to finally make good on his many threats.

Pharaun, fully aware of the irony of the situation, threw a spell that set a wall of invisible force between the uridezu captain and the advancing draegloth. Jeggred hit the wall hard, setting him back on his heels for a moment. Raashub cowered away from the draegloth then started to sniff the air in front of him, as puzzled by his unexplained, last-second reprieve as was Jeggred.

Quenthel threw an elbow at the uridezu that had bitten her, but the demon was able to avoid the blow. Quenthel's attacks were spasmodic and haphazard, and Pharaun knew it was only a matter of time before the two uridezu she faced managed to kill her.

The Master of Sorcere made his way quickly through a spell and sent its energy flowing out from him to the uridezu that had bitten Quenthel.

An enormous, disembodied black hand faded into existence from the thin air, and Pharaun took control over it with a thought. The uridezu that were harrying Quenthel stepped back from the hand but too slowly for the demon that had bitten her. The hand closed around the creature and began to squeeze.

Taking stock of the situation again, Pharaun saw that Jeggred had moved on to another uridezu, leaving Raashub to grovel behind the wall of force.

The wizard had only to will the spell-hand to squeeze as hard as it could and he could leave it to its own devices. As the uridezu trapped in the hand started gasping for air, Pharaun tightened his finger around the trigger of his hand crossbow and sent the bolt whizzing through the air. The missile slammed into the other demon's chest. It paused and turned to look at the source of the projectile.

The uridezu in the hand had its mouth wide open, but no sound came out. All the air had been squeezed from its lungs. Pharaun reloaded his hand crossbow, and the conjured hand squeezed even tighter. The demon's eyes bulged, and Pharaun couldn't help but watch.

The wizard launched another bolt at the demon that was still managing to dodge the high priestess's whip. The missile slammed home, pushing the uridezu toward Quenthel. The rat-man was staggered but far from dead—which was more than Pharaun could say for the creature in the hand. Its body bulged past the breaking point then burst in a torrent of blood and tissue. A few agonizing seconds later and it was dead.

Pharaun reloaded his hand crossbow again and watched the uridezu his last bolt had pushed toward Quenthel. The high priestess advanced quickly, scourge in one hand, the other wrapped into a tight fist.

The Mistress of the Academy hit the uridezu that faced her so hard its head burst into several large pieces that fell completely away from its shoulders. The rat-demon's glistening gray-and-yellow brain came free and went skipping out across the still surface of the lake. Pharaun knew that her strength was coming from a magic item, and he made a mental note to stop being surprised by feats of strength from the priestess.

Movement and light from below him caught Pharaun's attention. The uridezu he'd frozen in place had finally managed to break free, and it was moving with great whips of its ratlike tail. It swam up and toward Pharaun, who was still hovering and dripping above the water.

Pharaun cast a spell that let him push the advancing demon back down into the water. The Master of Sorcere continued pushing until the uridezu slipped beneath the layer of silt. He pushed harder until the creature finally hit the rocky lake bed, four feet under the drifting sediment. He pressed, crushing the monster into the lake bed. He could feel the thing's back break but kept pressing still.

Aliisza held her breath watching the drow fight off the uridezu. The rat-demons weren't necessarily the most impressive foes, but all things considered the dark elves made a fine show of it. Pharaun was especially alluring, hanging in midair over the water, so wet and intense. It made Aliisza all tingly.

The invisible alu-fiend drifted in the air over the regal female drow, who had been paralyzed by the bite of the uridezu she'd dispatched in a messy and uncreative way.

Another of the rat-demons swayed before the paralyzed priestess, its fangs bared and dripping with toxic spittle. It giggled in a shrill, excited way as it inched ever closer to the helpless drow female.

A low rumble drew Aliisza's attention to the draegloth. The half-demon growled in the face of another rat-demon then slashed the thing across the midsection with the razor claws of one hand. The demon bounced back on its heels only barely far enough to avoid having its guts opened onto the deck. A hiss exploded from the uridezu's quivering lips, and its tail lashed around at the draegloth. The half-drow, half-demon behemoth avoided the appendage with surprising agility.

The captain of the ship of chaos rattled his chain but remained bound to the deck. Aliisza sensed the presence of an invisible wall separating the captain from the rest of them. It was as if the air had turned solid there. She could see the magic shimmering in her Weave-sensitive eyesight.

Aliisza didn't particularly care what became of the uridezu captain or the uncouth, unappealing draegloth, but she couldn't stand the thought of the attractive, impressive drow priestess being eaten alive while paralyzed by a creature as lowly as an uridezu. The alu-fiend began to drain the life-force from that particular rat-creature while still hanging invisible in the air.

The uridezu looked around. It could feel that something bad was happening to it. Maybe it felt cold, or weak, dizzy, sick. Aliisza was killing it, and it had to know it was dying. The rat-demon drew its arms around itself, and Aliisza sensed that it was on its way back to the Abyss—but something kept it there on the ship. Aliisza could see that magic too, binding it to the very air around them. Only Pharaun could have been responsible for that.

The fact that the dark elf wizard had that power made Aliisza uneasy.

She wondered where the invisible wall had come from when she heard a horrid ripping sound and had to dodge an arc of dark-red blood. The draegloth ripped the arm off the uridezu that was stupid enough to stand up to him. Aliisza didn't like the smell of the rat-demon's blood . . . at least not as much as the draegloth seemed to.

The half-demon picked up the uridezu's arm and lifted it behind him until it bounced off the invisible wall. That startled the draegloth—no, not startled, *annoyed* him. Aliisza realized someone was trying to separate the uridezu captain and the draegloth.

That had to be Pharaun's handiwork. As the draegloth beat the rat-demon to death with its own arm, Aliisza sorted out why the wizard might be trying to protect the captain.

She whispered a quick spell and rose higher into the air so that no one but Pharaun would be able to hear her. She had to stop draining the life-force from the last survivor of the demonic boarding party, but the draegloth had already begun stalking toward it.

"Pharaun," she whispered over the intervening yards, her voice coming to the drow wizard as a whisper in his ear.

She saw the mage react and continued, "Yes, it's me. You're protecting the captain from your own draegloth?"

"What of it?" the wizard asked, his voice sounding as a whisper in her ear too.

"You don't need him," she said.

"Yes, I do," replied the mage. "It's a ship of chaos, Aliisza, and I'm a drow who isn't much for boats. I've never piloted one of these things before. Probably no drow in history ever has."

"It's not that hard," she explained. "The ship is alive. You simply *will* it to go where you want."

"It's that easy?" Pharaun asked, skeptical.

Aliisza watched the draegloth shred the weakened uridezu with a flurry of claws and fangs and said, "After a fashion, yes."

Barely missing a beat, the half-demon turned on the invisible wall and went at it with claw and fang, wild and feral. The sight made Aliisza's heart race.

The uridezu captain was cowering behind the wall. He didn't bother trying to pretend he didn't know what the draegloth was going to do to him if he got through the invisible barrier.

"Let the draegloth have him, darling," Aliisza said as her spell began to fade. "We can pilot the ship together."

Pharaun opened a dimensional rift and stepped through. In an instant he was standing on the deck of the ship of chaos next to the paralyzed priestess and directly under the hovering, unseen alu-fiend. She began to sink toward him.

"Jeggred," the drow wizard said to the draegloth, "stop it. Stop it, now. We need him."

The wizard turned to the high priestess, who stood, her hand dripping with uridezu gore. The snakes at the end of her whip hissed at Pharaun, warning him away.

"Mistress," he said to her, "tell him to stop it."

"She's paralyzed," Aliisza whispered in his ear, close enough then to do it without a spell.

Pharaun didn't flinch but smiled and said, "He won't listen to me."

"I told you it's all right, Pharaun," whispered the alu-fiend, "we don't need him."

"We?" he asked.

Aliisza blushed, though Pharaun still couldn't see her.

"If Raashub can pilot this vessel," she asked, "why can't we? Could it be that hard?"

Pharaun drew in a deep breath and let it out in a sigh.

"He's only going to keep defying me anyway, isn't he?" Pharaun asked.

"Who are you . . ." Quenthel said, her joints jerking as she recovered from the uridezu's paralyzing bite, ". . . talking to?"

"Wouldn't you, in his place?" Aliisza whispered, ignoring the high priestess.

Pharaun turned to her and looked her in the eyes, though she was sure he wasn't able to see her. He winked at her then turned back to the priestess.

"Jeggred means to kill the captain," he said.

"Let him," the priestess replied as she scanned the deck apparently looking for something with which to clean the blood off her.

"Well," Aliisza whispered into the wizard's ear, "it's her idea now, isn't it?"

Pharaun waved a hand and dropped the wall.

The draegloth leaped onto the uridezu captain. They both went over the rail. The chain that bound the uridezu to the deck—and to the material plane—snapped as if it were made of mushroom stem. There was a huge, echoing splash that sent lake water rolling onto the deck to mingle with the spilled demon blood.

Aliisza hovered over them as Pharaun and Quenthel ran to the rail and looked over into the black water. Bubbles peppered the surface, and there were ripples that made it obvious that some violence was occurring below the surface.

Then the bubbles stopped. The ripples played themselves out, and there was nothing.

"Go after them," the priestess said to Pharaun.

Aliisza caught herself before she laughed out loud.

Pharaun raised an eyebrow, looked at the priestess, and said, "I'm afraid I had to cancel the spell that allowed me to breathe underwater."

The priestess turned on him angrily, but any further discussion was stopped by the sound of another splash. Something arced out of the water and thumped onto the deck. The uridezu captain's head rolled to the other side of the ship and came to rest looking blankly up at nothing.

"Well," Quenthel breathed, glancing at Pharaun, "never mind."

The draegloth climbed slowly onto the deck behind the two dark elves. The half-demon shook himself hard, spraying water all over Pharaun and Quenthel. The two dark elves turned to regard the draegloth.

"That," the half-demon rumbled, "was almost worth the wait."

THIRTEEN

Danifae wanted them to meet her in a ruined temple on the edge of a swamp, on the east bank of which a wide river emptied into a sea. Halisstra spent the first night's walk explaining to Ryld what most of those words meant. By sunrise the first day, they had made the coast. The sight of the seemingly endless expanse of cold gray water took Halisstra's breath away. Like most of the rest of the World Above, it had made Ryld uncomfortable, even nervous. Halisstra was confident that he'd eventually get used to it, even grow to like it. He had to.

They followed the western shore of what the surface dwellers called the Dragon Reach for two long nights' march, using Ryld's keen senses, Halisstra's *bae'qeshel,* and Eilistraeen magic to avoid fellow travelers and unexpected dangers. In the hours before sunrise of the third day they stood at the bank of the wide Lis river delta, the Dragon Reach spreading out in angry, windswept white and gray to their right. To their left—north—was the river and intermittent woods and rolling, snowy hills. The weather was dark and bitterly cold, and Halisstra had to use spells to keep them from losing fingers and toes.

"We have to cross that?" Ryld asked, though he knew the answer.

They were concealed in a copse of sparse, leafless trees. The river delta crawled with boats of all sizes. Halisstra had never seen such vessels. Most bobbed on the angry waves, lanterns on their decks swaying in the chill wind. The drow caught the occasional glimpse of an armed human pacing the decks, wary of what, Halisstra couldn't imagine.

"It's an abandoned temple," Halisstra told him again. "An old temple to the filthy orc god Gruumsh. Danifae said it sits at the western edge of a vast swamp . . . a flooded place where water covers the vegetation, and many dangerous things hunt. The swamp is on the other side of the river."

Ryld nodded and continued to study the water as the sun's glow began to kiss the horizon.

"Would you know how to work one of those boats?" Halisstra asked.

The weapons master shook his head.

"Then we'll need help getting across," said the priestess. "It's too far and too cold to swim, and we'll attract too much attention using spells. If we keep our *piwafwis* up and over our heads, a less observant ferryman might not mark us as dark elves."

Ryld let out a sigh that told her he doubted that was possible but that he would try anyway.

They set out along the river's edge, working their way slowly northward in the pre-dawn gloom. Ryld stopped her occasionally to look around or study a boat that was either sitting on or adrift close to the riverbank. He never bothered to explain why he rejected first one then another and another, and Halisstra didn't ask.

Finally, they came upon a wide, square-keeled boat with a single long oar attached to a tall pole. The vessel had been pulled up on the riverbank, and a few feet away there was the indistinct lump of some humanoid creature asleep on the coarse sand. He'd built a fire before he drifted off to unconsciousness, and it sat next to him, the last of the embers quickly fading.

Ryld moved to within a few inches of the ferryman without making a sound. The weapons master slowly, silently drew his short sword and held it in a loose, easy grip. He crouched next to the humanoid, and the sleeper let out an odd sort of sustained, rumbling cough. Ryld half stood, looked at Halisstra, and shrugged. Halisstra returned the gesture. She had no idea what the sound could signify except that maybe the man—if it was a man—was choking.

Ryld rolled him over with a purposely harsh, violent push. The sleeper had the gruff grayish-yellow features of an orc, but not entirely. His eyes bulged, and he took a deep breath, his heavy brow wrinkled in anger. Ryld dropped the blade of his short sword to the boatman's neck, and the angry man stopped very suddenly. Halisstra stepped in. When she looked more closely at him, she saw that the ferryman was a half-orc. That was good luck for them. Half-orcs tended to be as despised on the World Above as they were in the Underdark, so he would be easier to manipulate into keeping their presence secret.

"Silence," Ryld whispered in the guttural trade tongue of the surface races.

The half-orc glanced once at Halisstra, then met Ryld's eyes and made a show of relaxing. He said nothing.

"We require a boat," the weapons master said quietly. "You will take us east across the river, and you will tell no one of it."

The half-orc looked at him, considering it.

Ryld nicked the man's neck with his short sword, barely enough to draw a half-inch sliver of blood.

"I wasn't asking," the weapons master added, and the half-orc nodded.

Within minutes they were on the boat. The horizon in front of them turned from black to a deep indigo. Halisstra had begun to grow accustomed to the sun, but Ryld still hated it, so they had been traveling at night. In order to make their arranged rendezvous with Danifae, they might have to continue through the morning, but Halisstra knew Ryld wouldn't complain.

"I think the ferryman expects us to pay him when we get to the other side," Ryld said in Low Drow, glancing at the half-orc who was pretending not to be staring at them. "Or do they breed half-orcs as slaves here too?"

At first Halisstra thought he was joking. It was hard to see his eyes with the cowl of his *piwafwi* pulled over his head. Halisstra wore her own hood the same way, but by the time they got to the midpoint in the wide river delta, the priestess realized that no one on any of the other boats was bothering to look at them and night-blind humans wouldn't be able to see them in the dark—not from a distance anyway. She slipped the hood off her head, eliciting an irritated scowl from Ryld, who kept his own cowl up.

"Why don't you ask him?" Halisstra said, nodding at the boatman.

Ryld shook his head.

"Danifae is going to kill you," he said, his voice flat.

"Is she?"

"I would," the weapons master replied. "She was your battle-captive for a long time, and now she isn't. Of course she will seek revenge for her years of bondage."

"Maybe," Halisstra had to admit, "but I don't think so."

"We don't get your kind around here much," the boatman blurted suddenly in heavily accented Low Drow.

The sound of the half-human, half-orc thing speaking the language of the dark elves made Halisstra's skin crawl. Ryld drew his short sword.

The boatman put up a hand, shaking, and said, "I mean no disrespect or anything. I was just saying . . ."

"You've seen drow before?" Halisstra asked then flashed a quick sentence in sign language: *An extra hundred gold pieces if you forget all about us.*

The half-orc had no reaction to the signed question. He didn't even seem to notice that she'd been trying to communicate.

"Sure," the boatman replied, "I've seen a drow or two. Not recently, but . . ."

Halisstra shrugged off the boatman's answer and signed to Ryld,

I think he wanted us to know he understood us, so we wouldn't say something that would make us want to kill him for hearing it.

That drew a smile from Ryld.

You can put your sword away, she added.

The weapons master sheathed his blade and said, "If he understands the sign, he should say so now or I will kill him."

The half-orc waved a hand and said, "No, no, sir. I swear to you. I didn't even know what you were doing. I just paddle, yes? Paddle? You don't even have to pay me."

"Pay you?" Ryld asked.

The half-orc looked away.

He heard us mention the temple, Ryld signed. *It goes without saying that he can't be trusted.*

Who can? Halisstra answered.

Not Danifae, the weapons master signed.

Eilistraee will guide us, she replied. *Danifae has no goddess to guide her.*

Ryld nodded, though he made his continued skepticism plain.

They rode the rest of the way in silence, and soon they were at the other side of the river. Halisstra stepped off the boat, wading in inches deep water to the rocky riverbank. She looked back for Ryld, who was stepping toward the half-orc. The weapons master reached behind the ferryman, unsheathed Splitter, took off the half-orc's head, and resheathed his weapon in precisely the space of one of Halisstra's heartbeats. The head splashed into the water, and the weapons master kicked the body in after it.

Ryld turned to wade ashore, and Halisstra looked away into the blue-gray light of the dawn. She could hear his footsteps in the water then on the rocks behind her, but she didn't want to look at his face just then.

Danifae materialized on the deck of the ship of chaos and was instantly struck by how much had changed. Valas appeared next to her, and she watched his expression change from his normal stoic, blank pragmatism to an uneasy curiosity—he'd noticed it too.

Pharaun and Quenthel both looked bad and smelled bad. The ship itself looked different. The deck, which had been a dull white expanse of stark bone, was covered in spots with pink tissue and crossed with gently throbbing arteries. Sinew and what might have been ligaments stretched between gaps in the bone. The ship felt alive.

Pharaun and Jeggred both looked up at them when they appeared, but only Pharaun stood. The draegloth looked to one side, and Danifae followed his gaze to Quenthel. Jeggred's eyes burned when he looked at the high priestess, who sat on the deck with her back to the others, one hand absently caressing one of the vipers that made up her whip.

"Welcome back to the Underdark's dull wet arse," the Master of Sorcere said. He only glanced at Danifae but approached Valas with his hand out. "You have what we need?"

The Bregan D'aerthe scout nodded and handed the wizard one of the magical sacks that held their supplies.

Danifae kept her attention on Jeggred, who made eye contact with her finally and nodded. The former battle-captive gave the draegloth a smile and a slight bow—then she noticed that the bound uridezu was missing.

"What happened here?" she asked Pharaun.

The wizard began to laugh, and at first it seemed as if he would be laughing for a long time. When no one joined him, he calmed himself and took a deep breath.

"Mistress?" Danifae called to Quenthel.

Nothing.

Jeggred stared at the high priestess's back, saying nothing as well.

"Are we . . . ?" the scout asked Pharaun.

"Oh, yes," the wizard replied, "we'll be setting sail as planned. It turns out that we didn't need the captain's services after all. Jeggred was kind enough to retire his commission for us. I will be piloting the ship to the Abyss and back."

Valas nodded, sat, and began to sort through their supplies. Pharaun stood over him, occasionally commenting on what the scout had purchased. Quenthel continued to sit with her back to the rest of them, saying nothing. Danifae approached Jeggred, gauging his mood as she moved closer. He seemed to want to speak to her, so she sat down next to him.

"Reverie?" she asked, nodding at Quenthel.

"No," said the draegloth, making no effort to lower his voice. "She has been unable to take the Reverie. The mistress is weakening."

Danifae took a deep breath, searching the draegloth's eyes for some hint that he was anything but genuinely angry with Quenthel. It didn't seem possible that Jeggred had come that far in the relatively short time that she and Valas had been gone, but obviously things had progressed much more swiftly than she'd hoped.

"The 'captain'," Jeggred grumbled, "gated in some of his kind. They attacked us, and we prevailed."

"Quenthel didn't fight?" Danifae guessed.

Jeggred looked at the silent high priestess and thought about that for a while.

"She fought," the draegloth said finally, "but she . . ."

Danifae waited a few heartbeats for him to finish then prodded, "We all serve greater mistresses, Jeggred. The Matron Mother of House Baenre, in your case, and in mine, Lolth herself—both greater mistresses than Quenthel. If you have something that either your matron mother or your goddess need to know, you must speak. Duty demands it."

Jeggred looked deep into her eyes, and she let him. She held the half-demon's gaze for a long time, never permitting herself the slightest twitch, the most miniscule sign of weakness or indecision.

"She's . . . sensitive," the draegloth said.

"Sensitive?" Danifae pressed.

"The Mistress of Arach-Tinilith has a sensitivity to beings from the outer planes," he said. "She can sense the presence of demons and communicate with them. It's not something that everyone knows about her, but I do."

"Then why didn't she know that Raashub was gating in . . . ?" She let the question fade away.

The look in Jeggred's eyes as he stared at Quenthel's still back told her all she needed to know.

"I am a priestess of Lolth," she told the draegloth. "I serve the Queen of the Demonweb Pits, and on this ship that means I serve Quenthel Baenre."

Jeggred tipped his huge head to one side, his wild mane of white hair spilling over his muscular, gray-furred shoulders.

"I serve her," Danifae went on, "whether she knows it or not, whether she appreciates it or not, and whether she desires it or not. Something is . . ."

Danifae wasn't sure how to finish that thought.

"She has succumbed," the draegloth said.

"Succumbed?" asked Danifae.

"To fear."

Danifae let that settle in then said, "She requires our services more than ever now. Lolth's servant demands our service, and we both live to serve, do we not?"

Jeggred nodded slowly, making it plain he was waiting to hear more.

The former battle-captive reached into her pouch and drew out one of the rings she'd taken from the cold, dead hand of her former House mage. She held it up so that only Jeggred could see it, sliding it between her fingertips so that it reflected the feeble illumination—enough for the draegloth's dark-sensitive eyes to see it. Jeggred opened one hand, and Danifae let the ring fall onto the half-demon's palm.

I need you to go somewhere with me, Danifae signed, her hands close to her stomach so none of the others could see, *and do something for me.*

Ask, he replied, also careful to keep his hands where only she could see them. *I live to serve, Mistress.*

FOURTEEN

They hadn't managed to kill each other yet.

Gromph floated in the still darkness above the Clawrift surrounded by a globe of magical energy. He'd conjured it from his staff, draining some of the item's magical essence in the process. The cost was worth it to keep out even the rudimentary spells the globe protected him from. Gromph knew the lich was capable of much more powerful castings—spells that would pass through the globe without the slightest degradation in power—but at least it would limit Dyrr's options.

Regardless of the globe, no matter what he tried, Gromph couldn't get within sixty yards of the lich.

The repulsion effect is coming from Dyrr's staff, Nauzhror whispered into Gromph's mind. *We are studying possible solutions.*

The repulsion was another petty defense, another meager drain on a powerful item, and in that way Gromph and Dyrr were even—again.

"What are you afraid of, lich?" the archmage called to his opponent. "I won't try to kiss you."

Dyrr, who was also floating above the black depths of the Clawrift, actually laughed.

"We could simply float here," Dyrr replied, "waiting for one of the defenses to go down—your globe, my repulsion . . . but where's the sport in that?"

"Good question," Gromph whispered, not caring if the lich could hear him or not.

The archmage began to cast a spell, and the lich pressed his fingertips together, waiting to defend against it. Gromph set himself moving through the air toward the lich the second he finished his incantation and knew it was successful when the distance between them abruptly closed. The repulsion effect successfully dispelled, Gromph swooped in quickly to get into range for a more damaging spell.

Dyrr, who didn't seem the least bit surprised, dropped out of the air. Gromph knew he'd dispelled the repulsion effect, not Dyrr's ability to fly. The lich was trying to escape into the black abyss of the Clawrift.

Gromph dropped after him. The air, moving fast over the surface of the magical globe that still surrounded him, made a curious humming sound that Gromph found distracting. Still, he managed to cast another spell as he flew and succeeded in closing the distance between them even more.

A bead of pulsing orange light appeared in Gromph's right hand. He looked up at Dyrr, brought his arm back to throw the bead, and hesitated. Dyrr, a cold light in his dead eyes, was coming at him. The distance between the two mages was closing faster and faster—and the lichdrow was casting a spell.

The words of Dyrr's spell—a series of almost nonsensical quatrains in an obscure dialect of Draconic—echoed around them both. Gromph drew his right arm back farther still, aiming the bead at his opponent's face while holding his staff in his left hand. Dyrr had something cupped in his own left hand and his own staff in his right. It was as if they were both looking in a mirror.

Dyrr threw his first. A cloud of sparkling red dust—*Crushed rubies,* Grendan reported—burst into the air around the lich. The dust swirled on some twist of wind for half a heartbeat then was gone. As the last grain of the powdered gemstone disappeared, Gromph threw the bead.

The archmage came to a sudden stop in the air. The breath was forced from his lungs, and he grunted loudly. His own staff hit him in the face, numbing his bottom lip and making his eyes water. His joints went limp for a few seconds, and his arms and legs flapped out of control.

The bead of compressed fire should have hit the lich in the face and exploded in a ball of flame six paces wide. It should have burned the lich's face off—but it didn't.

Gromph, as he finally gained control of his body and came to rest once again hovering in midair, could see the tiny speck of orange light fly true toward the lich's face then curve in the air and dive into the garish crown the Agrach Dyrr wizard had the audacity to wear. The bead blazed briefly to life in a splash of orange and yellow luminescence that lit the lichdrow's face but didn't come close to burning it off.

The crown, Gromph thought. I should have remembered.

The fireball has been absorbed by the crown, Nauzhror hissed into Gromph's mind.

Gromph was certain he'd see it again.

The item will allow him to redirect the fireball at you, Grendan warned.

Yes, gentlemen, Gromph replied. *Thank you.*

Dyrr drew to an abrupt stop and hung in the air, bouncing ever so slightly. He looked like a mushroom cap bobbing on the surface of Donigarten Lake. Gromph, on the other hand, was frozen in air, standing on what felt like a solid surface but looked like a dim, phosphorescent glow.

Gromph's globe was still up, but it wasn't the only thing that surrounded him.

An impressive spell, Nauzhror said. *Difficult to cast and expensive what with the ruby dust and all. It's nothing you can't handle, Archmage.*

"A forcecage?" Gromph asked.

The lichdrow didn't bother answering. Instead, he began to cast another spell. Clearly he thought he had Gromph trapped, so of course he would take advantage of the situation. The archmage brought a spell to mind and rushed through the casting of it, racing the lich, though he would likely still have to suffer through whatever Dyrr was throwing at him. He needed to get the forcecage off him. Being trapped in a magical box was hardly convenient at that moment.

Dyrr's spell took effect half a heartbeat before Gromph's. As the lich finished the last gestures and the final complex verbalization and crunched a lodestone and a pinch of dust in his right hand, something opened under the archmage's feet.

Gromph's spell went off, and his own globe fell victim to it—but so did the forcecage—and Gromph was falling into whatever it was Dyrr had conjured underneath him.

The archmage touched his brooch and made himself stop quickly, well before he contacted Dyrr's dramatic magical effect. As he drew himself up, moving farther and farther away from it, Gromph looked down—and into a whole other universe. The lichdrow had opened a gate beneath him, and a blinding, eye-searing light poured out of it. Gromph had seen light like it only a few times in his long life. It was sunlight, and the Archmage of Menzoberranzan didn't like it at all.

"Where are you trying to send me?" Gromph asked his opponent.

The World Above? Prath mused, though only Gromph could hear him.

Dyrr didn't answer but busied himself gathering some spell component or perhaps another magic item.

"You've imprisoned me more than once already," Gromph went on, "though they seem to hold me less time each attempt. Now you want to send me away? For pity's sake, Dyrr, why not simply kill me and get it over with? Or is it that you *can't* kill me?"

Gromph certainly wished that were the case—and maybe by some bizarre twist of fate it was—but Dyrr seemed to have something else in mind. The lich finished casting his spell. The immediate effect was that Gromph's stomach lifted in his gut. He caught his breath in a hissing gasp and started to fall.

He couldn't levitate—Dyrr had dispelled the magic that was keeping him aloft—and Gromph fell toward the rotating pool of daylight beneath him. Knowing Dyrr, it would be a worse fate than simply splattering at the bottom of the Clawrift. It was a fate Gromph would do anything to avoid.

The archmage extended himself, wiping more stored energy, more access to the Weave from his mind than he normally would have had to, but he needed the spell to take effect faster and couldn't spare the time for complicated incantations. The effect felt the same as Dyrr's dispelling of his levitation, but instead of falling down, Gromph drifted to a stop then started falling upward. The source of gravity, with enough magic, could be moved.

Gromph twisted in the air as he accelerated toward the roof of the cavern that housed Menzoberranzan. As the lich crossed his field of vision, Gromph could see him grimace in frustration. The archmage didn't waste time gloating. His brooch was useless to him—at least for the time being—Gromph would continue to fall upward toward the new source of gravity until he was dashed against the ceiling. He would have to stop himself.

The command word, Gromph sent to the masters of Sorcere. *Quickly.*

The staff that he'd used to surround himself in the globe of protective magic had been charged with more than one effect. He'd never used it, but the staff would grant him the same power of levitation as his brooch.

Sshivex, Nauzhror provided.

"*Sshivex,*" Gromph repeated and immediately began to levitate "up" and away from the ceiling.

In a fraction of a second—before he "landed" on the ceiling— Gromph once again drew to a halt in midair. The pool of blinding sunlight was far below him. The light made it difficult, but Gromph finally managed to spot the lichdrow, who was flying slowly, well away from the gate, and casting another spell.

"That was close, Dyrr," Gromph called out. "You almost—"

The words caught in Gromph's throat. His vision blurred. For a few seconds he couldn't breathe.

"You al—" Gromph started again, but the words were pinched off when his throat clamped shut.

Tears welled up in the archmage's eyes, and a wave of overwhelming despair passed through him, leaving his skin clammy, and his head spinning.

It's an enchantment, Grendan told him.

He was going to die. Gromph knew that with absolute certainty, but what was worse, Menzoberranzan would die soon after him. Everything he'd built over a life spent in the corridors of power had come to nothing. Menzoberranzan was eating itself alive. Everything Gromph had considered a strength—in himself, and in his race—had proven a weakness.

A compulsion, added Prath.

The hate and mistrust, the vendettas and animosities, had finally come home to roost. The once great City of Spiders had been reduced to a besieged, ragged, self-destructing ruin of its former glory—glory that was proving with every dead drow to have been a lie all along.

Fight it, Archmage, Nauzhror urged.

Lolth was dead, and Gromph would be dead soon too. Lolth was dead, and so was House Baenre. So was Sorcere. So was Menzoberranzan. It had all come to nothing, as he himself had come to nothing.

Archmage . . . Nauzhror prodded.

Gromph's body shuddered through an alien sensation: a sob. He wiped at his eyes with the back of his hand and tried to blink away the tears, but more came. Through the tears he saw that Dyrr had moved and was floating above him.

"That's it, young Baenre," the lichdrow said. "Lament. Cry for fallen Menzoberranzan. Cry for House Baenre."

Cry? Gromph thought. Am I crying?

"Slow," Dyrr said, his voice like a gentle caress against Gromph's pain-ravaged brow. "Stop, young mage."

No, a voice in Gromph's mind all but shouted.

Gromph hadn't realized he was moving—levitating slowly "down" toward the ceiling, moving away from the blinding light pouring from Dyrr's gate. The archmage slowed his descent and came to a stop, hanging only a few yards from the jagged stalactites that hung from the ceiling like fangs ready to puncture the neck of Menzoberranzan the Mighty, ready to punish them all for their weakness.

"There . . ." the lichdrow murmured, his voice sending a quivering chill down Gromph's spine. "There . . ."

The lich was holding something.

How did he get so close?

Archmage, the voice in his head asked, *shall I come help you?*

No, he thought back at the voice.

Gromph tried to flinch away, but the lichdrow touched him with a long, thin wand of gem-inlaid silver. The touch of it sent a wave of blinding agony ripping through the archmage's body. Every muscle tensed, joints popped, and the wizard clenched his teeth against the pain. His eyes watered more, and Gromph could feel tears streaming down his tingling black cheeks.

He turned away from the lich, rolling in the air, and faced down toward the gate. His eyes closed against the light, but he blinked them open and saw the briefest flash of a silhouette: Dyrr in shadow against the sunlight. The lichdrow was below him but had been above him. Gromph wasn't sure at that instant what he was seeing. Dyrr had fooled him, or he was disoriented . . . or he was dying.

Am I dying? Gromph thought.

"Am I?" he said aloud then clamped a hand over his face, closing his eyes and mouth.

No, Archmage, said the voice in his head. *You are under the effect of a powerful enchantment.*

In that moment, Gromph lost all memory of any plan, of any determination, of any purpose for the ruin of a life he'd been cursed with. He wanted to get away. He needed to run, but he was still the Archmage of Menzoberranzan, so he cast a spell that would get him away a little faster, a little farther. With a few words and gestures he'd repeated so many times that even in his confused, despairing state of mind he managed to get right, Gromph brought forth the magic to open a doorway through the dimensions—a break in space and time.

Gromph levitated toward it, but something hit him and hit him hard. It was Dyrr. The lichdrow had put away his wand. The slim magical weapon caused physical damage and pain, but it didn't cause an impact—not like that. The air was forced from Gromph's lungs again, and he found himself pinwheeling through the air.

The light from the gate grew brighter and brighter, and Gromph was only dimly aware that he was moving toward it. The pain was everywhere, still burning from the wand and joined by whatever it was that had hit him to send him falling toward the light. The pain turned to numbness in spots then was gone, and Gromph took a deep, shuddering breath.

The ring, he thought. I have a ring that will . . .

Yes, Archmage, the voice said, *the ring. The ring will keep you alive but not forever.*

Gromph closed his eyes tight again and let his body relax. The ring he'd slipped on at Sorcere before meeting Dyrr at the Clawrift would regenerate injuries: knit broken bones back together, seal cuts, even re-grow severed limbs. He remembered putting the ring on but couldn't for the life of him remember why. What could possibly have been the point? To live? To live in the shattered ruins of a Menzoberranzan ruled by the traitorous Dyrr and an army of stinking gray dwarves?

Gromph touched the ring, grabbed it with the opposite hand, and was about to rip it from his finger so it would let him die, when he saw the lichdrow swooping down at him, cackling. Laughing at him.

"Take it off," Dyrr chuckled. "It won't help with burns anyway."

Archmage! another voice shouted into his mind.

The lich blinked and jerked forward with his head and shoulders. From the grotesque crown on his head came a tiny ball of undulating orange light. It spiraled through the air, riding a sort of wave, and drew a long, curved trajectory directly at Gromph.

Your fireball, the voice in his head warned.

"My fireball . . ." the archmage whispered, as he instinctively tucked himself into a fetal position, wrapping his body around his staff and closing his eyes tightly.

Even with his eyes closed the flare of hot orange light burned his retinas. The fireball warmed his skin but didn't burn him. He and the other Masters of Sorcere had thought, of course, to protect him against fire.

"A little longer . . ." the archmage murmured.

"Gromph," the lichdrow spat back. "You live!"

"For now," was the archmage's shaking, muttered reply.

Dyrr didn't wait for Gromph to elaborate. He began to work another spell.

The fireball had broken Gromph's concentration on the levitation effect, and once again his stomach lurched up as he began to fall. Gravity was still upside down, and his fall took him away from the gate and toward the ceiling.

While Dyrr finished his spell, Gromph began to list in his own mind the many reasons he should simply let himself fall into the ceiling and die.

Before the troubled archmage could reach a conclusion, shards of jagged, half-molten rock burst into existence, flying with extraordinary speed toward the falling archmage. There were too many of them to count, and Gromph, mumbling to himself of his lost position and the bleak fate of his House, didn't bother trying.

When the meteors entered the area in which Gromph had affected gravity, their courses radically changed. They went everywhere, scattering, dipping, curving, colliding with each other, some even curving back at Dyrr.

One of the burning projectiles struck Gromph a glancing blow, sending him spinning as he fell. Pain blazed in his side, and without thinking he cast a spell. With only a few words and a quick gesture, Gromph's skin tightened, stretched—painfully—and took on the gleam, and the hardness, of cold black iron.

Very good, Master, the voice . . . it was Nauzhror . . . said.

Gromph watched one of the meteors come right at him. He might have twisted out of the way, but he didn't care. The rock hit him square in the chest, exploding in a shower of yellow-orange sparks and sending a deafening clang rippling away from him in the air. He started to spin in a different direction and began to wonder why he hadn't hit the ceiling. As he whirled around he saw Dyrr slip through a dark hole in the sky that was rimmed with purple light like faerie fire. The lichdrow was passing through a dimension door of his own to avoid the meteors that had come careening back at him.

Spinning, falling, Gromph saw the jagged, stalagmite-cluttered ceiling racing toward him, closer and closer—only inches from oblivion, from the sweet release of death—

—and the spell effect ended.

Gromph hadn't made it permanent after all. Gravity went back to its normal place, and once again Gromph hung in midair for a second—less than a second maybe—his stomach feeling as if it were rotating in his belly. He started to fall again but toward the floor—toward the Clawrift, toward the light, toward the gate, toward wherever it was that Dyrr was trying to send him.

Gromph didn't care. He'd go, then. He'd go anywhere as long as he could get out of Menzoberranzan, where every stone, every stalactite and stalagmite, every glow of faerie fire, reminded him of his failure and despair.

Archmage, Nauzhror said. *Gromph . . . no.*

Closing his eyes against the blinding sunlight, Gromph fell through the gate. Squinting, able only to see a vague play of shadow and light, he watched the gate close behind him. He was enveloped, enclosed in blinding light.

He hit the ground hard enough to break a leg, more than a few ribs, his left arm, and very nearly his neck. Quivering from pain and shock, blinded by the relentless sunlight, Gromph lay in a heap on a bed of what felt like some kind of moss. Blood roared in his ears, which were still ringing from the whine of the meteors and the rush of wind. Something in his chest popped, and his leg twitched out from under him, rolling him over onto his back.

Gromph put a hand over his face and realized that his broken arm was obeying his commands with only a little pain. His leg was numb and tingling, and he could actually feel his ribs popping back into place.

The ring, he thought again.

He almost wanted to laugh. It was his own fault after all, for insisting on wearing that cursed ring. He'd wanted to save his own life when he'd put it on, and it hadn't occurred to him then that all it would end up doing was keeping him alive in whatever blazing hell Dyrr had banished him to.

Gromph blinked his eyes open and found that he could actually see. The light was still uncomfortably bright, but something had moved between the brightest part of it and himself. The archmage blinked again, rubbed his eyes, and struggled to sit up. His face was still wet with tears, and he was breathing hard—panting like a slave at hard labor.

"Are you *keerjaan*?" a voice asked.

Gromph held out a hand, fending off the voice, and blinked some more.

It was all at once that he realized the thing that had come between him and the source of the light was a creature of some kind, and it was speaking to him.

"Am I . . . ?" the archmage started to answer.

He paused, rubbed his eyes, and found himself concentrating on a spell he'd long ago made permanent. It was a spell that allowed him to understand and be understood by anyone.

"Are you all right?" the strange creature asked, and Gromph understood.

He looked up and saw that he was surrounded by tiny, drowlike creatures—drowlike in that they were roughly the same shape, with two arms, two legs, and a head. There the similarity ended. The creatures that surrounded him had pale skin that was almost pink. Their hair was curly and an unsightly shade of brown-orange. Their skin was spattered with tiny brown spots. Plastered on their faces were the most childlike expressions of delighted curiosity. They hovered around him in a circle, several feet off the plant-covered ground, each of them borne aloft on a set of short feathered wings of the most garish colors.

Most of them were naked, though some wore robes of flowing white silk, and a couple wore breeches and fine silk blouses. They were no more than three feet tall.

"By all the howling expanse of the Abyss, Dyrr," Gromph murmured, curling his legs under him and resting his face in his hands, "where have you dropped me?"

Words began to pop into his mind like soap bubbles bursting:

Halflings.

Spells.

Crushing . . .

Crushing despair.

"Damn you," Gromph breathed, his body relaxing, his eyes drying, his mood lifting as if by magic.

It wasn't magic that was lifting it, he realized. It was magic that sank it in the first pace.

"Well played, traitor," Gromph said, looking up into the bright blue sky of the . . . where was he? The World Above?

"Who are you talking to?" one of the winged halflings asked, tipping its head to one side like a confused pack lizard.

"Where am I?" Gromph asked the strange creature.

The archmage, not waiting for an answer, stood, brushing soot, dust, and pieces of the odd, needle-like plant life from his *piwafwi*. He leaned on his staff, but thanks to the ring he was feeling stronger with each breath.

"You don't know where you are?" one of the winged halflings—a female—asked.

"Tell me where I am, or I'll kill you and ask someone else," Gromph growled.

The halflings reacted, maybe with fear—Gromph couldn't be sure. They bobbed up and down and quivered.

"Are you a cambion?" one of them asked.

"I am a drow," Gromph replied, "and I asked you a question."

The winged halflings all looked at each other. Some smiled, some nodded—some smiled *and* nodded.

"How did you get here?" the female asked.

"I asked you a question," Gromph repeated.

The female smiled at him, and Gromph had to squint from the brightness of her perfect white teeth.

"How could you come here from . . . where did you come from?" one of the males said.

"I am from Menzoberranzan," replied Gromph.

"Where's that?" asked another of the males.

"The Underdark," Gromph said, his crushing despair gone, being replaced by burning impatience. "Faerûn . . . Toril?"

"Faerûn," one of the males gasped. The others looked at him and he said, "I was from there. From Luiren. Faerûn is a continent, and Toril is a world. On the Prime."

The other winged halflings nodded and shrugged.

"So," the one who'd asked the question before repeated, "how could you come here from Menzoberranzan, the Underdark, Faerûn, Toril, and not know where you are?"

"You're not even on the Prime anymore, drow," said the halfling who'd claimed to be from Faerûn. Gromph could see contempt starting to manifest in that halfling's beady brown eyes. "You've come to the Green Fields, and you don't belong here."

"That's all right," Gromph said. "I'm not staying."

Looking over the vast landscape of gently rolling hills covered in a blanket of the tiny green, needle-like plants and punctuated with a scattering of rainbow-colored blossoms like delicate, paper-thin mushrooms, Gromph almost sank into despair again.

Dyrr had sent him far—sent him to another plane of existence altogether.

"The Green Fields," Gromph repeated. "Halfling Heaven. . . ."

Nauzhror, he thought, sending the name out into the Weave. *Grendan? Can you hear me?*

Nothing.

Gromph sighed. It was going to take him a while to get home.

FIFTEEN

"Oh, now, why the long face?" Aliisza purred.

Her hand slipped along Pharaun's waist, tickling him, but he didn't move. She smiled and wrapped her arm around him, sliding her hand onto his back and moving closer and closer until her body pressed against his. She was warm—almost hot, and she smelled good. She felt better.

"Your journey is barely beginning," the alu-fiend whispered into his ear. Her breath was so hot it nearly burned the side of his neck. "I almost envy you the sights you'll see, the things you'll experience. You will be in the presence of your goddess soon enough."

"Will I like what I see?" he asked. "Will the experience be a fulfilling one? Will my goddess speak to me?"

Aliisza stiffened, but just for a second, then she wrapped one leg around him and nestled in. The force of her embrace turned them slightly in the air. Pharaun glanced down at the ship of chaos and his companions, a hundred feet or more beneath them, oblivious to their presence there.

"Those are all things you'll have to discover on your own," she said.

"Then how can you be sure it'll be something to envy?" he asked, his voice playful but forced, his attention returning to her.

"I envy you the surprises," she replied with a wink.

"Have you been there?"

"To the Abyss?" she asked. "Not for a long time."

"The Demonweb Pits?"

The alu-fiend withdrew enough to look him in the eye, smiled, and said, "No, I've never been to the Demonweb Pits. Have you?"

Pharaun shook his head. He could answer her but not when she was looking at him. He leaned into her, and she squeezed him tighter.

"I was there twice, I think," he said into the soft warmth of her long neck.

"You think?"

"It was a long time ago," Pharaun replied, "and it might have been a dream. There was the last time, when we were all there in astral form, but I thought you might have been there once in the flesh. You're a demon. You can go there and . . ."

Pharaun stopped talking. He wasn't sure what he was trying to say.

"Have you been to Menzoberranzan?" he asked instead.

Aliisza stiffened again and for a little bit longer, and he knew that she had.

"Will there be a city for us to return to?" he asked.

Aliisza shrugged. Pharaun could feel the gesture against his body.

"Answer me," he pressed.

"Yes," she said, "or no. It all depends on what you find in the Abyss and how soon Kaanyr and his new friends can break your matron mothers' backs."

Pharaun found himself laughing. He was exhausted again. The Lake of Shadows had a way of sapping his strength.

"Honestly, Pharaun," she said, "you ask me questions as if I'm some sort of fortune teller or oracle . . . or goddess. I don't know what'll happen to you and your friends. No one, not even your Spider Queen I think, can predict what will happen from minute to minute in the mad chaos of the Abyss."

Pharaun looked her in the eye and decided not to say the first few things that came into his mind.

"Have you thought about my coming with you?" Aliisza asked.

"Why would you help me pilot the ship?" he asked her, gently pushing her away. "We enjoy each other, but I can't imagine you're asking me to simply trust you. I'll need an answer."

Aliisza resisted playfully and flicked the tip of her tongue against his cheek.

"You're pretty," she teased.

"Not as pretty as you," said Pharaun. "Answer me. Why would you help me find Lolth and help Vhok and the duergar lay siege to Menzoberranzan at the same time? You're the enemy—the consort of the enemy, at least—of the city I call home. One might be tempted to choose sides."

"Whatever for?" she asked. "When I'm with you, I like you best. When I'm with Kaanyr, he is everything to me. Either way, I'm amused."

Pharaun found himself laughing again.

"I'll assume that's the best answer I'll ever get from you," he said, "or any other tanar'ri."

Aliisza winked at him again.

As Pharaun let his hands explore her exquisite body, he said, "We should begin our lessons. Quenthel and the others are anxious to get underway."

Aliisza responded to his touch with a sigh, then replied, "As soon as you wish, love. You know how to get there from here?"

"Through the Shadow Deep," he said.

The alu-fiend nodded and said, "From there to the Plain of Infinite Portals—the gateway to the Abyss. There you'll need to find precisely the right entrance. The place you seek—the Demonweb Pits—is the sixty-sixth layer. There are guardians there and lost souls and things maybe even you can't imagine. You might actually like the Abyss, and you might not. Either way, it will change you."

Pharaun sighed. She was probably right.

He really didn't want to go.

Who is responsible? Quenthel asked.

Oh, Mistress, Mistress, K'Sothra answered. Of the five vipers in her scourge, K'Sothra was the least intelligent, but Quenthel listened anyway. *Mistress, it was you. You are responsible. It's all your fault.*

Quenthel closed her eyes. The skin on her face felt tight, stretched too thin on her skull. Her head hurt. She touched the viper just below its head, and K'Sothra writhed playfully under her touch.

Was it really my fault? the high priestess asked. *Could it be?*

She drew her finger away from K'Sothra, found the next viper, and cupped her head in two fingers.

I came back when she sent me back, and I served her as best I could, Quenthel sent to all five snakes. *I became the Mistress of Arach-Tinilith, and the worship of Lolth was never stronger. Isn't that what she sent me back to do?*

There was no answer.

What will become of us all? she asked Zinda.

The black-and-red-speckled snake twitched, flicked her tongue at Quenthel, and said, *That is also your responsibility, Mistress. What happens as a result of your having driven Lolth away from us will be washed away if only you can bring her back. If you can attract her good graces again, she will save us all. If not, we will be destroyed.*

Quenthel felt herself physically sag under the weight of that. Though she tried hard to muster all her training and natural fortitude, she wasn't able to sit up straight. What weighed most heavily on her was the feeling that the snakes were right. It was her fault, and she was the only one who could fix it.

When will Lolth answer? Quenthel asked, moving her fingers to Qorra.

The third viper had the most potent poison. Quenthel only let her strike when she wanted to kill, when she wanted to show no mercy at all.

Never, Qorra hissed into the high priestess's mind. *Lolth will never answer. Menzoberranzan, Arach-Tinilith, and your entire civilization are doomed without her, and she's never coming back.*

Quenthel's head spun. She was sitting on the deck of the ship of chaos but still felt as if she were about to fall over.

That isn't necessarily true, said Yngoth.

Quenthel had grown more and more dependent on Yngoth's limitless wisdom. It was his voice that tended to reassure her, and to Quenthel he sounded most like a drow.

Why was I sent back? she asked Yngoth. *Is this why? To find her?*

When you were sent back, the viper replied, *Lolth didn't need to be found. Haven't you thought all along that you were sent back to sit at the head of Arach-Tinilith? To hold that post for House Baenre and preserve Lolth's faith and Lolth's favorite in the power structure of Menzoberranzan?*

I'm not sure now, the Mistress of the Academy admitted.

You were sent back for this, Yngoth said. *Of course you were. You were sent back to become Mistress of Arach-Tinilith so that you would be the one they sent to find Lolth when the goddess chose to turn away. You were meant to be the savior of Menzoberranzan and perhaps even the savior of Lolth herself.*

Quenthel sagged a little further at that.

How can you be sure? she asked.

I'm not sure, replied Yngoth, *but it seems reasonable.*

Quenthel sighed.

It was Lolth's plan all along that I go back there, Quenthel asked, *to find her? How will I do that?*

Get to the Abyss first, replied Hsiv. The last of her vipers was never shy when it came to offering his mistress advice. *Go there first and you will be guided to Lolth by Lolth. You will know what to do.*

How do you know? Quenthel asked.

I don't, Hsiv replied, *but do you have any choice?*

Quenthel shook her head. She hadn't had any choice in a very long time.

☙ ☙ ☙

Valas looked around at the ragged drow who made up the expedition to the Abyss. They didn't look very good. Aside from Danifae, who had more energy than Valas had ever seen, who seemed transformed by their trip to Sschindylryn, they were tired, ragged, temperamental, and unfocused.

"May I ask a practical question?"

Only Danifae looked at him. Quenthel was in a world of her own, deep in her own obviously troubled thoughts. The draegloth was pacing, almost pouting if such a thing could be possible from a creature that was half drow, half demon. The wizard was nowhere to be found.

"Where has the wizard gone?" the scout asked.

Danifae pointed upward, and Valas followed her finger to see Pharaun slowly descending from the darkness above.

"Never fear, scout," the wizard said as he finally settled on the deck, "I wouldn't dream of abandoning this great expedition to rescue our mighty civilization from the brink of annihilation. We are nearly ready to begin, though there are a few more things I need to do."

Valas stopped himself from sighing. The never-ending string of delays was wearing on them all—especially when they came with little or no explanation.

"You're keeping us here," the draegloth said, giving voice to what Valas was thinking—and what the others were likely thinking as well. "You don't want to go."

The Master of Sorcere turned on the draegloth and lifted an eyebrow.

"Indeed?" said Pharaun. "Well, in that case perhaps *you* can attune the third resonant of the Blood Helm to the planar frequency of the Shadow Fringe."

There was a silence while the draegloth looked at him with narrowed eyes.

"No?" Pharaun went on. "I didn't think so. That means you're going to have to let me finish what I need to finish."

The wizard looked around at the rest of them, and Valas shrugged, casually meeting his eyes.

"This is not some mushroom-stem raft," Pharaun said to them all, "splashing about on Donigarten Lake. This vessel, if you haven't noticed, is alive. It is a being of pure chaos. It has a certain intelligence. It has the innate ability to shift between the planar walls from one reality to another. You don't simply paddle something like this. You have to make it a part of you and in turn make yourself a part of it."

He paused for effect then continued, "I am willing to do that—for the good of the expedition and for the pure curiosity of it. It's a unique opportunity to explore some fabulously outré magic. What you must all remember is that if I don't get it right, we could never make it out of this lake. Worse yet, we could find ourselves scuttled in the Shadow Deep or lost forever in the endless Abyss."

The Master of Sorcere looked around as if he was waiting for an argument. None came—even from Jeggred, but he went on anyway, "This time it will be different—the Abyss, the journey there, everything. Last time we were projected across the Astral. We were ghosts there. This time we'll actually *be* there. If we die in the Abyss, we don't snap back into our bodies. There will be no silver cord. We will be real there, and if we die . . ."

Valas wondered why the wizard stopped. Perhaps Pharaun didn't know what would happen if they died there. If you die in your own afterlife, is there an after-afterlife? Thinking about it gave Valas the beginnings of a nagging headache.

"Have any of you ever been to the Abyss before?" Pharaun asked. "Really been there, physically? Even you, Jeggred?"

The draegloth didn't answer, but his smoldering look was enough. None of them had been there, none of them knew—

"I've been there," Quenthel said. The sudden sound of her voice almost startled Valas. "I have been there as a ghost, as a visitor, and as a . . ."

Danifae took a few steps toward Quenthel then sank to her knees on the deck half a dozen paces away from her.

"What as, Mistress?" the battle-captive asked.

"I was killed," the high priestess said, her voice sounding as if it were coming from a great distance. Her vipers grew increasingly agitated as she went on. "My soul went to Lolth. I served the goddess herself for a decade, then she sent me back."

Valas's flesh ran cold, and he found himself stepping slowly away from the high priestess.

"Why?" Pharaun asked, a skeptical look on his face.

The Mistress of Arach-Tinilith turned and gave him a dark, cold stare.

"I think he means," Danifae continued for Pharaun, " why were you sent back?"

"I've never heard anything about this," the Master of Sorcere added.

"It was kept secret," said Quenthel, "for a number of reasons. There were circumstances concerning my death and the one who killed me that might have embarrassed my House. It's not a simple thing, attaining a position like the one I hold. Indeed there is no position like the one I hold . . . in Menzoberranzan, at least. It was not a position House Baenre was prepared to concede to any other House. For ten years I was simply 'away pursuing studies' or some other excuse alternating between ludicrous and clever. Eventually I returned, then things happened and I was elevated to Mistress of the Academy."

"And now you're on your way back," Danifae said in hushed, heavy tones.

"It's as if someone has a plan for you," said Pharaun.

No one said anything more. Valas walked back to the bags and finished sorting the supplies.

Danifae stood up slowly. Quenthel wasn't looking at her, but it was clear from her body language that the high priestess had finished speaking.

Danifae thought through the revelation quickly but thoroughly.

It didn't matter. It didn't change anything.

She turned, scanning the deck as she did so. The others had gone back to what they were doing. Each of them was undoubtedly going over in his own mind what Quenthel had said. She turned her back to them and stared at Jeggred. When the draegloth finally looked at her, she signaled him in sign language, careful to keep her hands close to her so the others wouldn't see.

It is time, she told him.

The draegloth nodded and glanced meaningfully at the tattered sails of human skin that sagged listlessly in the still air. Danifae nodded and began to ease her way across the deck.

It took them both several minutes to maneuver themselves behind the sail without making it obvious they were hiding.

When they were safely out of sight, Jeggred signed, *Where are we going, Mistress?*

Danifae smiled and replied, *Hunting.*

The draegloth's lips twisted into a fierce smile. The half-demon looked hungry.

Danifae stepped closer to him. She could see him stiffen, stand straight—almost at attention. The former battle-captive stepped closer still and wrapped one arm around the half-demon's huge waist. Jeggred's gray fur was warm to the touch and a little bit oily. He was surprisingly soft.

Danifae concentrated on the ring she'd taken from Zinnirit, and in the blink of an eye they were in Sschindylryn.

Jeggred took a deep breath and looked around at the dark interior of the gatehouse.

"Where are we?" he asked.

Danifae took his hand and led him to one of the gates. Not answering his question, she busied herself with the gate itself, activating it first, then tuning the location to the agreed-on meeting place. The portal blazed to life in an almost blinding torrent of violet light. Still holding Jeggred's hand, she stepped through. The draegloth didn't hesitate to follow, and they stepped out into a dimly lit ruin.

Even if Danifae didn't know exactly where they were she would have known they were on the World Above. The lighting was strange, a different color than anything found in the Underdark. The walls were made of mud bricks—very old, crumbling. Vines and moss grew in the cracks between the bricks, twisting in and out of every crevice, crawling up every wall, and matting the floor, eating away at the structure the way plants did on the World Above.

"It smells strange here," Jeggred grumbled. "What is this place?"

Danifae looked around to get her bearings. The dull gray light seeped in through dozens if not hundreds of cracks and holes in the decaying walls. On one side of the room a set of uneven steps led up to a floor above. On the other side was a similar staircase leading down. Danifae started up the stairs to the higher room, and Jeggred followed her.

"This was once a temple to the orcs' foul, grunting pig-god," she explained. "Now it's just another piece of rotting garbage being eaten away by the World Above. A suitable place to do what we've come here to do, don't you think?"

"What have we come here to do?" asked the draegloth.

Danifae, disappointed but not surprised that the subtlety was lost on the draegloth, replied, "The traitors are coming."

They came out into a more brightly lit room, and both of them had to shade their eyes with their hands. Danifae moved to a wide crack in the ancient wall and looked out onto the World Above. The sun had set, but the light was still difficult to take. In time, though, her eyes began to adjust. Half a dozen yards below her was what surface dwellers called a swamp. It was a place where water covered the ground—in most places at least—but it wasn't a proper lake. The whole area around the temple was choked with alien vegetation. The sounds of the myriad creatures of the World Above were almost deafening. The swamp crawled with life. Beyond the edge of the swamp, miles to the west, was a wide expanse of water: the end of a long river.

Danifae let out a slow breath through her nose and heard the drae-gloth scuffle on the loose rocks behind her.

"I hate this," she whispered.

"What?" Jeggred asked.

"The surface."

Danifae scanned the ground below the ruined temple. Finally she drew from a pouch one of the rings she'd taken from Zinnirit and turned it over in her fingers. The fading light played against its polished surface and picked out a scattering of ruby chips.

Pressing the ring into one of the draegloth's four hands she said, "Use this ring to return at will to the ship of chaos."

Jeggred nodded, slipped the ring on, and stood patiently behind her, listening attentively as she explained the proper use of the ring's magic. Confident that the draegloth understood, Danifae let the minutes drag on—and finally she saw them.

"There they are," she said.

The draegloth moved closer behind her, and she suppressed a gag when his breath rolled over her. She waited while he searched for them, and when he finally saw them he growled low in his throat.

"They're together," he said.

"They lied," said Danifae. "She didn't go to Menzoberranzan. She went to the Velarswood—a forest where there's a temple to . . ." She feigned difficulty in articulating the word. "Eilistraee."

Jeggred growled again and said, "And the weapons master?"

"He's made a choice," she replied.

Jeggred began to growl with every exhale. He was ready to kill. Danifae could smell it on him.

"Take the male," she whispered to the draegloth. "Just him for now."

She pushed Jeggred back away from the crack but held him so he wouldn't leave. Stepping up onto the bottom of the wound in the wall, Danifae drew herself up into the dimming light. She waved a hand over her head to attract her former mistress's attention.

It took an infuriatingly long time, but eventually Halisstra stopped at the edge of the swamp and pointed up at Danifae. Ryld looked up as well, and Halisstra waved in answer.

Danifae made exaggerated, wide gestures, an unsubtle form of the drow sign language, sending the message: *Only you.*

Halisstra turned to Ryld, and they conversed. Even from so far away Danifae could tell that Ryld was reluctant to let her go alone. The weapons master might have been a traitor to his city, his goddess, and his race, but he was no fool. Still, Halisstra managed to convince him—or command him—to stay behind. He stood with his arms crossed as Halisstra stepped gingerly into the swamp.

Danifae stepped down from the crack in the wall and took the draegloth by the shoulders.

Doing her best to withstand the half-demon's foul breath, she said, "Go. Don't let her see you."

The draegloth smiled, and a thick, ropy strand of drool dropped from his lower lip. His fangs glimmered in the dim light, and so did his burning red eyes.

Danifae thought he was the most beautiful thing she'd ever seen.

Chapter

S I X T E E N

The swamplight lynx didn't smell prey. The scent that filled the great cat's nostrils was something different. The lynx had never come across anything like it, but whatever it was, it was a predator—the odor of a meat-eater was unmistakable.

Padding softly, silently through the cold, shallow water, the lynx tipped its head up and waved its nose from side to side, honing in on the scent. A charge of energy thrilled through the cat. Its flesh tingled, its fur stood on end—a familiar feeling for the lynx, comforting, fore-telling of a kill ahead and food.

The lynx moved from shadow to shadow, still inside the treeline. It caught sight of the competing predator and recognized the shape of a man. Powerful and cunning hunters in their own right, men never respected another predator's stalking grounds. They ignored the scent markers, the scratches on trees, the most obvious signs. Its eyesight was the least of the cat's senses even in daylight, and the creature could see and smell only that the intruder was a man. It had no way of discerning the man's black skin, pointed ears, crimson eyes, and white hair.

The swamplight lynx gathered the Weave energy in its body, bared its fangs, and tightened into a crouch, ready to spring—when another scent all but slammed into its nostrils.

Another predator was approaching. It was bigger, and it smelled bad. It smelled like a scavenger.

The swamplight lynx relaxed but only a little. It watched the man, occasionally scanning the swamp's edge for the scavenger, and waited.

Ryld was surrounded.

There were noises everywhere. The place Halisstra had called a "swamp" was even more alive than the rest of the World Above, and the weapons master didn't like it at all. He could see things moving in the darkness around him. There were insects and spiders, all manner of flying creatures, and snakes . . . lots of snakes. The ground under his feet was spongy. He'd felt similar in some of the bigger fungal colonies in the Underdark, but down there it was at least quiet.

The ruined temple rose in black silhouette against the night sky in front of him. He'd watched Halisstra walk toward it through ever deepening water with an increasing certainty that she was walking toward her own demise. Going to meet Danifae was stupid, even if Halisstra had allowed him to come along, and Ryld wasn't sure why he'd let it happen. Could it be that she simply wished it and he was so accustomed to obeying priestesses that he'd obeyed her?

The weapons master took a deep breath, set his feet close together, and pressed his hands palm to palm in front of his chest. He steadied his breathing and cleared his mind as best he could, surrounded as he was by the unseen dangers of the swamp. He watched tiny yellow lights flicker in the air—some kind of bioluminescent insects moving slowly, sluggish in the cold night air. Pinpoints of light spattered across the black dome of the sky, not painful to look at and actually helping Ryld's natural darkvision. There was no other light except—

Except for a faint purple glow shimmering in chaotic waves over Ryld himself.

Faerie fire.

Ryld drew Splitter and stepped back, opening his stance, then he turned around once three hundred and sixty degrees looking for anything moving toward him—looking for Danifae. It was a dark elf who had picked him out from the dark background using the magical ability she, like all drow, was born with. Who else could it be?

She must have already killed Halisstra, Ryld thought.

The world exploded in agonizing light, and he could hear something big running at him.

Ryld had been trained to fight when unable to see, and as the foe that blinded him charged, he fell back on that training. The weapons master surprised himself with how well he'd adapted to the way sound traveled on the surface world. He timed Danifae's charge—and it had to be Danifae—so that when she was no more than three strides from him, he stepped to the side. The echoes were oddly spaced. It almost sounded as if Danifae had four legs.

That aside, Ryld had estimated correctly, and he stepped out of the way of the former battle-captive in time to feel her brush past him in a rush of cold air and an unpleasant, uncharacteristic strong musky smell.

Still blind, Ryld heard her scuffle to a stop in the ankle-deep, wet moss. She turned quickly and Ryld could feel her ready to come at him again.

Ryld heaved Splitter in front of him, again as he was trained to do. The blade never bit into flesh and bone, but the purpose of that attack wasn't so much to kill as it was to fend off. He had been blinded by some sort of conjured light, which meant that his eyesight would return in time. The first rule of fighting blind was keeping yourself alive until you weren't blind anymore.

It was exactly what he was supposed to do, but it didn't work. The moment Splitter passed to his left side, opening up his chest and face, she—it . . . something . . . dived on him. It was definitely not Danifae. It was no drow at all.

The thing that smashed Ryld to the ground was enormous and covered in thick, coarse fur. It had four strong legs each with a set of long, sharp claws that tugged at his armor but were unable to cut him through his dwarven mithral breastplate.

Ryld smelled hot, rank breath, and a name came to his mind: Jeggred.

Why would the draegloth be there with Danifae? Unless the former battle-captive had brought Quenthel with her, but would they all really waste their time running after him and Halisstra when there was still a goddess to awaken?

Ryld blinked, his sight returning in aching, cramping vibrations in his tired eyes. The claws worried at his armor and came dangerously close to his face as the creature—could it be the draegloth?—shifted in an effort to find some gap in his armor to exploit for the kill. Ryld pushed up with the flat of his blade and both his feet and rolled the heavy creature off him.

When it hit the cold, spongy ground, it wriggled on its side in an effort to get to its feet. The thing growled, and the sound was both higher in pitch and less intelligent than Jeggred's. Ryld blinked blotches of purple from his eyes and whirled around and up to his feet, Splitter in front of him to guard against the inevitable next pounce.

If it was Jeggred, the draegloth was down on all fours and attacking him only with fangs and one set of claws. Ryld batted away a rake from the thing with the flat of his blade but failed to slice off the paw. It bit at him, but he stepped back, leaning away from the attack so that the creature's fangs snapped down on thin air.

Ryld blinked again, and his eyesight returned to nearly normal. He wasn't fighting Danifae or Jeggred but some kind of furred surface animal. Ryld had seen similar animals: cats. The one that was trying to kill him was huge, ten feet from nose to tail. Mottled gray fur rippled over rolling muscles. Its tall, pointed ears twitched and moved independently of each other to track Ryld as it circled him, and the weapons master turned to keep the animal in sight at all times. Steam puffed from its nostrils into the cold air.

Ryld felt a chill run through the undersides of his arms. He had a strange feeling of relief that he was only being hunted—again—by a native surface animal. Danifae hadn't taken her revenge after all, certainly not with Jeggred as her second. The weapons master briefly entertained the idea that Halisstra was right about her former servant, but the reality of his situation intruded once again.

The animal leaped at him, and Ryld was ready for it. He had Splitter up and to the side and had just tensed his arms in preparation for a downward slice across his chest to dig at the animal's head when the thing stopped. The animal halted in midair for a heartbeat then fell. It made a sound that was halfway between a growl and a whimper when it hit the ground, already scrambling to regain its feet.

The weapons master hopped back, bringing Splitter quickly in front of him to guard against—

"Jeggred," Ryld said.

The draegloth held the huge cat by its tail, his eyes glowing red in the darkness. Even as the animal turned on him, Jeggred's lips pulled back over his teeth in a feral, hate-filled smile.

Halisstra stepped off the stairs onto what she assumed was the highest floor of the slowly crumbling structure and there she saw Danifae. A gasp passed across her parted lips at the sight of her former servant. Danifae had always been beautiful—that was part of what made her such a desirable possession—but though it hardly seemed possible, the girl had grown even more attractive. The ample curves of her strong body made an alluring silhouette in the dark space, and her bright white hair framed her round, beautiful face in a way Halisstra had never seen on her normally pragmatic and simple battle-captive.

"What's wrong?" Danifae asked, her voice quiet. "Do I look different?"

Halisstra nodded and stepped away from the top of the stairs, careful to keep her back to the wall.

"Yes, you do. Freedom agrees with you, Danifae."

"Yes, Halisstra," Danifae replied. Halisstra did not fail to miss the fact that Danifae had called her by name. "Freedom does agree with me," she continued, "but there is much to discuss and precious little time."

Halisstra arced an eyebrow and let a hand slip to the hilt of the Crescent Blade.

"You are in danger here," Danifae warned, her eyes darting to Halisstra's weapon. "I was careless and was found out."

Halisstra's blood went cold, and she said, "Found out?"

"I was gone too long," said Danifae. "I was questioned by the high priestess and the mage, and they . . . did things to me to make me tell them about you, about Ryld, and all of it. All of it that I know."

Halisstra tried to take a deep breath but found her chest tight with anxiety.

"Where are they?" Halisstra asked.

"Far away," replied Danifae, "and well prepared for their journey to the Abyss, but they sent Jeggred back with me."

Halisstra's blood ran even colder, and she said, "The draegloth? Why?"

"To kill you both."

Halisstra looked madly around the ruin and found the crack in the wall she'd earlier seen Danifae standing in. Though it meant turning her back on Danifae, Halisstra ran to the crack and began wildly scanning the dark swamp below for any sign of Ryld. There was a pain in her chest she'd never felt before. She couldn't see either the weapons master or the draegloth.

"He's out there, I assure you," said Danifae.

"So you drew me here?" Halisstra asked, not turning from her fruitless search of the swamp below. "You drew us both into a trap?"

"Yes, I did," said the former battle-captive, "but I can save you. I can save you, but I can't save you both."

"How can you stop a draegloth that has been sent to kill?" Halisstra asked. She scowled, still scanning the swamp. There were spaces where the trees were tall and thick enough to hide the surface all together.

Ryld must have gone in there, Halisstra thought, perhaps lured in by Jeggred.

"I can't stop a draegloth," Danifae admitted. "If Jeggred means to kill you both, he will, or Ryld will kill him, or I will kill him. Either way, there will be deaths tonight."

Halisstra sighed, not sure what to do and afraid that Ryld was already dead.

"I don't have to stop Jeggred," Danifae continued, "or kill him. Just go, and leave the rest to Ryld and me. If the weapons master can best the draegloth, fine. If not, I can convince Jeggred that I killed you."

"Why would he trust you?" asked Halisstra. "He'll want to see my body . . . or part of it at least. And what of Ryld?"

"Let me get you out of here," the former battle-captive said. "Get enough distance between yourself and the draegloth while he's still engaged with the weapons master and we can come to some arrangement. We'll have time to sort something out."

Halisstra shook her head and stepped away from the crack in the wall.

"I won't leave Ryld."

Halisstra smiled at the finality of her statement and the feeling that went with it.

"I can get you out of here fast," Danifae said, "and I can move Ryld almost as easily, but it has to be one at a time. Come with me now, and I'll go back for the weapons master."

Halisstra studied her former servant's face and saw nothing. Danifae didn't seem to be lying, but at the same time she didn't seem to be telling the truth. It was as if all expression had been sanded from her face. She was blank, impenetrable. That scared Halisstra.

"You've trusted me this far, Mistress."

Halisstra registered the return of the traditional title.

Danifae held out a hand to her former mistress, and said, "Trust me, Halisstra."

Confused, the First Daughter of House Melarn shook her head.

The former servant said, "The longer we do this, the longer your weapons master fights the draegloth . . . alone."

There was a brief moment of silence. Halisstra sighed, stepped toward Danifae, and took her hand. Eilistraee had been pushing her along for some time. Halisstra knew that, and she felt pushed again. She tried to remind herself of what she'd told Ryld, that Eilistraee was guiding her but no goddess was guiding Danifae.

As the interior of the ruined temple faded in a wave of vertigo and purple light to be replaced by a strange place somewhere that smelled and felt like the Underdark, Halisstra tried so hard to trust in Eilistraee that her head started to hurt. She thought about Ryld and her eyes filled with tears.

The animal turned on Jeggred, and it was all claws and fangs.

The swamp creature ripped a deep furrow in Jeggred's abdomen with its foreclaws. Blood welled up in the wound. Jeggred didn't flinch or cry out. Only a subtle narrowing of the half-demon's blazing red eyes indicated he'd felt the cut at all. The draegloth stepped in, slashing with two of his four sets of claws, but the cat leaped to the side, avoiding the attack, and at the same time stepped in again, forcing Jeggred to defend himself.

The cat was making a good showing of it, and Ryld knew it was the best chance he would have to run. By the time Jeggred managed to dispatch the beast—if he was able to at all—Ryld could be long gone. Even if he could leave Halisstra, wherever he went Jeggred would follow. If the draegloth had been sent to kill him, that's what he would do.

The cat bit at Jeggred, and the draegloth moved his arm in and allowed the creature to fasten its powerful jaws on his upper right wrist. The fangs dented the draegloth's skin but didn't puncture it. Smiling, steam pouring from his nostrils into the cold air, Jeggred drew the claws of both of his left hands along the cat's flanks. The animal opened its mouth to howl in pain, and the half-demon's arm came free.

Jeggred let the animal cut him. Four parallel lines of deep red blood traced behind the cat's raking claws. The animal was trying to hurt the draegloth in any way it could, but it was wounded and desperate and was making rash decisions. On the other hand, Jeggred only *appeared* feral. He was in control of himself. Ryld could see it in every twitch of the draegloth's eyes that anticipated the cat's attacks three or four moves ahead. Though the animal clawed him, Jeggred got in closer and wrapped one of his bigger, stronger arms around the animal's belly. The draegloth's claws made a popping sound when they punctured the cat's flesh, then a ripping sound as they opened its underside in three deep, ragged incisions.

Things started spilling out of the madly writhing animal. Long ropes of intestines, things that must have been its kidneys, and other organs rode a torrent of steaming blood onto the spongy moss. Jeggred held the animal close to him and squeezed until more came out and kept squeezing until the cat was dead.

Ryld stood a few paces away, watching, ready. He thought back on his training and the single overriding principal of defending against claws. Things with claws—any number of demons, trolls, and the like—stabbed then pulled down. Claw attacks always came high and ripped down. All he had to do was be ready for that. There was the fact that anything that attacked with claws would never parry. If Ryld set his blade against Jeggred's attack, the draegloth would avoid contact with the keen edge or risk dismemberment. Ryld could use that to his advantage simply by defending against the draegloth's arms as if they were swords. Jeggred would be put on the defensive by being unable to defend, and he wouldn't parry Ryld's attacks, but he would dodge.

The draegloth looked up from his still-quivering kill and bared his knifelike fangs at Ryld. The weapons master stood his ground. He wasn't as strong as Jeggred, and he might not be as fast, but he was smarter and better trained.

That might be enough.

"Why are you here?" Ryld asked the draegloth. "Surely you didn't come all this way just to save me from that cat."

The half-demon, covered in the animal's still-hot blood, was steaming.

"I was told things about you, weapons master," Jeggred growled. "Disturbing things."

Ryld held Splitter in both hands in front of him and said, "I can only imagine."

"The priestess I can understand," said the draegloth. He took a wide, slow step sideways, moving away from the dead animal. "They're feeling particularly betrayed by Lolth. They seek power and communion, so it seems only fitting that if one goddess turns her back on them, they might seek the embrace of another, but you?"

"I can't seek the embrace of a goddess?" asked Ryld, stalling as he examined the half-demon for wounds and weaknesses.

"Why would you," asked the draegloth, "when you can have the embrace of a flesh and blood female?"

"You have me all figured out," the weapons master said, surprised that the draegloth seemed to have done just that.

"My mistress has," Jeggred said with a shrug. He stepped to the side again, beginning to circle Ryld. "She even now stands over the corpse of your traitor priestess. I get the pleasure of ending your life."

"It'll be a particularly painful and violent death, no doubt," Ryld said, irony absent from his voice.

The draegloth smiled, coughed out a laugh, and charged.

The big claws came in first, high, aimed for his chest. Ryld whirled Splitter in front of him then abruptly stopped the blade's spin and sliced up to parry the draegloth's right arm. As he expected, Jeggred drew his arm back sharply in an effort to avoid the enchanted greatsword. Ryld quickly changed direction, tucking the blade in, stepping back, and stabbing at the dodging half-demon. The tip of Ryld's sword penetrated the draegloth's furred hide under his shoulder blade to a depth of an inch or two. The half-demon, bleeding, hopped back, sliding off the blade.

Ryld stepped back too, rolling the greatsword in both hands in a slow figure eight in front of him.

Soon, one of them would be dead.

S E V E N T E E N

"Where is he?" Quenthel asked, her red eyes wild with barely contained fury.

"He's gone to kill them," Danifae answered.

Pharaun watched the exchange from a distance. He had sat cross-legged in the exact center of the deck, right in front of the mainmast, precisely where Aliisza had told him to sit. He could feel the ship of chaos vibrating beneath him, reacting to the power he was exerting over it.

"On whose command?" the high priestess asked.

"On yours, Mistress," Danifae answered, "through me."

"Through you?" Quenthel repeated. "Through *you?*"

Pharaun pressed one of his hands against the deck and felt the pulse in a cluster of veins that was growing there.

The high priestess slapped Danifae across the face, but the battle-captive stood her ground.

"Halisstra Melarn and Ryld Argith are traitors," Danifae said. "They are traitors to this expedition, traitors to Lolth, and traitors to drow civilization. You know that, I know that, and Jeggred knows that. That's why he's there."

"On *your* command," the Mistress of the Academy pressed, "not mine."

"He's doing what has to be done," Danifae replied, her voice finally showing some emotion: anger and impatience. "You weren't able to give him the order, so I did it for you."

Pharaun laughed at the exchange and at the thrill of the ship reacting to his thoughts and touch. He found Danifae's hijacking of the draegloth fascinating.

"We have the time, Mistress," Pharaun offered in Danifae's defense—if only for the sport of it. "Why not let the draegloth clean up some messes? If Mistress Melarn is indeed a traitor, and after watching her in the face of Lolth's temple that's hardly a surprise, consider it a favor from a loyal young priestess in your service. Master Argith, on the other hand, is likely not a traitor to the City of Spiders. He lacks the necessary spark for rebellion, I'm afraid. If you wish to be concerned with anything it should be that the weapons master might actually kill your nephew."

Quenthel looked over at Pharaun, who met her gaze for a moment then returned his attention to the ship. The high priestess glanced at Danifae, who stood tall and resolute, giving no ground. The Mistress of the Academy held her scourge in one hand, and the vipers curled around the fingers of her other. She looked down at the vipers then back at Danifae. Pharaun watched the whole thing while feeling the ship's pulse momentarily quicken.

Quenthel took a step away and turned her back on Danifae, who sighed. Pharaun thought the battle-captive might have been disappointed.

"That," Danifae said to Quenthel's back, "is why Jeggred serves me now."

They began to circle each other, testing their steps on the spongy, uneven moss. Jeggred looked down and considered the puncture wound. He lifted one eyebrow in a sort of grudging salute then let his tongue unroll from his mouth. The black, rough tongue slowly licked the wound. When he smiled next, Jeggred's own blood stained his razor-sharp fangs.

Just keep your distance, Ryld told himself. Keep your distance and go for the hands.

The draegloth charged again, and again his claws came in high at first. Ryld had the wide, heavy blade of Splitter parallel to the ground. All he had to do was bend his knees, step in, then stand, and he met the draegloth's descending rake.

The weapons master stepped into the attack and parried precisely as if the huge claw was a sword blade. Jeggred brought his smaller claws down fast and hard so that Ryld barely had to press the parry. The draegloth drove his own arm down onto the blade. Ryld felt a tug, then release. Blood sprayed. Jeggred's right, smaller hand tumbled through the air and bounced once when it hit the moss.

Ryld didn't allow himself the time to celebrate having cut off one of the draegloth's hands. He stepped back away from the blood that was spraying from the half-demon's stump. Jeggred screamed—an unsettling, ear-rattling sound—and he started backing quickly away.

Well aware that the half-demon could change direction very quickly, Ryld stepped back too, though not quite as far.

"You will pay for that with your hands and feet, whelp," Jeggred hissed around clenched teeth. "I was following orders when I came here to kill you, but now—" he held up the stump from which blood was still pumping—"it's personal."

A refreshing cycle of darkness had passed during which Gromph alternated between brief periods of Reverie, infuriating sessions with the same handful of winged halflings, and the casting of powerful divinations.

The darkness was a welcome comfort to the archmage's light-ravaged eyes. He had spent nights under the open sky before—though not many—and he had seen stars. The stars in the Green Fields seemed a little brighter than those visible from Faerûn. Gromph wasn't familiar enough with either to sense any difference between the number and positions of the stars there and Faerûn's, but he knew they were different. The Green Fields was a separate reality all together.

The needle-like plant that covered the rolling hills was something he'd seen before as well. In the trade language of the World Above it was called "grass." The halflings of the Green Fields called it "ens." There were other things he'd seen before in the World Above: "flowers," "trees," and things like that. It made Gromph wonder if there was an Underdark of sorts somewhere beneath his feet—then he reminded himself that he wouldn't be there long enough to find out.

The halflings he'd first encountered had all but adopted him. A few of the little folk seemed genuinely happy to receive him. The one who called himself Dietr and who claimed to have been from Faerûn was suspicious but wanted something—something he wouldn't or couldn't ask for. However they approached Gromph, all of them were easy and casual with each other. They had a sense of hospitality and were determined to help him. They brought him food that fell into one of two categories: heavy and swimming in fragrant cream sauces or a confusing variety of sweet, fresh fruit. Neither appealed much to Gromph, but he ate enough to give him the energy he needed to prepare spells and collect himself for his return to Menzoberranzan.

Gromph hadn't moved far from the spot at which he'd first appeared. The Green Fields seemed to be exactly that: an endless open landscape of green grass and other plants. Gromph hadn't seen a building of any kind, and it appeared as if the halflings lived out in the open, slowly but constantly moving.

When the light returned, Gromph knew he would have to be on his way. He cast the last in a series of divinations that would help him not only return to the Prime Material Plane but go back to Toril, back to the Underdark below Faerûn, and back to Menzoberranzan herself. It was no mean feat, and certainly Dyrr hadn't expected him to be able to accomplish it, but then Dyrr hadn't expected him to break free of the imprisonment either. The lichdrow's insistence on underestimating him would, possibly, allow Gromph the luxury of beating him.

The archmage stood, shielding his eyes from the pervasive light and watched Dietr and one of the females approaching with another tray of fruit. Dietr held a waterskin.

"We thought you might want breakfast," Dietr said.

The halfling looked at Gromph with that same expression of vague hopefulness and fear. The female barely seemed to notice him at all.

"I've had enough of your food," the archmage said, "and I'm taking my leave of your pointless expanse."

"Pointless expanse?" the female repeated, her ambivalence all at once replaced by anger. "Who are you to dismiss the Green Fields?"

"Who are you to speak to me at all?" Gromph asked.

He waited for an answer, but all he got was a squinting sneer from the winged female. Dietr's eyes bounced back and forth between them, and his breathing grew shallow and expectant.

"Leave me in peace," Gromph commanded.

When the two halflings didn't immediately turn to leave, the archmage raised an eyebrow. The female did her best to stare him down, but her best wasn't anywhere near good enough.

"You were alive once," Gromph asked her, "weren't you?"

Neither of the halflings responded right away.

"This one"—Gromph indicated Dietr with a wave of his hand—"was a living, material being on Faerûn. Where did you live before you went to your Great Beyond?"

Again the female said nothing.

"I'll admit to being curious," Gromph went on. "If you died on whatever world you came from and your soul came here to rest in peace for all eternity, what happens when I kill you here? Does your soul go somewhere else, or are you consigned to oblivion? Will one of your weakling halfling godlings stop me? Even a halfling god on his home plane can be an inconvenience I'm sure, but it might be amusing to make the effort anyway."

"If you think you can kill me, interloper," the female sneered, "try it now or shut up."

Gromph smiled, and it must have been that expression that made Dietr finally step forward, his hands held out in a gesture of weak conciliation.

"Easy," he said. "Easy there, everybody."

Gromph laughed.

"That's better," said Dietr, a grin plastered across his cherubic face. "If the venerable drow would like to leave, then he's certainly free to go on his way."

"There will be no violence here," the female said, her voice even and strong. "If I have to blast you to pieces to ensure that . . ."

"We've all been blasted to pieces at least once, haven't we?" Dietr said. "No one wants to do that again, so let's all be friends."

Gromph took a deep breath and said, "I will be leaving, but there will be residual effects from the gate, and you won't want to go where I'm going. Back away or not, I'll leave that up to you."

The female continued to stare daggers at him, but still she drifted the slightest bit back from the archmage.

Gromph looked her up and down. She was half his size, and she looked ridiculous. The whole world looked ridiculous—the whole world *was* ridiculous. Dyrr had sent him there on purpose, and looking at the winged halfling in her grass-infested setting made Gromph angrier and angrier by the second. Dyrr was trying to get rid of him, was trying to dismiss him by sending him to that pastoral universe, and Gromph Baenre, Archmage of Menzoberranzan, would not be dismissed.

"Fine," Gromph said, and he began to cast his spell.

He was only vaguely aware of the female moving farther away, and he assumed that Dietr was doing the same thing. The words of the spell came easily enough, and the gestures went smoothly from one to another. There was a part of the spell that few of the experienced casters who'd ever done it knew could be manipulated, and Gromph began to maneuver it. He wove into the spell a subtle modification that would take him *precisely* where he wanted to go.

He finished and could feel himself falling backward out of the Green Fields—and he felt a hand on his arm.

There was light everywhere but it wasn't too bright.

There was sound coming from all around him but it wasn't too loud.

There were colors in the air but they weren't too vibrant.

They were moving in every direction at once but not too fast.

They appeared in Menzoberranzan, their feet on solid rock, their eyes comforted by the gloom lit by faerie fire.

Gromph turned and looked at the halfling. He was naked, shaking, his wings were gone, and he looked older, smaller, and weaker. His eyes were red, his skin dry and yellow. His face, twisted in a rictus of suffering, revealed gray, decaying teeth.

With a sigh, the archmage turned to survey his surroundings. It was Menzoberranzan—the Bazaar. He'd made it. There weren't many drow in the streets, and the few who were there recognized the archmage immediately. The smart ones scattered.

Nauzhror, Gromph thought, sending the name along the Weave to the Baenre wizard.

After a tense moment of silence a voice echoed in Gromph's mind: *Archmage. It is gratifying to hear you again. Welcome back to Menzoberranzan.*

It was Nauzhror.

Before he could reply, Gromph was distracted by a high-pitched whine. He looked down at the desiccated halfling.

"You are a fool," Gromph said to Dietr.

The halfling cowered from his gaze and quivered.

"I didn't ask you to come with me," Gromph added, "and you don't belong here any more than I belonged in the Green Fields."

"I wanted . . ." the halfling began then coughed. Dust puffed from his throat. "I wanted to live again."

"Why?" Gromph asked.

"My mother. She has been attending seances to contact me. She has no other family and needs me to support her."

Gromph laughed.

"It's not funny," Dietr said.

Gromph laughed more then cast a spell.

"An amusing diversion, traitor," he said into the air, "but a temporary one. We'll finish it in the Bazaar. Now."

He still had ten words left in the spell but had nothing more to say.

The lichdrow has been hiding in House Agrach Dyrr, Nauzhror sent. *The siege continues at a stalemate.*

"I don't understand," Dietr said.

Gromph turned to look down at the halfling again.

"Can you get me home?" Dietr asked. "Can you send me back to Luiren?"

Gromph raised an eyebrow at the little creature's audacity then slid his tongue around a quick divination. Obvious as it was by the halfling's appearance, it didn't hurt to be certain. The spell revealed a telltale glow around the slight humanoid.

Where have you been? Nauzhror asked.

Nowhere I'd like to visit again, he replied, *but someone's come back with me.*

I see, said Nauzhror. *The gate effect seems to have given him some kind of physical form.*

But he died on this plane, Gromph added, *so when he came back. . . .*

"Yes," the archmage finally answered the halfling. "I can take you anywhere you want to go. Of course, I won't."

The halfling shook, and Gromph thought he could actually hear the creature's bones rattle.

"Please . . . ?" the halfling whimpered.

"Your mother will not be happy to see you, Dietr," Gromph said. "You died. Remember? You came back to this world unbidden. You came back as a . . ."

It is a huecuva, Nauzhror provided.

"An undead creature," Gromph said to the halfling. "You're a huecuva. Do you know what that is?"

The halfling shook his head, terror plain in his bloodshot eyes.

Gromph, my young friend, the lichdrow's voice reverberated in the wizard's head, *welcome back. Of course I accept your gracious invitation. It will be my honor to attend you on your last day.*

Gromph nodded, mumbled through a simple necromancy, and directed it at the halfling. The archmage felt the undead creature come under his control.

"Stand up straight," Gromph commanded, and Dietr instantly complied, though it seemed to cause him some discomfort.

Gromph cast another spell on him, one that set a flicker of magical fire playing over the halfling's dead flesh.

"No . . ." the halfling muttered. "Please . . ."

Gromph tightened his grip on his staff and conjured a globe of protective force around himself.

"Please don't . . ." the huecuva pleaded.

Gromph looked around the Bazaar—abandoned tents and stalls, most with their wares secured under lock and key, and a few curious drow eyes watching from safe places in the surrounding stalactites.

"Won't you please just let me—?" Dietr begged.

"Silence," Gromph said, and the halfling was compelled to obey. "You decided to come through with me, Dietr, and now you're in Menzoberranzan, not Luiren. In Menzoberranzan, undead are property."

The huecuva's mouth worked in silence, and his skin crawled over his bones.

Gromph felt something, a presence, and quickly scanned the Bazaar again. At the far end of the wide thoroughfare was a splash of green light. The spell he'd cast on Dietr continued to give Gromph the ability to see a distinctive aura around undead, and the green light was just such an emanation, but all Gromph saw was the aura—a smudge of green light surrounding empty space.

Gromph rushed through another incantation, leaning his staff against his chest so he could use both hands to work the magic. Twisting tendrils of blue-hot flame leaped from his fingertips, growing as they made their way unerringly at the green shadow. The fire shuddered in the air and was drawn thin. It poured into a spot at the top of the shadow and disappeared into it.

The crown, Nauzhror sighed.

"Stand in front of me," Gromph said to the halfling.

The huecuva did precisely as he was told, even as the wave of blue fire shot back at Gromph. The flames hit the halfling full in the chest, and activated the protective spell Gromph had cast on him. The blue fire was replaced by a flash of red-orange that carried back along the path of the reflected spell. The green shadow was replaced by the fully revealed form of the lichdrow Dyrr, who was no longer invisible.

The fire from the huecuva's defensive aura burned the lich, making Gromph smile. He looked at the halfling and saw that Dietr was smoking, his dead flesh smoldering. His face was twisted with agony.

"Go," Gromph commanded. "Kill the lich."

Dyrr cast a spell on him, but Gromph's defenses proved capable of turning it away. It made the archmage a little dizzy, and that was all. Dietr staggered forward, reluctant but compelled to act. He wasn't moving fast enough.

"Kill the lich," Gromph called after him, "and I'll send you home to your mother."

Dietr believed the lie and broke into a run. Dyrr moved up to meet him and raked a clawed hand across the huecuva's face. Red-orange fire flared at the touch, blowing blistering heat into the lichdrow's masked face.

Dyrr threw up an arm, but the damage had been done. He roared, frustrated and angry.

Gromph was already working his next spell. Before Dyrr could strike again, it took effect, and the lichdrow's arm stopped in midswipe. Gromph hadn't quite expected the spell to work, but it had. Dyrr was frozen.

"Take me home!" the undead halfling shrieked.

He raked his own set of undead talons across Dyrr's sunken cheeks. The frozen lichdrow growled at the pain and humiliation of the wound and was able to move again.

Taking advantage of Dyrr's misdirected rage at the huecuva,

Gromph channeled the energy of a minor divination into a blast of arcane fire. He sent the silvery light pouring over the lichdrow and had to close his own eyes against its brilliance.

Dyrr had been casting a spell—likely one that would have blasted Dietr to flinders—but the arcane fire took him full in the face. His spell was ruined, and the lichdrow was burned again.

You're hurting him, Grendan said into Gromph's mind.

Dietr struck again, digging a deep furrow into the lichdrow's fore-arm. Thick, dead blood oozed slowly from the wound.

The lichdrow looked at Gromph, and the archmage could see in his undead eyes that he was hurt, and hurt badly. Gromph smiled, and—

Dietr exploded in a shower of black fire, dead flesh, and yellowed bones.

What's happening? Nauzhror asked.

The sphere of magical energy that surrounded Gromph winked out—its magic spent—as the archmage realized that the black fire that had destroyed his huecuva hadn't come from Dyrr.

The lichdrow looked up into the air over the Bazaar, and Gromph followed his gaze.

Nimor Imphraezl hung suspended on batlike wings a dozen yards above the floor of the Bazaar.

Wings? Gromph thought.

I knew he was no true drow, said Nauzhror.

"Well," Nimor said to the lich, his voice deeper, weightier than Gromph remembered, "seems you need me after all."

EIGHTEEN

Ryld stood knee-deep in the freezing water of the cold swamp. Jeggred was nowhere to be seen. The constant noise made it hard to pick out the sound of the draegloth moving. The strange smells masked Jeggred's rancid breath. The pinpoint stars and the odd patch of bioluminescence made it impossible to see the draegloth in the cold water and thick vegetation. The faerie fire the strange swamp cat had cast on him had long since faded away.

He saw things moving in the water from time to time, mostly snakes, but no disturbances big enough to be the draegloth. Something slid past his leg, but there was no sign on the slime-covered surface that anything had passed by. It was definitely something alive, but it couldn't possibly be Jeggred. It didn't touch him again, whatever it was.

Careful with each step, Ryld made his way across the swamp much more slowly than he'd hoped. The thin coating of bright green algae that covered the water made it impossible for the weapons master to see his feet. With each step his boot met some resistance: a rock, something soft, something that might have been alive, something that was solid and round like a quarterstaff—there were a lot of those—and something sharp like a dagger blade.

A bubble as big as Ryld's fist slowly expanded on the surface a few feet in front of him, sat there for a few seconds, then popped. Ryld stopped and watched it and winced when the smell of the air that had been trapped in the bubble finally wafted past his nose. The smell was reminiscent of the draegloth's horrid breath, but it was different enough that Ryld was sure that it wasn't Jeggred who'd sent up the bubble—and it wasn't the first such bubble he'd seen.

Ryld stepped forward, his foot again brushing past some hard object below the water. He used a Melee Magthere technique to slow his breathing and steady the shivering that threatened to slow his reaction time. He could see his breath condensing in the air in front of him in puffs of white steam when he exhaled, the air cold enough to make his teeth sting when he inhaled.

An explosion of water doused his face and made him close his eyes. The water was thick with slime and grainy bits of something—Ryld couldn't even guess what. His eyes blazed with flashes of yellow light and pain that made his jaw tense. Still, he brought his sword up in front of him and slashed twice at whatever it was that had splashed him. His blade met no resistance.

From much farther below, a set of claws grabbed at his left thigh, punctured, then pulled down. The claws dragged deep, ragged furrows in his skin, and Ryld could feel the heat of his own blood soaking his leg then cooling when it mixed with the cold water of the swamp.

Stepping back and stabbing down, Ryld tripped over something in the water that felt like a length of petrified rope. Though he did his best to judge where the draegloth must have been to have clawed him like that, Splitter sank into the spongy ground under the water, never touching Jeggred. Ryld fell backward until the water wrapped him in its freezing embrace.

The draegloth's next attack pushed one of Ryld's arms off the pommel of his greatsword and flipped it out to his side. Another set of deep cuts appeared on the underside of his left arm. Ryld wanted to scream, but he was under water, so he kept his mouth shut and brought his greatsword back under control. Even in the roar of swirling water that overwhelmed his hearing, the weapons master could sense the draegloth's jaws snap closed half an inch from his throat.

The draegloth was on top of him, and all the half-demon had to do was keep Ryld under water and eventually the weapons master would drown. The mistake the draegloth made was to reveal his position so clearly, though, and Ryld took full advantage of that mistake.

Pressing up with one leg, Ryld felt the heavy weight of the half-demon. The weapons master pressed harder, curling backward and straightening his leg—not an easy task since the draegloth outweighed Ryld by more than two hundred pounds. He almost had the draegloth rolled over his head, but—maybe due to resistance from the water, the cold, shivering, or exhaustion—Ryld's knees gave way, and the draegloth fell onto him.

Jeggred's claws found the underside of Ryld's breastplate and made some shallow but painful cuts in the weapons master's belly. The cold water slowed the flow of blood, though. Ryld almost subconsciously noted the irony in that. He would drown in the water that was keeping him from bleeding to death.

Ryld pressed again, using Splitter instead of his legs. Either the draegloth feared the greatsword or being totally submerged made him lighter, but Ryld managed to roll the half-demon off him. He made a few more blind jabs with Splitter to keep the draegloth at bay while he stood.

When Ryld's head finally cleared the water, he looked around for Jeggred even before he started to breathe again. The draegloth was nowhere to be seen. Ryld struggled to his feet, slipping twice on what felt like slime-covered rocks. Still he managed to get Splitter up in front of him in both hands and ready.

Ryld staggered through the water and across more odd obstructions under it, several paces from where he guessed that Jeggred should have been lying after the weapons master rolled him off.

He would have kept going but stopped when he heard another loud splash behind him.

Ryld spun, keeping his sword up and ready, and saw a disturbance on the water: what he thought looked like signs of a struggle. Puzzled that Jeggred would be so brazen after having effectively taken Ryld by surprise more than once in that cursed swamp, the weapons master took one step closer to the splashing with his sword in front of him and over his head in an effort to be ready for any eventuality.

The draegloth burst out of the swamp in a flurry of claws and legs. Water arced from his white mane as his head snapped back. He was wrapped in dark green ropes, some sort of plant he must have gotten himself tangled in. Ryld thought he saw the plants move, slithering against Jeggred's body like constricting snakes.

Jeggred had barely enough time to take a deep breath. As quickly as he came up, the draegloth disappeared into another swirling eddy that broke up the slime covering the water.

Ryld didn't have time to understand what he'd seen. Something wrapped itself around his ankle and pulled. The weapons master knew a hundred tricks to keep him on his feet even if someone really wanted to pull him down, but as much as he tried, whatever it was that had him was too strong.

So he cut it.

Splitter was still in his hands and still as sharp a sword as ever saw battle in the Underdark. Ryld brought the weapon stabbing down along the side of his body then in and through whatever had grabbed him.

It wasn't easy—the thing around his ankle was as sturdy as it was strong—but he severed it and stopped short of cutting off his own foot. Ryld struggled backward through the water then stopped and turned when he saw something moving in the corner of his eye.

Half a dozen of the green, ropy vines were sticking up out of the water like snakes scanning for their next meal. Ryld saw no eyes, no mouths, only green stalks as big around as one of the weapons master's sturdy wrists. They had no faces, but they were very much alive and appeared for all the world as if they were looking for him.

One of the vines burst toward him, unraveling itself from the water to snake quickly through the air at Ryld's throat.

The weapons master sliced fast and hard at chest level and took the first four inches off the end of the attacking vine. Greenish-yellow sap leaped from it like blood from a wound, and the vine quivered then fell into the roiling, slime-covered water.

Another vine tried to wrap itself around Ryld from behind, and he could feel even more of them worrying him from beneath the surface. Ryld kept Splitter moving in fast, fluid motions in front of him and to either side, cutting through the water, taking the ends off one animated vine after another.

Jeggred came back up, gasping for breath and ripping at a mass of the dark green vines. He was covered in the swamp slime, vine sap, and blood. One of the vines slipped around his face and into his mouth—a mistake. The draegloth bit down, and the bloodlike sap splashed over his cheeks. The vine quivered and went dead, but half a dozen more burst out of the water to take its place, and the draegloth was dragged under once again.

This swamp, Ryld thought as he chopped down two more attacking vines, will kill us both before we can kill each other.

Another reason to hate the World Above.

Jeggred came back up again for just long enough to take another breath, and Ryld got the feeling that the draegloth was finally getting the upper hand over the damnable vines. Ryld cut through another vine then sliced off one that had almost managed to get all the way around his wounded thigh. The vines were still coming at him one after another, and Ryld had no way of knowing how many there were or if, let alone when, they might finally give up or he might kill the last of them. That and the possibility that the draegloth might come at him again made up the weapons master's mind.

Ryld looked around, flicking his greatsword to his right to slice a vine then in front of him to cut through another, letting the movement of the vines in his peripheral vision chose his targets for him while he scanned for an escape route.

To his right—he had lost all sense of direction a long time before so had no idea if he was facing north, south, east, or west—the water gave way to slightly more solid if not entirely dry land. Larger trees with long, whiplike branches made a forest of thin lines. Behind those hanging branches Ryld saw a scattering of orange lights that must have been torches burning in the distance.

He knew there might be any number of sentient creatures that could have lit those torches, and surely none of them were drow. Still, he might be able to use any sort of habitation to his advantage. If Jeggred chased him there, and it was a human town, an orc town, or an elf town, they might not like dark elves, but they'd be terrified by the draegloth. That could buy Ryld time, if not allies.

Another vine managed to get around his ankle and tug. Ryld went down to one knee, his face almost falling under the slimy water before he managed to slice the vine off him. He left a cut in his boot that let in the water, and he shivered. Free of the vine, the weapons master ran. He didn't bother trying to be quiet but splashed headlong through the knee-deep water. Behind him, Jeggred surfaced again, tore at the vines still covering his midsection, roared, took a deep breath, and went back down.

Ryld stepped onto dry ground and hopped in an unseemly fashion as a set of vines worried at his heels. The ground was slippery and muddy, covered in patches with slick moss, but Ryld continued running, working past the occasional loss of footing. From behind him came the draegloth's peculiar growl and a flurry of splashes. As Ryld ran through the stinging, whiplike branches, dodging between the close-set trees while barely managing to keep on his feet, he could hear the half-demon panting, tearing, and growling behind him. Jeggred had surfaced again and was fighting his way free of the vines.

The weapons master ran on, and soon the sounds of the struggling draegloth were joined by the faint echo of voices ahead. He came out of the forest of whiplike branches, still at an all-out run. The clearing was wide and relatively dry. A collection of stumps replaced the trees, and Ryld jumped up onto one of them then hopped to another and another, making his way toward the settlement. The stumps provided more even footing and were less slippery than the muddy, mossy ground.

The torches burned from long poles stuck into the ground in a circle around a collection of a dozen small shacks and tattered tents. Even Ryld, who knew little of the World Above, could tell that the settlement was a temporary one and not an established village. The voices he heard echoing from one of the more permanent-looking buildings sounded human. The weapons master could pick out the occasional word in the human's common trade language. He'd learned the language at Melee Magthere but had few opportunities to use it, and many words were still unfamiliar to him.

Off to one side of the settlement was a huge pile of trees, cut down, stripped of their branches, and stacked carefully in a pyramid almost ten feet tall. In Menzoberranzan it would have been a king's ransom in wood.

Ryld made his way one stump at a time toward the bigger building but paused briefly to sheathe Splitter—and he was hit hard from behind. He fell forward off the stump, the greatsword still in his right hand, and pain blazed from his back. He fell onto a stump, pushed off, rolled forward, and saw the dark shape of Jeggred scrambling up behind him. The weapons master kicked out hard with both feet and smashed the draegloth between his legs. Jeggred grunted and backed off, long enough for Ryld to get to his feet.

Splitter in both hands, Ryld sent a feint at the draegloth's midsection. Jeggred fell for it, spinning to the side. The weapons master hopped back up onto one of the stumps and jumped backward again from stump to stump. The soaking-wet draegloth was covered in slime, sap, and blood. His crimson eyes blazed in the darkness, and steam poured from his mouth and nostrils.

Ryld tried to think of something to say, perhaps to taunt the draegloth, but his mind was a blank. Pharaun would have had a thousand irritating quips on the tip of his tongue, enough to drive his opponent to distraction, but Ryld could only keep his mouth closed and his mind on the fight. The two of them had gone well beyond conversation anyway.

The Master of Melee Magthere knew that the building was behind him. He could see the orange firelight from the windows growing brighter and could hear the voices growing louder. There didn't seem to be any change in the tone of the random bits of conversation that drifted out the window. No alarm had been raised.

Jeggred clawed at him with one of his larger hands, and Ryld stepped in to cut his arm but found out the hard way that the attack was a feint. The claws of the draegloth's remaining smaller hand ripped across Ryld's face. The weapons master stepped back, and there were suddenly no more stumps behind him. He slipped on the muddy ground and at the same time slashed across his opponent's midsection. The tip of his greatsword traced a line of red across Jeggred's thigh, and the draegloth drew away long enough to allow Ryld to get his footing and jump three long paces backward.

Orange firelight lit the battle-ravaged draegloth and glittered off his massive, daggerlike teeth. With a fang-lined sneer, the draegloth launched himself at Ryld. All the weapons master could do was bring up his hands—and his sword—to meet him.

Jeggred hit him hard enough to drive the air from Ryld's lungs and push his greatsword into him so hard it sliced into the side of his face, nearly cutting the weapons master's ear off. Ryld felt his feet leave the ground, his body completely at the mercy of the draegloth's inertia. They went through a window, glass shattering into millions of tiny knives that cut them both in a hundred places. Ryld could only close his eyes and grunt when he hit a wood floor so hard with the heavy draegloth on top of him that at least one of his ribs snapped like a twig.

The draegloth rolled, and Ryld pushed him off. Before he knew what was happening, they were both sitting on the floor of some kind of ramshackle tavern surrounded by a dozen very surprised humans.

Let it in, Aliisza whispered into Pharaun's mind, *but not too far.*

Pharaun sat on the deck, his legs crossed, his eyes closed, and his palms pressed down against the pulsating surface of the living vessel. He tried to sort out the sensations that were coming at him. Some were physical, some were emotional, and some came in forms Pharaun had never imagined. He could smell something like algae cakes being grilled over an open fire. Flashes of light pulsed behind his eyelids and left trails and tendrils in their wake. The sound of the ship's pulse hummed in his ears. He grimaced when a horrid taste like rotting fish rolled across his tongue. That all happened at once then changed.

You will use your body to steer it, Aliisza continued, *as much as your mind.*

Pharaun could feel that she was right. A wave of hopelessness came from nowhere and made his flesh crawl. Almost at the same time he was charged with adrenaline and felt as if he could lift the ship physically over his head and throw it across the endless Astral and into the Abyss that way.

Like that, Aliisza whispered. *Yes . . .*

It wasn't wind or water that powered the ship of chaos but desire, entropy, malice, and confusion—those things and others like them.

You will have to gather the will to move, Aliisza went on, *which should be easy enough for you. Learn how to channel it through the ship and into the planar medium around you. There's no way to learn how to do that. You simply have to give yourself over to it, while keeping it at bay at the same time. Do you understand?*

Pharaun nodded, not wanting to speak.

Something entered his skin at the wrist—a thin tendril like a length of string. The Master of Sorcere could feel it slip into a vein, tapping his blood. He tried to jerk his hand away, but his fingers were stuck to the deck.

Don't panic, Aliisza sent. *It won't take enough of your blood to weaken you, but it must have some or the connection will fail.*

You're asking me to trust it? Pharaun asked her. *To trust this construct of demonic chaos?*

He felt her touch his cheek, her fingers warm and dry, but he couldn't see her. She remained invisible, insisting that he not reveal her presence to the others. Pharaun was content to keep her a secret.

Another wave of conflicting emotions rolled through him, and he rode it out.

The ship will feel what you feel, Aliisza told him, *even as you feel what it feels. It will follow your commands now. When you're ready, will it into the Shadow Fringe and on from there.*

Will it? asked the mage.

The same way you would lift your arm or open your eyes, she answered.

That easy?

The alu-fiend laughed and said, *There are three sentient creatures out of a thousand that can do what you have done, my dear. Bonding with a ship of chaos is a dangerous proposition.*

How so?

If it hadn't accepted you, it would have killed you, she replied, *and in a very ugly, mean way.*

Pharaun sighed, interested but not surprised.

You would have let it kill me? he asked.

Aliisza thought about it for a long time then said, *You have to do this, one way or the other. I had faith in you.*

Pharaun caught the sarcasm in her tone and cracked a smile. She was an alu-fiend and by all rights on opposing sides of a bloody, ever-unfolding war. Why would she care if the ship of chaos killed him or drove him mad?

The tendrils slipped out of his wrists, and his palms came free of the deck.

Navigating the ship will require your full attention, Aliisza advised, *but if you're adrift or on a predetermined course, you will still be able to speak with your comrades and even cast spells.*

Convenient, the mage remarked.

The ship of chaos was a war ship, Pharaun, she replied. *It was created to fight, and the tanar'ri who built it had no interest in having the most powerful spellcaster among them bound to the deck, helpless and mute. The ship will require a lot of you but not everything. Don't give it any more than it needs.*

Cryptic, the mage shot back. *I like that.*

"Are you all right?" a voice asked, and Pharaun thought at first that it was Aliisza.

You know perfectly well, he thought to her, *that if I wasn't well I would simply—"*

He realized that it wasn't Aliisza who'd spoken but Quenthel.

"Master Mizzrym. . . ." the high priestess said.

Pharaun opened his eyes but had to blink several times before he could see clearly. The Mistress of Arach-Tinilith was standing over him, arms folded across her chest, her eyes stern and cold but distracted.

"I am well, thank you, Mistress," Pharaun replied. "I have reason to believe that I am fully in command of the vessel and that it is suitably powered."

He looked around at the others, who were standing behind Quenthel, also looking down at him. All he saw were Valas and Danifae.

"When the draegloth returns," Pharaun finished, "we can be on our way."

"We won't be waiting for Jeggred," Quenthel answered, eliciting a sharp look from Danifae and a lift of one eyebrow from the mercenary scout.

"Mistress—" Danifae began, but Quenthel held up a hand to silence her.

"Anyone who breaks off from this expedition," Quenthel said, "without my permission will be considered to have deserted it."

"Surely that wasn't the intent of your nephew," Pharaun replied. "I think it was hardly the intent of Master Argith either. Where we're going it seems to me that we'll need their str—"

"We won't," the high priestess interrupted. Looking off into the darkness she continued, "They are both strong, but where we're going there will be things around every stalactite that could rip them both to shreds. We're not going on a jaunt in the Dark Dominion. What we'll encounter will not be defeated by brute strength but with a clear and steady mind—the single-minded pursuit of one's own desires."

Pharaun frowned and waited for one of the others to say something.

Valas stood waiting for the females to sort it out.

"You seem to know what we'll see," Danifae said to the high priestess, "but you don't know, not for sure."

Pharaun, surprised by the way Danifae had pinned the high priestess down, looked at Quenthel, curious to hear her answer.

"I know that I can't stay here anymore," Quenthel answered. The vipers writhed slowly at her hip. "This place is killing me. We know what needs to be done. Live or die, we live or die in the Abyss at the side of the Spider Queen."

Pharaun lifted an eyebrow and smiled, glancing between the two females.

"We've not even begun," Danifae warned. "There will be much for Jeggred to do. We should wait."

"That, my plaything," the Mistress of Arach-Tinilith shot back, "is not for you to decide. You've presumed enough."

Pharaun recognized that it took considerable effort for Danifae to look down, letting her smoldering red eyes linger on the deck instead of boring into the high priestess. The battle-captive had come a long way, and Pharaun caught himself smiling at her.

"Master Mizzrym," Quenthel said, "take us to Lolth. Now."

"I will require a brief rest," the mage lied. Even as the words passed his tongue, he wondered why he was lying. He didn't look at Danifae. "One more period of Reverie for us all. We should face the goddess rested and at our best."

Quenthel didn't answer but turned and walked away. Danifae lingered.

What are you doing? Aliisza whispered into his consciousness, startling the mage. He'd forgotten she was there. *That's not true.*

The Mistress of the Academy, he told the alu-fiend, *isn't thinking clearly.*

Don't want to travel without your draegloth? Aliisza asked.

Would you?

Pharaun could feel her laugh in his mind.

"Thank you," Danifae said.

Pharaun looked up at her with a smile. Quenthel and Valas had both wandered off, but he used sign language to be sure they weren't overheard.

Why should I continue to help you? he asked. *What are you doing?*

She thought about it for a long time then signed back, *I want you to promise me that you won't leave without Jeggred.*

And if I do?

Danifae had no answer.

The Mistress irritates me, the mage went on. *I've made no effort to mask that. She's tried to kill me in the past. She has treated me with less respect than I deserve, but she is the Mistress of Arach-Tinilith, the most powerful priestess in Menzoberranzan if not in the whole of Lolth's faithful—the matron mothers included. This is her expedition, and her orders are law where I come from.*

Not where I come from, Danifae replied, *and I serve Lolth as well.*

"Perhaps," Pharaun replied aloud, confident that the high priestess had gone back to her quiet, oblivious sulking, "but in what way do you serve me?"

Danifae looked puzzled, her eyes inviting him to continue.

"You wish something of me," he explained. "You ask me to put my life at risk and my future in Menzoberranzan. You ask me to defy the sister of the archmage, my master, and the Matron Mother of the First House, his mistress."

"You want to know what I will give in return?" she asked.

It was his turn to let his eyes invite an answer.

"Answer this," she said. "Do you really want to travel through the Plane of Shadow, into the Astral, through the Plain of Infinite Portals, and to the sixty-sixth layer of the Abyss without Jeggred?"

"He would be of service to us all, I'm sure," said Pharaun, "as he has been, but he doesn't serve me. He doesn't really even like me, if that can be imagined. You, on the other hand, have made an important and powerful new ally to replace the one you've used up."

You think Quenthel is "used up"? Danifae asked silently.

"She's not herself," answered the mage. "That much is obvious, but the question remains: Why should I do anything for you?"

"What do you want?" she asked, and Pharaun got the feeling he could have asked her anything and she would have at least considered it.

"I would feel more comfortable if Ryld was here," he said, not caring if it made him sound weak.

Danifae nodded and said, "Even if he has gone over to Eilistraee?"

"I doubt that that's happened," replied the mage. "Master Argith isn't the religious type."

"His sword arm works for you, as Jeggred's claws work for me," she said.

Pharaun smiled, winked, and nodded.

"I suppose that's fair enough," she said, "but don't ask me to spare Halisstra."

"Who?" Pharaun joked.

That drew a smile from Danifae.

"Keep the draegloth away from Ryld," the mage said. "Bring the Master of Melee Magthere back here, kicking and screaming if you have to, but alive, and I'll take him from there."

"Agreed," Danifae said. She touched a ring on her right hand and disappeared.

That took Pharaun by surprise.

Interesting, Aliisza said from somewhere. *Who is she?*

A battle-captive, Pharaun replied, *or at least she used to be.*

Seems more like a priestess to me, said the alu-fiend.

Yes, Pharaun replied. *Yes, she does, doesn't she?*

Chapter

NINETEEN

She spoke entirely in movement, in the subtle nuance of gesture and rhythm, and it all seemed like a glorious dream.

Halisstra felt her body moving. The air swirled around her, cool and invigorating. In the movement she sensed the presence of Danifae. The subtle curve of her former servant's hip turned in a way that suggested duplicity and with a grace that bespoke ambition. Danifae breathed discontentment and stepped into the Demonweb Pits.

Halisstra didn't watch, she danced. She was there, though she had no idea where "there" was. There was no space, only the movement within it—the movement that was the voice of Eilistraee.

Danifae and Halisstra both stepped in time to a different song. They moved toward the same endpoint but for different reasons and were surrounded by the same chilling stillness. In the sway of a shoulder, Eilistraee warned Halisstra not to trust Danifae but pushed her servant along the former battle-captive's path. Halisstra would lead some of the way, and Danifae would lead some too. Both goddesses would push and pull them from the edges, sending them toward a place and a time that no sane drow could possibly imagine except in a goddess-birthed nightmare.

Halisstra felt herself move through a still, empty space, and she knew that space was the Demonweb Pits—the home plane of Lolth, bereft of souls, an empty afterlife with no hope and no future. Halisstra felt Danifae whirl through that same dead space with her and look at Halisstra with the same dull fear. There would be no service, no reward but oblivion, and Danifae would arrive at the same conclusions, be dragged to the same realization.

Danifae can be turned, Halisstra danced.

Eilistraee hesitated.

It was with that wordless sense of uncertainty that the movement ceased. There was a solid, unmoving floor of sanded stone beneath her and dead gates all around. Halisstra rolled onto her back, wiped her face with her hands, and tried to steady her breathing. Sweat poured off her, and her body ached. She felt as if she'd been dancing for hours though she wasn't sure she'd actually been dancing at all.

Halisstra looked around at the interior of the gatehouse, searching for Danifae. The former servant was nowhere to be found. Even Halisstra's shouts went unanswered, so she wandered outside.

The cave's dull light revealed a large and complex structure. Halisstra knew she was in Sschindylryn but knew little else about the city. Not sure if she was coloring the world through her own filtered perceptions, she felt that the air in the City of Portals was heavy with dissent and nascent violence. She'd sensed the same thing before—in Ched Nasad.

An image of Ryld came to her mind—not so much an image but the memory of the way he moved with her and the touch of his night-black skin. She'd led him to Danifae, who had led Jeggred to them on Quenthel's behalf. Quenthel knew that they—or at least Halisstra—had turned their backs on Lolth in favor of Eilistraee.

However, Ryld hadn't actually done that. A male, and not particularly religious, the weapons master served Lolth because everyone around him did. Ryld, like all drow in Menzoberranzan was raised with the words of Lolth never far from his ears. Halisstra had been raised the same way, but she had the sheer force of will to step back and examine the reality of the situation as it continued to unfold.

Danifae had a choice too, and the realization of it hit Halisstra the moment Danifae stepped out of the suddenly blazing-purple archway. The gate had burst into life, revealing Danifae and momentarily blurring Halisstra's vision.

Blinking, Halisstra stood and said, "Ryld?"

Danifae shrugged. It was a rude, dismissive gesture that set Halisstra's teeth on edge. The Melarn priestess's face flushed, her teeth clenched, but she did her best to swallow the anger at the same time pushing away memories of punishing her battle-captive, beating her, humiliating her, and breaking her.

"Where have you been?" Halisstra asked.·

"With Mistress Quenthel," Danifae replied. "They're proceeding. I was sent back to retrieve Jeggred."

"You know where the draegloth is?" asked Halisstra. "If you do, then you must know where Ryld is."

"Jeggred was sent to kill him," replied Danifae. "I told you that."

"You did," Halisstra said, "but . . ."

"You want to know if the weapons master has prevailed," Danifae replied, "or if the draegloth is feeding even now."

Halisstra swallowed in a parched throat and said, "Does he live? Has Ryld won?"

Danifae shrugged again.

"You can get me back to him," Halisstra said. "Using these gates of yours, you can send me to his side."

"Where Jeggred would shred you as well and eat you both in alternating bites," said the former servant, "or, you can move forward as opposed to backward."

"Forward? Backward? What is that supposed to mean?"

"The way I see it, Mistress Halisstra," Danifae said, "you have two choices: Go to your lover's side and die there, or go back to the surface temple and your new sisters in Eilistraee."

Halisstra let out a breath and looked the ravishing dark elf up and down. Danifae smiled back, though the expression looked more like a sneer.

"They're leaving," Danifae pressed, "and they're leaving soon. If you go back to the temple where I first contacted you, if you tell them that Quenthel and her crew are on their way to the Demonweb Pits in search of Lolth herself, the Eilistraeeans might have enough time to help."

"To help? To help whom?" whispered Halisstra, then more loudly: "I should go back to the Eilistraeeans and tell them that we can follow Quenthel and the others to the Demonweb Pits. Would you stand by and watch that and not warn them . . . and not warn Lolth?"

"I'm still a servant," said Danifae. "I can't make the decision for you or ask you to trust me. I can give you no promises, no assurances, no guarantees about anything. For that, you'll have to look to your goddess. Either way, I can send you wherever you want to go."

She saw it. Only a flash, but there was the unmistakable look that had wrapped within it uncertainty, fear, embarrassment, and more. Danifae was jealous in a very immature way that Halisstra was once again serving a deity who would answer the prayers of her faithful while Danifae still clung to the memory of a dead goddess.

"I have a choice?" Halisstra asked, slowly shaking her head.

"I can send you where you want to go," Danifae repeated. "Tell me if you want to go back to your temple to organize the priestesses there, or—"

"Organize?" Halisstra interrupted.

Danifae was irritated, and Halisstra was momentarily taken aback by the reaction.

"Surely Eilistraee grants them spells still," Danifae said. "They will be able to travel the planes without a ship of chaos. Eilistraee should be able to take you right to them."

Halisstra watched her former servant's face change again—saw that fear return.

"Or," Danifae said, her voice deep and even, "you can go try to help your weapons master against the draegloth and die."

Halisstra closed her eyes and thought, occasionally stopping to wonder at the fact that she was thinking about it at all.

"My heart," Halisstra confided in Danifae, "wants me to go to Ryld, but my head tells me that my new sisters will want to know what you've told me and that they'll want to go to the Demonweb Pits."

"The time you have to gather them," warned Danifae, "is drawing increasingly short."

Halisstra clamped her mouth shut while her throat tightened.

"Choose," Danifae pressed.

"The Velarswood," Halisstra blurted out. A tear glimmered in the faerie light and traced a path down her deep black cheek. "Take me to the priestesses."

Danifae smiled, nodded, and pointed toward a purple-glowing gate.

The two of them stared at each other while a few heartbeats went by. Danifae's eyes darted back and forth between Halisstra's as if they were reading something written across her pupils. Halisstra saw the hope in Danifae's eyes.

"How bad is it?" Halisstra asked, her voice almost a whisper. "What has she sunk to?"

"She?" Danifae asked. "Quenthel?"

Halisstra nodded.

"She can go lower," the former battle-captive said.

"Come with me," Halisstra said.

Danifae stood silently for a long time before she said, "You know I can't. They won't leave without Jeggred, and I have to bring him back."

Halisstra nodded and said, "After he's murdered Ryld."

Danifae nodded and looked at the floor.

"We'll see each other again, Danifae," Halisstra said. "Of that I'm certain."

"As am I, Mistress," Danifae replied. "We will meet again in the shadow of the Spider Queen."

"Eilistraee will be watching us both all the way," Halisstra said as she crossed to the waiting portal. "She will be watching us both."

Danifae nodded, and Halisstra stepped into the gate, abandoning Ryld to the draegloth, Danifae to the Mistress of Arach-Tinilith, and herself to the priestesses of the Velarswood.

※   ※   ※

"You seem as surprised as I am," Gromph said to the lichdrow, "that your friend Nimor has sprouted wings."

Dyrr didn't answer, but his ember-red eyes drifted slowly to the winged assassin.

"Duergar," Gromph went on, "a cambion and his tanarukks, and a drow assassin. Oh, but the drow assassin isn't even a drow. You've allied yourself with everything but another dark elf. Well, you haven't been a dark elf yourself for a very long time either, have you, Dyrr?"

If the lich was offended or affected in any way, he didn't show it.

"He could be allied with a drow, though," Nimor said. "We both could."

"You actually think I'm going to join you?" Gromph asked.

"No," Nimor answered, "of course not, but I have to ask."

"If I do," Gromph persisted, "will you kill the lich?"

Dyrr raised an eyebrow, obviously interested to hear Nimor's answer.

"To have the Archmage of Menzoberranzan himself turn on his own city," Nimor said, "betray his own House, and overthrow the matriarchy with a wave of his hand? Would I kill the lichdrow? Certainly. I would kill him without the slightest moment's hesitation."

That brought a smile to Dyrr's face, and Gromph couldn't help but share it.

Nimor looked at the lichdrow, bowed, and said, "I would try, at least."

The lich returned the bow.

"You're not going to do any of those things, are you?" Nimor asked Gromph. "You won't turn your back on Menzoberranzan, House Baenre, the matriarchy, or even Lolth, who has turned her back on you."

"That's all?" Gromph asked. "That's all you plan to say to try to turn me? Ask a question then answer it yourself? Why are you here?"

"Don't answer that, Nimor," the lichdrow commanded, his tone as imperious as ever. "He's drawing tales out of you. He wants time to try to get away or to plan his attack."

"Or," Gromph cut in, "he may simply be curious. I know why my old friend Dyrr wants to kill me, and I can guess at the motivations of the duergar, the tanarukks, the illithids, and whatever else crawls out of the crevices and slime pools of the Dark Dominion, drawn to the stench of weakness. You, though, Nimor, are half drow and half dragon, aren't you? Why you? Why here? Why me?"

"Why you?" Dyrr said, his voice dripping with scorn. "You have power, you simpleton. You have position. That makes you a target on a good day—and this isn't a good day for Menzoberranzan."

Gromph ignored the lich and said to Nimor, "My sister said the assassin she captured named you as an agent of the Jaezred Chaulssin."

Nimor nodded and said, "I am the Anointed Blade."

Gromph didn't know what that meant but gave no indication of that to Nimor or Dyrr.

"Ghost stories come true," Gromph said.

"Our reputation precedes us," replied Nimor.

"Chaulssin has been in ruin for a long time," said Gromph.

"Her assassins survive," Dyrr said.

His dragon half, Nauzhror said into Gromph's mind, *has been identified, Archmage. He is half-drow, half-shadow dragon. More than one generation, perhaps. An incipient species.*

"We have placed ourselves in city after city," Nimor said, "all across the Underdark. We've been waiting."

"And breeding," Gromph said, "with shadow dragons?"

Nimor's smile told Gromph how right Nauzhror had been.

"It's over," Dyrr said, and Gromph found it difficult to deny the finality in his voice. "All of it."

"Not yet," Gromph replied, and he started to cast a spell.

Nimor beat his batlike wings and shot up into the darkness. Dyrr followed, more slowly, wrapping himself in additional protective spells.

Gromph finished his spell and held his hands together. A line of blackness appeared between his palms and stretched to the length of a long sword blade. The line was perfectly two-dimensional, a rift in the structure of the planes.

Lifting into the air, the Archmage of Menzoberranzan threw his hands apart, and the blade followed him up. Using the force of his will, Gromph set the planar blade flying in front of him. Choosing a target was simple.

Nimor has to die first, Prath suggested, though it was unnecessary. *The extent of his true abilities is the only unknown.*

Gromph set the blade hurtling at the half-dragon assassin. Nimor flew as fast as anything Gromph had ever seen fly, but the blade moved faster. It cut into the assassin, and Nimor convulsed in pain. What makes a blade sharp is the thinness of its edge. The blade that Gromph conjured didn't actually have any thickness at all. Being *perfectly* thin, it was perfectly sharp. Anything that Nimor might have had on him to protect him from weapons would be of no consequence.

Blood pattered down over the floor of the Bazaar, and Nimor roared. The sound rattled Gromph's eardrums, though he didn't hesitate to send the black blade at the assassin again—but it disappeared.

Gromph whirled in midair to face the lichdrow. Dyrr held his staff in both hands. Gromph assumed he'd used some aspect of the weapon's magic to dispel the blade

Disappointing, Nauzhror commented. *That was an impressive spell. And effective.*

Nimor wasn't flying quite as fast, and he was still bleeding. Gromph had to keep his attention shifting back and forth between the assassin, the lich, and his own next spell, so he didn't actually see Nimor heal himself, but he did—enough to keep himself alive.

Gromph was nearly finished with his next incantation when Nimor blew darkness at him—it was the only way the wizard could think to describe it. The assassin drew in a breath and exhaled a cone-shaped wave of roiling blackness. Gromph tried to drop away from the darkness, but he couldn't. The twisting void washed over the archmage. It was as if all the warmth were drawn out of him. He shivered, and his breath stopped in his throat. His spell was ruined, cut off in mid-word, the Weave energy unraveling.

Part of the layers of defensive magic that he and the Masters of Sorcere had cloaked him in protected Gromph from the full extent of the freezing darkness's power. If not, Gromph would have shriveled to a dead husk.

"I was right," Gromph said to Nimor, trying not to gasp. "It was a shadow dragon, wasn't it?"

"More than one shadow dragon, Archmage," Nimor replied—and Gromph thought the assassin was trying not to gasp himself, "and more than one drow."

The half-dragon assassin drew a needle-thin rapier that glowed blue-white in the gloom of the abandoned Bazaar.

Caution, Archmage, Prath warned.

Gromph winced at the idiocy of his inexperienced nephew. The archmage was always ready for anything—though he wasn't fast enough to dodge out of the way of the rapier as it slashed across his chest.

Nimor had disappeared from where he'd been hovering, several paces away and appeared right next to Gromph and a little above—perfectly in a blind spot. All of that had happened in the precise same instant.

The assassin was gone again just as fast.

The slash in Gromph's chest burned, the wound crisp and jagged. He looked down at the cut. Frost lined the wound, and the blood that oozed from it was cold when it touched his skin. Gromph shivered.

Something hit Gromph from behind, and he grunted and doubled over when the air was smashed out of his lungs. It was a painful second or two before he was able to draw in another breath. Dyrr had hit him with something—a spell or a weapon—from behind.

The spell didn't pass through all of your defenses, Archmage, Nauzhror told him. *If it had, you would have been disintegrated.*

"Good for me," Gromph muttered under his breath, then he spoke the command word that brought the defensive globe from the staff.

Circled again in protective magic, Gromph turned in the air, trying to catch sight of at least one of his foes. He saw Nimor flying at him with that freezing rapier poised for another slash. Behind the assassin and off to one side, the lichdrow was moving his free hand through the air, his fingers leaving streaks of crackling white light behind them.

Pain blazing in his chest and back, Gromph twisted in the air when a cone of twinkling white light shot forth from the lichdrow's extended hands, threatening to engulf him in a blast of freezing air and cutting ice.

The archmage managed to twist out of the way of the spell, but he lost sight of the assassin in the process. Gromph braced himself for another icy slash from the rapier, but it didn't come.

The assassin had to dodge the cone of cold as well, Master, Prath said.

Gromph took advantage of the respite and drew two slim, platinum-bladed throwing daggers from a sheath in his right boot. Even as he drew the knives up along the length of his body, he spoke the words of a spell that would enchant the weapons to a greater keenness. The spell would make them fly truer as well, and farther, and he was sure they would pierce at least some of his target's magical defenses.

Gromph got his arm up to throw and finished the spell. When he turned to find his target, the pain was gone. The ring was working still, healing him almost as fast as the assassin and the lich could wound him.

A fraction of a heartbeat before Gromph could throw his ensorcelled daggers, Nimor appeared next to him again. The rapier made a shrill whistling sound as it whipped through the air, drawing a frosted white line across Gromph's right side. The pain was extraordinary, and Gromph's fingers twitched along with most of the other muscles of his body. He almost dropped the two daggers but didn't.

He's gone, said Prath.

Gromph had expected that.

I think it might be the ring, Nauzhror said.

The ring? Gromph sent back.

That allows him to slip from one place to another in an instant, Nauzhror explained.

Gromph had expected to fight Dyrr alone and had expected to fight him spell to spell. The archmage had to admit, at least to himself, that he was unprepared for hand-to-hand combat and that in that regard at least, Nimor was likely superior.

He put those thoughts out of his mind when he heard Dyrr casting another spell. He turned to look at the lich.

Dyrr had a strange look in his eyes, as if something was going to happen, but he wasn't sure exactly what. Gromph didn't like that look at all.

He's summoning something, Nauzhror said.

By the time the last syllable of Nauzhror's warning sounded in Gromph's head, the lich's spell had done its work. Lurching out of thin air, a set of insectoid legs slammed down onto the rock floor of the Bazaar—then another set, and another and another and another. The insect's head was wider than Gromph was tall, maybe even twice as wide. On either side of its grotesque mouth was a curved, jagged-edged pincer. Two bulbous, multifaceted eyes scanned the abandoned expanse of the marketplace as the rest of the huge beast drew itself out of the Weave.

It was a centipede the size of a whole caravan of pack lizards, and behind it, Dyrr was laughing, and Nimor was flying at Gromph again.

One at a time, the archmage told himself.

He worked another spell on the pair of enchanted throwing daggers. The centipede lurched at Gromph, but it was moving slowly, still unsure of its surroundings and the extent of the lich's control over it. That gave Gromph time to finish the spell and throw the daggers. He didn't bother to aim. He tossed them in Nimor's general direction and let the spell do the rest. The daggers whirled through the air, their paths twisting around each other in a perfect beeline for the winged assassin.

With impressive agility, Nimor slipped sideways in the air in an attempt to avoid the daggers, but once set on their course, nothing so simple would deter them. The assassin had to twist in the air again, swatting at the blades with his rapier. The flash of steel—Nimor's thin blade and both daggers—became a whirling blur around the assassin.

Well played, Master, Prath commented. *That should keep him occupied.*

Again ignoring his nephew, Gromph called on the levitating power of his staff to launch himself straight up in the air. The centipede's hideous sideways jaws crashed together an inch below the soles of his boots, and it immediately drew back for a second lunging attack. Gromph, hoping he was well above the monstrous insect, twisted and rolled in the air, his eyes taking in every detail of the Bazaar and the surrounding stalagmites as he went.

The archmage stopped, hanging in the air between the confused centipede and the hovering lich.

"You don't like my new pet?" the lichdrow taunted. "All he wants is to give you a little kiss."

"I don't—" Gromph started, but the air was pushed from his chest once again when Dyrr, his staff held in front of him, used its power to thrust Gromph away.

The archmage could feel the giant insect behind him, looming like a stalactite fortress. Dyrr drew himself up higher in the air and the repulsion pushed Gromph down and away—directly into the centipede's greedy jaws.

The right spell came to Gromph's mind in an instant, and he wasted some extra energy to cast it quickly. The effect was one he'd felt hundreds of times, but he'd always hated it. His body felt as if it were drawing itself thin. He shivered despite himself and had to force himself to keep his eyes open when his vision blurred a little and the world around him became both distorted and somehow brighter, sharper.

He was surrounded by the inside of the gigantic insect. Muscles and rivers of green semiliquid that served it for blood, the odd line of sheets the thing seemed to be using as lungs, the husks of other too-big insects that it had recently eaten—then another thick layer of armorlike chitin, and he was through it. He had passed through the centipede, his body more a part of the Ethereal than the Prime Material Plane.

The centipede had no idea what was going on—how could it? Gromph knew the insect wouldn't have been able to feel him pass through it, but the tasty morsel of drow flesh it thought it was going to bite and swallow was somehow behind it.

Gromph caught a flash of movement out of the corner of his eye and turned fast to see Nimor coming at him again. The daggers were gone, and the assassin had a few new cuts, but he was no less deadly for the experience.

The centipede turned, moving its massive body—one that must have weighed several hundred tons—in a shockingly quick and agile twist. Gromph's ethereal body was still visible, though he appeared ghostly, oddly translucent. The centipede didn't seem to see him. Instead, its bulging eyes locked on Nimor.

Nimor slipped sideways in the air again and, fast as the insect was, the assassin slipped past its jaws in time to save his own life. The centipede would have bitten him cleanly in two.

Gromph levitated up past the reach of the centipede as his body faded back into its solid form.

"Dyrr," Nimor raged, "mind your pet, damn you."

Gromph smiled at that, but Dyrr's response was to begin another incantation. Nimor might have been angry at his undead ally, but they were far from turning on each other. The archmage knew that Dyrr's spell would be directed at him. Despite having spent a little time in ethereal form, the globe was still around him, so Gromph knew that Dyrr was going to be using powerful magic. The archmage turned in the air to face the lich, but all he could do in the seconds it took for Dyrr to cast the spell was hope the defenses he already had in place would be enough to save his life.

There was no visible effect when the lich finished his spell, no trail of light or clap of thunder, but Gromph could feel the magic wrap itself around him. The protective globe did nothing to keep the spell out, but other defenses came into play, and Gromph concentrated on those. Still, his body began to stiffen. The archmage could feel the moisture being drawn from his skin. He found it difficult to bend his elbows. It was as if he were being turned to stone.

He started to drop, and before he could take control of his levitation again, the centipede turned and bit at him. One of the insect's pincers caught the archmage on the thigh as he dropped past. It might have bitten his leg off, but it had the wrong angle, so instead it ripped his skin open and dragged its serrated edge deep into the muscle until it vibrated against Gromph's thighbone.

The archmage ground his teeth against the pain. Even with his muscles stiff and his breath coming in slow, shallow gulps, he used the staff to pull up into the air away from the centipede, which came at him again.

Blood oozed like thick mud out of the deep gash in his leg, and Gromph found it ironic that it was Dyrr's spell that seemed to be saving his life. The ring Gromph had been depending on didn't seem to be functioning.

Nimor hit him again, and the cold of the magic rapier made Gromph stiffen even more. A breath caught in his throat, and his stomach convulsed until he was wrapped in a ball in the air. He tried to blink, but he had to close his eyes, pause, then slowly open them again.

He tried to turn you to stone, Nauzhror said, his voice clear in Gromph's groggy mind. *You've resisted it thus far, Archmage. Don't let it in.*

Gromph turned his head slowly to the right—all he managed from an attempt to shake his head. The globe of protective magic that enveloped him disappeared, its energy spent. Gromph saw Dyrr draw himself up, only a few yards away. The lich cast a quick spell, and a flurry of green and red sparks, each as long as an arrow, streaked at him. Gromph managed to move his leg and extend his arm but couldn't get his jaw to open fast enough to utter the command word. The bolts of Weave energy smashed into him, burning him, shocking him, making him twitch, making his muscles extend then contract. The archmage's skin rippled, and his joints popped.

It was painful, and he was bleeding in wide, hot sheets across his thigh, which was open to the bone. He could move again but not fast enough to avoid the centipede.

The insect reared up, its massive pincers wide open, and closed on him in a lunge. Gromph hung in the air barely within its reach. The pincers came down and came together over his already wounded thigh.

Gromph felt himself tugged down by the centipede, then something gave and he bobbed back up. Before taking stock of his new wound, he levitated farther up, dimly aware that he was trailing something. He cast a spell even as Nauzhror and Prath shouted into his head. Something was wrong, but he needed to finish the spell before he could do anything else. He had to get rid of the centipede or it would eat him piece by piece while the damned lich stood by safely watching.

Gromph looked down and saw a spray of blood play across the centipede's wide, flat head, then fall through it as it faded. The spell took full effect, and the centipede was gone, but the blood still fell in a grisly rain onto the floor of the Bazaar far below.

Gromph reached down to his leg and felt something hard and jagged. He cut his finger on a sharp edge—the sharp edge of his own thigh bone. His leg was gone. The centipede had bitten it off. Gromph clenched his fists in anger and looked down. He could see his severed leg lying amid a shower of blood that still rained from his open wound.

Sparkles of light off to one side caught Gromph's attention. Nimor threw something, and Gromph instinctively blocked his face, fearing a spell. Instead, he saw the hilt of the winged assassin's enchanted rapier spinning to the ground far below. The trail of sparkling light was what was left of the freezing blade. Gromph's spell had done more than banish the centipede.

Nimor, to say the least, was not happy.

As the assassin launched a string of invectives his way, Gromph flexed his muscles and found that the stiffening effect was gone. He was in pain but not as much as he would have imagined. His ring was already starting to fight against the grievous wounds the archmage had suffered. Gromph knew that he'd survive, but there was still the matter of the leg.

Nimor swooped over him then disappeared into the darkness. Gromph couldn't see the lichdrow. He dropped slowly to the floor, coming to rest in a pool of his own blood. When weight started to return to him, he staggered and had to reactivate the staff's levitating power before he fell in a sprawl into the puddle of cooling gore. He hadn't thought about trying to stand on one foot. Instead, he let himself hover an inch off the ground, bent, and picked up his own leg.

It was a curious feeling, holding his leg in his hand, but the archmage brushed it off. The assassin and the lich were obviously regrouping after Gromph's powerful spell had disjoined the magic all around him—all the magic save his own—but they would be back.

Gromph felt the bone on his stump again and was pleased that the skin hadn't yet begun to grow over it. He turned the leg in his hand and—

A blast of cold air surrounded him, engulfed him, pushed him back and down, grinding him into the stone floor of the Bazaar and dragging him along. Gromph's head smashed into something that broke, splintered, and fell all around him.

He shook his head, and bits of giant mushroom stem and glass fell from his white hair. He was half buried in a shattered merchant's stall, but all Gromph could think about was how relieved he was to still be holding his leg. His body was covered in a thin layer of chilling frost that was already starting to melt in the cool damp air of the Bazaar.

The lich, Nauzhror said into Gromph's mind, *was outside the disjunction.*

I see that, the archmage answered, letting a wave of frustration follow the thought.

Gromph looked up and around. Dyrr was casting, while Nimor arrowed fast through the air at the archmage. He set another protective globe around himself, briefly worrying that the staff's power was being too quickly drained. It couldn't keep protecting him and levitating him forever.

The lich finished his spell, and Gromph smiled when a bolt of blinding yellow lighting crackled from Dyrr's hands, arcing through the air and splattering in a shower of sparks against Gromph's protective globe. Even as the lightning spent itself on his defenses, not even making Gromph's hair stand on end, the archmage cast another defensive spell on himself. Flames flickered almost invisibly along his body.

I see, Prath said. *It worked on the huecuva, but . . .*

Nimor was upon him, and Gromph tucked his body into a ball against the assassin's attack. The half-dragon's hands were bigger than they were in his drow guise, and each of this fingers ended in a thick, sharp talon of jet-black ivory. Nimor raked Gromph's shoulder with those formidable claws, but they skipped harmlessly along the sparking surface of the archmage's fire shield. Bright orange flames blazed up from Gromph's shoulder, covering the assassin's face. Nimor roared in pain and beat his wings once so hard that stinging shards of glass from the ruined merchant's stall whirled around the archmage. Each time one of the little shards of glass hit him, a spark of fire burst out in answer. The spell never burned Gromph, but for a few unnerving seconds he was surrounded in a cascade of roiling flame.

Nimor disappeared into the shadows in the cavern's vault.

The flurry of glass and fire subsided, and Gromph worked his way out of the wreckage of the merchant's stall. When his stump was clear, blood still oozing from it, the pain reduced by his ring to a dull, annoying throb, Gromph took a second to make sure his foot was pointing in the right direction and stuck his leg back on.

He held it in place and closed his eyes. His breath came in short, sharp gasps as the dull throb turned into a skin-quivering shiver. The feel of the bone reattaching, each fine blood vessel rejoining its severed end, nerves blazing back to life with a wild flurry of pain, itching, pleasure, then pain again, and his skin drawing itself together made Gromph gasp and shake.

The lich, Nauzhror warned.

Only then did Gromph become aware that Dyrr was casting another spell. The response that came to Gromph's mind was a powerful deterrent, one that would protect him where the staff's globe could not. Not pausing to consider any greater implications, Gromph drew together the required Weave energy, and the antimagic field was up in time to block a huge explosion of searing heat and blinding fire.

It also suppressed the regenerative power of the ring.

No magic was working anywhere near Gromph Baenre, and his leg was only half repaired. He shuddered, clenching his jaw and eyes tightly shut as pain roared up from his leg to wrap his whole body in a spasm of agony.

"Well played, my young friend," the lich called down to him, "but that field will come down eventually. Meantime, you'll be bleeding—and I'll be waiting."

Gromph didn't bother to consider the lich's threat. He was in too much pain to think.

TWENTY

Piet squeezed the handle of his axe, hoping that his sweating palms would still be able to grip it when the fighting started—and the fighting would start soon. He glanced at his friend Ulo and could tell that Ulo was thinking the same thing. Piet could even see Ulo's fingers worrying at the handles of his two big knives, and he knew that Ulo's hands were sweating too.

They had come to the Flooded Forest to do some logging, make a couple of silvers, and mind their own business. Since they'd been there they'd seen ten of their comrades killed. Some had died in the inevitable accidents that one might expect at any logging camp, but most of them fell to the local wildlife. The swamp held all manner of arcane threats, from animated vines that dragged men down to a watery grave to lizardfolk who picked off stragglers at the edges of the clearing seemingly out of spite. Still, the ring of torches and the gods only knew what else—maybe even some sort of swamp etiquette—kept the really dangerous creatures out of their camp. The makeshift tavern where the men spent virtually all of their non-working time (and there wasn't much of that) seemed like a safe enough place.

Now a dark elf and some kind of huge demon-thing had smashed through the window, and all bets were off.

Piet and Ulo faced off against the dark elf. Of the two of them, he appeared merely lethal, where the demon-thing might have really done terrible things to someone. Piet's knees were shaking. So were his hands, and his jaw felt tense.

On the other side of the common room four of the other loggers, Ansen, Kinsky, Lint, and Arkam, were facing down the huge demon-thing. They were all armed—no one with half a brain went unarmed in the Flooded Forest—but their weapons looked puny against the massive creature. Ansen had grabbed a torch from a wall sconce, Kinsky had his axe with him, Lint was hoping to keep the monster at bay with the spear he used to fish in the swamp, and Arkam waved a broken axe handle in front of him. They all looked suitably terrified.

The dark elf had a huge sword—Piet had never seen a sword so big—but he was holding it in a loose grip, dangling to his right, the tip scraping the rough wood floor. The drow was wet and bleeding from his face, from his leg, and maybe other places as well. Piet had never seen a dark elf before. He'd actually always thought they were a myth, so it was impossible for him to get a read on the creature, but he seemed to be weak, exhausted, maybe even dying.

"Who are you?" Piet asked, not liking at all the terrified quaver he heard in his voice. "What are you doing here? What do you want?"

Difficult as it was for Piet to tell what the drow was thinking, the logger was convinced that the outsider understood him. The look he gave Piet in answer seemed haughty at first then wasn't so much haughty as . . . Piet didn't know what to call it. He thought he remembered a word: disdainful, but he wasn't sure he remembered what that meant.

The drow didn't answer. Instead, he started to bring his sword up, and Piet, afraid the drow was going to cut him, chopped down with his axe. Piet had spent his entire adult life—since he was eleven-and-a-half—chopping wood. He knew how to swing an axe, and he did it with speed, power, and precision. Still, he didn't come within an armslength of the dark elf.

Piet barely saw him move. He was a couple of feet to the right all of a sudden, standing between Piet and Ulo. The drow had his sword up, but it looked as if he was defending himself, not attacking. Ulo, surprised that the dark elf was suddenly standing so much closer to him, waved his knives in front of himself madly—cutting no one—and scrambled backward until he hit the wall.

"Stab him, Ulo!" Piet shouted, but it didn't look as if Ulo even heard him.

The dark elf came at Piet with his sword low, and Piet dodged out of the way instinctively. A rush of adrenaline coursed through him. He'd never moved so fast in his life.

He changed his grip on his axe and swung it sideways at the dark elf, who leaped back to let the axe head pass a few inches in front of his face. Piet reversed his grip at the end of the swing, twisted the axe around and swung again. He knew the dark elf would lean back again and was ready for it. He actually aimed at a point several inches behind the drow's head. The only thing he could see was the drow, and when the axe came at the dark elf's head, Piet closed his eyes, expecting a splash of blood.

The axe stopped, and hot, thick liquid splashed over Piet's face. He closed his eyes tighter to keep the blood out of his eyes and tried to wrench the axe out of the dark elf's skull, but it was stuck. The falling body dragged Piet down with in and he slowly sank to his knees. Piet's forehead bumped the wall, which surprised him. He didn't think he was that far forward.

He wiped his eyes with one sleeve as he said, "I got him, Ulo! I split the black devil's sku—"

Piet stopped cold when he opened his eyes and saw exactly whose skull he'd split. Ulo's dead eyes stared back at him, glassy and vacant. Piet's axe head was jammed into the side of his friend's head, and blood was still oozing out from around it.

Piet's body shook, wracked by a spasm, but he kept himself from vomiting by pressing a hand tightly to his mouth, letting go of the axe that was still stuck in his friend's head, and rolling off onto the floor.

He looked up and saw the dark elf looking down at him, making no move to kill him, though the drow would have had an easy time of it. Piet met the black creature's gaze and got the sinking feeling that the drow was not only pleased with himself for getting Piet to kill Ulo but that he was thinking about trying something like it again.

"Men!" Piet barked, his voice cracking.

He wanted to warn them, but his throat was tight, and he had trouble forcing the words out. Looking up at the other four loggers, Piet saw the huge, gray-furred demon rip Arkam's throat out with one hand, as if he were digging a handful of shortening out of a pot. Blood poured out everywhere, and Arkam was dead before his gore-soaked body hit the floor.

Piet knew the second the two bizarre creatures burst in through the window that things were going to end badly for the logging crew, but there was something about the way matters were unfolding—the casual manner in which the gray demon ripped Arkam's throat out and the conniving, almost mean-spirited way the dark elf made Piet kill his own friend—that made it seem too personal, as if they'd come there for that reason.

Piet's palms weren't sweating anymore. His jaw was still tight, but for a different reason. His blood pounded in his ears. The dark elf was watching the demon toy with Ansen, Kinsky, and Lint. He didn't even think Piet was dangerous enough to keep an eye on.

That, Piet thought, is your second and last mistake, drow.

Piet coughed back the bile that rose in his throat when he put his heavy-booted foot on his friend Ulo's split-open head and pushed while pulling on the axe handle. The axe head came loose with a nauseating sucking sound, but Piet managed to ignore it.

Axe in hand, Piet stood then lunged at the dark elf. The slippery drow dodged him again, quickly and easily enough that Piet thought he must have eyes on the back of his head. Undaunted, the logger swung again but sliced through nothing but air. The drow danced back, not even parrying with his huge greatsword, just stepping back, leaning to either side or backward as Piet swung again and again.

Piet finally gave up. His lungs were burning. He tried to speak but couldn't. He wanted to run but his legs felt like twigs ready to snap—he'd already spent a long day cutting down trees. All he could do was stand there and watch the dark elf watch the demon-thing kill the rest of the men in the room.

The demon had one of the heavy oak tables in his hands—the larger two of the thing's three hands—and was pressing Ansen, Kinsky, and Lint into the wall. Their weapons were caught between the tabletop and their own bodies. Ansen's torch burned his face, Kinsky's axe handle cracked his collarbone, and Lint's spear wagged impotently from behind the table, digging deep furrows into the roof beam above him.

The men were grunting and coughing. Ansen screamed. Smoke billowed up from his hair, and the flesh around his right eye was crisping and beginning to flake away.

"Stop it," Piet gasped.

Neither the drow nor the demon even looked at him.

"Stop . . ." he moaned and was about to drop his axe when the door burst open, and five men all but crawled over each other to get into the common room.

Piet knew them all: Nedreg, the tall man from Sembia who was one of two men in the camp who'd brought a sword with him. Kem, the short guy from Cormyr who also had a sword and who hated Nedreg as much as Nedreg hated him. Raula, the only woman in the camp, had a spear she said was magical but no one believed her. Aynd, Raula's husband, had a spear that was so warped he didn't bother telling anyone it was anything but an old piece of Impilturan army garbage he'd found on the side of a road.

The first of the five to get into the room was the foreman of the camp: a big man named Rab who claimed to have been a sergeant in the Cormyrean army, who was on the battlefield the day King Azoun was killed. Everyone believed what Rab told them—whatever Rab told them—because everyone was afraid of him. Piet never liked Rab, but seeing him burst into the blood-soaked tavern with his greataxe at the ready was the most beautiful thing Piet had ever seen.

It was then, for no reason Piet could understand, that the dark elf finally attacked him. The greatsword moved so fast Piet could barely see it. Still, he managed to stagger back away from the blade. He tried to parry with his axe, but the dark elf never touched it. His greatsword whirled around it, flipped over it, pulled away from it.

Piet had taken maybe ten steps before he even realized he was walking. He was closer to the demon than he'd intended to go, but the monster was still pushing against the table behind which Ansen, Kinsky, and Lint were trapped. Ansen was still screaming. The tone of his voice had taken on a more desperate, almost girlish quality, and Piet found himself wishing the man would hurry up and die. It was the only humane thing.

The other two men looked as if they were trying to scream but couldn't. The demon-thing glanced up at the men who'd burst into the room but who were hesitating at the door still trying to understand the grim scene. The demon took advantage of their hesitation and pressed harder. Piet could see the thing's legs tense and the sharp claws on its feet dig into the floor. Kinsky's eyes popped out of his head, followed by a waterfall of blood. Lint coughed out a mouthful of blood, gurgled, and died. Kinsky tried to scream. The room filled with a series of loud cracking noises, and he went limp. Ansen finally stopped screaming, though he continued to burn.

Rab and the others charged at the demon. Piet wasn't even sure they noticed the dark elf.

"Why?" Piet asked the drow, who was watching the others charge the demon. "What are you doing here? Why are you doing this? What do you want?"

The dark elf turned to him and raised an eyebrow, looking down his nose at Piet—though the human was easily six inches taller.

"What do you want here?" Piet asked again.

"Nothing," the drow said in strangely accented Common.

Piet was aware of some motion below him—something that looked as if the dark elf had shrugged—then he felt something wet on his neck, warm liquid pouring down his chest. Piet put a hand to his throat and his fingers met a pulsing jet of hot red blood shooting in a four-foot stream from his throat. When he tried to speak, his lungs filled with blood, then his eyesight blurred.

The dark elf turned away from him, and as he died, Piet knew that the drow would never give him a second thought. He didn't live long enough to decide how he felt about that.

Ryld didn't give the dead human a second thought. Five more of them had come in, and though Jeggred had dispatched the first three humans he'd encountered with minimal effort, at least one of the newcomers looked like someone who could actually fight. Ryld didn't entertain for a second the thought that Jeggred might not be able to handle the five humans—even the one with the greataxe—but the five of them together might slow the draegloth down a bit, and that would have to do.

Ryld sheathed Splitter, and before the blade was entirely covered his feet were off the ground. He intended to jump through the window and almost made it when someone grabbed his foot. Ryld knew before he turned that it was Jeggred.

The draegloth pulled hard on Ryld's foot, and the weapons master twisted in his grip and kicked Jeggred in the face. The half-demon's head snapped back into one of the onrushing humans—one armed with a sword—who took the opportunity to slice at the back of the draegloth's head. The sword tangled in Jeggred's still-wet mane of thick white hair.

Two more of the humans came up on either side of the half-demon and jabbed their spearheads into Jeggred's back. The spearheads sank into the draegloth's flesh, and Jeggred let out a loud growl. He let go of Ryld, who landed on his feet, face to face with the draegloth. The humans withdrew their spears, and Jeggred and Ryld shared a look that said Jeggred wanted the human male and female with spears. The swordsman drew his weapon back to stab the draegloth from behind.

Jeggred spun away, sending the two humans with spears scattering. The human with the sword was left facing Ryld.

"The draegloth will kill you all," Ryld said, reasonably certain he got the Common right.

The human seemed more frightened that Ryld could speak his language than he was of the dark elf himself. That was a mistake the man wouldn't make twice.

"Don't—" Ryld warned as the human pulled his sword up to hack down at the dark elf.

With an impatient sigh, Ryld flicked his sword in a fast arc in front of him and took the human's sword arm. The man staggered back, bulging eyes fixed on the blood pumping out of his stump. He looked at Ryld, made eye contact with him for the space of a heartbeat. The human seemed to be waiting for Ryld to say something, to explain why the drow had taken his arm. Humans were an odd lot.

Ryld shrugged. The man opened his mouth to speak then fell over dead.

The female human jabbed at Jeggred, and the draegloth grabbed the spear. He snapped it like a twig, and the woman backstepped away, her hands up in front of her face in a feeble attempt to fend off the half-demon.

Ryld suppressed the urge to laugh. Instead, he bent quickly and ripped the dead human's hand off the sword. He had to break a few of the man's fingers to get the weapon free, but it certainly didn't matter to the swordsman anymore.

The other spearman went for Jeggred with renewed fury, his hopelessly warped spear jabbing again and again at the draegloth, who danced out of its way, toying with the man. The woman had her hands on her mouth, apparently concerned with what might happen to the other spearman. There was something about the look on her face that Ryld recognized, and in response he tossed her the dead man's sword. She didn't notice the blade coming at her until it was halfway there, but she caught it just the same.

The woman met Ryld's gaze, and the weapons master nodded at the draegloth.

"Take the dark elf, girl!" the man with the greataxe yelled to the woman.

The man with the greataxe had been barking orders all along, but Ryld hadn't paid much attention. Hearing someone order his death wasn't an entirely alien experience for Ryld, but there was something about the circumstances that frustrated him. He'd just tossed her a weapon . . . so what if he'd taken it out of the severed limb of one of her comrades?

The woman hesitated, looked at the sword as if she wasn't sure what to do with it, then looked at Jeggred. The draegloth stepped into the man with the spear, deftly slipping past the spearhead, and grabbed the logger's head in one of his huge, clawed hands. With a twist of the draegloth's wrist and a bend of his elbow the human spearman's head came free of his shoulders in a shower of blood.

The woman screamed, and Ryld was taken aback by the sound. It was soaked with emotion—a sound Ryld hadn't heard often in Menzoberranzan. He looked at her and she met his gaze. Tears streamed down her face. She looked back at the draegloth, who was meeting the advance of the man with the greataxe.

The woman dropped the sword and ran, rushing past Jeggred and the man with the greataxe to stumble out the door. Ryld heard her footsteps recede into the night.

The weapons master longed to follow her.

Rab Shuoc was born in the Year of the Striking Hawk in the Cormyrean city of Arabel. He grew up there, the son of a city watchman, and spent his childhood hunting rats with his friends in the back alleys and occasionally following his father on his rounds in the wealthier sections of the city. It wasn't the slightest bit surprising to anyone who knew him when he joined the army. Rab was fiercely loyal to the kingdom of his birth and the king he admired more than anyone but his father.

He worked his way up the ranks, slowly, and was a sergeant when the ghazneths and goblins ravaged Cormyr and all but destroyed Arabel. He was nearly killed in the same battle that resulted in the death of the king, and he watched the city of his birth burned. His father was killed when part of a building fell on him. With the king and his father both dead, and no family of his own to tie him down, Rab simply walked away.

He went on to become alternately a sellsword, a tavern bouncer, an innkeeper, a weaponsmith, then a logger. He was strong and smart, so he soon became foreman. His employers paid Rab a considerable sum in gold to gather crews to go deep into some of the most dangerous places in Faerûn to find exotic woods. He quickly built a solid reputation among the lumber mill owners and loggers alike as a fair but tough leader who knew how to get the job done, and Rab always delivered.

During those hard forty-six years of life, Rab Shuoc had missed out on a lot. There had been women but never a wife and never any children. Since the war he hadn't even had a home. He rarely worked with the same men more than one season at a time and had no real friends to speak of.

He wasn't the kind of man who worried about his own happiness or even expected to be happy. He wanted to live, work, and be left alone.

When he stepped into his common room and saw some of his crew already dead at the hands of a dark elf and some kind of giant demon monster, he knew that if he wanted to live, he would have to fight harder than he ever had before. It was with that thought foremost in his mind that he stepped toward the two interlopers and got started with the last thirty seconds of his life.

Raula was smart enough to run, and Rab let her go. The dark elf watched her go too, and the demon ignored her. The huge, gray-furred creature locked its blazing red eyes on Rab and advanced on him. Rab hefted his greataxe and stepped into the demon's attack. He was aware of the drow facing him as well.

The drow came in faster than the demon, swinging his enormous greatsword in a wild, chaotic fashion. Rab was sure he could parry the uncontrolled assault with ease and he held the steel haft of his greataxe in both hands so the greatsword would bounce off it—but it didn't.

The tip of the greatsword wasn't where it was supposed to be. It didn't seem possible to Rab that someone could move such a huge, heavy weapon so quickly, but that strange dark elf had, and it was Rab who paid the price. The tip of the sword drew a deep cut across the logger's chest. Pain flared, and blood poured, and in that half-second of shock, the demon took his axe.

He'd been disarmed before but he'd never had an opponent actually reach out and take the weapon right out of his hand.

Rab was still puzzling over that when something even stranger happened: the dark elf drew his greatsword across the demon's back, cutting it deeply enough that blood sprayed from the wound and the creature roared. The drow said something in a language Rab didn't even recognize let alone understand. There didn't seem to be any anger, any emotion at all on the drow's face, but he was definitely trying to kill the demon.

The huge creature spun on the much-smaller dark elf, and Rab backed away. He only got one step back before the demon reached around and grabbed him by the shirt, taking some skin with it. The monster lifted Rab, who weighed well over two hundred pounds, right off the floor without any sign of strain.

Rab grabbed at the thing's massive clawed hand, but the demon's skin was like steel coated in coarse fur. There was nothing Rab could do but wonder at the monster's intentions. It whirled on the dark elf, who had his sword ready. The demon still held Rab's greataxe in one hand but almost seemed to have forgotten it.

The demon threw Rab at the dark elf. The human barked out an incoherent, scared sound that might have been a scream or a shout. He didn't even know. It was the sound a man makes when he knows he's got less than a second to live and there's nothing he can do about it.

Rab was impaled on the dark elf's greatsword. He could feel every inch of the cold steel as it slid through his chest. Strangely enough, it didn't hurt.

Ryld held the human up and looked past him at the draegloth. The man died trying to make eye contact with him—Ryld would never understand why humans insisted on doing that. Ryld tipped his sword down in hopes that the man would slide off but instead had to quickly jerk back to avoid the blade of the human's greataxe, wielded by Jeggred, as it chopped down.

The greataxe hit Splitter and sliced clean through. Ryld felt his eyes bulge and his blood at once boil and run cold. Splitter was broken. His greatsword. The weapon he'd practically lived for, had developed his skills around for years, was destroyed.

The human's axe must have been enchanted after all.

The man fell away on the remaining length of the greatsword blade, and the sudden loss of his weight made Ryld fall backward. He let go of the shattered sword, and it clattered to the floor next to him.

The weapons master reached for his short sword and almost had his fingers wrapped around the pommel when the axe blade came down again, split his dwarven mithral breastplate as if it were made of parchment, and buried itself into his chest. Ryld could feel the weight of it not only on him but in him. There was no pain, just a heavy, even pressure.

The draegloth stood over him, drool hanging from his exposed fangs in shimmering tendrils, his eyes aglow in the orange torchlight.

Ryld tried to breathe but he couldn't. No air was getting past his throat at all. He wanted to say something, but there was no way to form words. Besides, he didn't know what to say. He'd turned his back on everything he knew for a woman he didn't know at all, a woman who chose a path for herself that would inevitably lead to her own destruction as surely as it had led to his. Part of him wished he'd been killed by anyone but the filthy half-demon, but another part was satisfied that it took a draegloth to bring him down. He almost wanted to thank Jeggred for fighting him in the first place. It was more than he deserved.

Jeggred moved closer, and Ryld was thankful that he couldn't breathe. He couldn't smell the half-demon's breath.

Jeggred leaned on the axe blade and broke open Ryld's chest. The sensation was something beyond pain—a mind-twisting agony that only death could possibly cure.

He watched the draegloth reach into his chest. Ryld's body started to jerk, and he couldn't stop it. The draegloth grabbed and groped inside his chest, and Ryld's vision faded in and out.

When Jeggred pulled his hand away, Ryld's eyesight came back long enough for Ryld Argith, Master of Melee Magthere, to see that his heart was still beating when the draegloth began to eat it.

The weapons master's heart was strong, and Jeggred relished the texture as well as the taste of it. Ryld Argith was a worthy opponent, a good kill, and the draegloth wished he could stay and devour more of him. The drow was dead by the time Jeggred finished eating his heart, and he knew that Danifae and the others were waiting for him.

Not bothering to wipe any of the blood, slime, or sap off himself, the draegloth touched the ring that Danifae had given him and used its magic to return to Sschindylryn.

T W E N T Y - O N E

"Ryld Argith is dead," Danifae said to Quenthel, her eyes darting at Pharaun.

The mage sat quietly, legs folded, in front of the mainmast. He didn't look back at her, seemed to have no reaction at all. Danifae chewed her bottom lip, her eyes flickering back and forth between Pharaun and Quenthel.

"And?" the Mistress of Arach-Tinilith prompted.

"I killed him," Jeggred grumbled.

Danifae looked at the draegloth, whose eyes were locked on Pharaun. Still the mage made no move and never looked at either the draegloth or her. She'd promised to spare the weapons master but had lied. Danifae half expected the mage to burn her to ciders where she stood for the betrayal. Either he was too busy with his preparations for the journey, or he didn't care . . . or he was planning something for later.

"And Halisstra Melarn?" Quenthel asked.

"I tore his body to shreds," Jeggred went on, oblivious to his aunt's question, "after I ate his heart. There's barely a piece bigger than a bite left of him, spread out over that freezing mud hole."

"Yes," Danifae said, smiling at the draegloth, who was still looking at Pharaun, "well, be that as it may, Halisstra has in fact done the unthinkable. She enjoys the protection of Eilistraee now, and there's no longer any doubt."

"You have evidence of that?" Pharaun asked, his voice quieter, weaker somehow, or maybe just bored.

"She told me," Danifae replied, still looking at Quenthel.

"It's true," the draegloth added.

Quenthel turned on Jeggred, her face tight, her eyes blazing. Still, she looked tiny in front of the hulking creature.

"How would you know, fool?" Quenthel spat. "You weren't brought here to think."

"No," the draegloth answered, not shrinking the slightest in the face of the high priestess's rage, "I was brought here to act. I was brought here to fight and to kill. How much of that have I done, my dear, dear aunt?"

"As much," Quenthel replied, her voice coming out almost as a growl, "or as little as I tell you. As *I* tell you, not Danifae."

Jeggred loomed over her, the muscles under his gray fur rippling with anticipation.

"Mistress Danifae," the draegloth said, "is at least trying. She's acting—"

"Without my direct orders," Quenthel finished for him.

Danifae was afraid that Jeggred would continue, so she said, "Only on your behalf, Mistress."

Quenthel lifted an eyebrow and stepped closer to Danifae.

"We talked about that, didn't we, battle-captive?"

"I am no one's captive now, Mistress," Danifae replied, "but still I serve Lolth."

"By turning my draegloth's head?" the high priestess said.

Danifae felt the skin on her arms and chest tingle.

"No," she said. "Jeggred helped me help you."

"Help me?" asked the high priestess.

The draegloth turned and skulked away. He found a spot near the bow and sat with his head bent downward. Quenthel was still looking at Danifae as if she expected an answer.

"Mistress," Danifae said, "I am without a home. You said you would bring me back to Menzoberranzan with you if I served you. That, and a host of other reasons, is precisely why I did what I did."

"*Did I ask?*" Quenthel roared. "Did I send you to do this?"

Danifae lifted an eyebrow herself and waited.

Quenthel took a deep breath and turned away from the former battle-captive to stare out at the black water, lost in thought.

"My loyalty is with Lolth," Danifae said, "and to the House of your birth."

"House *Baenre*," Quenthel said, her voice icy, "has no room for upstarts, traitors, or battle-captives."

"I think you'll find, Mistress," the former servant pressed on, "that I am neither an upstart, a traitor . . . or a battle-captive. It is not I who dances under the gaze of Eilistraee. I am here, and I am ready to serve you, to serve Lolth, to serve Arach-Tinilith, Menzoberranzan, and the entire dark elf—"

"All right," Quenthel snarled, "leave it out. I don't need my arse li—"

"Never, Mist—"

"Silence, child," the Mistress of Arach-Tinilith said. "Interrupt me again and taste venom."

Danifae got the distinct impression that it was a hollow threat, but she silenced herself just the same. It wasn't easy for her to do. There was much she burned to say to Quenthel Baenre, but she decided that she would say it to her corpse instead. Besides, the vipers at Quenthel's command were still dangerous, and all five of them stared at her, their cruel poison glistening on darting tongues.

"Everyone," Pharaun called from where he sat, his eyes closed. "Now that we're all here . . . what's left of us anyway . . . we'll be on our way.

"As the Mistress ordered," the mage added.

Danifae took a deep breath and a last look at the dreary Lake of Shadows and said, "We're ready, Master Pharaun."

Quenthel turned to look at her, but only out of the corner of her eye. A thrill raced through Danifae at the emotions plain in that look. The Mistress of Arach-Tinilith was terrified.

The ship began to move in response to Pharaun's will, and the wizard shuddered. Through his connection with the ship he could feel the cold of the water, the heat of his own body and the bodies of his comrades on the deck, and he could feel the lesser demons still being digested in the hellish transdimensional space that was the vessel's cargo hold. He found it an unusually pleasant mixture of sensations.

Still water rippled and tapped against the bone hull as the ship glided slowly across the surface of the lake. Other than that, nothing changed at first.

The walls are thin here, Aliisza whispered into his consciousness.

They are, he agreed.

The walls she referred to were the barriers between planes. In certain places and at certain times those barriers drew thinner and thinner and often broke all together. The Lake of Shadows was very close to the Plane of Shadows. The barriers between the two planes were especially thin there.

It's good that you're starting slowly, Aliisza sent. *It won't take much before we slip into the Sha—*

They were there.

It took even Pharaun, who'd had quite a bit of experience in planar travel, by surprise. As they passed from the Lake of Shadows onto the Shadow Fringe Pharaun saw what little color there was drain from the dimly lit cavern.

The movement of the ship was smooth but disturbingly random. The deck rose gently, then fell gently, then rose a little farther, then fell not as far, then rose the same amount, then fell less far. Pharaun couldn't tell if, on aggregate, they were going up, down, or staying the same. Sometimes they slipped straight to one side or rolled gently to the other. His stomach rolled with the ship, and he felt increasingly nauseous.

Don't ride it, Aliisza advised. *Be it.*

Pharaun concentrated on the deck, on the palms of his hands pressing against the warm, living bone. He watched random memories from the devoured souls pass across his consciousness then looked deeper into the ship itself.

Though the vessel lived, it didn't think. He felt it react to stimulus, riding the cool water of the lake into the freezing water of the Fringe. It knew it had crossed into the Plane of Shadow by feel but had no way to form the word "shadow." The ship didn't like the Shadow Fringe, it didn't fear the Shadow Fringe, and it didn't hate the Shadow Fringe. All it did was ride the water from one universe to the next at the command of the Master of Sorcere.

Pharaun's stomach felt fine.

Valas had traveled the Shadow Fringe before and was not impressed. It was a world devoid of color and warmth—two things the scout had little appreciation for anyway. Every turn in the caverns of the real Underdark had a requisite turn in the Shadow, but distance and time was distorted there, less predictable, less tangible.

The scout had been hired to guide the expedition through the Underdark, but they had left the Underdark. They were in a realm more suited to the wizard, on their way to a world only a priestess could appreciate. The time for Valas Hune to step aside was at hand.

Among the trinkets and talismans that adorned his vest was a cameo made of deep green jade that he wore upside down. He looked around, making sure that none of the others were looking at him. They were all too busy standing in awe of the difference in the air and water, obsessed with the feel of the ship moving across the shadow-water, to notice him. Touching the cameo with one finger, the scout whispered a single word and closed his eyes while a wave of dizziness passed through him.

Having sent his message back to his superiors at Bregan D'aerthe—a simple message they would easily interpret along the lines of "I'm no longer needed here"—Valas let go of the cameo and joined the others in marveling at the sometimes subtle, sometimes extreme differences in the world around them.

Bregan D'aerthe would answer in their own time.

Danifae could barely contain herself. The feel of the deck rocking beneath her was thrilling. The draining of color from the world around her was exhilarating. The thought that they were on their way, and that thus far everything she'd planned had come to fruition excited her. The presence of the draegloth next to her reassured her.

Danifae had never felt better in her life.

"The wizard will avenge him," Jeggred grumbled in what sufficed for a whisper from the hulking half-demon.

"The wizard will do what is best for the wizard," Danifae replied.

"I don't know what you mean," said the draegloth.

Danifae could hear the frustration in his voice.

"You don't fear him," she said. "I know that. Forget the wizard. He won't put his own life at risk to defend Ryld Argith, who's dead anyway and no longer of use to anyone. Even now, if he isn't too busy piloting the ship, he's coming to the realization that the weapons master had abandoned us all—including him—anyway, so to the Hells with him."

"And to the Abyss with us," the draegloth said, "at Pharaun's mercy."

"Pharaun has no more mercy than you and I, Jeggred," said Danifae, "but he has his orders from his archmage and his own reasons for remaining with the expedition. If he puts anything at risk at any time in the Shadow Plane, the Astral, or the Abyss, he dies. Until then, I want you to leave him alone."

"But—"

"No, Jeggred," Danifae said, turning to face the draegloth and look him directly in the eyes. In the dull gloom of the Shadow Fringe, his eyes glowed an even more brilliant shade of crimson. "You will not touch him unless I tell you to, and even then only in the way I tell you to."

"But Mistress . . ."

"Enough," she said, her voice flat with finality.

There was a moment of silence intruded upon only by the creak of the rigging and the strangely echoing water splashing against the living bone of the ship of chaos.

"As you wish, Mistress," the draegloth said finally.

Danifae forced herself not to smile.

You will grow accustomed to the motion after a time, Mistress, Yngoth reassured her. *Eventually, you won't notice it at all.*

The vipers could speak to her, directly into her mind, but Quenthel didn't know they could sense what she was feeling. She hadn't articulated, aloud or telepathically, how uncomfortable she was with the motion of the undulating deck.

It's the water that's pushing us up and down, K'Sothra offered.

Quenthel ignored her, choosing instead to look out into the cold gloom of the Shadow Fringe.

"Care, all," Pharaun said, his voice distant and echoing in the strange environment. "We'll be crossing into the Shadow Deep. There are dangers there . . . creatures, intelligences . . . keep your arms and legs inside the rail at all times, please. Try not to make eye contact with anything we might pass. Be prepared for any manner of strange effects and all manner of strange creatures."

Only a wizard, Zinda hissed, *could offer such vague and meaningless warnings. Does he expect any of us to jump overboard in the Shadow Deep?*

He's right, Yngoth argued. *The Shadow Deep hides many dangers.*

"Hold onto something," the Master of Sorcere advised.

Perhaps the draegloth could keep you from falling, Mistress, Hsiv advised.

Quenthel's lip curled in a sneer, and she flicked the offending snake under his chin. She looked over at the draegloth. Danifae's hand absently stroked his mane, and the draegloth stood very close to her.

Quenthel looked away, trying her best to rid her mind of the image. She kneeled on the deck and wrapped her arms around the bone and sinew rail. No sooner had she tightened her grip than the world—or the water—dropped out from under the ship.

They fell, and Quenthel's stomach lurched up into her throat. Her jaw clenched, and all she could do was hold on, her body tense and ready for the inevitable deadly stop at the bottom of whatever they were falling into.

It took a terribly long time for that to happen. Finally Quenthel began to relax—at least a little—even though they were still falling and she continued to hold on to the rail for dear life. Quenthel gathered her wits enough to survey the rest of the expedition.

The ship's deck was elongated and twisted, as if it had been pulled at either end by a strong but careless giant. Pharaun seemed twice as far away, Valas twice as close, and Danifae and Jeggred appeared to be hanging upside down. The draegloth held the battle-captive in one arm and the rail in the other.

All around them black shapes flitted in and around the rigging, up and under the hull, and between the falling dark elves. The air was ribboned with black and gray, and there was a dull roar like wind but not wind that all but deafened her. The flying black shapes were either bats or the shadows of bats. In the Shadow Deep, Quenthel knew, the shadows would be the more dangerous of the two.

We're stopping, Qorra said, and Quenthel knew it to be true.

The sensation of falling had wafted away. It wasn't that they had slowed in their fall, and they certainly hadn't hit bottom, they simply weren't falling anymore.

"Sorry, all," Pharaun apologized, his voice cheerful and bright. "A bit of a rough transition, that one, but you'll forgive my general inexperience with the whole piloting a ship of chaos thing, I'm sure."

Quenthel didn't forgive but also didn't bother to say anything. The ship was perfectly still, as if it had come up on solid ground, and the high priestess risked a glance over the rail.

They hadn't come to rest on the ground, she saw, but had stopped in midair above a rolling landscape of gray cluttered with vaguely translucent silhouettes of trees. The shadowy, batlike things still raced all around them.

"Oh, yes," Pharaun added suddenly, "and don't touch the bats."

Quenthel sighed but never touched a shadow-bat.

Pharaun extended his senses out into the Shadow Deep, using the properties of the ship of chaos in a way that felt natural to one who had become part of the demonic vessel. He did it the same way he would have strained to hear some distant sound.

The Shadow Deep is not unlike your Underdark after all, Aliisza said, *and like the Underdark it has its own rules.*

Pharaun nodded. He didn't pretend to understand those rules in any but the simplest way. He'd always been smart enough not to linger in the Shadow Deep.

We won't linger now, Aliisza said.

She touched his shoulder, and Pharaun took a deep breath. He was reassured by her touch, and not only for her help navigating and piloting the ship. With Ryld dead, he was alone with a group of drow who'd be as happy to see him dead as not. The alu-fiend might be more enemy than friend, but still Pharaun couldn't help thinking she was the only one he could trust.

Can you feel it? she asked.

Pharaun was momentarily taken aback. He thought she meant—

The gateway, she said. *Can you feel it?*

There was a lightness in his head and an itch on his right temple that made the ship turn and accelerate. His fingers curled, instinctively gripping the deck.

I feel it, he said. *The barrier is thinnest there. The ship will pass through.*

Yes, the alu-fiend breathed.

She wrapped an arm around him from behind and pressed into his back. Pharaun's heart beat a little faster, and the wizard was amused with himself. He couldn't see her, but he could feel her, he could smell her, and he could hear her voice echoing in his skull. He liked it.

At Pharaun's unspoken command the ship drifted across vast distances in insubstantial leaps. Like shadow walking, the ship slid across the Plane of Shadow faster than it should have, the distance compressing beneath it.

Will we fall again? Pharaun asked Aliisza as they neared the place where the Shadow Deep gave way directly to the endless expanse of the Astral.

No, she said, *it will be different.*

It was.

The ship was through in an instant. The darkness of the Shadow Deep with its sky of black and deep gray blazed into a blinding light. Pharaun's eyes clamped shut and were instantly soaked with tears. The ship shuddered. It felt as if the vessel were being battered on its side. Pharaun's breath caught in his chest, and there was a hard pressure there, a tightness. Fear?

Don't be afraid, Aliisza whispered.

Pharaun cringed at the word but had to admit to himself at least that he was afraid.

He blinked his burning eyes open, and his head reeled so he almost fainted. There was such an expanse of nothing on every side of them that he felt too out in the open, too vulnerable, too . . . outside to be anything but tense and jumpy.

The sky around them was gray, but it also held what Pharaun could only describe as the essence of light. There was no sun or any other single source of luminescence. The light was simply there, coming from everywhere at once, saturating everything.

Bright streaks of multicolored luminescence rippled across the backdrop of saturated light—brilliant and chaotic aurorae.

The ship rocked and shuddered, and Pharaun tensed again, fully prepared for the thing to shake itself apart. He held his teeth closed, then closed his eyes, and would have closed his ears if he could.

No, Aliisza advised, *don't close your eyes. Don't shut yourself off from it.*

Pharaun opened his eyes, mentally brushing off the resentment that boiled to the surface. He didn't like being told what to do, even when he knew he needed it.

She squeezed him tighter and whispered in his ear, "Think it. Think the name of it."

It? he thought to her.

Again she whispered with her real voice, her lips so close to his ear Pharaun could feel them brushing against the sensitive skin there: "The Abyss."

The Abyss, he thought. *The Abyss.*

There it was.

"What is that?" Quenthel asked.

"We're heading right for it," the draegloth said.

Pharaun laughed and moved the ship faster toward the disturbance.

That's it, Aliisza prodded.

They were moving toward a black whirlpool in the sky. It was as big as Sorcere itself, maybe bigger. It was huge. The closer they got to it, the bigger it became, and not only because they were moving closer to it. The thing was actually growing.

"We're not projections here," Valas said. "If we fly into that thing . . ."

"We'll end up where we meant to go," Pharaun said.

His own voice sounded strange in his ears, as if he hadn't spoken in ages.

Tell them to hold on again, Aliisza said. *They won't need to, but it'll reassure them.*

"Hold on," the wizard repeated. "Hold onto something, and hold on tight or you'll be tossed overboard and lost in the limitless expanse of the Astral Plane for all eternity, set adrift for all time to come, never to be seen or heard from again."

Aliisza giggled quietly in his ear, her breath tickling him.

They made straight for the whirlpool, and when the tip of the bow hit the trailing end of the disturbance, all Hell broke loose.

Literally.

Pharaun couldn't help but scream as the ship was whirled so madly around that his head snapped back and forth. His hands threatened to come away from the deck. Something hit him in the back of the head. Aliisza squeezed him, then let go, then squeezed him again. Pain flared in his legs and side, and he didn't know precisely why. The others were making noises as well: screaming, growling, calling out questions he couldn't understand, much less answer.

"This is it," Aliisza shouted into his ear. He still couldn't see her. "This is what you came for. This is where you're going. You brought yourself here, but now it's time for the Abyss to decide if you live to walk its burning expanse. The Abyss will decide if you get what you want."

"What?" Pharaun asked. "What do you mean?"

"The Abyss decides, Pharaun," the alu-demon said, her arms slipping away from him, "not you."

"We're almost there," the wizard said. "I feel it. It'll let us in."

Not me, Aliisza whispered into his mind. *I leave you here.*

"Why?" he asked, then thought to her, *Come with me.*

The alu-demon giggled then was gone, and Pharaun screamed again.

Until the roaring of the whirlpool dropped to nothing and his own screaming rattled his eardrums.

The ship stopped spinning but continued to fall, accelerating down and down while Pharaun struggled to regain control. Aliisza was gone, and the subtle help she provided, the extra consciousness at the helm, was gone with her. He tried to think of some spell to cast, but his mind, tied to the ship that was damaged in ways he was only dimly aware of, wouldn't form the list of spells.

The sky had gone red, and there was a sun, but it was huge and dull. The heat was stifling, and Pharaun had trouble drawing a deep breath. Sweat poured from him, stinging his eyes and soaking his forearms.

"Pharaun," Quenthel screamed, her voice shrill and reedy, "do something!"

Pharaun formed a number of replies as they continued to dive, faster and faster downward, but he didn't bother with any of them.

"Do something?" he repeated.

The wizard started to laugh, but the laugh turned into a scream when the ship rolled over upside down.

Below them was a level plain that went on and on forever in all directions with no horizon. Tinted red by the dull sun, the sand shimmered with heat. Scattered all over were deep black holes—thousand of them . . . millions of them.

He knew where they were. He had heard it described.

They had come to the Abyss. To the Plain of Infinite Portals.

They were falling and falling and screaming and screaming until they hit the ground.

The ship of chaos shattered into a thousand shards of bone and sinew, the human-skin sail ripping to shreds. The sound was a wild cacophony of snapping and booming and tearing and cracking. The four drow and the draegloth aboard the ship were sent spinning into the air, rolling and tumbling to a stop on the burning sand.

TWENTY-TWO

It was raining souls.

All around Pharaun, one after another, transparent wraiths dropped from the burning sky onto the blasted sand of the Plain of Infinite Portals. He could pick out representatives of a thousand different races. Some he recognized, and some he didn't. There was everything from the lowliest kobold to enormous giants, humans by the hundreds, and no shortage of duergar. Pharaun could only hope that the latter were coming straight from the siege of Menzoberranzan.

Someone stepped close to him, and the Master of Sorcere turned to look. It was then that he realized he was lying on his back on the uncomfortably hot sand looking up. The wispy shade of a departed soul passed by him. The newly dead orc looked down but didn't seem to see Pharaun. Maybe the creature didn't care. It was headed to some porcine hell to serve its grunting god or demon prince, probably as a light supper. So what if it passed a sleeping dark elf along the way?

Pharaun blinked, expecting the passing orc to at least kick sand in his face, but the thing's feet were as insubstantial as they looked, and it made no sign of its passing on the dead ground. The Master of Sorcere slowly rose to a sitting position under painful protest from a dozen muscles, at least three of which he hadn't realized he possessed.

Taking a deep breath, he looked around.

The wreckage of the ship of chaos seemed oddly suited to their surroundings. Jagged fingers of bleached-white bone stood up like a more substantial line of souls against the red sky. The parts of the ship that had been alive with blood and breath sat shriveled and gray on the unforgiving sand.

Jeggred stood slouched in the center of the wrecked ship, his wild mane of white hair blowing madly in the hot wind. The draegloth stared at Pharaun expectantly. He looked even more battered and bruised, and he was bleeding again from a number of small wounds.

Danifae stepped out from behind the enormous half-demon. She held a long shard of broken bone and was dusty and disheveled but otherwise looked no worse for wear. The battle-captive looked down at the bone fragment she carried then absently tossed it to the ground where it clattered to a stop amid a myriad of shards like it. Danifae followed Jeggred's eyes to Pharaun.

The sound of a sigh startled the mage, and he spun, still sitting, to see Valas crouched next to him. He hadn't seen or heard the scout approach.

"Are you injured?" the mercenary asked him.

The scout's voice rose and fell on the wind, sounding distant though it came from only the few inches between his lips to Pharaun's ear.

"No," Pharaun answered, hearing his own voice echo in the same way. "I'm quite fine, actually. Thank you for asking, Master Hune."

"I'm no one's master," Valas replied, not looking the mage in the eye.

He stood and began to wander slowly back in the direction of the debris field.

Pharaun asked of all three of them, "Has anyone seen Quenthel?"

"I will thank you," Quenthel said from behind him, "to refer to me as 'Mistress.' "

Pharaun didn't bother to turn. Quenthel walked past him, looking all around, apparently not giving the mage a second thought.

"My apologies, *Mistress*," he said. "I will extend Ma . . . Valas's question to the rest of you. Are you all all right?"

Quenthel, Danifae, and Jeggred variously shrugged, nodded, or ignored him, and Pharaun decided that was good enough.

"Frankly," Pharaun added, "I'm utterly shocked we survived that crash. That was impressive, even by my standards. What an entrance."

The others only sneered at him, except Valas, who shrugged and began to shift though the wreckage.

"Yes, quite an entrance, but I'm getting worried about our exit," Danifae said. "How do you plan to get us back?"

Pharaun opened his mouth to speak then clamped his teeth shut.

He didn't say anything to Danifae but assumed his silence was explanation enough. Pharaun had no idea how they were going to get back to their home plane, home world, and home city without the ship of chaos.

"Lolth," Quenthel said, "will provide."

No one looked at the high priestess or commented on how little faith was evident in her voice.

Danifae scanned around her and up into the air as the phantasms continued to drop from the sky, only to form columns then pitch themselves headlong into one of the endless array of black, puckered pits that looked like bottomless craters scattered around them as far as the eye could see in all directions. None of them were marked in any way that Pharaun recognized, and he hadn't the faintest clue which of the pits would take them to the Demonweb Pits, the sixty-sixth layer of that endless infernal plane.

"What are they?" Danifae asked, looking around at the falling apparitions.

"The dead," Quenthel answered, her voice barely audible through all the unnatural echoes that the air around them threw in and around her words.

"Departed souls from all over the Prime," Pharaun added. "Anyone who served one of the Abyssal gods in life will pass through here then jump into the appropriate portal and they're on their way. Each of these pits leads to a different layer, almost an entirely different world. There are an endless number of them. This plain literally goes on into infinity in all directions."

Jeggred snorted, stood, and shook blood, water, and sand from his fur.

"So?" the draegloth asked.

Pharaun shrugged and said, "Actually I was hoping you could tell us more, Jeggred. After all you were sired by a native of the Abyss, and even a half-blooded tanar'ri should have some sensitivity to—"

"Never been here," the draegloth grunted. "You've mentioned my sire for the last time, too, wizard."

Pharaun was interrupted before he could answer the draegloth's unsubtle threat.

"How do we find the right one?" Danifae asked. "The right portal, I mean."

Jeggred growled once and said, "There is only one entrance for each layer, but there are an infinite number of layers. We could be standing right next to the pit that will take us to the Demonweb Pits, or it could be a thousand miles or more in any direction . . . a million miles even."

"Not likely, actually," said Pharaun, "but thank you for the vote of confidence anyway, honored half-breed—" Danifae put a hand on Jeggred's arm when the draegloth lurched for Pharaun at the sound of that word—"but I was guiding the ship, at least up until the very end there, and I was willing it not simply to take us to the Plain of Infinite Portals but to the one portal that would take us where we wanted to go. Even though we crashed, we must be close by it. The ship was moving us at least in its general direction before things went astray."

"Well it's good to know that you're not entirely inept, Pharaun," Quenthel said, her voice louder and oddly more confident than it had been in a long while, "but I will take it . . . take *us*, from here."

Pharaun watched another ghostly orc step past him. It dropped into a deep back hole in the ground. There was no sound, nothing at all to signal that it had hit bottom or that anything had happened to it at all. It was gone.

"My first instinct," Valas said, "would be to pick out a column of drow and follow them."

"Do you see any drow?" Quenthel asked.

"No," Danifae whispered.

The sound of her voice made Pharaun's skin crawl.

"So what do we do?" the draegloth asked.

"Follow me," the high priestess replied. "I'll know the right pit when I see it."

"How?" Pharaun asked.

Quenthel said, "I've passed through it before."

The Mistress of Arach-Tinilith set out before any of them realized she meant to leave right away. Danifae and Jeggred watched her go then shared a look that made it obvious that neither of them believed the high priestess.

Valas followed her, as did Pharaun, albeit as reluctantly as Danifae and Jeggred.

Aliisza watched from a safe distance as the dark elves brushed themselves off and regrouped.

Have I underestimated you? she thought, watching Pharaun struggle to his feet.

She whispered, "Probably not," to herself and mulled over her next move.

Kaanyr Vhok's instructions were clear, even if they hadn't included helping the drow get to the Abyss in the first place. She was supposed to watch them, so she would do that at least until she got bored.

Aliisza looked out over the Plain of Infinite Portals, the gateway to the Abyss, and sighed. It had been a very long time since she'd been home, and at first it looked the same. She watched the ship of chaos fall through a red sky she used to fly through as a girl, then crash on sand she once sculpted into monsters from faraway universes— monsters like solars, ki-rin, and humans. It looked the same, but it wasn't—not quite.

Perhaps she had spent too much time with the goddess-obsessed dark elves, but Aliisza was sure there was something different about the Abyss, as if a piece of it were missing.

The feeling didn't make sense, and it confused the alu-fiend and made her uncomfortable, so she pushed it out of her mind.

Aliisza forced herself to smile even though she didn't feel like smiling, as she followed the drow from a safe distance and invisible.

The alu-fiend wasn't the only demonic creature that watched the drow just then. Another looked on from a similar far vantage point, cloaked in invisibility and other defensive spells. The creature seethed with hatred.

Floating in the air high above the Plain of Infinite Portals, the glabrezu touched the ruined stump of its legs and growled, "Soon, drow. Soon . . ."

Halisstra ran a finger along the warm, glowing edge of the Crescent Blade and marveled at its beauty. It was a magnificent weapon, and one she would never feel worthy of. Ryld should have drawn that blade, not her. Ryld would have known what to do with it.

The Melarn priestess felt the absence of her lover in a physically painful way. There was an emptiness in her chest that burned, that ached, that throbbed with uncertainty and longing, and a host of other emotions both alien and familiar.

"If you can't do it," Feliane whispered to her, "you need to tell me now. Now, before we go any farther."

Halisstra looked up at Feliane and her eyesight blurred with tears.

"Tell me," the Eilistraeen prodded.

Halisstra wiped her eyes and said, "I can do it."

The elf priestess stared at her, waiting for Halisstra to go on.

Halisstra looked down at her tear-soaked hand with blurred vision. Her eyes were hot, her throat so tight it was painful. She hadn't done much crying in her life and had certainly never cried over the fate of a male, a soldier . . . anyone.

I've changed, she thought. I am changing.

"He didn't want me to," Halisstra whispered.

"He wanted you to go back to the Underdark," said Uluyara, "if not to Lolth."

Halisstra looked up at the drow priestess. Uluyara stood in the doorway, framed by the blinding twilight behind her. She was dressed for battle, covered in tokens made of feathers, sticks, and shards of bone. Halisstra nodded, and Uluyara stepped in.

The drow priestess crossed to the bed that Halisstra had once shared with Ryld Argith and kneeled. She took Halisstra's chin in one rough-fingered hand, holding her gently and forcing their eyes to meet.

"If they killed him," Uluyara said, "it's but another reason to do what you've been doing, another reason to leave them behind at least and defeat them forever if possible."

"By killing Lolth?" asked Halisstra.

"Yes," answered Feliane, who still stood leaning against the weed-covered wall, also dressed for battle and for a long journey.

"I need you to tell me something," Halisstra asked, her eyes darting back and forth between the two women. "I need you to tell me that this is possible, I mean even remotely possible."

Uluyara smiled and shrugged, but Feliane said, "It's possible."

Both Halisstra and Uluyara looked over at her.

"Anything is possible," Feliane explained, "with the right tools and with a goddess on your side."

"Eilistraee can't go where we're going," Halisstra said, "not to the Demonweb Pits."

"No, she can't," Uluyara agreed. "That's why she's sending us."

"If we die there," Halisstra asked Uluyara, who dropped her hand from the priestess's chin, "what becomes of us?"

"We go to Eilistraee," Uluyara replied.

Halisstra could hear the certainty in the drow's reply and see it in her eyes.

"I don't know that for sure," Halisstra said.

"So," said Feliane, "what do you know for sure?"

Halisstra looked at her and the elf returned the gaze with almost perfect stillness.

"I know . . ." Halisstra began even as she was thinking it through. "I know that Lolth abandoned me and was a cruel mistress who let our city, our way of life fall into ruin, perhaps simply to satisfy some whim. I know that her temple on the sixty-sixth layer is sealed and there are no departed souls there. I know that eternity is closed off to me, thanks to her."

"What has changed?" asked Feliane.

Halisstra looked at Uluyara when she said, "Eilistraee."

"Eilistraee hasn't changed," Uluyara whispered.

"No," Halisstra agreed, "I have."

Uluyara smiled, and so did Halisstra, then the Melarn priestess began to cry.

"I miss him," she said through a sob.

Uluyara put a hand on Halisstra's neck and drew her closer until their foreheads touched.

"Would you have been able to miss him," asked Uluyara, "if you were still Halisstra Melarn, First Daughter of House Melarn of Ched Nasad, Priestess of Lolth? Would that ever have entered into your mind?"

"No," Halisstra replied without hesitation.

"Then Eilistraee has touched you," said Uluyara. "Eilistraee has blessed you."

Halisstra looked up at Feliane and asked, "Do you believe that too?"

Feliane looked at her for the span of a few heartbeats then said, "I do. You wield the Crescent Blade, if for no other reason . . . but there are other reasons. Yes, I think Eilistraee has blessed you, indeed, and blessed us all with your presence."

Halisstra nodded then looked to Uluyara. The other drow female nodded and hugged her. The embrace was a quick one, sisterly, warm, and reassuring.

"Well," Halisstra said when the embrace ended, "I think we should begin. There's a long road ahead for us and the most frightening opponent of all at the end of it: a goddess on her home plane."

Uluyara stood, helping Halisstra up with her. Halisstra dressed for travel and for fighting as the other two had, but when she was done she felt heavy and stiff.

Gromph's world had been reduced to a series of circles.

The antimagic field surrounded him in a circle of null space that would dissipate any spell that tried to pierce it and suppress any magical effect within it. The pain in his leg circled all the way around, where the interrupted regenerative effect of the ring had only partially reattached it, leaving a ragged, seeping wound all the way around the middle of his thigh. Past the outer edge of the antimagic field a tiny circle—a sphere really—of condensed magical fire orbited slowly around and around. It was Dyrr's next explosive blast of fire, held in check, circling, waiting for the field to drop. The lichdrow was circling him too, and like his fireball, waiting.

Gromph sat on the cool rock floor of the ruined Bazaar trying not to actually writhe in agony, concentrating on his breathing, and making himself think.

"How long can it last, Gromph?" the lichdrow taunted from well outside the antimagic field. "Not forever, I know. Not as long as my own would. Am I that frightening to you that you have to hide so, even in plain sight?"

Gromph didn't bother answering. He wasn't afraid of the lichdrow. In fact, he was more concerned with Nimor Imphraezl. The winged assassin had disappeared into the shadows, back into his natural element. He could be anywhere. Dyrr, a being literally held together by magic, would no more cross the threshold of the antimagic field than he would throw himself headlong into the Clawrift. Nimor, on the other hand, had likely lost most if not all of his magic in the disjunction anyway and needed no spell to cut with his claws.

The Weave was blocked by the field, but that was all. Gromph, weak and in pain from loss of blood and the morbid wound in his leg, was all but helpless against anything but spells. Nimor could walk right up—anyone could walk right up—and kill the Archmage of Menzoberranzan with a dagger across the throat.

At least, Gromph thought, I don't have to listen to Prath remind me of that.

The field blocked the telepathic link he'd established with the other Baenre mages. Gromph was entirely on his own, though he was sure Nauzhror and the others were still watching.

"Please tell me you aren't going to just sit there and die," Dyrr said. "I've come to expect so much more from you."

"Have you?" Gromph answered, every word coming with a painful effort. "What have you . . . come to expect . . . from Nimor?"

"Why, Archmage," the lich replied, "whatever do you mean?"

"Where is he?" Gromph said. "Where has your half-dragon gone? He could kill me easily enough, and we both know that. Has he—" Gromph winced through a wave of pain—"abandoned you?"

"I never trusted Nimor Imphraezl," said the lich. "What's your excuse?"

Gromph puzzled over that last comment.

Still, some of what the lich said rang painfully true. If he didn't drop the antimagic field, the ring would never finish reattaching his leg. If he sat there he would succumb to shock, loss of blood, even infection soon enough. The only thing keeping Dyrr from killing him was killing him.

Gromph did nothing to alert Dyrr to his intentions. He didn't draw in any dramatic, shuddering breath. He didn't move his trembling, pain-ravaged body. He didn't even look at the lich or at the bead of compressed fire waiting for its chance to immolate him. Everything that was happening was occurring inside his mind.

Gromph mentally arranged spells, bringing the opening stanzas to mind, willing his fingers in advance to form the gestures. He kept one hand on his staff, knowing that its magic wasn't gone but was simply suppressed, waiting the same way Dyrr's fireball—and Dyrr himself—was waiting.

He dropped the antimagic field, and in that same instant the globe burst back around him and the spell tripped rapidly past his lips. The bead of fire dropped out of its lazy orbit and shot at him as fast as a bolt from a crossbow, but Gromph's spell was a split second faster. The spell enabled him to push the bead of fire away with a wave of invisible force. Using the power of his mind, Gromph seized control of the nascent fireball and sent it hurtling back at the lichdrow.

Dyrr backed quickly away from it then turned and flew fast. Gromph kept the fireball racing toward the lich, gaining on him.

The pain in his leg began to fade and was replaced once more by pulses of nettling as it drew itself together. Concentrating on chasing the fleeing lich with his own fireball, Gromph didn't see the blood that still surrounded him—his own blood—being soaked up by the skin of his leg. As it drew into his tissue, the blood itself warmed, and one by one the cells came back to life.

The bead of fire was within a handspan of the fleeing lich when Nimor stabbed Gromph in the back.

The archmage might have thought that he'd be accustomed to the odd blast of mind-ravaging agony by then, but the pain hit him full force. He could feel every fraction of an inch of the blade's path through his skin, into and through the muscles of his back. He could feel the cold steel pierce his heart.

Gromph gasped and lost control of the spell that held the fireball. He closed his eyes against the flare of it exploding—too far from Gromph to burn him but too far from the lich to damage him either.

That wasn't the only fire. The flickering shield of arcane flames that had surrounded him before he cast the antimagic field had returned to him as had the globe. Fire poured over the wound in Gromph's back even though it hadn't protected him from the dagger. Fire washed over Nimor, who released the knife and staggered back, waving off the flames that once again seared his shadow-black face.

The dagger was still in him, still in his heart, and Gromph lurched forward to sprawl on his stomach on the unforgiving floor of the Bazaar. The ring fought second by second to keep his heart intact, to keep it beating, to keep his blood flowing, but it did nothing for the pain. The archmage's vision blurred, and when he tried to reach behind him to pull the dagger out of his back he could only twitch his arm uselessly at his side.

The archmage was vaguely aware of heat, light, and the sound of crackling, a dull roar . . . fire.

He blinked. His vision cleared enough to see a row of burning merchant's stalls and a thick column of smoke rising into the still, warming air. Hovering in stark, spindly silhouette against the blinding orange flames was the figure of the lichdrow Dyrr.

Gromph coughed and felt something warm and thick trickle from his lips. The dagger twitched in his back, and Gromph was afraid that it was Nimor, turning the blade, driving it deeper, or withdrawing it only to plunge it home again.

No, Nauzhror said into Gromph's confused, slowing mind. *It's the ring. Don't move, Archmage. Try not to move for a few seconds more.*

Gromph looked up at the hovering lich and saw another black silhouette join him to hover far above the burning stalls. The second silhouette had huge, semi-transparent wings traced with veins.

The dagger twitched again, and Gromph coughed more blood as it came free of his heart, only to knick his lung.

A few more seconds, Master, Nauzhror said. *Patience.*

Gromph let that last word play in his mind. He had no choice but to be patient. To him, it felt as if the pain were actually pushing him down, driving him into the rock beneath him.

The two black figures started to grow against the roiling backdrop of uncontrolled fire. They were coming for him. They meant to end it.

The dagger slipped out of Gromph's back to clatter on the stone floor beside him. He shuddered through a last spasm of pain and clenched his chest when his heart skipped a beat then started up again, strong and regular. The archmage began to cast a spell.

Gromph rolled into a seated position as he cast, turning to face his enemies with fire reflected in his stolen eyes. Nimor was closer, coming at him with his shadow dragon's claws, so Gromph directed the spell at him. The archmage sent a rolling wave of blinding fire at the assassin, but Nimor stepped quickly to one side and was gone, sinking into the shadows like a rock slipping under the surface of Donigarten Lake.

The conjured fire flared past the spot where the assassin had been standing, burning nothing but empty air.

Gromph cringed.

It's all right, Archmage, Nauzhror said.

No it's not, Gromph shot back at him. *I'm using too much fire against Nimor.*

It's true— Prath began but stopped so abruptly Gromph was sure it was Nauzhror who silenced him—lucky for Prath.

The lichdrow stopped his advance and waved his hands in front of him. Gromph tightened his grip on his staff, sighing as the last of the grievous wounds were closed forever by the magic of the ring.

A faint mist coalesced in the air in front of Dyrr, adding to itself one mote at a time until a wide, flat cloud of churning mist rolled out away from the lich and toward Gromph.

The archmage got to his feet and uttered the single triggering command that activated another of his staff's array of powers. Gromph couldn't see it, but thanks to the magic of the staff he was keenly aware of the confines of the invisible wall he'd conjured in front of him.

The cloud of—Gromph assumed—poisonous gas that Dyrr had conjured mixed with the smoke from the burning stalls, slowing it but not stopping it. Gromph set the wall of magical force between himself and the cloud, and in a moment the mist began to spread along the flat surface of the wall, well away from the archmage.

Dyrr, obviously not surprised by Gromph's simple solution to the killing cloud, arced high into the air and flew over the wall of force.

The lich drew a wand from the folds of his *piwafwi* and stared at Gromph with a face devoid of emotion.

Gromph began to cast, judging the time necessary by the lich's flying speed. Even when Dyrr accelerated, Gromph had the opportunity to finish the spell and step through the doorway he opened in the air next to him. Like passing through an ordinary door, Gromph stepped out the other side having traveled a dozen yards across the burning Bazaar. He watched the lich swoop down, swing his wand through the spot where Gromph had been standing, then come to rest on the ground growling in frustration.

Gromph dropped the wall of force and smiled.

The cloud of poisonous gas—Dyrr's own spell—burst through when the wall fell, and the lich only had time to look up before the mist engulfed him and he disappeared inside its black-and-green expanse.

Gromph took a deep breath and glanced down when the fire shield finally faded from him. The spell he cast next was one of his most difficult. He worked it carefully and reveled as its effects washed through him. All at once he got the distinct impression that someone was behind him, and he knew that the spell was warning him. No one was behind him yet, but someone would be.

Gromph spun in place then stepped back when Nimor appeared from the shadows, already bringing one black-taloned hand down at the archmage's face. The tips of the claws passed within a finger's breadth of the archmage's nose. Nimor let the surprise show in his eyes, and Gromph had to admit to himself at least that he was just as surprised.

The archmage skipped back several steps, and so did the assassin. Nimor looked at Gromph with narrowed eyes that glowed in the smoky shadows of the burning Bazaar. Gromph had a clear vision of Nimor stepping in then quickly to the left and slashing at his side—then Nimor did just that. Gromph managed to step away again, and again the assassin was taken aback by the archmage's newfound reflexes. What Nimor didn't know was that it wasn't reflexes but foresight.

Gromph reached into a pouch—an extradimensional space that held much more than it appeared capable of from the outside—and drew a weapon. The duergar's battle-axe was heavy, and the weight and heft of it was unfamiliar to Gromph. The archmage had been schooled in the use of a number of weapons, but the battle-axe was hardly his cup of tea. It was unwieldy and unsubtle, almost more a tool than a weapon. However, there was more to that particular axe than its blade and a handle.

He knew that Nimor was going to step back and give himself a chance to examine Gromph's weapon. The archmage also expected that Nimor would move a few steps to one side in order to turn Gromph around and place himself between the half-dragon and the cloud that still concealed the lichdrow. Gromph gave him the chance he wanted to study the axe but didn't oblige him with the superior position.

Archmage, Nauzhror said, *are you certain?*

Gromph assumed that the other mage was referring to the battle-axe, and the obvious fact that Gromph meant to actually fight the assassin with physical weapons.

Gromph sent back the answer, *I know what I'm doing,* at precisely the same moment that Nauzhror repeated, *Archmage, are you certain?*

Gromph realized he hadn't heard Nauzhror the first time. It was the spell, showing him the future.

I see, Nauzhror replied and Gromph could feel that the other Baenre mage understood that Gromph had armed himself with perhaps the most potent weapon imaginable: the ability to perfectly anticipate every move of your opponent.

The voice came to his head for real: *I see.*

Gromph knew that Nimor was going to rush him in an attempt to push him back toward the cloud of poison gas, so the archmage stepped quickly to the side and circled. Nimor took one step then stopped, eyeing Gromph.

The lich burst out of the cloud, trailing tendrils of toxic mist as he rose into the air. He turned and faced the archmage.

"Go ahead," said the lichdrow with a leering, evil smile, "try to fight him with your stolen axe. I'll enjoy watching Nimor shred you."

The half-dragon assassin smiled at that, and Gromph saw him

coming in with one wild slash after another, a flurry of claws and kicks and head butts. Gromph had no idea what to do.

In the instant that Nimor started to run toward him, Gromph realized that knowing what your opponent intended to do might not be enough.

TWENTY-THREE

How could there be any sense to a world that existed in a universe made of chaos? In a place where the only rule was that there were no rules?

When they were there last, not very long ago, they walked enormous strands of spiderweb and saw nothing alive until they were beset upon by a horde of feral demons at the gates to a temple sealed by the face of Lolth herself. There, a god tried to break through but couldn't.

Though they had been away from the Demonweb Pits for only a short time, much had changed.

The smooth expanse of the gigantic webs was pitted and worn. Patches of what looked like rust went on for acres at a time. In spots they had to climb or levitate up and down cliffs of crumbling webbing and traverse craters big enough to hold all of Menzoberranzan in their uneven bowls.

All around them was the stench of decay, so intense at times Pharaun Mizzrym thought he would suffocate.

The wizard had been walking for hours in uncharacteristic silence. None of the drow or the draegloth commented aloud on the state of the Demonweb Pits. It was too difficult to voice the palpable sense of despair the ruined place imbued in them all. They stopped occasionally to rest, and minutes would go by where they didn't even look at each other.

Constantly on their guard for the plane's demonic inhabitants, at first they were all on a knife's edge, but as the hours dragged on and they saw nothing alive, let alone threatening, they soon began to relax. That was when the despair deepened even further.

They walked on and on and finally came to Lolth's temple. The once imposing, otherworldly structure stood in ruin, infected by the same decay as the universe-spanning web. The obsidian stone had turned brown and was crumbled away in spots. Huge columns of smoke rose from the interior. Many of the great buttresses stood like shattered stumps, amputated by some inconceivable power. The surrounding plazas were difficult to traverse, littered with boulders of carved stone and iron rusted and twisted out of shape. Bones lay everywhere—the bones of millions stacked in great piles or scattered as if by the cruel winds alone. The petrified spider-things they had marveled at before were gone, leaving holes in the floor of the plaza and along the buttresses as if they'd pulled up their feet from the stone and marched away.

The party traced the same path they had taken when in astral form and came once again to the entrance to the temple. The great stone face was itself shattered, revealing glimpses of the visage of Lolth but only in tiny, enigmatic fragments.

The doors swung wide.

"It was the gods," Valas whispered, his voice echoing in a million tiny pings across the ruined plaza.

Vhaeraun, who had come to kill Lolth because of their own rash decision to lead one of his priests there, had been confronted by Selvetarm—Lolth's protector—at the temple gates. Their duel was a sight that would be burned into Pharaun's memory if he lived to be ten thousand years old, and the contest had caused much damage, but. . . .

"Not this," the Master of Sorcere said, his own voice echoing, though in not quite the same way. "This is different. Older."

"Older?" the draegloth asked, his eyes darting from rock to rock.

"He's right," said Danifae, who was crouching, holding the skull of something that might have been half drow, half bat. "These bones are dried and bleached, almost petrified. The stone itself is crumbling to dust. The webs are rotten and brittle."

"This place was razed a century ago or more," Pharaun said.

"That's not possible," Valas argued, staring up at the open doors. "We were just here—*right* here, and the doors were sealed, and . . ."

The others didn't expect him to finish.

"Lolth has left this place," Quenthel said, her voice so quiet it barely managed to elicit an echo at all.

"She has left the Demonweb Pits?" Danifae asked. "How could that be?"

"She has left the Abyss," the Mistress of Arach-Tinilith said. "Can't you feel it?"

Danifae shook her head, but her eyes answered in the affirmative. The two females shared a long, knowing look that raised the hair on the back of Pharaun's neck. He sensed similar reactions from Jeggred and Valas.

"That's it then," said the Bregan D'aerthe scout. "We have come here to find the goddess but instead we have found nothing. Our mission is at an end."

Quenthel turned to glare at the scout, who returned it with a steady, even gaze. The vipers that made up the high priestess's scourge writhed and spat, but Valas paid them no mind.

"She isn't here," Quenthel said, "but that doesn't mean she isn't . . . somewhere."

The scout took a deep breath and let it out slowly, looking all around at the ruined temple.

"So where is she?" he asked. "How much farther do we go? Do

we search the limitless multiverse for her, plane by plane, universe by universe? She's a creature of the Demonweb Pits, and here we stand on the sixty-sixth layer of the gods-cursed Abyss and she's gone. If you don't know where she's gone to—and she could be anywhere—and she won't tell you where she is, maybe we all have to accept the fact that she doesn't want to be found."

It was the most Pharaun had ever heard Valas say all at once, and the words made his heart sink.

"He's right," said the Master of Sorcere.

To his surprise, Quenthel nodded. Danifae's eyes widened, and Jeggred growled low in his throat. The draegloth moved slowly, in that fluid, stalking way of his, and went to stand next to the former battle-captive.

"This is sacrilege," Danifae whispered. "Heresy of the worst sort."

Quenthel turned to look at the other priestess and silently raised an eyebrow.

"You presume to allow some—" Danifae turned to briefly glare at Valas— "*male* to speak for Lolth? Does he decide the goddess's intentions now?"

"Do you?" Pharaun couldn't help but ask.

Surprisingly, Danifae smiled when she said, "Perhaps I do. Certainly I have more claim to that right than Master Hune. Capable a scout as he is, this is the business of priestesses now."

Quenthel stood a little straighter, though her shoulders still hunched. Pharaun marveled at how old she looked. The high priestess had aged decades in the past tenday, and exhaustion was plain in her heavy-lidded eyes and blunt temper.

Pharaun couldn't look at her, so he looked down at the floor of the plaza. He scuffed his boot through brown-powdered stone.

"I was wrong," the Master of Sorcere said. He could feel the others looking at him, could sense their surprise, but he didn't look up. "This didn't happen a century ago. This place was destroyed . . . no, a battle was fought here, and it was fought a millennium past at least. At least."

"How can you say that, wizard?" asked the draegloth. "You

were just here. Weren't you? Isn't this the same place Tzirik brought you?"

Pharaun nodded and said, "It is indeed, Jeggred, but the fact remains that what we see all around us is an ancient ruin, the corpse of a battlefield that's lain cold for a thousand years or more."

"We were only just here," said Valas.

"We aren't in the Underdark anymore, Master Hune," said Pharaun. "Time might move very differently here, in fits and starts like distance in the Shadow Deep. This could all be more illusion than real, the whim of Lolth or some other godly power. It could be that we simply see a ruin where there is nothing, see a ruin where there is in fact an intact temple, or everything we see is real and made a millennium old by a power so vast that it can manipulate time and matter and the æther itself."

"The Spider Queen isn't here," Valas added.

"If the priestesses say that she is not here," Pharaun replied, "then I'm content to believe that's true."

The Master of Sorcere looked up at the enormous open doorway, big enough for House Baenre to pass through it intact. The others followed his gaze.

"These doors were sealed shut before," Pharaun said, "but now they're open. Why?"

"Because Lolth wants us to step through them," Danifae said, her voice carrying a certainty that surprised Pharaun. "Who else could have opened them?"

Pharaun shrugged and looked at Quenthel, who was nodding slowly.

"We go on," the high priestess said.

Without a glance at the others, Quenthel walked toward the mammoth doorway. One by one the others followed: Danifae, then Jeggred, then Pharaun, and Valas at the rear. Each stepped more reluctantly than the last.

On the planes of chaos there were so many names for it, Aliisza didn't remember them all: temporal flux zones, slipped time layers, millennia sinks. . . . It had been a very long time since she'd seen one, and it took her almost as long to realize what was happening.

The sixty-sixth layer of the Abyss had been abandoned. The glue that held the planes together was the gods themselves, and in the planes of chaos, just as in the planes of law, when all the gods left a particular place, entropy progressed in fits and starts, and even chaos itself spiraled out of control.

In the case of the sixty-sixth layer, there was the rest of the Abyss to hold it together and to provide echoes of its past that were strong enough to keep its physical form—in that there still was a sixty-sixth layer. Time was moving forward faster at times, then slower, then it might reverse itself. It was impossible to pin down, even for a tanar'ri like Aliisza. Places like that were better left alone, better avoided, better forgotten.

She watched Pharaun and his companions walk through the massive temple gates with a heavy heart. She didn't know exactly what they would find in there, but she was sure that whatever it was it would be disappointing for them. They had traveled to the sixty-sixth layer to find Lolth, but Lolth wasn't there. It was a guess on her part, but an educated one: the plane had been abandoned for longer than anyone imagined—longer than Lolth had been silent.

"There's a lot you never told them," Aliisza whispered to the Spider Queen.

If the goddess could hear her—and Aliisza had no reason to believe she could—Lolth didn't answer.

The alu-fiend absently scratched a doodle in the brown dust on the underside of the massive web strand onto which she clung: a bit of graffiti no eyes would ever see. Her mind was racing; she had a lot to think about.

Aliisza had abandoned Pharaun and the others, leaving them to crash into the Plain of Infinite Portals simply on a whim. It pleased her that Pharaun survived, but she didn't give the others a second thought. Still, Aliisza had made her choice, and it was an obvious one. She chose Kaanyr Vhok.

Though she knew she would go back to him, she also knew that she had helped Pharaun and his expedition along a bit more effectively than Vhok would have approved of. He might not have asked her to stop them, but he certainly hadn't asked her to help them. Aliisza knew the cambion well enough, though, to know that the more she came back with, the more forgiving he would be.

Pharaun and the other drow disappeared into the abandoned ruin, and Aliisza closed her eyes.

She was a tanar'ri and as such could move about the planes with a bit more ease than most. With a thought she was back in the Astral, floating free in the endless æther.

"You left the Abyss," Aliisza whispered to herself, though she addressed Lolth, "before you fell silent, so . . ."

She didn't bother finishing the thought, only concentrated on a name: Lolth.

She closed her eyes again and let the name roll over and over again in her mind, and after a time, her body began to move. Any god's name has power, if you know how to use it.

When she opened her eyes she was surrounded by ghosts.

Translucent gray shades floated all around her, all of them with similar features: the pointed ears, almond-shaped eyes, and thin, aristocratic faces of the dark elves. There were a lot of them—a war's worth—and they were all headed across the Astral Plane toward the same destination.

Aliisza drifted in front of one of them, a strong-looking male dressed for battle, regal in his armor and helm.

"Can you hear me?" she asked the spirit. "Can you see me?"

The dead drow looked right at her and lifted an eyebrow. He stood stock still, but his body continued to drift through the endless expanse, unerringly falling sideways toward its final destination.

"My name is Aliisza," she said. "Do you know where you are?"

Yes, the drow answered directly into her mind. His mouth was open, but his lips didn't move. *I can feel it. I'm dead. I died. I was killed.*

"What is your name?"

I was Vilto'sat Shobalar, the soldier answered, *but now I am nothing. My body rots away, my House forgets me, and I pass on. Are you here to torment me?*

"I'm sorry?" the alu-fiend asked, confused by the drow spirit's sudden change of subject.

You're a demon, he said. *Are you here to torment me? For my failure on the battlefield or simply to satisfy your cruel nature?*

Aliisza's hackles rose, and she couldn't help but sneer at the dead drow. He had obviously mistaken her for a different sort of tanar'ri altogether, and she didn't find it flattering in the least.

"If I was here to torment you," she said, "you'd know it, mushroom farm."

Vilto'sat Shobalar turned away from her with a look of haughty contempt that was the only thing, apparently, dark elves took to the grave.

Aliisza moved on along the line of dead drow, and as she progressed in the direction of their travel, moving faster than the wandering souls, the density of the ghosts increased, as if they had been stacking up, one after another, for a long time. Finally, her curiosity getting the better of her, she stopped another drow spirit: a female dressed in finery that made the alu-fiend momentarily jealous.

"Lady," she said, sketching an overwrought bow that the dead dark elf seemed to find insulting, "may I speak with you briefly as you complete your journey?"

There's nothing you can do to torment me, demon, the shade said into Aliisza's mind, *so move on and let me be dead in peace.*

Aliisza hissed and almost reached out to grab the female by her throat then realized that her hands would pass through the priestess. The dead female would have no physical form again until she arrived at her final destination. The Astral Plane was only a way to get from one universe to another. There, the dead drow were incorporeal ghosts.

"I'm not here to torment you, bitch," Aliisza said, "but I will if you don't answer a question or two."

Lolth has turned her back on us, the priestess replied. *What worse could you do?*

"I could leave you in the Astral forever," Aliisza replied—a hollow threat, but the ghost didn't need to know that.

What do you want? the drow replied.

"Who are you," she asked, "and how long have you been here, awaiting Lolth's grace?"

I am Greyanna Mizzrym, the ghost replied—and Aliisza thought something about the name was oddly familiar. *I have no idea how long I've been here, but I can feel myself moving. That only just started. Is Lolth ready to take us in? Has she sent you?*

"Can you feel her?" Aliisza asked, ignoring he dark elf's questions. "Does she call you?"

The priestess looked away, as if listening for something, then she shook her head.

I'm moving toward something, Greyanna said. *I can feel it, but I do not hear Lolth.*

Aliisza turned to look in the direction the line of drow souls were moving. At the end of the very long line was a whirlpool of red and black—a gateway to the outer planes that was drawing the souls in.

"That's not the Abyss," Aliisza said.

It's home, whispered the bodiless soul of Greyanna Mizzrym. *I can feel it. It is. It's the Demonweb Pits.*

Aliisza's heart raced.

"The Demonweb Pits," the alu-fiend repeated, "but not the Abyss."

Aliisza stopped herself and hung in the gray expanse off to one side of the procession of dead drow.

"Well," Aliisza whispered to an unhearing Lolth, "moving up in the world, aren't we?"

The alu-fiend closed her eyes and concentrated on Kaanyr Vhok. She let her consciousness travel through the Astral and back to the cold, hard Underdark. There she found her lover's mind and dropped a message into it.

Something is happening with the Demonweb Pits, she sent. *It's a plane unto itself now, and the gates are open. Lolth welcomes home the dead. She lives.*

That was all she could say, and she hoped it would be warning enough. Aliisza could have shifted back to the Underdark in an instant and been by her lover's side, but she didn't. She wanted to stay where she was, though she didn't know why.

Nimor had given up trying to claw Gromph. Instead, he started to work on forcing the archmage to attack him, but the drow wouldn't oblige. The feeling Nimor had that Gromph somehow knew what he was thinking—maybe before he even thought it—grew stronger and stronger and made Nimor start to second-guess himself. It was no way to fight.

Nimor stepped back and so did Gromph. The assassin could see Dyrr slowly circling them both from a safe—some would say cowardly—distance. The assassin was about to speak when a familiar nettling buzzed in his skull.

Aliisza is in the Demonweb Pits, the voice of Kaanyr Vhok sounded in his head. *Something is happening, and it will be bad for us all. I'm not waiting to find out how bad.*

For the first time in a very, very long time, Nimor's blood ran cold.

Gromph twitched, almost gasped, and Nimor couldn't help but look at him. Their eyes locked, and an instant of understanding passed between them. Nimor stepped back, and Gromph nodded. The archmage still kept the ghostly battle-axe in front of him but didn't advance. He breathed heavily, sweat running down the sides of his face and matting his snow-white hair to his forehead.

Again, Nimor was about to speak, and again he was interrupted.

"What are you doing?" the lichdrow demanded. "Kill him!"

Nimor let a long, steady breath hiss out through clenched teeth. It was bad enough that a key component of his alliance was abandoning the cause, worse still that Lolth was somehow, for some reason he might never understand, choosing that moment to finally return—or do something that scared Kaanyr Vhok, anyway, and the cambion wasn't the type to scare easily. All that, an opponent he should have been able to dispatch with nary a thought but who was able to out-think and outfight him at every turn, and the damned lich was barking orders at him.

Dyrr began shouting again, but Nimor didn't understand what he was saying.

"I can't—" the Anointed Blade started to say then stopped when he realized that the lich was casting a spell.

Gromph heard him too. With one hand still holding the axe in front of him, the archmage tapped his staff on the pockmarked floor of the smoldering Bazaar and was instantly enveloped in a globe of shimmering energy. No sooner did the globe appear than Dyrr finished his muttering, and the sound of the lich's voice was replaced by a low, echoing buzz.

Nimor, eyes still locked on Gromph's, blinked. The archmage glanced over at the lich, and one side of his mouth curled up into the beginning of a smile. Nimor had to look, and he knew that Gromph had no intention of attacking him anyway.

The buzzing sound grew louder, escalating to an almost deafen-ing roar. Nimor saw what looked like a cloud of black smoke winding through the air at him, and it was a few seconds before he realized it wasn't smoke. The cloud wasn't a cloud at all, but a swarm of tiny insects—perhaps tens, even hundreds of millions of them.

The swarm descended over Gromph, but they didn't penetrate the globe that surrounded the archmage. Nimor had to assume they were being directed by Dyrr, so when the insects turned on him, he took it personally.

Before the first of them could land on him, sting him, bite him, or do whatever they were meant to do to him, Nimor stepped into the Shadow Fringe. The act was second nature to him. He was there in the Bazaar, then he wasn't. The swarm became a shadow, the Bazaar a dull world, barely corporeal, drenched in blackness.

Nimor looked at his claws. His mind was strangely blank, his mood impossibly serene.

"Is that it?" he said aloud into the unhearing shadows. "Have I lost?"

He closed his eyes and thought of the lich . . . and stepped back into the solid world right behind him.

Nimor grabbed the spindly undead mage from behind and beat his wings hard to pull him up and away from the floor of the Bazaar. The lich stiffened and drew in a breath—perhaps to cast a spell—but was wise enough to stop when Nimor pressed one razor-sharp talon into the lich's desiccated throat.

"You might not bleed, lich," Nimor whispered into the lichdrow's ear, "but if your head comes away from your neck . . ."

"What are you doing?" Dyrr asked, his voice a thin, reedy hiss. "You could kill him. Our moment is at hand, and you turn on me? *Me?*"

"You?" Nimor sneered. "Yes, you. I should kill you now, but then you're already dead, aren't you, lich? All you did was waste my time, and now the Spider Queen is rattling in her cage, and our time together is spent."

"What?" Dyrr asked, honestly confused. "What are you saying?"

"Not that you deserve to know it before I let Gromph Baenre kill you," Nimor replied, "but it's over."

"No!" the lich shouted.

Nimor grunted when something pushed hard against his chest His hand came away from the lich's throat, and he was forced backward, driven through the air by some unfathomable force. Despite any attempt to fly, Nimor was repulsed.

The assassin spared a glance down at Gromph, who had put away his stolen duergar battle-axe and was looking up at them, laughing.

Nimor laughed too. Why not?

"We failed, lich," Nimor called to Dyrr, "but at least for me there will be another chance."

"*We* failed?" the lich wailed. "We? No, you wretched son of a wyrm, *you* failed. You'll go back to the Shadow with your dragon's tail between your legs, repeating your feeble excuses to yourself over and over again. Blame me if you wish, Nimor, but I'm still here. Live or die, I'll still be here, in Menzoberranzan, fighting."

"Perhaps," Nimor said, the first waves of a profound exhaustion beginning to soften his tired muscles, "but not for long."

The lich screamed his name, but Nimor didn't hear the first echo before he drifted into the Shadow Fringe and was gone from Menzoberranzan forever.

TWENTY - FOUR

Inside the temple walls was a city twenty times the size of Menzoberranzan. Like the walls and the surrounding plazas, the city was a battered, war-ravaged ruin that looked to Pharaun as if it had been abandoned for a thousand years or more.

The architecture throughout mimicked all manner of dark elven dwellings, from the calcified webs of Ched Nasad to the hollowed-out stalagmites of Menzoberranzan. The only thing the structures had in common was that they were all at least partially collapsed and they were devoid of life.

Valas appeared behind the mage as he always did, as if by magic. Pharaun didn't bother trying to pretend the scout's sudden appearance hadn't startled him. The time for keeping up appearances and jockeying for position in the party had come and gone.

Valas nodded once to the Master of Sorcere and said, "There's more metal the deeper in we go."

Pharaun found himself shaking his head, unsure at first what the scout was trying to tell him. He looked around more closely and saw that Valas was right. Though they had seen jagged, twisted chunks of rusted iron and scorched steel in the plaza outside, the deeper into the temple they walked, the more they all had to step around larger and larger pieces.

Valas stopped and reached out to touch a gently curving wall of steel three times the scout's height.

"It looks like it was ripped off of a larger piece," the scout said. "I've never seen this much steel."

Pharaun nodded, examining the relic from a distance.

"It looks like a piece of a giant's suit of armor," the wizard commented, "a giant bigger than any you might find on the World Above, but this is the Abyss, Valas. There could be such a creature here."

"Or a god," the scout replied.

"Selvetarm was that big," Danifae said. Both the males turned to look at her, surprised that she'd stopped to join the conversation. The former battle-captive had been walking in silence with the draegloth never far from her side, apparently unfazed by her surroundings. "So was Vhaeraun."

Valas nodded and said, "There are other pieces, though, and there are things that don't look like armor."

"The mechanical bits," Pharaun interjected. "I've noticed those too."

"Mechanical bits?" the young priestess asked.

Pharaun continued walking as he said, "The odd moving part. I've seen hinges and things that seem to act almost like a joint, like a shoulder or knee joint in a drow's body but with wires or other contraptions in place of muscles."

"Now that you mention it," Valas said, "some of them did look like legs or arms."

"Who cares?" the draegloth grumbled. "Are you two really wasting your time examining the garbage? Do you have no understanding of what's happened here?"

"I think we have at least a rudimentary understanding of what's gone on here, Jeggred, yes," Pharaun said. "By 'examining the garbage,' as you so eloquently put it, we might gain some understanding beyond the point where it can still be described as rudimentary. Alas, that's not a state of mind with which you tend to be familiar with yourself, but those of us with higher—"

The air was forced out of Pharaun's lungs in a single painful grunt. The draegloth was on top of him, smashing him into a crumbling pile of bricks that had once been part of a soaring cathedral. The wizard brought to mind a spell that didn't require speech but stopped himself from casting it when Danifae's voice echoed across the temple grounds.

"Jeggred," she commanded, "leave it."

It was a command someone might give a pet rat distracted by a cave beetle. As the draegloth withdrew and Pharaun struggled to his feet, he wondered which was a greater insult, Jeggred smashing him to the ground or Danifae's rude remark. The Master of Sorcere brushed off his *piwafwi*, did his best with the wild mop his hair had become, and cleared his throat.

"Ah, Jeggred, my boy," the wizard said, letting the sarcasm drip freely, "was it something I said?"

"Next time you talk to me like that, mage," he draegloth growled, "your heart will follow Ryld Argith's through my bowels."

Pharaun tried not to laugh and said, "Charming as always."

"Come, Jeggred," Danifae said, waving the draegloth into step behind her.

Pharaun finished assembling himself, and as he was about to move on he stopped and turned, having caught someone looking at him from the corner of his eye. Quenthel Baenre stood partially blocked by another huge, jagged hunk of steel. The look the wizard saw on her face was ice cold, and if they had been back in Menzoberranzan it would surely have presaged Danifae's death.

After the echoes from Dyrr's last, barely-coherent shout finally died away, came a moment of almost complete silence. The lich hung in the still air, trembling with rage. Gromph took a moment to survey the ruined Bazaar.

The fires had burned themselves out, and the smoke slowly dissipated. Dozens of stalls, tents, and carts were ruined—burned or shattered. Great cracks and pits had been dug into the stone floor, which was scorched in large swaths of dusty black.

A few whispered words drifted across the otherwise quiet space, and Gromph saw a few inquisitive—and unwise—drow beginning to wander into the edges of the ruined marketplace. They had sensed that the duel had come to an end, but Gromph knew how wrong they were. Something, and it wasn't only Gromph's ability to outthink him, had scared Nimor off, had given the Anointed Blade the impression that he had lost.

Why did Nimor abandon the fight, Archmage? Nauzhror asked. *What does he know?*

Find out, Gromph ordered then turned his attention to Dyrr.

"We can finish this now, if you like," Gromph said.

The lich took a deep, shuddering breath and shook his head.

"It's as it should be," the archmage added.

"I suppose it is, my young friend," the lich answered, his voice steady. "You, the highest ranking wizard in Menzoberranzan, and me, the most powerful. It's only symmetrical that we eventually face each other. Power abhors that sort of imbalance."

"I don't know," Gromph answered with a shrug. "I don't consider balance. I worship a demon. I serve chaos."

Dyrr's answer was to begin casting a spell. Gromph stepped back and used his staff to levitate, hopping a dozen feet up into the air and hovering there. He looked down and could see a small group of drow— fifteen or twenty and mostly older males—begin sifting through the ruined stalls. They must have been the merchants themselves, finally unable to stay away, not knowing the fate of their livelihoods.

Gromph thought to warn them off but didn't. He didn't want to.

Dyrr finished his spell, and at first it looked as if the lich burst. He grew, ballooning up to twice, then three, then four times his normal size and bigger. He changed in every conceivable physical way and dropped from the air with a resounding crash that made the merchants scatter back past the edges of the Bazaar. Gromph watched the bystanders gape in awe and fear at what Dyrr had become.

It's a gigant, Nauzhror said. *A blackstone gigant.*

Gromph sighed. He knew what it was that Dyrr had turned himself into.

Under normal circumstances, a blackstone gigant was a construct, created by priestesses of any number of dark faiths to be used as servants, guardians, assassins, or instruments of war. Carved from solid blocks of stone, they were formidable creatures that could destroy a whole city if left unchecked. What Dyrr had done was change his form from his normally thin, aged drow frame to the form of a gigant. In the process he had become, for all intents and purposes, that new creature.

The gigant was easily forty feet long from the top of its massive, drowlike head to the tip of its curling, wormlike tail. It had four sets of long arms with drowlike hands big enough to close over Gromph entirely, though the hands were oddly twisted with three multijointed fingers ending in black talons not unlike Nimor's. The lich had opted to retain his black coloration, but the creature's eyes blazed a bright blue. Shafts of light extended from them, cutting through the haze of smoke that still hung in the air. It opened its mouth and revealed fangs the size of short swords, set in rows. Slime dripped from its twisted lower lip. It was in constant motion, twitching and squirming like a maggot. The weight of it dragged ragged scars in the floor, and the sound of grinding, cracking stone overwhelmed all other sounds.

The creature started to destroy everything it could reach, and it could reach a lot. What merchants' stalls were still intact and unburned were ground to splinters under the colossal beast's raw tonnage. The once curious merchants ran for their lives, but as the gigant writhed across the Bazaar, it rolled over one fleeing drow after another. When it rolled on to reveal them once again, instead of the mass of unrecognizable paste Gromph expected to see, there was left behind an array of what looked at first like statues. The petrified forms of a score of drow lay perfectly still, scattered across the ruined Bazaar. The touch of the gigant had turned them to stone.

Its fit of destructive rage finished, the gigant turned its attention to Gromph. The shafts of light from its eyes fell on the archmage, illuminating him where he hovered a dozen yards above the floor of the Bazaar.

Gromph cast a spell as the gigant came at him, gnashing its massive fangs and petrifying a handful more of the careless drow merchants. The spell made Gromph difficult to see. His form became cloudy, indistinct, and he dropped quickly to the ground. The boots he was wearing would help him run faster than any drow. Difficult to see and moving fast, Gromph managed to stay out of the raging gigant's way.

"Can you hear me, Dyrr?" Gromph called out.

The lich didn't answer. Gromph wasn't sure if he could in his current state. The gigant growled and gnashed its teeth and came at him again. Gromph literally ran in circles in an effort to contain the dangerous beast in the Bazaar. Any living thing it touched turned to stone, and too many Menzoberranyr had perished already. If the siege truly was coming to an end, it was time for the wasteful killing to stop too.

"Dyrr, answer me," Gromph tried again, but again there was no response.

Instead, the gigant glanced down at the petrified drow left in its wake. When the beam of light from its eyes played on their stone forms, the rock-hard drow lurched into motion. The petrified merchants drew themselves up, staggering slowly like zombies, and each one turned its head up to regard the gigant as if listening for orders. Dust fell from them in gently wafting clouds.

The gigant hissed at each of them, and as it did so one after another of the animated statues turned to face Gromph and began to stagger slowly toward him.

Gromph could move many times faster than the petrified drow, but there were a lot of them: a dozen, then more, and he knew that eventually he would have to do something about the blackstone gigant and its cadre of animated statues in the heart of Menzoberranzan.

The lich isn't answering you, Master, Nauzhror said. *Perhaps he can't. Perhaps he's more gigant now than lich.*

What does that mean? Prath asked.

It means, Gromph answered, *that what a lich might be normally capable of, normally resistant to, may no longer apply.*

Like what? Prath asked.

Gromph and Nauzhror projected the same word at precisely the same time: *Necromancy.*

"That's impossible," Valas said. "It's the size of a castle."

Pharaun shrugged, nodding, looking up at the enormous wreck.

"Bigger," the Master of Sorcere replied, "but it walked."

The wreck was once a sphere of polished steel three hundred feet or more in diameter. It lay amid the ruins of half a dozen smaller stone and web buildings, one side of it gone completely. On the whole it resembled a discarded eggshell, but in fact it had once been a walking fortress. Pharaun tried to imagine the sight of the thing intact, standing on legs that were left bent and torn underneath its bulk.

"Some kind of clockwork contraption," Valas persisted, "that big . . . It would have to have been built by a . . ."

"A god?" Pharaun finished for him, when he sensed Valas hesitating to draw the same conclusion. "Or in this case a goddess. Why not?"

"What would you use something like that for?" asked Danifae.

"War," Jeggred offered, though there was enough of a lilt in his voice to make it almost sound like a question. "It's a war machine."

"It's a fortress," Quenthel said. There was a finality, a certainty in her voice that made the others turn to look at her. "It's . . . it *was* Lolth's own fortress. It once resembled a clockwork spider, and from within Lolth herself could traverse the Demonweb Pits, protected and armed with weapons the likes of which no drow has yet imagined."

"I think . . ." Danifae said. "I think I remember reading something about that but always thought it a fantasy, a bit of harmless heresy to thrill the uninitiated."

"You know this for sure?" Pharaun asked Quenthel, though he could see in her face that she had no doubts.

The high priestess looked the Master of Sorcere in the eye and said, "I've been inside it. I've seen it move. It was inside that spider fortress that I first came before the Spider Queen herself."

Pharaun turned from Quenthel's gaze to look at the massive wreck again.

"She seldom left its confines," Quenthel went on, her voice growing softer and softer as if she were receding over a great distance. "I don't think I ever saw her leave it, in fact, in all the years I . . ."

Pharaun didn't turn back to look at the Mistress of Arach-Tinilith when he said, "We should go inside. If Lolth never left that fortress, perhaps she's still in there."

"She isn't there," Quenthel said.

"The mistress is right," said Danifae. "I can feel it—or, rather, I can't feel her."

"She might still be inside there," the wizard said, knowing that he was taking his life in his own hands again by suggesting the possibility—even though he was sure each one of them had at least briefly considered it. "Her body might be, anyway."

No one said anything in response, but they did follow when Pharaun began the long walk to the fallen spider fortress.

As minutes dragged, the walk grew increasingly difficult. Fatigue had long since made itself known, and though they occasionally stopped to eat and drink from the supplies that Valas had given each of them from his dimensional containers they were all hungry, thirsty, and ready to drop. That, coupled with an increasing denseness in debris and intervening walls of stone, web, bricks, or steel, reduced their speed to a quarter of what they hoped for.

Still, the draegloth managed to get close to Pharaun's side. The mage was reasonably confident that the defenses he already had running would prevent the half-demon from taking him down before he could defend himself, so he didn't stop and challenge the draegloth.

"You would like it," Jeggred whispered to Pharaun. The draegloth's whisper was as loud as a drow's normal volume, but still no one seemed to have heard him. "If Lolth is dead in there and all we find is a skeleton, you'd be happy. Admit it."

"I admit nothing," the Master of Sorcere replied. "As a matter of policy, actually. Still, in this case I truly hope we don't find Lolth dead in there. If I did, what would you care anyway, draegloth? Would you run and tell your mistress on me? Which of your two mistresses would you tell first? Or would you even tell Quenthel at all? Honestly, Jeggred, you're acting as if you expect never to see Menzoberranzan again."

"Am I?" the draegloth asked. He was fundamentally incapable of sarcasm. "How so?"

"You're ignoring the wishes of Quenthel *Baenre*—" the wizard stressed that House name—"in favor of the whims of a servant. Here, in the very heart of Lolth's power."

"Danifae is a servant no longer," the draegloth said. "I have seen many—"

Fire.

The word formed in Pharaun's mind even as his skin blistered and his clothing threatened to catch. The flames came at them in a wave, engulfing all five of them in blinding tongues of orange, red, and blue. Pharaun could hear his defensive spells crackling to hold out the heat, and though he was still burned, he survived it. Not all of the others were in as good shape, though, and Pharaun immediately searched his mind for a spell that would protect them all—and if not them all then Valas, Quenthel (she was the sister of the archmage, after all), Danifae, and Jeggred . . . in that order.

He didn't have a chance to bring any spell to mind, though, before another wall of fire passed him, burning him even worse as it went.

Foul, coughing laughter echoed down from above, and Pharaun looked up to see a vicious tanar'ri hanging, by dint of at least some simple magic, in midair above them. The thing was like some kind of mad, twisted bull, and it lacked feet.

Pharaun recognized it at once, even as he was conjuring a sphere of Weave energy around himself to protect him from certain spells. The tanar'ri was a glabrezu, and it looked familiar.

"The ice . . ." Danifae suggested, her voice hissing through clenched teeth.

Danifae and Quenthel bore shiny patches on their black skin. They had been burned worse than Pharaun but not quite enough to raise blisters. Quenthel drew the healing wand and lost no time passing it over her own skin.

"I had it trapped in ice," said Pharaun, "and left it there."

The mage glanced quickly around for Valas, but the scout was nowhere to be seen.

"Typical demon," Quenthel mumbled. "Chewed its own legs off to get out of there."

Jeggred roared with rage. Smoke rose from his singed fur in black-gray wisps.

"You followed us all the way here, Belshazu?" the Mistress of Arach-Tinilith asked. "So we could kill you?"

"Quite the opposite," said Jeggred's father.

Halisstra Melarn was flying.

Though that wasn't an entirely accurate description of what was happening to her, it was what all her senses told her. Below her stretched an eternity of gray nothing punctuated by swirling storms of color and distant chunks of drifting, turning rock as big around as a mile and as small as a single drow. Above her and to every side was precisely the same thing.

She had recently visited the Astral Plane with the party of Menzo-berranyr and her former battle-captive, but that had been a very different experience. At that time, under the care of a priest of Vhaeraun, she'd felt like a ghost being pulled along by a chain. Through the power of Eilistraee, however, she was actually in the Astral, not projected there, and there was nothing anchoring her to the plane of her birth.

Halisstra Melarn felt more free than she'd ever felt before. Her lips turned up into an unashamed smile, and her heart raced. Her hair blew out behind her though there wasn't technically any wind. Her body responded to a mere thought in the æther medium of the Astral Plane, and she soared and swooped like a darkenbeast at play.

The only restraint she felt was the need to keep close to her companions, Uluyara and Feliane. Halisstra could see that the surface elf and the drow priestess were enjoying their flight through the Astral as much as she was, and both of them shared her smile. Still, the gravity of the mission that brought them there was never far from their minds.

Halisstra had risked everything and lost everything to be there. Ryld was surely dead, as dead as Ched Nasad, and any life she might ever have had in the Underdark was behind her. Ahead was uncertainty but acceptance. Ahead was risk but at least the potential for reward, where all she left behind was hopelessness.

"There!" Uluyara called to her fellow travelers, breaking into Halisstra's thoughts. "Do you see?"

Halisstra followed the other priestess's black-skinned finger, and found her body shifting in the "air" to begin flying in that same direction. Uluyara was indicating a long line of dull black shadows, and Halisstra had to blink several times before she began to understand what she was seeing. It was as if she were looking at a vast gray screen behind which, like actors in a shadow play, a line of drow were slowly drifting toward a common goal.

"Approach them slowly," Feliane warned. "They may not even be able to sense our presence, but we don't know for sure, and there are so many of them."

"Who are they?" Halisstra asked, though even as the last word left her mouth she realized what she was seeing.

"The damned," was Uluyara's whispered, heavy reply.

"So many . . ." Halisstra whispered in the same stunned monotone.

"All the drow who died while Lolth was silent, I would suppose," said Feliane. "Where are they going?"

"Not to the Abyss," Uluyara replied.

As they came closer and closer Halisstra couldn't help but pick out faces among the slowly drifting forms of the recently deceased. All of the dark elves appeared uniformly gray, as if they were merely charcoal renderings and not real drow. When she looked directly at one of them, a female probably too young for the Blooding, Halisstra could see right through her to the spinning rock that was passing behind.

One of the shades noticed her and briefly made eye contact, but the departed soul didn't slow in its progress or make any move to speak to her.

"Where are they going?" Halisstra asked, seeing first one, then another of the ghosts wearing a symbol of Lolth or other trinkets and heraldry that showed them as devotees of the Spider Queen. "If not the Abyss, if not to Lolth's domain, then where?"

Hope leaped in Halisstra's chest. If the dead among her loyal followers weren't going to Lolth's side but were going *somewhere*, perhaps there was some hope for a follower of the Spider Queen besides oblivion.

"Eilistraee's own spell," said Feliane, "was drawing us to the Abyss, and we weren't going this way."

"When I was in the Demonweb Pits with the Baenre sister and the others," Halisstra recounted, "we saw no souls such as these. Quenthel remarked on their absence. The sixty-sixth layer held only hordes of feral demons, two warring gods, and a sealed-off temple."

"Should we follow them?" Feliane asked Uluyara. "If they are Lolth's followers, they might be moving toward her, even if they aren't moving toward the Abyss."

"Could Lolth have abandoned the Abyss itself?" Halisstra asked.

Both Halisstra and Feliane looked to Uluyara for answers, but the drow priestess only shrugged.

Halisstra willed herself closer to the line of souls and watched them go by, waiting for an older priestess to pass, someone who looked as if she might have some insight. As the dead filed past her, Halisstra saw mostly males, warriors obviously, and a few driders in the mix. From their costumes and heraldry, Halisstra could tell that the drow came from a number of cities spread across the length and breadth of the Underdark.

Finally, a priestess approached whom she thought looked suitable, and Halisstra drifted closer still. She reached out her hand to touch the passing soul, when someone called to her.

Halisstra, the voice said, echoing directly into her mind.

Halisstra blinked and slapped her hands to her head. She was only dimly aware of Uluyara and Feliane asking after her condition.

The sound of the psychic voice echoed in her skull, the gravity of it pushing all other thoughts away.

"Ryld. . . ." she said through a jaw tight and quivering.

I'm here, the Master of Melee Magthere whispered into her consciousness.

Halisstra opened her eyes and was face to face with the ghostly shadow of Ryld Argith. The drow warrior stood tall and proud in his shadowy armor, his hands at once reaching out for her and pushing her away. Tears burst from her eyes, blurring her vision of her lover's disembodied soul.

I loved you, he said.

Halisstra had been trying not to cry, but with those three words she broke into body-racking sobs that sent her drifting slowly away from him in the Astral æther. She wanted to say a hundred things to him, but her throat closed, her jaw clenched, and her head throbbed.

I gave up everything for you, he said.

"Ryld," Halisstra managed finally to say. "I can bring you—"

He didn't so much say "no" as he imparted that feeling into her consciousness. Halisstra gasped for air.

I go to Lolth now, said Ryld. *I don't belong with Eilistraee, even if I belonged with you.*

"I didn't choose her over you, Ryld," Halisstra said, though she knew she was lying. "I would have turned away from her if you'd asked me to."

Again, the feeling of "no."

"I wanted you," she whispered.

You had me, he said, *for as long as you could.*

"Halisstra," Uluyara whispered into her ear. Halisstra realized that the other drow priestess was holding her arm. "Halisstra, ask him where he's going. Ask him where Lolth has gone."

"He's going to her," Halisstra said to Uluyara, then to Ryld: "I love you."

She blinked back her tears in time to see him smile and nod.

"To Lolth?" asked Uluyara. "Where is she?"

"That's why we're here now, isn't it?" Halisstra asked the slowly drifting soul of Ryld Argith. "Because we loved each other."

Because we left our world behind, he said. *Because we left ourselves there. You were able to create a new Halisstra, but I was not able to make a new Ryld. I'm here because I deserve to be. If not, the draegloth could never have beaten me.*

"And we would still be together," she said.

Tell your friends, he said, *that Lolth has taken the Demonweb Pits out of the Abyss. We have been waiting, some of us for months, to feel her pull us across the Astral to her, and only now are we compelled so.*

"Lolth," Halisstra said to the other priestesses, her voice tight with regret, anger, hate, and too much more to bear, "is bringing them home."

"The Demonweb Pits is no longer part of the Abyss," Uluyara guessed.

She's changing, Ryld said and his thoughts had the feel of a warning. *She's changing everything.*

Halisstra felt Uluyara's grip on her arm tighten, and the priestess whispered to her, "Let him go. There is only one way to serve him now."

"W-we can bring him . . . bring him back," Halisstra stuttered, watching Ryld turn from her and drift slowly away with the other uncaring shades.

"Not if he doesn't want to go back," Uluyara whispered, and the hand on her arm slipped into a snug embrace.

Halisstra wrapped her arms around Uluyara and wept as Ryld dwindled from sight farther and farther along the line of the damned.

Chapter

TWENTY-FIVE

"Welcome to the Abyss, corpse," the glabrezu said. His voice was a low, rolling growl. "Welcome to my home."

"Belshazu," Quenthel said, her scourge in her hand, vipers writhing expectantly.

The demon didn't look at her. Instead, he kept his burning eyes locked on Pharaun.

"I'm going to rip your soul from your body, mage, and eat it raw then vomit it up so it drips all over your quivering corpse and soaks into your shriveling skin and runs into your gaping mouth so it knows that you're dead," the demon ranted.

"Well," Pharaun replied, "if you say so."

"You will die," Belshazu said to Pharaun, "in the shadow of your dead goddess's ruined fortress."

The Master of Sorcere saw Jeggred step up next to him from the corner of his eye. The draegloth was growling almost as low and as thunderously as the glabrezu—the demon that happened to be his father.

The glabrezu, its severed legs dripping dark blood onto the ancient battlefield, turned slowly to the draegloth and said, "When I'm done with the drow, son, you can join me—have your freedom from the dark elves at last."

Jeggred drew in a breath, and Pharaun could tell he was ready to pounce, though the glabrezu was hovering well out of his reach.

"Jeggred . . ." Quenthel started but stopped when the draegloth whirled on her.

"It's meat to me," Jeggred growled. "Just another tanar'ri scum. That thing is no parent of mine." He turned to the glabrezu. "Call me 'son' again, demon, and it'll still be on your lips when I rip off your head."

"Fear not, draegloth," the demon replied with a feral grin. "Even if you were full-blood I wouldn't give you a second thought. For a half-breed I won't even bother killing you." Belshazu turned his attention back to Pharaun but spoke to the rest of them. "All I want is the summoner. Give me the wizard, and you can go on to meet your Spider Queen."

"Only him?" Quenthel asked.

Pharaun looked at her, and she tried to avoid his gaze, keeping her attention on the hovering glabrezu.

The demon glanced down at his severed legs and said, "The trick with the ice . . . I had to snip my own legs off." He held up one of his four arms, one of two that ended in a hideous, sharp pincer claw. "They won't grow back. At the very least, the whoreson owes me two legs. Give him to me now, and be on your way."

"Everyone," Quenthel said, her voice faraway and bored, "step aside."

The draegloth growled, and Valas appeared from behind a pile of broken bricks, shifting his feet in an uncharacteristically audible way. Pharaun looked at Quenthel, and she met his gaze evenly.

"Are you serious?" the wizard asked.

"Yes," Quenthel replied. "You summoned him, you bound him, you froze him in ice. The rest of this expedition is too important to waste fighting every monster we stumble across—not anymore anyway, and not to settle vendettas you bring upon yourself with your own simpleminded carelessness."

"Pharaun summoned that demon on your command, Mistress," Valas reminded her, but she didn't acknowledge the scout at all.

Pharaun looked at Belshazu, who was quietly laughing, obviously surprised that Pharaun's companions had so quickly and easily sold him out. The wizard scanned the glabrezu quickly and found that he was flying thanks to a thin platinum ring on the little finger of his left hand.

"It's all right," Pharaun said. "All we're talking about here is one legless glabrezu. Go on ahead, and I'll catch up in a minute or so."

The glabrezu roared and moved closer. Pharaun's first impulse was to run, his second to stand and swallow. He forced himself to do neither. Instead he prepared his first spell.

Something drifted past Pharaun's face. He leaned back a bit to avoid it, but something else tapped him under the chin. Dust rose up from the ground all around him—and pebbles, shards of petrified bone, and little bits of twisted, rusted iron. He looked at the glabrezu, who was holding up one of his two proper hands, a knowing grin on his canine face.

Pharaun's stomach lurched, and he felt himself being pulled upward. His boots came off the ground, and he was falling—but falling upward along with the debris around him. The others backed out of the area where gravity had been reversed. Quenthel watched with a look of irritation, as if she were disappointed that the demon was taking so long to kill him. Valas drew his kukris but seemed unsure if he should intercede. Jeggred looked at Danifae, who waved him off but watched expectantly.

With a sigh, Pharaun went to work.

He touched the Sorcere insignia and used its levitation power to counter the gravity reversal. It was disorienting, but he managed to hover at the same level as the glabrezu. He then touched his steel ring and brought forth the rapier held within it.

The weapon flew at the demon. As the blade flashed through the air, the glabrezu slashed at it with his claws and snipped at it with his pincers. The demon had the advantage of being able to fly with the enchanted blade, and they quickly matched speeds so that Belshazu and the rapier were evenly paired.

Pharaun took advantage of the stalemate to cast a spell. His stomach lurched again, and his levitation started to pull him up instead of down. The demon's upside-down gravity was gone.

Belshazu could parry the animated sword's attacks but couldn't hurt it. At the same time the rapier nicked the demon here, slashed him there, and blood started to drip onto the dead ground from half a dozen cuts.

"Unfortunate," Belshazu hissed, almost to himself, "but I would have liked to keep this one after I kill you."

The demon made a gesture difficult to define—a blink, a shrug, a shudder—and the blade shattered into a thousand glittering fragments of steel that rained down onto the ancient battlefield.

Pharaun felt his blood boil, his face flush, and his breath stop in his throat.

I should have remembered, he scolded himself. I should have known he could do that.

The Master of Sorcere wanted to hurl a string of invectives into the air, at Belshazu and the cold, uncaring multiverse, but he swallowed it. Still, he'd always liked that rapier.

"I'll take the value of that blade out of your guts, demon," Pharaun threatened.

The glabrezu's animal face twisted into a feral grin again as he rushed through the air toward Pharaun.

From behind him, the mage heard Valas say, "You'll leave a fellow drow to a filthy demon? You'll leave us without a mage?"

"Yes," Quenthel replied with an utter lack of regret that Pharaun actually found refreshing.

The tanar'ri approached quickly, and Pharaun pulled an old glove from a pocket of his *piwafwi*. He started the incantation even before the glove came out of the pocket, and by the time the glabrezu was in striking range, the spell was done.

A hand the size of a rothé appeared in the air between the wizard and the demon. Though Belshazu tried to avoid it, he couldn't. The hand opened and pushed him through the air, forcing him away from the wizard no matter how hard he resisted the conjured hand.

Pharaun turned to Quenthel, who looked at him blankly when he said, "What I'm about to do, I should do right here and let you all taste it, but I won't. I'll push him away first and keep you at a safe distance. Nonetheless, I want you to remember, Mistress, that I can do this again, and by all rights I *should* do it again."

He didn't bother to wait for a response—none came anyway—instead he turned back to the glabrezu who had been pushed by the spell several paces away in the air over the ruined temple grounds. Pharaun started to run over the uneven, debris-scattered ground, counting his paces as he went. Belshazu ripped and slashed at the conjured hand in a mad flurry of uncontrolled, frustrated attacks but to no effect. The magic held.

When Pharaun had gone twenty paces away from the rest of the expedition, he stopped. He held the hand in the air, no longer pushing the glabrezu, but keeping him at bay. As he ran he'd gone over in his mind again everything he'd learned about tanar'ri in general and glabrezu in particular. When he stopped he cast a spell—not a terribly complicated one—that would prevent another inconvenient manifestation of the tanar'ri's natural magic. A ray of green light leaped from Pharaun's outstretched hands and found its way unerringly to the floating demon. The spell would hold him to the sixty-sixth layer of the Abyss, preventing the glabrezu from teleporting even within the confines of the plane.

"Tell me the—" the wizard called out to the demon, stopping when Belsahzu's huge pincer burst through the conjured hand.

Solidified magic burned away from the surface of the black fist like blood clouding in water. The glabrezu grinned, grunted, and slashed at the hand. The great fingers twitched, their grip loosening.

The wizard had never seen anything tear through that spell in the same way. The glabrezu was more powerful, more uniquely talented than Pharaun had given him credit for. Even as those thoughts passed through his mind, the drow mage pulled another spell out of the Weave.

The demon's hideous pincer broke through one of the fingers. When it came away from the hand, the black magic burst like a bubble and the finger was gone. Belshazu pushed at the quivering, dissipating hand with one severed leg and his all-too-intact arms. As Pharaun's next spell began to form in the air above the demon, Belshazu fell out of the conjured hand and onto the wreckage-strewn ground.

The demon roared at him, and it was all Pharaun could do to force himself to appear unaffected by the deafening, terrifying sound. Belshazu stood but didn't look up—didn't see the slab of stone assembling itself bit by bit in the thin air above him.

"Tell me the truth." Pharaun slid a loose strand of hair away from his eyes and asked, "Can you tell I haven't washed my hair in over a tenday?"

The glabrezu growled, roared again, and leaped into the air—

—just as the wall of stone fell.

The demon disappeared under it, and the ground shook. The wall cracked as it came to rest on the uneven surface. Belshazu lifted the several-ton slab off him just enough to turn his head and reveal burning eyes sunk in a bleeding, animal's head.

The look of the battered creature made Pharaun smile. The spell he'd had to move so far away from the others to cast safely came to his lips as the tanar'ri continued to slowly dig itself out from under the stone slab. When he completed the incantation, Pharaun opened his mouth wide and screamed.

The sound came not from his lungs, throat, or mouth but from the Weave all around him and inside him. The sound rolled up, louder and louder, then shot out of him: a mad, keening shriek that smashed into the demon so hard it even blew the massive slab of stone into smoky vapor, then blew that smoke away into nothing. The sound crashed into the glabrezu, shaking him and spinning him into the air. Bruises exploded on Belshazu's tough red hide, and his bones cracked loudly one by one. The demon couldn't muster the breath necessary to scream, though Pharaun reveled in the obvious fact that he wanted to.

Especially when pieces of him started coming off.

Pharaun kept screaming, continued pushing air out of himself. The sound shredded the glabrezu, taking off skin, plates of exoskeleton, divots of fur, claws, fangs, eyes, then blood and entrails. The whole mess whirled in the air as if it were being stirred in a great invisible cooking pot, then all at once the spell—and the hideous shrieking scream—was gone, and the shredded remains of Belshazu fell in a heap on the battle-scarred ground. Blood continued to rain down in tapping spatters for a minute after the last big piece hit the ground.

Pharaun sighed, pushed away his errant hair again, and stepped gingerly into the mess. He kicked pieces this way and that with the toe of one boot until his eyes settled on the thin platinum band. He bent and retrieved the ring, making some effort not to touch the tanar'ri's blood.

"You owed me a ring," he said to the demon's mute remains then slipped the ring on a finger and turned back to rejoin the drow who had been more than happy to let him face the glabrezu alone.

"It looked big from a distance," Pharaun said as he ran a hand along a cold, rusted metal rib. "It's even bigger from the inside."

The Master of Sorcere looked up along the line of the gently curving steel beam and tried to guess how far above his head it ended—a hundred feet, maybe a hundred and fifty?

"Why was this just left here for a thousand years?" asked Jeggred. The draegloth was sniffing the outer surface of the great spider fortress and seemed dissatisfied. "It should have been cleaned up. Wouldn't the goddess want it cleared away?"

"It hasn't been here a thousand years," Quenthel said. She was standing inside a huge tear in the side of the broken sphere, her arms crossed in front of her. "I told you all, I was here."

"How long ago?" asked Danifae.

The high priestess looked at her with open contempt but answered, "Ten years."

"Ten years ago," Pharaun asked, "was this thing intact and moving?"

The Mistress of Arach-Tinilith nodded.

"How were you here?" Danifae asked.

Quenthel turned to Pharaun and said, "If there is anyone alive in here, could you sense them?"

The wizard glanced at Danifae, who offered him a bored shrug.

"There are spells," he answered Quenthel, "that will do that, yes. Do you think we'll find someone alive in here? Lolth herself, perhaps?"

"If the Spider Queen is anywhere," said the Baenre priestess, "she'll be here. This is her palace. Still, I don't sense her presence. I still can't feel her here at all."

Pharaun nodded and looked around at the ruin again.

"Far be it from me to argue, Mistress," he said to Quenthel, "but I find it impossible to believe that this construct was in operation a mere ten years ago. I'll admit I've never seen materials like this—steel beams big enough to hold up a building, a magical construct as big as House Baenre—but I've seen steel both old and new, and this steel has been laying out here for somewhat longer than ten years. I will accept that you're reluctant to tell us how you came to be here a decade ago, but . . ."

"But what?" Quenthel snarled.

Pharaun stopped to think. The Mistress of Arach-Tinilith watched him the whole time, and finally he shrugged and shook his head. Quenthel turned and strode deeper into the wrecked spider fortress.

Pharaun could feel someone looking at him, and he turned to see Valas lurking at the edge of a shadow. The scout was standing outside the wreck. Following Valas's glances, Pharaun watched Danifae and Jeggred follow Quenthel into the ruin. When the three of them had disappeared into the maze of twisted metal, Valas stepped closer.

"Do you really think she's alive in there?" the scout asked.

Pharaun shrugged and said, "At this point, my dear Valas, I'm willing to accept nearly anything. Time seems to have no meaning here—a different meaning anyway. Everything Quenthel says may be true, but then here we are at the very heart of Lolth's domain, and where is she?"

"Where are the souls of the dead?" asked the scout.

"We should be swarmed by departed ancestors, shouldn't we?" Pharaun agreed. "There should be all manner of creatures here: demons, driders, draegloths . . ." Pharaun paused to chuckle. "All manner of things that start with 'd' . . . but all there is is wreckage and ruins, calcified bone and rotting stone. It's the stuff of an epic lament."

Valas stared into the darkness inside the spider fortress and sighed.

"I don't know my way around in there," the scout said, his voice barely above a whisper. "Why am I still here?"

"You were hired," Pharaun said. "House Baenre pays Bregan D'aerthe . . . everyone knows why you're here."

"No, I said, why am I *still* here?" the scout asked. "I was hired as a guide to get this expedition through the Dark Domain, and I have done that."

"You have indeed," Pharaun replied.

"I never said I knew . . ." Valas started, but ended with a sigh.

"You're out of your element," Pharaun said, "as are we all, but we could still certainly benefit from your skills."

"I could have helped you with the demon," said the scout.

"Quenthel wouldn't allow it," Pharaun replied.

"You got us here," Valas said, "and as far as I know, even with the ship destroyed, you're the only one who can get them home, yet she risks you to prove a point that no one needs proven? Does that make sense to you at all?"

Pharaun smiled and shook his head, sliding an errant strand of hair out of his face, then said, "I have been a thorn in the high priestess's side since we stepped out of Menzoberranzan. I've lost track of the various different reasons why she might want to kill me, as I've stopped counting the reasons I'd like to see her dead, too. Still, perhaps she was confident that I could handle the demon on my own. I did, after all."

"There might have been a time when I'd have thought that

was good enough," Valas went on, "but after all this, I can't help thinking it's just stupid, and potentially wasteful. Her behavior is erratic."

"I think we're all a bit erratic," Pharaun admitted, "but I agree in principle with what you're saying. I think the snakes are whispering to her more and more. She's lost control of both the draegloth and Danifae, has never had control of me, and knows that you're only here because of House Baenre's gold. We finally get to the Demonweb Pits and this is what we find? An ancient ruin? She should be insane. We all should be."

Valas thought about that for a while, and Pharaun waited for him to respond.

"My contract is at an end," the scout finally said.

Pharaun nodded, shrugged, and said, "I will leave that for you to decide, but I have to admit I'd rather have you stay with us than leave. I can use spells, as the priestess asked, to find anything that might still live here, to find any latent sources of magic. If I'm the guide here, fine, but we could well need you again soon. Besides, can you even get back on your own?"

The scout tipped his head up, raised an eyebrow, and gave the hint of a smile that faded before it was completely recognizable.

"Well," Pharaun said, "perhaps you can then. I'm going inside anyway, and if you'd like to join us, so be it. We can discuss why, if you're capable of returning to Menzoberranzan on your own, you're concerned that I might be the only one who can get you back and Quenthel's tried again to kill me."

The scout bowed ever so slightly and held back a smile.

"Why do you care, anyway?" Valas asked.

"About what?"

"All of this," said the scout. "Lolth . . ."

The scout nodded and Pharaun replied, "I'm curious. It's a unique challenge for a spellcaster, and my hard-fought position in Menzoberranzan depends on the harder-fought position of my superior, who depends on the matriarchy for his power—his political power, anyway."

Valas nodded and Pharaun gestured toward the rip in the wall of the spider fortress.

"After you?" Pharaun said.

Valas walked past him, but his reluctance was plain in each forced step.

Halisstra couldn't move. She let herself hang in the æther, crying, holding her head in her hands, fending off both Uluyara and Feliane who were trying to comfort her. She could hear them repeating one reassurance after another and could feel them touching her, hugging her, wiping away her tears, but she didn't care. She didn't know what to do, and something was wrong with her.

We brought you along too fast, a voice hummed in her head. It was a female voice, quiet but strong. *I'm sorry.*

Halisstra blinked open her eyes and looked around for the source of the voice. Uluyara and Feliane had moved away from her—what would have been a few paces if they'd been standing on ground—and both of them stared with open mouths at an apparition floating only just within reach of Halisstra. It was the ghost of a drow female, resplendent in robes of flowing silk, all color drained from her, a wind that Halisstra couldn't feel carrying her long white hair in a halo around her head and brushing her robes out behind her.

"Seyll," Halisstra whispered, the name almost sticking on her tongue.

The shade, who was looking Halisstra directly in the eyes, nodded, and again the voice sounded in her head. *Eilistraee has many gifts to offer our sisters from the World Below. Pain, unfortunately, is one of those gifts.*

"You can keep it," Halisstra shot back, anger rising to replace the crushing remorse that the disembodied soul of Ryld Argith had left in its wake.

Feliane and Uluyara reacted to her reply with puzzled expressions, and Halisstra realized they couldn't hear Seyll.

I know, the dead priestess replied. *Believe me, I know what it's like to experience these emotions all at once and for the first time. Your mind has been trained not to recognize them, but they've been there all along, waiting for you to find them and set them free. Freedom isn't always easy. You've gone on a long journey within yourself to a place where the emotional consequences may be more painful, but the rewards will be greater than you've ever imagined.*

I don't care, Halisstra thought back. *I don't want it. Right now, I'd go back to the Underdark if I could.*

Would you?

In a second, Halisstra vowed. *There when I was being manipulated I knew it and knew the ends to which I was being pushed. There I was a priestess and a noblewoman.*

And here? Seyll asked. *What are you now?*

An assassin, Halisstra answered. *I'm an assassin in the service of Eilistraee.*

What do you suppose is the difference between an assassin and a liberator?

A liberator? Halisstra asked.

When you kill Lolth, Seyll said, *and you* will *kill her, you will set thousands free . . . millions.*

Dooming them to a life of despair and remorse?

And love, contentment, trust, and happiness, Seyll replied.

Halisstra paused to think about that, but her mind was blank. Her eyes burned, her jaw ached, and she felt heavy—so heavy she actually began to sink in the weightless æther of the Astral Plane.

Feliane and Uluyara appeared on either side of her, holding her gently by the arms. Halisstra didn't look at them or at the ghost of Seyll. Instead, she let her eyes wander up and down the long column of silent souls. The dead were returning to Lolth. Everything she had feared had not come to pass.

"I could go back to her," Halisstra said.

She could feel both Feliane and Uluyara stiffen. From Seyll she felt a wave of disappointment mixed with fear.

"If she would have you," Feliane whispered.

That stopped Halisstra. Had she passed a point of no return, one where Lolth would reject her or worse, punish her for the heresies she'd already committed? Would Eilistraee abandon her for even considering a return to the Spider Queen? Would she manage to work herself into a godless afterlife by her own indecision?

No, Seyll whispered into her mind, obviously having sensed her thoughts. *Eilistraee understands doubt and weakness and forgives both.*

"Do you understand, Halisstra," Feliane said, "what Seyll has given up by coming here?"

Halisstra shook her head in an effort to gently shake off the elf's words.

"She has abandoned Arvandor to come here," Feliane continued. "Seyll has doomed herself to an eternity in the wild Astral, and she's done it for you."

"Has she?" Halisstra asked, eyeing the ghost of Seyll, who floated there staring at her. "Or has she done that for Eilistraee? Did she come here on her own, or was she sent by a goddess who fears the loss of her assassin?"

Yes, Seyll said. *Yes to all those questions. I have come here on my own, for Eilistraee, to protect you from Lolth, to protect you from yourself, and to assure that you will do what you must do.*

"Why?" Halisstra asked. "Why now?"

Because something is going to happen, Seyll replied.

"Something is going to happen," Uluyara repeated.

Right now, Seyll asked, *this very moment, do you want to go back to Lolth? If she poured her "grace" over you right now, would you accept it, accept her, and turn your back on Eilistraee?*

"I don't know," Halisstra answered.

You must decide, said Seyll, *and you must decide now.*

The apparition gestured behind her at the long row of disembodied souls. Something was different, and it took Halisstra a few seconds to realize what was happening. The line of souls disappeared into the gray distance, what might have been miles away. The colorless ghosts were changing, one another as if a wave was passing through them. Color and life, even substance returned to each soul in turn, but only for a brief moment, then the effect passed to the next dead drow in line. As the color passed in and out of them they convulsed, twisting in the air more from pleasure than from pain. The wave drew closer and closer, scattering the line of drow in its wake.

"She's back," Halisstra whispered.

Seyll came closer to her, wrapping her ghostly body around Halisstra, who stiffened but didn't push the apparition away.

She is back, Seyll whispered into her mind. *Soon her power will course though you. I can protect you, but you have to want me to. You have to want Eilistraee, not her. Not that demon. Please.*

"Please," Uluyara whispered.

Halisstra closed her eyes and tried to return Seyll's ghostly embrace, but her arms closed over nothing.

"Eilistraee," Halisstra called, her voice breaking, "help me!"

Seyll grew solid in her arms, and Halisstra felt the priestess's body quiver. Seyll screamed, and Halisstra heard it both in her rattling ears and in her tortured mind.

"Seyll," Uluyara shouted over the sound of pure agony that was ripped from Seyll's momentarily corporeal throat. "No . . ."

Seyll's body disappeared, and Halisstra's arms wrapped around only herself. The scream echoed in her mind but left her ringing ears to the silence of the Astral Plane. She opened her eyes and saw Seyll floating in the gray nothing in front of her. The priestess's body was twisted and broken, her face wracked with pain. She had grown more transparent, and was quickly fading away.

"Seyll . . ." Halisstra whispered.

The priestess looked her in the eyes one last time, and though it seemed to cause her a considerable amount of pain to do so, she smiled as she faded from sight.

Halisstra felt her body sag even as she was infused with an energy and confidence unlike anything she'd felt before.

"She's gone," Uluyara whispered.

"She didn't abandon only Arvandor," Feliane said, her eyes wide with horror. "She let the power of Lolth pass into her."

"To protect me," Halisstra whispered.

"It killed her," Feliane said. "She didn't choose the Astral, she chose oblivion."

"The thing that I most feared myself," said Halisstra. "It was oblivion that drove me to Eilistraee."

"She sacrificed herself," Uluyara said.

"For me?" asked Halisstra.

"And for Eilistraee," Feliane said.

Halisstra's mind reeled, but her eyes cleared of tears, and blood began to flow in her tired muscles. She felt alert, refreshed, even as she was overwhelmed.

"She sacrificed herself," Halisstra repeated, "so I could . . ."

"So you could serve Eilistraee," Uluyara finished for her. "So you could wield the Crescent Blade."

Halisstra put a hand on the hilt of the weapon that could kill a goddess and said, "I hesitated, but I hope not for too long."

"She's awake," Feliane warned, "or resurrected. She'll fight back."

Halisstra thought about that. She tried to imagine facing Lolth herself in battle, and for the life of her she couldn't.

"We'll follow the souls to Lolth," Halisstra said, moving in that direction even before she finished speaking.

Feliane and Uluyara fell in behind her.

TWENTY - SIX

"No," Pharaun muttered, "this way . . . ?"

He turned left when the corridor forked. He had cast a number of divinations and was doing his damnedest to follow them all.

"None of your spells are working," Quenthel asked, "are they?"

Pharaun didn't bother looking at her but continued along the corridor hoping he would stumble on something that might get them on the right track.

"I'm getting . . . contradictory information," he shot back, "but at least I'm doing something. You said you've been here before—why aren't you taking us right to her?"

Quenthel didn't answer, and they shared a look that served as an agreement not to continue bickering.

"It's as if the farther we go into this spider fortress, the stranger our surroundings become," Danifae said. "There were no right angles anywhere when we first walked in, but now there are. They seemed to appear the moment I got comfortable wandering the corridors without them. Still, we have seen nothing alive, haven't been harried by a single guardian, and for all intents and purposes we have the run of the place. What does it mean?"

"That Lolth wanted us to come," Quenthel replied, shooting a contemptuous glance at Danifae.

Pharaun and Valas exchanged a look that told each other they'd reached very different conclusions.

The wizard paused in a section of corridor that had widened out to well over twenty feet. The ceiling was low, the darkness comfortably dense, and the smell of rot fortunately not as overwhelming as it had been most of the time. He cast another spell and concentrated on his surroundings, searching for signs of life. He could sense dead spots through which his magic couldn't penetrate—walls perhaps lined with lead or some other particularly dense substance. Still, far at the edge of the limits of his perception, Pharaun could make out signs of life.

"A light wash," he whispered to himself, "but it's there."

"What?" Quenthel asked. "What's there?"

The wizard opened his eyes and smiled at Quenthel.

"There is something alive in here with us after all," he said, "but the sign is strange—diffuse and distant as if the creature is either very far away, only barely alive, cloaked in magic that protects it from divination, or some combination of those things. I can't get a . . . Mistress?"

Quenthel dropped to her knees, and Pharaun instinctively backed away. The air was charged, and the Master of Sorcere's skin tingled, but whatever was happening had a much more profound effect on the two females.

Quenthel dropped to her hands, her face coming dangerous inches from smashing into the cold, rusted steel of the ruined spider fortress. Her muscles jerked and spasmed, and her face was twisted into either a rictus of agonized pain or a grin of some kind of feral pleasure—Pharaun couldn't tell which.

Danifae fell to the floor as well, but she was facing up. Her back arched, and soon she was touching the floor only from one tiny spot on her head and the tips of her toes. Pharaun couldn't help admiring the curve of her body, marred as it was by the same petty wounds—cuts, abrasions, welts, and bruises—that they'd all accumulated along the way. Not sure he wasn't seeing only what he wanted to see, Pharaun thought Danifae's expression was one of total pleasure, complete physical abandon.

Next it was Jeggred's turn to fall. The draegloth dropped to one knee, his three remaining hands reaching out to grab blindly at the walls. He ripped jagged rents in one steel partition. Brown dust covered his fur, clinging to it in clumps until it looked like the half-demon was rusting the same as the spider fortress. Jeggred screamed so loudly Pharaun had to clamp his hands over his ears.

Even as the draegloth's scream faded into panting—desperate gasps for air—Pharaun looked at Valas. The scout seemed entirely unaffected, and Pharaun himself felt no burning desire to writhe around on the floor.

"Whatever it is," Pharaun said to the scout, "it only seems to be affecting the—"

He thought at first that he was going to say "the females," then he realized that it was affecting the *priestesses* and the one creature among them born of Lolth's peculiar hell.

It ended as abruptly as it began.

Jeggred, who had been the one least affected by the sudden rapture, was the first to stand and begin to brush himself off. His face—normally difficult to read—gave Pharaun nothing.

"What happened?" the wizard asked, but the draegloth ignored him. "Jeggred?"

Quenthel sat back on her haunches and held her hands up to her face. Her eyes scoured her rust-dusted hands as if searching for something.

Danifae took longer to recover, rolling into a fetal position on the unforgiving rusted steel floor and making a noise Pharaun at first thought was crying.

"Mistress?" Valas asked, crouching to get to Quenthel's eye level but not stepping any closer than the half dozen paces that already separated them.

Quenthel didn't speak, didn't even give any indication that she had heard Valas. Pharaun didn't bother asking what happened. He was beginning to understand what he'd witnessed.

Quenthel began to speak.

At first she moved her lips in a mute pantomime, then she whispered at the edge of hearing, then she chanted a litany in an ancient tongue not even Pharaun recognized.

She continued for a minute or so then stopped. Pharaun's eyes played over her, and he watched as all the cuts and bruises, scrapes and welts faded away, leaving her skin a perfect, almost glowing black. She even seemed to gain back some of the weight she'd lost. Her hair appeared cleaner, softer, and even her *piwafwi* and armor shone with renewed life.

Quenthel Baenre stood and looked down at Danifae, who had uncurled herself to sit with her back to the wall, smiling as she whispered a prayer of her own that sealed her cuts, made her bruises disappear, and brought the twinkle back into her big, expressive eyes. A tear traced a path down one of her perfect ebony cheeks, and she didn't bother to wipe it away.

Pharaun looked back at the Mistress of Arach-Tinilith, who stood tall and still in the darkness of the spider fortress, seeming to glow. Her eyes were closed and her lips were moving.

In one fluid, graceful motion Danifae swept up to her feet, her perfect white teeth shining in the gloom as she grinned from ear to ear. Pharaun found himself returning that smile. Jeggred rolled up onto his feet but in the same movement sank down to his knees in front of Danifae and Quenthel. The draegloth was breathing hard.

"They are alive, and they're here," Quenthel whispered. She looked at Pharaun and more clearly said, "They are behind walls that shield them from your spells, and they are further protected from most divinations, but they are here."

"Who?" Valas asked.

"I sense them too," Danifae said. She put a hand on Jeggred's wild mane and absently stroked it back into place. "I think I could find them. I think they're actually waiting for us."

"Wait," Pharaun said, stepping closer to Danifae—until a fierce growl from Jeggred stopped him. The young priestess patted the half-demon's head. and he calmed quickly. "Did what I think happened actually happen? Did she . . . ?"

"Lolth has returned to us," Quenthel said.

"She has," Danifae agreed.

She appeared as if she wanted to say more.

"Is there something else?" Pharaun asked. "Is that it? Is our journey at an end?"

"Mistress?" Jeggred said, looking directly into Danifae's eyes. "What did the voice say? I couldn't quite . . . it was too far away to . . ."

Danifae ran her fingers through his fur and said, "The voice said—"

"*Yor'thae,*" Quenthel finished for her.

"*Yor'thae. . . .*" Danifae whispered.

"High Drow?" Valas asked, correctly identifying the language.

"It means, 'Chosen One,' " Pharaun explained.

"One . . ." Quenthel whispered, shaking her head.

At the same time, Danifae mutely mouthed the word, *"Yor'thae."*

Quenthel used her eyes to get Pharaun's attention then said, "Our journey is far from over, Master of Sorcere. Lolth has not only returned but she has asked me to come to her, has invited me to be her chosen vessel. This is why she brought me back, all those years ago. This is why she dragged me from the Abyss and back to Menzoberranzan. I was meant to come here, now, and to be her . . . to be *Yor'thae.*"

Deep in the heart of the First House, in a room protected from everything worth protecting a room from, Triel Baenre watched her brother fight for the life of Menzoberranzan.

He was losing.

She could see what was happening in the Bazaar, every detail of it, through a magic mirror, a crystal ball, a scrying pool, and half a dozen other similar items, most of which had been created by Gromph himself. She paced back and forth across the polished marble floor, looking from scene to scene, angle to angle, as the transformed lichdrow made a mess of the heart of her city.

Wilara Baenre stood in one corner, her eyes darting from one scrying device to another, her arms crossed in front of her, her fingers drumming against her shoulders with barely contained frustration.

"The archmage will prevail, Matron Mother," Wilara said, not for the first time that day.

"Will he?" Triel asked.

It was the first time she'd replied to one of Wilara's hollow reassurances, and it took the attending priestess by surprise.

"Of course he will," Wilara answered.

Triel waited for more, but it became obvious that Wilara had nothing else to say.

"I'm not entirely certain that this is a fight he can win," Triel said, as much to herself as to Wilara. "If we're all being tested and this is Gromph's test, he will pass or fail on his own. If he fails, he deserves to die."

"Is there nothing we can do to help him?" asked Wilara.

Triel shrugged.

"There are soldiers and other mages," the attending priestess went on.

"All of whom are required elsewhere. The duergar still press, even if the tanarukks are turning away," said Triel. "The siege of Agrach Dyrr goes on unabated . . . but, yes, there are always more soldiers, always more mages, and there is Bregan D'aerthe and other mercenaries. If the lich kills Gromph I certainly won't let him rampage through the rest of Menzoberranzan turning our citizens to stone and smashing the architecture."

"Why not send those forces in now?"

Triel shrugged again and considered the question. She had no answer.

"I don't know," Triel said finally. "Maybe I'm waiting for a sign from—"

She was back.

Triel fell to the floor, her body going limp, her head spinning, her mind exploding in a cacophony of sound and shadow, voices and screams. Tears welled up in her eyes so she could only barely see Wilara lying in a similar confused, twitching, limp state on the floor across the room.

The Matron Mother of House Baenre felt every emotion she'd ever known simultaneously and at their sharpest and most intense. She hated and loved, feared and cherished, laughed and cried. She knew the endless expanse of the limitless multiverse and saw in crystal detail the square inch of marble floor right in front of her eye. She was in her scrying chamber and in the Demonweb Pits, in her mother's womb and in the smoldering Bazaar, in the deepest Underdark and flying through the blazing skies of the World Above.

She took a deep breath, and one feeling after another fell away, each a layer of confusion and insanity. Pieces of her mind began to function again, then pieces of her body. It took either a few minutes or a few years—Triel couldn't be sure how long—for her to realize what had happened and sort through the sensation that had been so familiar all her life, then was gone, then returned.

Lolth.

It was the fickle grace of the Queen of the Demonweb Pits.

Triel didn't try to stand at first but lay there and stretched, luxuriating in the wash of power, exulting in the return of Lolth.

Gromph knew of so many ways to kill someone, he'd forgotten more than most drow ever heard of. There were spells that would kill with a touch, kill with a word, kill with a thought, and Gromph searched his mind for precisely the right one as he ran to both avoid the rampaging gigant and keep it contained in the ruined Bazaar.

He wore the skull sapphire that gave him even more choices

and afforded him protection from negative energy—like Nimor's enervating breath. In his memory he stored a few more, and in time Gromph settled on one spell, with some input from Nauzhror and the small circle of Sorcere necromancers. The archmage gathered the Weave energy within him and brought the words and gestures of the incantation to mind. However, in order to cast the spell—and it was a powerful spell indeed—the archmage would have to stop running.

It wasn't the first time that the battle with Dyrr came down to timing. Would he have enough time to cast the spell before the gigant rolled over him?

We can help you choose your moment, Nauzhror said.

I know, Gromph answered, *but there are always . . . variables.*

The archmage stopped running, turned, and began his casting.

The gigant looked down at him, bathing Gromph in the light from its mad blue eyes. Gromph was sure he had time. The animated, petrified drow were too far away and moving too slowly to be of any concern, and the gigant had been slapping its tail around the Bazaar at random, as if Dyrr had little control over his new body. Gromph trusted in that.

He was wrong.

One set of trigger words from completing the spell, the enormous black tail of the blackstone gigant rolled over him. Gromph felt the words stop in his throat and felt his joints stiffen then nothing.

Triel stood and looked from scrying device to scrying device, trying to sort out what she was hearing. The magically transmitted voices of a hundred mages, priestesses, and warriors filled the air in an incoherent tangle of confusion and undisguised bliss. The doors of the scrying chamber burst open, and a priestess whom Triel recognized but whose name she couldn't instantly recall staggered into the room. Tears streamed down her black cheeks, and her mouth worked in silent, incoherent attempts to put into words what she, Triel, Wilara, and every other servant of the Queen of the Demonweb Pits all across the endless expanse of the multiverse had experienced.

The matron mother's attention fell on one image: Gromph, petrified.

He had lost. The lich, in its freakish monster form, had turned the Archmage of Menzoberranzan to stone.

Triel felt her jaw tighten then she stood for a moment, letting the anger wash through her.

"Is this a sign?" she asked the Spider Queen.

Lolth didn't answer, but Triel knew she could if she wanted to.

"It's a sign," the matron mother whispered.

Triel pressed her fingertips together, bent her neck in a slight bow, and willed herself to the Bazaar. There was a momentary feeling of upside down weightlessness, a black void, then she was standing in a deep crack in the stone floor of her city's marketplace. The blackstone gigant reared up high above her, apparently having sensed her passage through the dimensions from House Baenre to the Bazaar. The creature opened its mouth to roar at her, but Triel spoke a few words, and it froze. The great, thrashing tail came to a sudden stop. It was as if time itself had taken a moment's pause. Smoke still rose around her, and the animated stone drow lumbered on.

"This has gone on long enough, lich," Triel said, "all of it. I will have no more dead drow, no more of my city ruined, no more challenges to my power or to the power of Lolth."

Triel doubted the lichdrow could understand her. He seemed to have been subsumed by his adopted form, but she said it to everyone she knew was listening in, from House Baenre, Arach-Tinilith, Sorcere, and perhaps beyond the city into the command tents of her enemies.

She called directly upon Lolth, beseeching the restored goddess for her most potent spell, asking for nothing less than a miracle.

Lolth didn't answer in a drow's voice as she had in the past. There were no words, only a feeling, a swelling of power, a rush of blood in the matron mother's ears.

Triel sank to her knees amid a scattering of rough gravel and broken glass and pressed her forehead to the cool ground. She didn't express her desires in words. She didn't have to. What she was working was a wave of emotion, of feeling, of pure fear.

The terror of Lolth herself blasted out in all directions at once, in an expanding circle of fear with Triel at its center. All across the City of Spiders, drow stopped in their tracks, fell to their knees, or lay prone. Some leaned against walls or collapsed on stairs, but all of them knew the purest fear, the fear of a goddess, the fear of the eternal, the fear of chaos, the fear of darkness, the fear of the unknown, the fear of the certain, the fear of treason, and a thousand other horrors that brought the city to a full stop.

The blackstone gigant trembled and broke apart. Triel, still kneeling below it, didn't dodge the falling black boulders, the pieces of the titanic construct, which disappeared before they hit the ground. Within seconds all that was left of the rampaging creature was the lichdrow, stunned, reeling, kneeling on the crumbling floor of the Bazaar a few paces in front of the matron mother. The animated statues stopped moving and stood frozen in place.

The wave of fear moved onward, past the walls of the city's vault and into the crowded approaches to the Underdark beyond. It passed through the duergar lines, overtook the retreating tanarukks, and blindsided the scattered illithid spies. It affected all of them in different ways, but it affected all of them. By the time it was done—and it didn't take long—there was no question, anywhere, that Lolth was back.

Triel stood and surveyed the damage. She looked down at Dyrr and knew she could simply step over to him and kill him with a thought—or at least a dagger blade across his undead throat—but she didn't. Killing the lich was someone else's job.

The matron mother stepped to the rigid, calcified form of her brother. The expression frozen on his face was one of anger. Triel smiled at that.

"Ah, Gromph," she said. "You couldn't do it alone after all, could you? There are limits to your power as there are limits to mine, but together . . ."

Triel embraced the petrified form of her brother, wrapping her arms around his back as she whispered a prayer to Lolth.

Warmth came first, then softness, then a breath, then movement, and Gromph's knees collapsed. Triel held him up, and he grasped her around the waist, his head lolling on her shoulder as he drew in a series of ragged, phlegmy breaths. When his legs came back under him, Triel released him and stepped back. Their eyes met, and Gromph opened his mouth to speak.

"No," Triel said, stopping him. She glanced at the quickly recovering Dyrr, and her brother's eyes followed hers. "Finish what you started."

He opened his mouth to speak again, but Triel turned her back on him. She could hear his feet shifting on the loose gravel and glass, and she knew he was facing his enemy.

Triel walked away.

TWENTY - SEVEN

Anger, hatred, and exhaustion passed between the archmage and the lichdrow. They were done with each other. Both only wanted to finish it. They stood a dozen paces apart, eyes locked. Dyrr began to cast a spell, and Gromph surrounded himself in another globe.

Gromph began to cast a spell too, and the lichdrow kept casting. He was doing something complex. He meant to finish it indeed.

Before Gromph could finish his spell—one meant to burn the already wounded lich once more—Dyrr whispered something the archmage couldn't quite hear, and the spell took effect. The skull sapphire burned red-hot against Gromph's forehead, and he reached up to throw it off him—but it disintegrated before he could touch it. The dust that fell over the archmage's face was dull gray and power-less. There would be no more protection from the skull sapphire and no more stored necromancies. Gromph knew it had taken a wish to destroy it.

His own spell ruined, Gromph brought another to mind and said, "Well, everyone's using the big spells today, aren't we?"

The lich ignored the jibe and started casting a spell the same time Gromph did. It was the archmage's that finished first: another minor divination spent to create a blast of arcane fire. The preternatural flames poured over the lich, who threw his arms over his face to block them but to no avail. Dyrr's dry flesh crisped and curled, and the lich staggered in pain.

When the fire burned out, the lich lurched forward, red eyes bulging, his ever-present mask burned away, his face twisted in hatred and agony. Gromph could feel that despite the arcane fire Dyrr had finished his own spell.

Cold coursed through Gromph's body, and he shook—and Gromph was getting painfully tired of shaking, shivering, and quivering—but the lich wasn't through with him yet. He could feel the warmth, the life itself, being drawn from him. He staggered backward, barely managing to stay on his feet.

"I'll drain you dry, Gromph," the lich grumbled, his voice raspy and haggard. "You'll die with me, with my House, and my cause."

The lich began to cast again, and Gromph recognized the peculiar cadence and structure that revealed the incantation as a powerful necromancy. Gromph knew many ways to kill, but he also knew that Dyrr probably knew more.

The archmage's hand tightened on his staff, and his arm jerked. A dull pain and a hard pressure settled in his chest, and when he tried to take a breath, no air came to him. His knees finally buckled, and he fell. Gromph forced air into his lungs, but barely a whisper made it in. Dark shadows began to coalesce at the edges of his vision, and his ears went numb with a roaring rush of blood as his body fought in vain to keep his brain alive. The ring was of no help. The lich wasn't wounding him, he was killing him soul-first.

Gromph tried to speak, to utter the words of a spell that might save him, but he couldn't. Dyrr stepped closer, moving to stand over him. Gromph barely managed to turn his head to look up at the gloating lich. The archmage had other means of escape but couldn't force himself to activate any of them. He could feel Nauzhror and Prath trying to speak into his head, but their words never fully formed. Gromph feared that his body was already dead.

He tightened his grip on the staff, and his arm jerked again—the staff.

Gromph forced every ounce of will he had left into pulling his other hand beneath him. He felt his fingers wrap around the staff.

"Fight it, Gromph," the lich growled at him. "Suffer before you die."

"Arrogant—" Gromph coughed out, surprising himself with his ability to speak, even if it was only that one word.

"What was that?" the lich asked, taunting him. "The last words of Gromph Baenre?"

"Not . . ." the archmage gasped.

Gromph's arms tensed, his hands tight around the staff of power—an item so prized hundreds had died just to possess it for a day.

". . . quite," Gromph finished, and he broke the staff.

The ancient wood snapped in response less to the force of Gromph's arms and hands than to his will. The staff broke because Gromph wanted it to break.

Dyrr had time to take in a breath, Gromph had time to smile, then the world around them both became a raging hell of fire, heat, pain, and death. Gromph couldn't see the lich blasted to pieces. He was too busy worrying that the same had happened to him. He closed his eyes, but the light still burned them. He felt his flesh peel away in parts, sizzle, and crisp.

It was over as fast as it started.

Gromph Baenre drew in a breath and laughed through waves of burning agony. The ring started to bring him back to life a cell at a time and he lay there, waiting.

"You've done it," Nauzhror said, and it took a few murmuring heartbeats for Gromph to realize he'd heard the Master of Sorcere's voice with his ears and not his mind. "The lichdrow is dead."

Gromph coughed and dragged himself up to a sitting position. Nauzhror squatted next to him. The rotund wizard began examining the archmage's wounds.

"Dead?" Gromph said then coughed again.

"The cost was high, and not only the staff of power," Nauzhror said, "but he's been utterly destroyed."

Gromph shook his head, disappointed with Nauzhror. The lich's physical form was blasted to flinders when the staff unleashed all its power in one final burst, but a lich was more than a body.

"Dead?" the archmage said. "Not quite yet."

Nimor Imphraezl stepped out of the Shadow Fringe and into the ruins of Ched Nasad. High above him, clinging to the remains of a calcified web street, was perched a massive shadow dragon, an ancient wyrm magnificent in the terror it inspired in all who gazed upon it.

It was a dragon Nimor recognized instantly. It was the dragon Nimor had gone there to see.

Stretching his own aching, exhausted, wounded wings—wings that were puny in comparison to the great shadow wyrm's—Nimor lifted himself up off the rubble-strewn floor of the cavern and into the air below the dragon. If the wyrm took any notice of him, it gave no sign. Instead, it continued as it had been, directing the clearing of the rubble in the preparation for the rebuilding of Ched Nasad. It was a huge task, even for the dragon.

Nimor coasted to a slow, respectful stop on the web strand next to the dragon and bowed, holding the posture until the dragon acknowledged his presence. He was still bowing when the enormous shadow wyrm shrank into the form of an aging drow with thinning hair but a solid, muscular form, dressed in fine silks and linens from all corners of the World Above, every stitch as black as the assassin's heart.

"Stand," the transformed dragon said, "and heed me."

Nimor straightened, looked the drow-formed dragon in the eyes, and said, "I am less than satisfied with the results at Menzoberranzan, Revered Grandfather."

The dragon-drow returned Nimor's look and held it until Nimor had to look away. The assassin heard footsteps approaching but didn't turn around to look. Nimor knew whose they were.

"Nimor," someone said. "Welcome to Ched Nasad."

Nimor pretended to look around at the still smoldering ruins.

"Of course," the source of the second set of footsteps said, "it will look quite different when we're finished."

"I clearly remember your promise," the transformed dragon said. "Do you?"

"Of course, Revered Grandfather," Nimor replied, head held high, showing no outward sign of weakness.

Patron Grandfather Mauzzkyl drew a deep breath in through his nose then slowly said, "You promised to cleanse Menzoberranzan of the stench of Lolth. Have you done that? Is that why you're here?"

Nimor didn't nod, shake his head, or sigh—nothing to make it seem to the patron fathers that he was guilty of anything. The two patron fathers who had approached him from behind stepped around him on either side and stood before Nimor flanking the once majestic wyrm.

"No," Nimor said.

"I have come from the City of Wyrmshadows," the patron grandfather went on, "to aid Patron Father Zammzt in the reconstruction of Ched Nasad. Is that why you've come from Menzoberranzan? To aid in the cleanup?"

"No, Revered Grandfather," Nimor replied.

"Tell your tale to Patron Father Tomphael and Patron Father Zammzt," Mauzzkyl said, his voice cold and final.

Nimor closed his eyes and said, "I answer to—"

"Tomphael," Mauzzkyl said. "You will speak to me through Tomphael from this day until I order otherwise."

Nimor had no time to argue, but that was the last thing he intended to do. Instead he watched, barely breathing as Patron Grandfather Mauzzkyl turned his back then transformed again into a dragon. The great wyrm stepped off the edge of the shattered web and disappeared into the gloom of the ruined city.

"Tell me what you came here to say," Patron Father Tomphael said.

Nimor looked Tomphael in the face but saw no anger, pity, or contempt. Nimor had fallen in the ranks of the Jaezred Chaulssin, and he'd done it just like that.

"Something has changed," Nimor said.

"Lolth has returned," Tomphael finished.

Nimor nodded and said, "Or she will soon. Very soon. The lich-drow failed, and the tide is turning in Menzoberranzan. I thought we'd have more time."

"Dyrr is dead?" Tomphael asked.

Nimor nodded.

"And the cambion?"

"Alive," said Nimor, "but already withdrawing. He had an agent in the Abyss who gave a strange report. I still don't know what happened to the spider goddess, where she's been, or why she fell silent, but she has managed to pinch the Demonweb Pits off of the Abyss."

Tomphael raised an eyebrow, and he and Zammzt shared a glance.

"So," Tomphael said, "your tanarukks are deserting. What of the duergar?"

"Horgar still lives, and when I left him he was still fighting," Nimor said. "However, with the priestesses again able to commune with their goddess and the tanarukks marching home, the gray dwarves won't stand a chance."

"Menzoberranzan," Zammzt said, "is the greatest prize. It was always the one thing most out of reach. We have had successes in other cities. The Queen of the Demonweb Pits was gone long enough."

"Was she?" Nimor asked.

"Look around you," Zammzt replied. "Once this was a drow trade city, openly obedient to the priestesses. Now it is a blank slate, and even as we speak it is being transformed."

"The other patron fathers and I," Tomphael said, "under Patron Father Zammzt's expert guidance, will be concentrating our energies here."

"As you always intended?" Nimor concluded.

Tomphael sighed and said, "I know you've always considered me a coward, Nimor, but you were wrong. Only the fool misses the difference between the coward and the pragmatist."

"Only the young seek glory over success," said Zammzt.

"I could have won in Menzoberranzan," Nimor argued.

"Perhaps," said Tomphael. "If you had, this conversation would have taken a very different tone. It was your opportunity to surprise us, Nimor. That is what you failed to do—surprise us. Our plans did not depend on the City of Spiders being delivered to us on a silver platter, nor did they assume that Lolth was never going to return from wherever it is she's been. We had this one opportunity, and we took all there was to take. There will be other opportunities to take more."

"Other opportunities. . . ." Nimor repeated, rolling the words over on his tongue.

"You could be Anointed Blade again, Nimor," Tomphael said.

Nimor nodded, bowed, and said, "I will return to the City of Wyrmshadows . . . with your leave, Patron Father."

Tomphael nodded, and Nimor turned and stepped into Shadow.

Pharaun hadn't felt so good in so long, he'd almost forgotten what it was like to be healthy. The priestesses, perhaps reveling in the return of their spells, were almost continuously chanting healing prayers. They conjured a banquet and clean, cool water. They healed every wound and soothed aching muscles.

Stretching, feeling too good to bother with Reverie, Pharaun stood and watched Quenthel and Danifae work on Jeggred. Again, likely because they couldn't resist using the spells that had been denied them so long, the two females worked together. As they sat cross-legged on either side of a nervous, reclining Jeggred, Pharaun sensed flashes of the old physical relationship the two priestesses had shared not too long ago. There was the accidental touch that turned into a lingering caress, the heavy-lidded eye contact past the draegloth's wild white mane, and the occasional play of a tongue along parted lips as the words to a series of complex healings taxed even their spell-rejuvenated throats.

The result of all of it was that Jeggred's severed hand grew back. Pharaun found the sight of the thing slowly taking shape from the dead end of the stump even more fascinating than the exchange between the two females. The hand came together in layers: bone, sinew, muscle, blood vessels, skin, fur, claws.

When they were done, the draegloth stood, flexing his hand, jaw agape, body quivering.

The two priestesses stood with him, separating, their eyes once again going cold toward each other.

Jeggred looked first to Danifae and said, "My thanks, Mistress." Then to Quenthel, "Mistress Quenthel. . . ."

Anger poured over the high priestess's face like fog, and she turned away from her nephew, quickly gathering her pack.

"We've rolled around on the floor long enough," she said, already walking swiftly down the corridor. "This way."

Danifae motioned to Pharaun to proceed, and the wizard gladly went after Quenthel. Valas followed behind the wizard, and Danifae and the draegloth took up the rear. Any distance, any buffer between the two priestesses was a good thing, and Pharaun was happy to provide it as long as they got moving. The Master of Sorcere was all but overwhelmed with curiosity.

Quenthel led the way with a confident stride and such assurance that none of the rest of them argued or second-guessed her at all. They went from one corridor to another, passed through rooms, sometimes through doors that Jeggred had to force open by brute strength. All the while the interior of the spider fortress maintained its cold, dark, dead, rusted feeling. Though Lolth's power had definitely returned to the two priestesses, the construct was as dead as ever, and Pharaun got the distinct impression that wherever that power was coming from, it wasn't the sixty-sixth layer of the Abyss.

When they saw light at the end of one of the passageways they all stopped, clinging to the walls and the concealing shadows. As he ran through the spells still available to him and closed his fingers over a wand that would send bolts of lightning crashing through the air, the Master of Sorcere took stock of the rest of the expedition. Quenthel and Danifae both looked down the corridor with hopeful, excited expressions. Jeggred looked at Danifae in the same manner. Valas was nowhere to be seen—as was usual for the scout.

"What is it?" Jeggred asked, his voice as quiet as was possible for the massive half-demon.

Pharaun guessed, "A gate."

"It's where we have to go," Quenthel said.

"She's correct," said Danifae.

"Well, then," Pharaun replied, "we ought to proceed right away. Should we be prepared to fight our way through?"

Quenthel stepped away from the wall and started walking quickly, back tall and straight, toward the strange purple glow.

Pharaun shrugged and followed, still holding the wand in one hand and the list of spells in his mind. The high priestess hadn't actually answered his question after all.

By the time they got to the end of the corridor Pharaun's instincts were telling him to approach more slowly, more cautiously—but he'd also grown accustomed to following the lead of the highest ranking priestess in attendance, so he followed Quenthel into the chamber at the end of the corridor with a hesitation in his mind but not in his step.

The corridor opened into a huge, round, high-ceilinged chamber walled in the same rusted steel as the rest of the spider fortress. In the center of the otherwise empty space was a circle that appeared to be welded together from jagged, rusted pieces of the fortress construct itself. The circle stood up on its end, perhaps eighteen feet in diameter. The center of the ring was filled with opaque violet light, swirling and folding in on itself as if it came from a luminescent cloud of vapor trapped in the confines of the circle.

Pharaun heard footsteps and brought the wand out from under his *piwafwi*.

"You will not require that here, mage," a voice echoed in the chamber.

As the others filed into the room, Pharaun looked for the source of the voice. He sensed a figure lurking in a particularly dark shadow.

"There," Pharaun whispered to Quenthel. "See it?"

Quenthel nodded and said, "You will cast no spell; you will make no move toward it unless I order it. Do you understand?"

Pharaun said, "Of course, Mistress," but the others stood silent.

"I said," the high priestess reiterated, "do you understand?"

Danifae and Jeggred nodded, and Pharaun again said, "Of course, Mistress. Can you at least tell me what it is?"

"I prefer to be referred to as 'she'," the voice said, "being female."

The figure stepped out of the darkest part of the shadow and strode confidently into the purple light from the active but untuned portal. The sight of it took Pharaun's breath away.

The figure of a drow female slowly twisted and writhed a good ten feet in the air. The drow was perfectly formed and nude, her body more like Danifae's in its fullness than Quenthel's modest, strong frame. She dragged her hands over her body in long, slow caresses for which no part of her was forbidden.

From her sides grew two sets of long, segmented spider legs. It was those four legs—and four more like it all together—that held the drow female up above the rusted floor.

Pharaun had seen too many driders to count, but what stepped out in front of him was no drider. Everything about the spider-drow creature demanded the wizard's full attention. The drow form was beautiful—beautiful in a way that Pharaun had no words to describe. Her long, spindly spider legs simply reminded him of where he was: the home plane of—

The Master of Sorcere shook his head slowly from side to side. It couldn't be.

"Lo—?" he whispered.

"I am not the Queen of the Demonweb Pits, Master of Sorcere," the spider-drow said in accented High Drow. "To even say it would be blasphemy."

"I've only read about you," Quenthel whispered.

A second spider-drow appeared, stepping lightly out of the gloom, and a third hung suspended from the ceiling, both their drow bodies those of a writhing naked drow female.

"Abyssal widows," Danifae said.

The name meant nothing to Pharaun.

"You are her handmaidens, and—" Quenthel started.

"And her midwives. We were only legend," the first abyssal widow purred. "We were only prophecy."

"Prophecy. . . ." Quenthel whispered.

"We exist now," the abyssal window said, "to guard the entrance to the Demonweb Pits."

"But," Pharaun said almost despite himself, "we're *in* the Demonweb Pits."

The beautiful drow female smiled, her teeth perfect and clean, the skin of her cheeks smooth and utterly devoid of blemish or imperfection.

"No," the creature replied, "not anymore."

"What's happened?" Quenthel asked. "Where is the goddess if not in the Abyss?"

"All your questions will be answered, Mistress," said the widow, "when you pass through the gate."

"It's a plane all its own now," Pharaun guessed.

The abyssal widows all nodded in unison and moved to stand on either side of the portal—guards along a procession route.

"You have come this far," one of the widows said.

"And so have proved you are worthy," continued another.

"To face Lolth and speed her into her new form," finished the third.

"Her new form?" asked Pharaun.

The abyssal widows all shared a coy look and gestured to the yawning violet portal.

"Did you . . ." the Master of Sorcere said, his throat dry, his hands shaking no matter how hard he tried to stop them. "Did you call yourself a midwife?"

"Pass," one of them said. "You are expected."

Quenthel stepped forward, Danifae close on her heels, and boldly walked into the roiling mass of purple light. She disappeared instantly, Danifae only steps behind her. Jeggred was a bit more reluctant, regarding the abyssal widows with blazing eyes as he passed them. Soon enough, he was gone as well.

Pharaun turned to Valas, whose eyes were darting from one widow to another. He had a hand on one of the many garish trinkets he wore pinned to his vest.

"So, Master Hune," Pharaun said, "here we are."

Valas looked at him and nodded.

"Where we're going . . ." the wizard said, pausing to gather his thoughts—not easy with the prospect of stepping through that particular portal looming so close. "It could be that your services are no longer required."

Valas locked his eyes on Pharaun's and said, "My services are no longer adequate."

Pharaun took a deep breath.

"Well," the wizard said, "as I said before, we would benefit from your skills and experience wherever we go, but here we've come to a point where you must make a decision."

"I have," said Valas, the look in his eye inviting no more conversation.

"Yes, well," Pharaun said, "there it is."

The wizard turned and without a backward glance stepped into the portal, leaving Valas Hune behind.